THE REBEL FOXES

The Sirione Chronicles: The Dome

Noah Hawthorne

Neshama Publishing

Contents

PREFACE

Please read before beginning your adventure.

This is an adult fantasy fiction, and contains mature themes such as sex and violence. Other warnings include gore, torture, off-page child death, reference to previous sexual assault, ableism, and religious trauma caused by on-page abuse. There is a glossary in the back of this book, which can be read along with the story.

The Rebel Foxes is a story of healing, overcoming the impossible, and creating your own hope in a world that so desperately fights against you.

DEDICATION

To those who rebel against the world by merely existing.
I see you. I am you.
You are not alone.

TERMINOLOGY

Ancient Sirione is based on the Hebrew language, some meanings have been adjusted to fit the story.

Aleph – Alpha.

Chaya – Life.

Chayal – Royal Guards.

Kanah Bosem – Cannabis.

Meira – Light, a weekly light ceremony.

Me'od – Strength.

Mishpoke – Family, or pack.

Syzdon – God of Deliverance.

Tchotchke – Little Thing.

In the Citadel, people are referred to by their parentage, and it's done so in one of three ways.

Ben – Son of

Bat – Daughter of

Xir – Child of

CITADEL
WOODS
JUNGLE
CHUTE
REPTILLIAN
ROOST
CLUBHOUSE

PROLOGUE

I never forgot the boy with amber eyes, and he never forgot about me.

Paw stuck in a trap.

Pull, push, struggle.

Friends yip and cry. Why aren't they running?

The Hunters are coming. Heavy boots, guns, and death.

I lock eyes with the golden pup holding a fox kit by the scruff of her ginger neck. I send out a call of distress, ordering my friends to save themselves. *Leave*.

The Hunters are coming. Metal spikes, hatred, and nets.

I fight once more against the steel jaws, but my leg is broken. A tall Hunter approaches at last, replacing my agony with pure terror. I steal another look at my friends, they're gone. When I turn my attention back to the Hunter, I am met with amber eyes brighter than the popping neon signs lighting this apocalyptic hell.

The Hunter is disproportionate. A small face hides behind the respirator hissing in the space between us. Black hair falls forward when he reaches for me, and I snap despite the fact I can hear his heart. It's so *loud*.

He giggles, muffled by his mask. "It's okay, I won't hurt you." Dirty fingers move to the mechanism in the trap. I bare my teeth, wary of his kindness. He sounds like a child. Someone like me. "I've never seen a fox like you before, you look special," He says softly, otherwise focused on his work and unbothered.

He is delicate, and I find myself trying to memorize his face beneath the mask. But shouts fold my ears, and he hurries anew. I keep my wary attention on him, listening to his ragged breathing through the mask filtering out smog. He's ... different. There's something about the gentle way he moves, and the care he shows me.

It takes me a second to realize I'm free.

"There, go on," He says with a satisfied smile, unmoving. I slowly stand, holding my lame leg close to my side. He waves me off, glancing over his shoulder at flashlights reflecting off the buildings forming the alleyway. The Hunters are coming.

I take a few tenuous steps towards the kind Hunter and lick my blood from his fingers. A small gasp escapes the respirator with a click, and he turns his hand over. When I press my nose to the place where hard lines intersect in the center of his palm, his eyes brighten to a faceted amber, full of many different shades of gold and earth. I want to shift, to tell him to come with me. I tug on his thumb, but he pulls back.

Harsh voices bellow from behind him, starkly contrasting the only human who has ever shown me kindness. "It's okay, go on," He whispers, standing. I take a nervous step back as he does, neither of us break eye contact.

Then I run away, and I don't look back.

Even though it feels like I'm leaving part of me behind.

THE HUNT

Two Decades Later

The Chute that delivers life-sustaining supplies to the underworld will be under attack in precisely 72 seconds.

The Rebel Foxes wait in the shadows, ready to pounce on our rivals who have had tight control of this valuable and extensive territory for far too long. Common people are dying in the oil-slick streets, deprived of fresh oxygen tanks and proper respirators to fight the perpetually smog ridden atmosphere. Starved and dehydrated corpses are a daily obstacle for the cabs, but those who are able to afford a vehicle don't care about the bones they drive over. They don't care about the territory war over the Chute, either. Only the impoverished do.

It's been four months since the Jungle and Reptilian gangs became allies and stole this territory from the Roost, hoarding an entire underworld's worth of resources for themselves. The Rebel Foxes, and our new allies in the Roost, only take what they need and give away the rest to the common people. The other gangs aren't so generous.

But that ends here and now.

I search the side of a tin-coated skyscraper where my chemist hides in the darkness. I can't see them, but I know Hotaru's there. All around the plaza, my Foxes wait in position, their excitement palpable through the strong as steel bonds between us all. We've been planning this retaliation for months, more or less waiting until Sorin was ready to reclaim what's his.

"Ready to blow this joint, Taru?" I relay over the radio strapped to my shoulder, voice transformed into a neutral, crackling tone by my respirator.

"Do you even need to ask?" Hotaru buzzes through, bored as ever. "Let's just blow it up already."

"*No*, the labs aren't evacuated yet." Balderik snaps, his labored breathing heavy over the mild static.

"Hurry the fuck up, Erik," I order, tensing. They should've been out by now.

"The drones are almost there, 42 seconds." Mairin's modulated voice warns through the wavelengths stretching from here to the distant Clubhouse.

"Xylia, are you two ready my darlings?" I ask, trying to lighten the mood.

"*Ugh*, save that shit for the party. We're all out now." Jaromir scoffs through the radio, his breathing just as heavy as Erik's.

"We're ready, my lovely," Takara sighs over the radio, and Xylia laughs in that bright way she does in the background. Despite the distance, Takara's voice and Xylia's laugh fortify me.

A bone shaking *hum* vibrates the ground level of the Dome, ironically named the Garden. It is not called this due to any legendary nature growing in the fuel soaked dirt and stone, but due to the fact the upper world, the Citadel harvests its needs from the bugs crawling beneath it. The skyscrapers buried into the Garden are a mishmash of modern and decrepit, and not all of them are accessible from the ground.

Most are tin, but the more modern ones are aptly named Concrete Towers, made from concrete, rebar, and pretty reinforced glass. Those are for the wealthy and do not shake beneath the Chute's warning siren. The Tin Scrapers are from the Old Days, an echo of the steel monoliths they used to be. Now they're precariously stacked tin sheds and crumbling stone foundations, mostly reserved for the middle-class. These do tremble in anticipation of the Chute's incoming delivery, and collapse isn't an uncommon thing.

High above the Garden's traffic and trash filled streets are skyscraper tops and skiff ports, all connected by elevated stone walkways that hold the beautiful and modern world of the Upper City, and the governing Citadel. I'm sure the nobility of this godforsaken place are placing bets on who will take control of this month's supply drop. The struggles of the poor are naught but entertainment for the wealthy. The distant artillery guns silhouetted by purple glass and black stone aren't powered up, but I'm keeping an eye on them.

The yawning mouth of the Chute rattles, shaking dust and soot onto the gangs standing guard around the plaza. They protect the cracked, circular stone or more specifically, the dual steel crates waiting to be filled. They look no different than the average person, other than their matching black leather bombers with upturned collars. Green paint spray painted onto the Jungle respirators, red on the Reptilian's.

A swarm of people, families and otherwise, surround the abruptly fenced off plaza, anxious and desperate, but no one dares take a step closer to the organized groups wielding automatic rifles. At least, not at first.

"Hotaru, start the countdown."

"10."

When the siren goes off once more, hundreds of civilians start rattling the chain link fences, haphazardly placed and poorly fortified by the gangs themselves. People beg for something, *anything* to eat. I'd heard rumors that some of the humans had resorted to cannibalism, and that's when we decided to hasten our plan.

"9."

Muzzles of black steel rise to the crowd of innocents, prepared with ammunition that is far from ordinary. Bullets designed for my kind, not humans, but they kill indiscriminately all the same. Well disguised shifters in the form of humans shout for people to '*stay back,*' their harsh voices echoing all around the space.

My comrades express worry over the radio.

"8."

I tell them to wait.

"7."

Blood-red lights trimming the outer rim of the chrome-plated Chute blink on, drawing the attention of the gathered crowd. Away from the Rebel Foxes clinging to the sides of buildings and elsewhere, preparing to attack.

"6."

Someone breaks through the crowd, scales the fence.

"5."

They run to Talay, Jungle's leader, standing at the forefront of the stone plaza. They drop to their knees, hands up and words lost to the chaos.

"4."

Talay is known for being merciless, the person won't make it. Distantly, I hear Mairin confirm her drones are in position. Talay raises a pistol to the person's face, and a child in the crowd screams. A faint, green glow emits from the other side of the Chute, where Xylia and Takara are hiding.

"3."

Talay pulls back on the hammer of her pistol with a feral grin. She's one of the few in her group *not* wearing a mask. Shifters don't need masks, but it helps us blend in with the humans. Idiot.

"2."

Reinforced crates filled with dehydrated food packets, medical supplies, respirators, and so much more, rattle down the Chute.

"1."

A searing white implosion rocks the Dome.

Then another, and another.

Concrete towers known for housing Citadel labs and other operations collapse like fallen dominoes. The plan was for Balderik and Jaromir to evacuate all the innocents first, which in those places are often shifters, and those who give up without a fight. Not *all* those who work for the Citadel do so willingly, but still. Taru's implosions are only a distraction from the real show. Several things happen at once, executed perfectly.

A gnarly net of vines ejects from the shadows and sweeps beneath the Chute, filing with a month's worth of supplies. The projectile greenery latches onto Mairin's drones stationed at four equidistant points around the Chute. They hold up each corner of the net, remotely piloted by my best mechanic safely tucked away in the Clubhouse. Xylia and Takara stand on a fifth drone, and the neon green emitting from Xylia's body draws attention from the crowd below.

Unnatural vegetation explodes from the ground around the opposing gang members, flying to the nearest enemy. Vines and roots take hold of an ankle or calf, a limb or neck. Talay's attention diverts from the civilian on their knees, which is all the person needs to sweep her legs out from beneath her and steal her gun. I chuckle, they were playing coy.

Golding and Sallow, a deadly couple that I'm constantly thankful are on our side, appear behind the remaining gang members attempting to flee, blades in hand and mischievous grins present as they apprehend their targets.

Once the net is full and sagging, the drones lazily pull away from the Chute and fly past the spire I cling to. I leap from my post and take hold of an extending vine, welcoming the shock that rides up my arm. Xylia's power overwhelms my senses, filling my heart with warm strength.

I steady my footing on the net while I'm taken for a slow victory lap around the Chute, its red lights winking out one by one. I unstrap the narrow megaphone from my back using my free hand and project my words to the awe struck people below.

"Good people of the Dome, let's not spend tonight fighting! There's enough here for everyone to *share*. In fact," I gesture to the distant smog hiding the southeastern quarter, "you all know the lovely Sorin, don't you? Take a look at what he's brought!"

An oblong airship protrudes from the smog, and its chrome reflects the sickly yellow of the city's perpetually lit gas lamps onto the buildings all around us. Thick, black smoke trails behind the behemoth, and the ship promptly joins our drones in their orbit around the chute.

Sorin hangs off the prow, seemingly back from the dead after last month's near fatal ambush on the Roost. We weren't allied during the time he was attacked, but we weren't enemies either. After receiving a distress call from his Lieutenant, we dug through the remains of the Roost and healed those we could, and helped Sorin put together his base of operations.

You always made sure your enemy was well and dead before turning your back on them. Survival 101. Talay's failure to abide by this rule will be her undoing, and Conlead's saving grace.

The owl shifter wears a respirator similar to mine, one of the many we gave him during our last visit. Tiny leaves, flowers, and tendrils escape from the vents resting on either side of Sorin's nose, providing a rejuvenating air that you can't get anywhere else besides the Foxes. The Roost members have their rifles drawn on the port and starboard sides, the remaining enemies in their sights.

All those left alive are on their knees, subdued by my people. Talay and Conlead are at the forefront, the gang leaders who brought destruction to the Roost, and starved out all the common people. Shifters like *them* give people like *us* a bad name, providing all the dirt the Citadel needs to slap our faces across billboards dripping with fatal propaganda. I'm mildly surprised the troops haven't come to rain on our parade yet, but I'm sure they weren't expecting so many of us to gather for this showdown.

I suppose they're waiting for the Hunt to take place a few days from now. They'll try to kidnap and murder as many Shifters as they can, then. When the whole damn affair can, and will, be televised and broadcast upon every television set and radio. Announce every shifter tag as its filled, every human that falls due to retaliation. Every life as it's stolen. Fear is the Citadel's weapon, along with the posters and billboards that depict life in the gaudy Citadel and ask, *'What could you be, if only you were here?'*

A mere five tags, and you're granted visitor's access to the Upper City.

Ten tags, and you're granted a furnished apartment in the Upper City.

Twenty tags, and you're granted a furnished manor in the Citadel.

Thirty tags, and you're granted a household staff to maintain that manor.

And fifty. Fifty tags, and you're granted a place by the Emperor's side. The ranking of a Crystal Star.

I wish I could say no one person has achieved that many in a single Hunt, but it's happened. In my lifetime, there have been eight Crystal Stars given to civilians that now hold a place in Emperor Drazen ben Matzliach's dynasty. The last Crystal Star to be bestowed was three years ago, and it was the most fucked Hunt we've encountered in a long time. It's taken three years to grieve, and now we're just pissed.

Hunts are an effective way to cleanse the shifter population. Why use an army when you can use civilians?

Generally, shifters only leave their hideouts for Chute drops, and we're well disguised when we do. To attack us when we're all gathered at once would be like walking into an early grave, at least without the artillery. But then there's collateral damage, and the Emperor doesn't care for that. There's only one sure-fire way to tell if someone is a shifter. But if they're hostile and you're close enough to tell, chances are you're about to die.

The *problem* with this would be advantage, is none of us get along. We're selfish and feral and bloodthirsty. If this many of us are gathered, it's to fight for scraps of land, as we are now. There is one thread that connects us though, one besides the power granting mutations we've inherited. We *will* fight to the death, rather than surrender to the Citadel. And it's time we acknowledge that similarity.

Dual green dots appear on Talay and Conlead's foreheads. Hotaru's latest invention makes long-range shots infinitely easier, much to Madlock's delight, my designated sniper. My quad of drones tail Sorin's ship from a short distance away and I wave to him, earning a dramatic bow in return.

"Jungle and Reptilian, I'm giving you *one* chance to leave here now." I announce through the megaphone, voice crackling through the distance. Sparking flashes of light erupt from multiple cameras, bulbs shattering.

"Fuck you, Rajni! We've won this territory, fair and square!" Talay spits, her disgust audible to my dull hearing through Taru's earpieces. "I told you, no *goddamn* survivors, Conlead! But there's that fucking—!"

Talay thrusts a menacing, gloved finger at Sorin, but a bullet splits apart her skull and sentence. I smile as a weight tumbles off my shoulders, and her own. She's been in my way for far too long, more concerned about fighting among her own people than turning on the Citadel.

Conlead immediately leans forward and presses his forehead to the ground, as do the rest in his gang. Talay's people do the same, who are now leaderless. Shifters without protection are as good as dead in the Dome, especially with the next Hunt knocking on our door.

Drystan takes the male by the back of his jacket and yanks him to standing, then forces Conlead to stare up at me. A short distance away from them, Takara dismounts the drone she and Xylia had been riding on. She approaches her old kin, nervousness tainting the pack connection between us.

My radio buzzes. "He's listening," Takara says once reaching Conlead's other side.

Sorin and I descend with each circle around the Chute, and the hungry civilians are growing more eager with every pass. "Conlead, darling. How're you?"

He chances a look at Takara standing beside him, then glances back up to me. "Been better, devilish fox. What tha' fuck do ya want from me?"

"Only reason *you're* alive is because Sorin is. Leave this place, and never claim it again. The Chute belongs to the Roost now, and the Rebel Foxes are their protection. You dare lay a hand on his people again, or mine, and you'll be wishing you came to such a clean end as our dear friend, Talay. Claim Jungle's turf as your own, and be happy with that."

"You'd leave me alive?" Conlead scoffs, and the distance does nothing to hide his confusion. "What if I change my mind, come after ya?"

Takara swiftly injects a tracker into his thick neck, unbeknownst to the crime lord until it's too late. I sigh, watching the male curse and sputter, flailing about until Drystan forces Conlead's attention on me once more.

"What the fuck did she just do ta' me!" Conlead curses over the radio.

"You like that? Taru's been doing some tinkering, these lil' trackers are brand new. You know my apprentice, don't you? Taken to explosives lately, and I must say, their work is just *exquisite*. Get where I'm going with this?"

Conlead's head lowers, and Takara shoves the radio closer to his face.

"You so much as look at me and mine, your head will be blown off quicker than you can say please. Still think you'll change your mind?"

"You're a fuckin' piece of work, Rajni." He grumbles in defeat.

"How original of you." I check my watch, then salute Sorin. He nods, and large wooden barrels decorated with green runes are thrown over the railing of his ship. They plummet in various directions towards the plaza below, and thousands of people scream in unison.

Mutation-born blackwood explodes into mushrooming clouds of jade dust upon impact, releasing nothing more than great plumes of powderized nature. Upon making contact with the little oxygen there is in the air, wild vegetation blooms all throughout the center of the Garden.

Flora takes root beneath the enraptured swarm of weeping civilians, spreading outwards from the central plaza like a massive carpet that gently sways those on their feet. We've learned how to compress our power into aerosol cans and frequently spray vegetation onto building sides and leave small gardens in the shards of dirt breaking through the stone underbelly of the Dome, but we've never done something like this.

I'd bet money more than half of these people have never seen flora in their entire lives. Not like this.

Flower bushes ranging from every color of the fabled rainbow fill in the weak spots on several of the Tin Scrapers, along with sturdy roots and vines that weave over numerous gaps that expose many apartments to the elements. Where rust and decrepit buildings once stood, are pillars of natural creation.

Enormous trees break through the streets encircling the plaza, rivaling the revitalized high risers. Low hanging branches fill with rapidly growing fruit of red, orange, purple and blue varieties in all sorts of shapes. The twisted limbs stretch towards the crowd once begging for food, ignoring those stepping out of their cabs and staring at the world in wonder.

Bushes taller than a human sprout all around the plaza and at intersections, uprooting traffic signals. Black, white, and purple berries grow until they can't anymore, reaching the size of a fist before tumbling off the plants and into the streets. People collect fruit into their aprons, trouser and jacket pockets, or directly into their mouths. A group of children kick a large red fruit back and forth a short distance away from the loose crowd which has begun to disperse in favor of exploration.

Filament thin vines form thick webs, weaving around the circumference of all nearby Concrete Towers. The vines trap inhabitants within their apartments filled with wealth that is only hinted at, but we've all seen the rich peering at us from above, shining in their layers of privilege. Stomping on us beneath their boots when they come down for 'extra' entertainment.

Layers upon layers of canopies bury the Garden in life and hide us from the Upper's prying eyes. Tree tops, crawling ivy, and prismatic flowers the size of tires flourish throughout. The crowd cries with delight, and their happiness is magnified when the burdened net of supplies gently releases over a fresh cushion of grass nearby the Chute. The plaza is now secured by *my* people, disguised as humans like the rest of the shifters.

Jaromir, the polar bear who loves to bake.

Balderik, the golden canine with healing hands.

Hotaru, the black fox who likes chemistry *too* much.

Xylia and Takara, the foxes who share my bed and dream.

More Foxes are there too, standing their ground, and three times as many are waiting at home, tending to the young and preparing for Koa's party.

Their first Change.

The Rebel Foxes create orderly lines and I watch from my drone that's detached from the net, keeping an eye out for the inevitable Citadel forces. The artillery still hasn't engaged, apparently deeming Sorin's ship as a non-threat. Once the platoons stationed at the bottom of the strangled Concrete Towers finish hacking through the webs blockading the elevators to the Upper City, the Citadel will send in more troops to seize whatever produce and goods the civilians can't hoard and hide in time.

They'll come, eventually.

Sorin's ship docks behind the pile of resources, anchored by sand bags which slam to the ground in quick succession. Smoke escapes in one last cough before his engines enter a hibernation state, using only enough energy to hover. A ramp unfolds from the side and his crew unloads crates filled with more supplies. The truth is, we gave him our excess so he could rebuild. And most importantly, there's respirators with filters made of mutated nature, our specialty.

Hundreds of them.

It's not illegal for civilians to possess respirators, and there's nothing in the latest reform barring them from using ones that don't require oxygen tanks. I'm sure another reform will be introduced after today to address that. Our respirators have been a shifter secret until now, but the humans need them more than we do. Each mask should last one adult human eight months with daily use, much longer than the week usual that the hard to find oxygen tanks offer. And that's if you have a mask in good condition.

The Rebel Foxes only take what we need, and give back what we don't. It was Sorin's idea to bring what *he* didn't need now that his stocks are full. Pride warms my heart as I watch him pass his wealth along. Sorin needs a good reputation and people to believe in him, which won't be hard. He's a good one, and I'm thankful to have his help this year. A hot sense of approval escapes me and rolls down the bonds between my packmates and me, which brings forth a series of howls. Although they're all in human form, there's a distinct animalistic quality to their cheers.

What surprises me is the responding howl from the crowd of humans. I can't find who started it, as a wave of grateful cries and hollers quickly swell all throughout the Garden. I chuckle, breathless for a moment at the sight and sound. In this corner of the world, there is nothing but harmony and life. Sweet, ever so green life. I fill my lungs with it, then release a mighty cry of my own.

The Citadel's distant black spires are illuminated as the spotlights in the distant northern quadrant of the Dome blink awake. "It's time for dinner," I shout through the megaphone, the code phrase for *'hurry the fuck up.'*

Takara assigns new leaders from the crowd to take over the distribution, and shifters are seamlessly replaced by humans who are eager to see us leave, if only to protect their new overlords. Thankfully, the peace is kept despite our withdrawal.

Sorin's crew boards his ship with haste, the engines kick up a notch and spit smoke onto the ground, but it's immediately absorbed by the shimmering green vegetation we've left behind. He catches my attention and waves, smiling wide. I salute him once more, then watch him go.

The Rebel Foxes disappear into dark alleys, past manhole covers leading to underground tunnels, and on the remaining freed up drones that cut through the air at a swift and steady pace. I'm the last to leave, studying the most important detail of our takeover. At this altitude, our massive message spelled out across the overturned plaza and rooted into the ground is clear.

'The Hunt is On'

Before the drone takes me home, a flash of honeyed amber catches my eye from below. I narrow my eyes, searching the crowd for the source of unnaturally gold light. In a nearby alley

I notice the person who confronted Talay staring up at me from a dislodged manhole. At this low altitude, despite their respirator with full head-straps, I can sense they're a fierce looking man.

He waves to me, and it almost looks like his eyes are crinkled by a hidden smile. I can't find where the gold came from, so instead I wave at the brave and somewhat foolish civilian, then disappear.

What a terrible mistake.

Big Boy Wolf

Outside of the central plaza, labyrinths of roads and streets dominate the Garden floor of the Dome. Our world is thick with towering metal and stone coated with decades of smog and oil. Makeshift villages are tucked inside narrow alleys and along rare vehicular streets. The ground is the most dangerous of all the Dome's levels, but there are ramshackle houses and shacks built into every nook and cranny available. Thin walls are better than none at all.

Each quadrant of the Dome houses a few nameless settlements, places where businesses, the middle class, and Citadel outposts dominate. The Foxes hide in the most remote and treacherous section, the southeastern quadrant. Our mediocre part of the maze is crime free and only mildly depressing. Layers of people live atop one another in a cacophony of underground dwellings and surface homes. The Tin Risers in this section have long crumbled into stone and violently twisted steel. Homes have been built on the bones of those old apartment buildings, already beginning new stacks.

Metal-grate walkways connect the creative buildings, providing more vertical room to build on. Not to mention the new steel homes shaped like light bulbs which hang from the walkways. Our territory is the only one with communities of humans and shifters living together in such harmony.

Most of the humans just don't know it.

To the common people, we're nothing more than a well to do hostel for Metalworkers Union #53. A select few of the laborers from said Union are long-held allies, and they provide a perfect cover for our base of operations. In exchange, they receive protection, respirators, and fresh produce. A treasure trove, one might say.

I stand on a suspended balcony playing host to a patchwork tin cottage with rusty crooked shutters that were once painted purple. I'm not sure who hung the shutters in the first place, there's no wind or any great scenery outside the singular window. A construct disguised as a gaslamp hides in plain sight, standing guard at the corner of the balcony where a set of stairs leads down to the ground. I stand there, transfixed by the fat flame flickering against the thick green glass of the lamp.

We're living in harmony, but we're still hiding.

Takara steps out of the cottage, and I break my vigil to give her a small smile. The sight of my companion eases the hollow ache in my chest a fraction, but my unease doesn't disappear. She's changed out of her tactical gear and into a torn pair of denims, along with a sheer, off the shoulder blouse which I belatedly recognize as mine. A gift from someone, one I've never worn.

Takara scrubs a hand over her cropped, dark hair upon joining my side. She gives me a tiny smile in return, revealing a singular dimple once hidden in the patch of pink and white splashed across her cheek. I could stare at the birthmarks contrasting her dark brown skin for hours, and I have.

She says, "You did good tonight. Everyone's home, safe and sound."

"Mm, so why do I get the feeling something's wrong?"

Takara lifts a shoulder. "Hunt's almost here, Koa's of age."

I search her heart-shaped face for answers, but find none. I flash my emerald eyes at her, and her dark brown ones brighten in turn. Part of what drew me to Takara was her spirit, how it speaks to mine nearly as strong as Xylia's does. Whilst Xylia and I have been mated for years, she has taken lovers of her own, the same as I have. Sometimes, those lovers are shared.

Such is the case with Takara. She defected from Conlead and sought sanctuary here, which was granted in exchange for her invaluable knowledge and work of constructs, something that Mairin and many of the other technologically inclined shifters have benefited from. Shortly after she came, Xylia and I found ourselves drawn to Takara, and her to us.

While the three of us have been mutually bonded as partners for quite some time, Takara isn't ready to take the final step, which is a mating bond. She may never be, and it's something I've always been fine with. But lately, I find myself second guessing every decision. Every word uttered and action taken, or not taken. I trust Takara. I do.

But that doesn't stop the crawling beneath my skin.

Without looking at her I say, "No one will be touched in Fox territory this year, or the others if I can help it, and I'm leaving Koa in Drystan's care. Plus we actually have help this year. The Hunt isn't what's bothering me."

"Talk to me, Raj." Takara whispers, and one of her hands cups my elbow. The hairs on my arms stand on end, brushing against the inner leather of my jacket. I can feel her concern, and I know that it's genuine.

I shrug, allowing her to pull me against her broad chest. "There's nothing to say, you know how it goes. I get a *feeling*. If I could grasp anything more than fear, shreds of vague truth, then perhaps I wouldn't be so afraid in the first place."

"Xy told me you dreamt about him again, Raj." Takara murmurs, warily treading the line called *'shit we don't talk about.'*

"If *he* was part of the problem, I'd know." I shake my head, gently stepping out of her comfort to lift the collar of my jacket. I tuck my chin down, nestling into the collar, and her hands fall to her sides. "Besides, it was only a dream."

"What does that mean? How would you know?"

"It doesn't matter, let's not keep Koa waiting. You're right, it's a good day, and we can't fight an enemy we don't know, so we'll wait. That's all we can do."

I reach for her and she reluctantly takes my hand, squeezing tight.

"I'm here for you, *Aleph*. Did I not prove that tonight?"

"Oh, Takara." I kiss her knuckles, then press them to my cheek. Guilt for doubting her overrides my worry as I recall the sight of her standing over Conlead, waiting for my orders. She would've killed him if I asked. I know it.

"You've never needed to *prove* it to me. I trust you, through and through. Honestly, when I know *what's* wrong, I'll tell you, I promise. Until then, worrying does nothing."

Takara chews on her lip and nods, then bends down and presses her forehead to mine. "Thank you, for not killing him." A neon sign sparks in the distance, someone's light popped.

"Besides the fact he's your kin, Conlead spared Sorin. I believe there's good in him, hidden deep within like all of us. We can only do so much with the opportunities we're given, so let's see what he does with this."

"*Deep*. I didn't think it existed in him at all anymore, but now I wonder how much of it was Talay's doing." Takara sighs, breath heavy on my lips.

My dream plays at the edges of my mind, the one that started this anxiety storm. Takara walking away from me.

Abruptly I ask, "You're not thinking of leaving, are you?"

Her fingers dig into the loose fabric of my trousers as she pulls me close. Takara breathes, "*Never*," onto my lips.

I smile, but my heart doesn't slow. "Good, because I won't let you."

She smiles, too, nose brushing against mine. "Is that so, Rajni, Queen of the Foxes?"

"If I'm the Queen, that makes you and Xylia royalty too, you know." Both my hands slide past her jaw, skimming her scalp.

"I'd have never gotten this far without any of you. You know how much I appreciate you, don't you?"

"Take the compliment, yeah?" Takara teases, then cuts off my protest with a soft kiss. Her full lips are tender, her dexterous tongue curious. I allow myself this moment and take my own advice. I let go of my worries and absorb the essence of Takara. The scent of rust and oil, endless hard muscle, and two decades of scars.

Heat simmers to life in my core, and my stiffening arousal grinds against Takara's pelvis which draws a moan out of me. She swallows it greedily, and I absently wonder if we have enough time to slip into a closet before hitting the party.

The gas lamp above us flickers in a rhythmic pattern, green dances across our bodies in a chastising manner. I curse Hotaru in a grumble, and Takara laughs. I shut her up with a particularly sharp kiss, allowing my canines to partially shift and drag across her lips. She moans, and the sweet sound coupled with the even sweeter taste of her blood temporarily satisfies the beast within.

"We're being paged." I manage a moment later, unable to hide my smile.

Takara kisses my forehead, upturned lips brush against my skin in the barest of there gestures. "There you are."

"Here I am."

I follow her into the cottage, cringing as the hinges squeak and the off-kilter door swings open to the inside. A shudder rides my spine and I scan the area behind me, then shut the pointless door. I don't bother locking it, instead I follow close behind Takara through an impossibly long and narrow hall of darkness. At the end waits a panel filled with numbers, inlaid directly into the wall.

Takara enters today's code and I shake out my wild, dark blonde hair, then straighten my jacket. The floor hidden by darkness vibrates my combat boots and a soft hum emanates around us. I take Takara's hand as our platform descends into nothing.

"So, we're alone ... what do you think Koa's spirit is?" Takara asks after thirty three seconds of our elevator scuffing metal. She elbows me, and I chuckle. "What? I won't tell."

I jab at her ribs in retaliation. "We don't hypothesize such things, Takara."

"Such a hardass." She scoffs, but it's light.

In all honesty, Koa is ... unpredictable. That kit surprises me at every turn, and I'm thankful they pulled through, a testament to their strong spirit. I suspect Koa will be a bear like Jaromir, but I don't like to put expectations on the kids, or favor one species over another. The other gangs are more specific on who they accept, but our group has no rhyme or reason. Despite the fact we're called the Foxes, there's many more different types of species living here than that. One thread connects them all, and that's the kernel of good in their soot covered hearts.

Excited voices meet my ears and I squeeze Takara's hand as we lower through the last bit of the elevator shaft. "Strong. Koa is strong, whatever form such a spirit takes, that's what Koa's will be." I whisper.

I earn a kiss to my forehead at the same time warm light spills in from the concrete bunker known as the Clubhouse. "I love you, Raj," Takara says.

"And I you, Takara."

Our moment is promptly interrupted by a herd of kids, but I don't mind.

"You're home! Home! She's Home!" Small voices sing in a chorus and I laugh, hugging armfuls of half-shifted orphans at a time. Seven years of intercepting Hunts have given these children safety and a home, but it's not enough. Not anymore. I tease kits and tussle fur, but suddenly my heart aches like before, twisted with something wrong.

"Alright kiddos, let *Aleph* in the door so we can get this party started. Seats! All of you." Noemie calls as she enters the vestibule from a side hall, shooing the reluctant kits off me. The teacher adjusts the red bandanna holding back a thick mass of curled brunette. Her left hand, constructed of metal and mutation, clicks and hums as she does so. Layers of *'junk jewelry'* as Drystan calls it, cover Noemie from head to toe, lending to her eccentric style. Arms enveloped in a loose knitwork wrap around my waist, and I bend over to hug the woman.

"Mairin said everything went well, and that Conlead agreed to terms," Noemie says after pulling away. Her narrow, bright yellow eyes flick to Takara briefly, then back to me. Only a few people know of Takara's relation to Conlead, and Mairin isn't, or *wasn't*, one of them.

"Yes, this Hunt we'll have friendly eyes in nearly all the territories." I affirm. "You and Drystan ready for a new batch of wild ones? I heard they found quite a few."

Noemie smiles wide, almost too far like she's overcompensating, all thin red lips and pointed chin. "You know how that panther is, bitchin' the entire time he built the new classroom, but you can tell he's excited. Painted it all up nice. There *is* something, though." Noemie's joy fades when she glances at Takara again, who nods. I raise a brow, confused.

Noemie reaches into her rainbow knitted duster, retrieving a folded piece of paper from an inside pocket. "Balderik found this in one of the labs, and the shifters they brought back ..." She shakes her head and I take the note from her, temper rising at the fact I'm just now finding out there's *something*.

The paper reads like a death sentence.

Test Subject 587
Physical Sex: Male
Age: 26
Shifter Form: Canine

Remarkable Features: Twin (Sibling Deceased), Healing Mutation

Notes: When this subject shifted under the last astrological event, everyone in a five block radius was healed immediately, regardless of ailment. The old were made young and the youthful were invigorated. Transfer to the Breeding Program; Phase 3

Test Subject 432
Physical Sex: Female
Age: 12
Shifter Form: Feline
Remarkable Features: Feral, Metal Manipulation
Notes: Subject is highly dangerous, refer to Metal protocols and restrain in a five point system. Refer to the Super Soldier program; Phase 1.

"They can't be serious." I whisper in horror, covering my mouth with my free hand. The sounds of impatient children and the adults tending to them waft through the nearby doorway, like the nasty outside world doesn't exist at all. "I should have been told. If I had known—"

Takara cups my cheek and I flinch back. Undeterred, she says, "You would've postponed Koa's party, and Koa needs this. *You* need this, we all do. *We* need something good, Raj. Balderik and Jaromir are taking care of the new ones, and we can slip away after the ceremony. Noemie and Drystan will keep the kids up here entertained while we do. From what I hear, Taru and Mairin have some new toys for the kits too. You don't have to take care of everything alone, we're *mishpoke*. We've got your back, like you have ours."

"That was not for you to decide, Takara. I—"

"Jaromir actually gave the order," Noemie says quietly, and I cut a glare at her that immediately causes the shifter to bow her head.

"Regardless, I need to be made aware of any and *all* changes, especially if it concerns people we've brought into our home. I will rest when I'm dead, and it's not for anyone else other than me to decide when that is. Are we clear?"

Takara nods, bowing her head. Her and Noemie say, "Yes, *Aleph*."

"Let's go, we've kept them waiting long enough." I lead the way into the Long Room, tucking the paper into my leather jacket.

Our main gathering hall of the Clubhouse, the Long Room, is filled to the brim. It's not often that everyone is in the same room at the same time, everything occurs here in shifts. From mealtimes to leisure time, meetings and everything in between. But for special events like today, everyone takes a break from their duties to be a part of it. I wish that Balderik and Jaromir were up here, and I have to drown my irritation once more.

I stand at the head of the Long Room with Xylia to my right, and Takara to my left. The once chaotic wave of children are situated in a semi-circle before us, flanked by most of the adults in the Rebel Foxes.

A child's first shifting has long been a source of fear for our kind. Their constantly shifting bodies do not settle until the mutation sparks around ten years old. Always transforming between humanoid and various animal forms that aren't per-manent. Due to this, children are hard to hide during everyday life, and *especially* during the Hunt.

Over time, Hotaru and I learned that our animal spirits are particularly pulled upon for one day out of a thirty day cycle. I theorize that's when the moons are full, but Hotaru isn't so sure. The Dome is buried deep beneath the earth, insulated by granite and aluminum, and the possibility of seeing the moons are non-existent. Nevertheless, the Hunt always falls on a '*maybe full moon*' as Hotaru calls it, when the kits have no control. Not to mention stress aggravates the shift, and nothing is more stressful than an entire world trying to kill you.

Before I started this gang with Balderik and Xylia, shifters were close to extinction. Abandoned by human parents or worse, their own kind, for fear of being caught by the Citadel. Or, eventually losing their child to poverty or violence. There's no rhyme or reason to shifters, we just *happen*. Best guess is a mutation, a way for humans to evolve and replace themselves.

After the day I was given a second chance, the three of us vowed *no more.*

We vowed children like us would no longer grow up on the streets, orphaned and hunted.

We vowed shifters like us would no longer struggle under the heel of the Citadel, and we would take our place in society.

We vowed friends like us would no longer fear losing another, ever again.

We don't always win, but shifter numbers *are* growing, and it's thanks to us. The only gang brave enough, *strong* enough, to house any and all shifters we can find. The other gang leaders offer refuge to a select few, but none have come close to our success, and no one else takes in kids. There's been mistakes made, lives stolen, but for the most part we have lived pretty well for the past decade or so.

When things really started to change, and more than the three of us were trying. Trying to be better. Trying to help. Trying to be *more*.

I inhale sharply and glance at Xylia beside me, finding the breathtaking redhead is full of freckles and tears. She's thinking about *that* day, too. The day we found the cottage and turned it into a home. We haven't lived up there in quite some time, not since building the bunker, but it was some of the best days of our life. We weren't on the streets anymore.

I wish Balderik was by our side, but if the refugees are that traumatized, I'm glad he's with them. I have a gnawing feeling in my gut about the identity of *'Subject 587,'* but Noemie didn't say anything. Unless Balderik didn't recognize him ... no, that would be impossible.

Hotaru hides under a rusty beret at the rear of the crowd, accompanied by many of the teenagers. Much to Taru's chagrin, I'm sure. My apprentice feigns boredom, but there's a gleam in those black eyes as Drystan escorts Koa through the throng of children.

A panther in fur or skin, the ebony tattooist clad in a denim jacket and a white shirt tucked into his jeans takes a knee before me. Drystan's waist-length, white locs are tied back, but a few frame his face. He takes Koa's small hands in his, and the toughest, 'meanest' of our group, sheds a tear for his youngest student. Koa was an accident, one that Drystan has personally felt responsible for ever since, and for reasons unknown. We usually never go into the old Woods territory as it's heavily fortified and guarded by the Citadel, but that day I was on the run in places I shouldn't have been.

I had found a hole in the barricade, which provided a perfect place for me to hide from the Citadel troops I'd been antagonizing. What I found inside was a bomb-wrecked portion of the Dome, devoid of any type of skyscraper or ground dwellings. Save for a singular warehouse situated at the far end of the section, close to the Citadel. I wanted to get a closer look, but I was pushing my luck as it was. I settled for scouting the immediate area beyond the hole, and subsequently found Koa.

After that, nothing else mattered but bringing them back to where it was safe. No one has lived in Woods for ages, not since the Citadel wiped out everyone living there nearly twenty years ago and put their barricade up. We have no idea where Koa came from, or how they ended up in the most desolate part of the city and survived. Koa hasn't spoken since I found them, but in the year since we took Koa in, they've started to cling to Drystan less and make friends with the others, surprising us with their ability to read and write. Most of the older kids we find aren't literate, but having that way to communicate seemed to break down a few more of Koa's walls.

But we never learned anything about Koa's past, and no one's pushed.

The gangly child with the remnants of acid burns covering the left side of their face smiles at Drystan, a beautiful and twisted thing. Something unspoken occurs between them, and I bow my head in deference to their moment. Drystan is more father to Koa than teacher, and I'm waiting for the day he asks to officially adopt the kit. The Long Room's clock tower chimes, and the other kits murmur and gasp, '*It's time.*'

"Koa, come forth." I beckon, hand extended.

Drystan and my lovers leave us in favor of standing in the back with Hotaru, Noemie, and Mairin, behind the children. Koa raises their chin, tilting the brim of their patchwork hat up, a gift from Balderik. Koa's thin lips set firm as they take my hand. I lead Koa to the only cement wall untouched by yarn, art projects cast in paint, or wrinkled newspaper clippings, evidence of our famous goodwill.

We face the Wall of Foxes, a textured white stucco that forms the face of the Long Room. Dual sconces flank either side of the enormous wall, illuminating green prints that trail from floor to ceiling. There's paw prints large and small, bird tracks and slither marks. Symbols of all those who came before Koa, no matter their animal spirit.

Located at chest height are three familiar, and faded tracks. A large paw print from a golden canine, flanked by two smaller ones. The one on the left is from a white and black fox, and the other a red fox. We were so young, and we had no idea what we were doing. Now, the wall is nearly full.

I raise Koa's hand, bringing their palm to rest over Balderik's. Koa gasps, and big brown eyes flicker up to me. They flash for the first time, a brilliant gold that temporarily bring me back in time. To *him*.

I bury the thought and smile, tapping into the pride over-flowing my being. A shift tugs at my skin, but I hold it back.

"I can hear them *all*," Koa whispers, entranced by the prints once more. Perhaps to ordinary ears, such tiny and hoarse words would be lost, but we all hear them. A tear slides down my cheek but I don't fret, and neither does anyone else. Even the youngest children feel the weight of this moment, in perhaps the only sacred place we have.

"What are they saying, Koa?" I ask quietly, drawing the child's attention back up to me.

"*Mishpoke*," Koa says.

I flash my eyes at Koa, and a fluorescent green plays across their cheeks. Koa flashes their eyes in return, and their golden irises absorb the emerald power dancing across them.

"Shift with us. Run with us. Grow with us. Fight for those less fortunate than you, with us. Your *mishpoke*. Your family. You are important, Koa, and this family would not be the same without you. Each of us contribute in different ways, and the form we take is an extension of that. There is a place for *everyone*, and tonight you find yours. Tonight, your print will join ours, and in a few years, when you're ready, you will choose a mentor and help our pack. Are you ready?"

Koa nods, body vibrating. "I'm ready, *Aleph*. I can feel it. He wants to come out."

I rest my hand on their shoulder, squeezing lightly before releasing them. "Let go when you're ready, Koa. Close your eyes, breathe, and open your heart to the spirit within. *Your* spirit."

Koa obliges, trusting me completely. There is not a singular feeling in the world better than that. Tell-tale spirals of magic come to life, beginning at Koa's forehead where it takes hold of skin cells, transforming them into something refractory and blinding. Ancient symbols cast in green and gold unfurl alongside paw prints, unbeknownst to the child whose eyes are shut tight. Across their cheeks, down their throat. A thick sweater covers their torso, but symbols make an appearance on Koa's small, shaking hands. Koa's heart *thuds* one singular time down the pack bond between us. Their body quakes beneath the oncoming shift, then stills completely.

"*Oh*, hello." Koa murmurs through a growing smile, eyes blissfully closed now instead of shut tight.

Slowly, they step back and *shift*. A flurry of gray and white fur overwhelms the air before me. Bones snap in violent succession, and there's an enormous groan of muscle as Koa lurches forward, crying out. Their voice twists into a marrow crushing howl as their face stretches into an elongated snout, complete with ferocious teeth that could easily pop my skull.

I'm nearly swiped by a paw bigger than my head, and claws the length of my arm. I take a few steps back, not recognizing the incoming animal at first. My heart races in anticipation, and the nervousness spreading throughout my pack is palpable. I glance towards them, finding Drystan and Noemie have herded the wide-eyed children back. A few of my enforcers have shifted into active positions. Not aggressive, but at the ready.

"By the Gods ..." Hotaru murmurs, the only one who dares to speak.

I turn my attention back to the great timber wolf when it whimpers, struggling to stand under its own great weight. From shoulder to paw, Koa is a few feet taller than Jaromir and thrice as wide, the largest in our pack. Koa falls back to rest on their haunches, and their head scrubs the distant ceiling. Never, not once, have I thought the ceilings were too low in the bunker.

Chest rising and falling unsteadily, I close the distance between us. Koa whines, and I whisper soothingly. "Hey, it's me." I bring the full force of *Aleph* to the surface, and extend my hand to Koa, palm facing out. Koa whimpers frantically and scurries in an effort to get to me, but the weight of their paws surprises them and they stumble forwards.

We collide, but I hold my ground (barely) and steady them. Koa exhales a long sigh of relief, forehead pressing to my chest. I run my fingers through their thick and ever so soft fur, and close my eyes. I seek Koa out between the singular bond between us, excluding all other packmates. *"Koa, can you hear me?"*

"Yes. Big Dog. Big Wolf. Big Boy Wolf." That same soft, hoarse voice echoes in the confines of my mind, nearly overshadowed by the *thump thump* of a tail.

I laugh breathlessly. *"Yes, such a good big wolf. Are you ready to make your mark?"*

Koa whines. *"Yes."*

I take a step back, then gesture for Xylia to take my place. Long curls of ginger flow behind her as she moves in that effortless way she does, and she kisses my cheek before I take my leave. I make my way through the crowd, exchanging placating comments and a promise to speak later for questions.

I settle at Hotaru's side and look at my blank-faced apprentice. Well, to anyone else it would be blank-faced, but I'm well versed in Taru. Their black eyes flash to a *deep* maroon upon cutting to mine through shaggy black hair, then back to Xylia. We watch her conjure emerald dust and sprinkle Koa's paw with it. Drystan's there too, a hand in Koa's fur.

"*That* was unexpected. Has there ever been a wolf? I thought they were something of myth." Hotaru mumbles, not unkindly.

"Nay, not that I know of. By the way, Koa said, 'big *boy* wolf.' And yes, he's *obviously* ... a giant wolf. What the fuck are we going to do?" We watch Koa press his enormous paw to the end of the highest row, beside Hotaru's small fox sized one. My shoulders relax an inch as cheers break the holy silence.

"Ah. I'll let the others know 'bout that." Hotaru replies, leaving the new pronouns where they lay. They turn to me, lowering their tone. "But to answer your question, you'll keep him safe. Like you've always done."

"He's a target, Taru."

"Only if you make him one."

I blink, slightly taken aback. "What is that supposed to mean?"

Hotaru shakes their head minutely, lips pressing tight.

"Tell me." I ask, having to keep the Alpha, and my irritation in check.

Hotaru glances towards Drystan and Koa, then back to me. "There's been talk that you're sending them out too young, especially since it was found out that Daisy and Liam are going on the Hunt."

"Do you really think so poorly of me that I would send Koa out at a mere ten years old because his spirit is fearsome?"

Hotaru's eyes widen. "No, I didn't say that."

"But people are comfortable enough around you to assume that you agree."

Hotaru opens their mouth, but I shake my head.

"We will discuss this later. As far as Daisy and Liam go, I trust Raith and Golding's judgment. We cannot shelter them forever, Taru. We were fighting for our lives at much younger than fifteen, and they have a right to it."

"Rajni, I *don't* think poorly of you," Hotaru says, stepping closer. They stare me in the eyes, daring me to say otherwise once more. "And I don't doubt you. You're right, we *will* discuss this later, because you have the wrong idea, and I have more to tell you."

Their eyes flash, igniting the darkest of wine. A beat passes, and panic spreads through the bond between us when I don't acknowledge them. I grumble, then gently thump their forehead with mine and flash my eyes in return. I sigh, then say what I came over here to say in the first place.

"Taru, you did good tonight. I don't tell you enough, but I'm proud and honored to have you as my apprentice," I say through the bond that is many things. Mentor and apprentice. Guardian and charge. Siblings. Alpha and Beta. Friends.

Hotaru's porcelain skin flushes to match the deep crimson of their studded leather jacket, and they hug me. *"Promise?"*

"Promise?"

After a few more moments we separate, then locate my mechanic not far away, standing on the outside of the crowd. An enormous cake has been unveiled, and Drystan is holding back Koa's massive tongue while Noemie cuts the masterpiece crafted by Jaromir. A few other Foxes hold back the young ones while the teenagers sneak around Noemie to steal a bit of frosting, and it's a beautiful sight.

I sign to Mairin, asking, "You got this?"

The raccoon shifter nods, dressed in nothing but a loose undershirt, overalls, and a crooked grin. Oil taints her tightly curled locks of blue, left cheek, and the back of her right hand. She slides a hand into her chest pocket, retrieving a palm sized tube with nothing but mischief in her brown eyes. She wiggles the concoction, raising her brows as she does.

"Oh yeah, we got this. Get outta here before the mess starts." Taru snickers.

A hand brushes up my spine before soft words meet my ears. "Raj, we got a problem downstairs."

I sober immediately and nod to Takara now at my side, then the others. Taru and Mairin's smiles fade, but the light in their eyes is bright. They trust me to make things right, that in the end, everything will be okay.

I hope that's true.

Super Solider

Smash.

Over and over again.

Teeth and claws and the entire weight of a feral bobcat slams into reinforced glass. Glass that has held true for far more wild shifters than I care to admit, but now a spider-like crack fractures throughout the length of the modest cell separating Subject 432 from Takara, Jaromir, Balderik, and me.

"I can't even get close to them." Balderik admits, pushing light curls away from his tired eyes. Takara is silent at my other side, arms crossed and chin raised. She tracks every movement the bobcat makes, and I'm once again struck with the fact that this was kept from me. While we were celebrating, this shifter has been hurting themselves again and again.

"I wouldn't let you get close to me either if I was strapped to a fucking *table* for who knows how long," Jaromir says from behind me.

Whenever we are together Jaromir stands at my back, an unspoken agreement that echoes the day I found him. When I stood between him and Citadel troops, blood oozing from a gash in my head. Thirty *dead* soldiers that I massacred in retaliation for killing his family in broad daylight. Jaromir was subdued, beaten to near death. I don't remember killing them all, but I do remember taking him home.

He doesn't remember much of that day either, but enough to haunt him for the rest of his life, that's for sure.

"They were in human form then, when you found them?" I ask, glancing back at the bear shifter. I haven't let on my irritation with him yet, but we'll be having a talk.

He nods, tendrils of white escape from his hip-length braids and stick to his sweaty, thick neck. "All of the shifters were drugged. Some were kept in cages, others were strapped down like 432 was. But the moment we took out these," Jaromir reaches into his woolen vest pocket, "they shifted and went absolutely feral. The others we could at least calm down, but not her. This one's a fighter. It would seem the chips are not only for tracking, but to restrain their shift."

I rub a hand over my face, then fix Balderik in my gaze. He's staring at the bobcat, hiding under the upturned collar of his knee-length black overcoat. His attention slides to mine and his usually steel blue eyes don't flash, in fact they're quite dull. I gesture to Takara and Jaromir, and both of them leave the bright hall filled with holding cells without question.

The basement is everything I don't want the children to see, if I can help it. Private and common infirmaries. Storage rooms filled with weapons, locked but dangerous nonetheless. Mine and Hotaru's lab, along with Mairin's shop. Jaromir's training arena is down here, along with the firing range. There is one more level below this one, but that's only in case of emergencies.

Once the pair step out of the hall and into an infirmary room, Balderik slams into me. The bobcat crashes into the glass as he does. Tears fall onto my shoulder as his arms sweep around my waist. I stumble backwards a step or two, wordlessly holding onto him with all my might. My life long friend breaks like rare ceramic. I've only seen him cry a handful of times in our life, and it's violent when he does.

Today is no exception.

After long minutes filled with tears, saliva and choked sobs, he manages words into my hair. "He's alive, Rajni. My brother's alive, and he doesn't remember me. And the things they put him—"

"Erik, eyes." I order softly.

He drags his face from my shoulder until our noses brush. Our foreheads meet and he hyperventilates, eyes dancing between silver and blue. I cup the back of his neck, fingers digging into his sweat ridden curls. "He's *alive*. We can work with that. That's what's important, right? Let me help this one first, and then we'll see to him. Together."

Balderik shakes his head without breaking contact with me. "You don't *understand* what they were doing in that last place Raj." He inhales sharply, steeling himself. "They were using him ... for *breeding*. Why? Wh-why would they do that? They *hate* us. Why, *why*—"

"Hey, hey, come here. Shh." I crush him back into me, lungs seizing as tears burn my eyes.

"It could've been me." Balderik cries.

Anger reignites my breathing. He presses his nose against my throat, inhaling my scent. I hold onto him for another moment, then gently push him back. "Erik, *you're* safe. *He's* safe. We cannot change the past, all we can do is make those bastards pay. You understand? Tonight, we make them safe. In two days, we exact our vengeance. But I can't do that if I don't know what's going on."

He blinks, confused. "What do you mean?"

I search his face, then flick my attention over his shoulder to where Jaromir and Takara had disappeared. "We'll talk later."

Erik nods, shoulders slumped and mutation under control. "Gods, I fucking missed you. It's been what, six hours? No wonder why they call us codependent."

I laugh, then kiss his forehead. "There he is."

Balderik smiles, and it highlights his thin cheeks. He hasn't been doing well, and I resolve to pay more attention to him. This certainly won't help his melancholy. I exhale a shaky breath and roll out my shoulders, then approach the sliding door attached to the bobcat's empty holding cell. I punch in a code that brings down the ward keeping mutation powers inside the cell. We have metal manipulation protocols, too.

"Want me to come with?" Balderik asks.

I shake my head. "No, I'll be fine."

I enter the last series of codes, and the door slides open with a hiss. I step inside the wild animal's territory, slow and steady. The bobcat doesn't charge me. Thick white foam drips from curled lips, and their pupils are extremely constricted. Upon making direct eye contact, I flinch at the cat's red hot defenses aggressively fighting my influence.

I close my eyes, and breathe.

The cat keens lowly.

The spirit in me, one that others recognize as Alpha, attempts to connect with the lost spirit. It's glorious and bright as it free falls through the universe, no threads are attached to it. She is unbonded, packless. Without a family.

Teeth snap dangerously close to my neck and I side-step the advance, doubling down my influence until they're whimpering at my feet. I kneel, looming over the cat. My eyes explode with such great power that neon green light reflects off her dappled fur and the walls of the cell.

The cat wants nothing more than to look away from me but she *can't*. A singular gasp cuts through her feral haze, one I've heard many times before. Claws dig into my arms as a terrified, foreign voice bounces in my mind.

"Don't leave me, Alfa."

I don't withdraw my influence until she's forced out of her full shift, reducing the bobcat to a trembling, adolescent girl. A girl, once fated to become a super soldier. I rise and take a step backwards, but she scrambles closer to me, an effect I was hoping to avoid.

Repeatedly, she cries, "No, no, no, *Alfa*, *Alfa*, please, PLEASE."

I kneel once again, unable to do anything else. The girl wraps around me like a monkey, sobbing. Fingers tug my hair and toes kick across my thighs. The sliding door opens, and a moment later Takara covers the naked girl with one of the standard woolen blankets given to all Foxes.

"Thanks, love." I murmur, then stand with the girl in my arms. By the time I straighten fully, she's snoring in my ear. Strawberry blonde locks lay over her bruised face, rather sweet looking when she's not trying to kill you.

Super Soldier.

My gut turns as I carry her out. Past the other empty cells, beyond the infirmaries. Through the cement maze until reaching a hall lined with plain, spare bedrooms. Ones used for new members as they acclimate to the life here. Balderik and Jaromir are nowhere to be seen, but I can hear the bear's low tone echoing from an infirmary back the way we came.

Takara opens the last door on the right, before the hallway splits at an intersection. She holds it open for me and I lay the girl down in a bed, complete with a frame, mattress, and freshly made linens. Has she ever slept in a real bed before? I was about her age, maybe a little younger, when I was given another chance.

Set free from a vicious trap, and released into an even more vicious world. My parents died when I was a child, a rare breed of people, especially now. Both were human, and they loved me. I don't like to think about them, because the force of their love and the sacrifice they made to keep me alive is enough to sink me deep below this Gods forsaken earth.

I was alone, mostly, for quite some time. Years. A period of time that I remember all too well, and not enough of. It was a haze of starvation, constant festering injuries and cold feet.

Such a small thing, but that's what stands out the most. Cold feet, and never sleeping in the same place twice. To this day I wear double layers of socks. Then Isaac took me in, protected me. Later on, I found Xylia and Balderik.

He was protecting her from a group of kids who weren't even old enough to be called teenagers, but they had all the meanness of such. My soon to be friends weren't even shifted, but the humans could tell they were something Other. Poor, to begin with. Weird. Disgusting. They especially poked at Xylia. Called her dumb, because she didn't speak, didn't defend herself. Not until that point, at least. And not with words. A brawl ensued, and she was the first to swing. Balderik was always the strongest, he was the leader of our little pack. It was never supposed to be me.

I was nothing more than a scared kid destined to be a super soldier.

I tuck the girl in and brush errant hair away from her eyes. The girl nestles deep beneath the covers and her dire need for *Alfa* fades. I sigh as the weight lessens, then roll out my neck. Hesitantly, Takara asks, "Will she turn again?"

I leave my place at the bedside, turning to Takara. She's standing near the door, hands clasped behind her back. "If she does, I'll be here. But, no. I think she was scared and lost to her spirit, that's all. Assign Noemie to her, will you? She needs a gentle touch."

Takara bows her head. "Of course. Erik's waiting for you, his brother is awake again."

I take her hand and pull her close. She rewards me with a deep kiss, and I exhale a question onto her lips. "What am I in for?"

"They're identical, Raj. It's ... eerie. And he doesn't remember anything other than ..." Takara bites her lip, steadfast attitude gone. "We can't let that go on. I never thought the Citadel would stoop so low."

I lead her out of the bedroom, then gently shut the door. I stare at her for a long, hard moment. "There's only one reason they're creating shifters, Takara. Fighting fire with fire, it's quite simple, really. Something we should've seen coming. It does not surprise me in the least, so why does it surprise you?"

Takara blinks rapidly, taken aback. She releases my hand, stiffening. "We can't all be as clever as you, Rajni."

We stare at each other and the wrong feeling creeps up my spine again.

I am the first to break. Time and place, time and place. I sigh and run a hand through my knotted hair, then look away. "It's been a long night and I shouldn't be taking it out on you. Like I told Erik, tomorrow is a new day."

She studies me. "Are we good?"

"Yes. Come, let's take care of the next."

We walk side by side, and I become lost in my thoughts. The look in the girl's eyes as she submitted to the power of the Alpha. The first time I used my influence was an accident, forcing Balderik into a painful submission when we were rough housing and he nipped me too hard. Not with my mutation, but the power of the Alpha.

The only one there's ever been, that I know of.

Few know besides the Foxes, and I'd like to keep it that way. If I get too close to unfamiliar shifters, I have to be in full control in order to hide the pull my spirit has on others. It's almost like holding my breath. I think it's part of why I'm always stumbling upon people who need someone. Someone to follow. Someone to protect them.

I attempt to hold my breath now, but the moment we step into the private infirmary room housing Erik's twin, my presence acts as a siren's call. Thick waves of blonde are cast behind my shoulders as thin arms encapsulate my neck, taking me by surprise.

He's tall like Erik, but much more malnourished than his willowy brother. His own hair is cropped short, scrubbing against my scalp as he rubs his head against mine. He's dressed in the standard issue, loose linens we have for all new members, and they hang off him. I force myself not to think of the fact he was naked when they found him. I focus on one thing and one thing only. This one, this one needs me.

No one moves as Willoughby Alaric, long thought to be killed in the same building collapse that took the rest of Erik's family, cries onto the top of my head.

He whispers, "Alpha, help me, *please*, Alpha."

My palms come to rest on Willoughby's sides and I carefully kneel, bringing him down with me. I cradle the male against my chest, eyes flicking up to Jaromir, Takara, and Balderik, then to the door. One by one they leave, except for Erik.

"A moment," I say to him through our bond, a connection that's deeper than pack. His jaw flickers, then he leaves without a word. The moment he does, Willoughby relaxes in my arms. I fight the urge to cry. I can't break down. Not yet.

His sobs don't stop, but they're softer, quieter.

I breathe with intention, long and slow, encouraging him to fall into sync with me. When he does, I bring my fingers under his chin, lifting his face to mine. His steel blue eyes are hollow, and his exposed neck is marked with ...

Anger washes through me at the sight of *'587'* inked into the column of pale freckled skin, but I bury it deep within. My eyes simmer with the spirit of Alpha and Willoughby inhales sharply, like the first breath after a long, good cry. I hold Willoughby tight to me, and he holds me just as firmly. I run a hand up and down his back, unable to fathom how identical he is to Erik, even after all this time. How easily my best friend could've had the same fate. I have so many questions for this male, but instead I ask only one.

"Have you ever tried cake?"

After many hours, two *whole* chocolate cakes which Jaromir ended up baking after the kids went to bed, and a gallon of soy milk later, Willoughby lies curled up in a pile of blankets and crumbs. I sit on the floor beside his cot, petting his scalp.

"I have something else for you." I whisper.

His eyes open a crack and a hint of silver light flashes there, warming my heart. A purr of approval escapes my throat and his pulse quickens in response. The thready and paper-thin pack bond that's formed between us in the last few hours reverberates like a plucked string, strengthening as his trust in me grows. Betas seem to bond to their Alpha quicker than each other, so I try not to think much of it.

"Yes?" Willoughby asks, and it's rough, but hopeful.

"It's your name. Do you want it?"

He frowns, looking away. "That ... man, he already told me. I do not like it."

I almost smile, his tone borders on a familiar pout. "No? Is there a different name you'd like?"

He glances back at me, pupils blown like that never crossed his mind. Eventually he says, "I'll think about it."

I nod. "Good. Sleep now." I resume petting his head and he leans into my touch, closing his eyes. He doesn't fall asleep, not at first.

"Alpha, that man. I thought I finally lost my mind. But he's real, isn't he?" His eyes shut tight, and he grimaces. "He, *we* ..."

I softly pick up the words he cannot carry. "He is real, and his name is Balderik. He looks a lot like you, doesn't he?"

He shakes his head, eyes still closed. "He's my brother. That's what he said, but I can't *remember*. I'm trying, but it hurts. I've been there for so long, I don't ... there's only ever been this." He absently reaches up and touches the block style numbers along his neck, blinking away tears.

"That's okay, you know. If you don't remember."

"It is?" His eyes open, and his hand falls from his neck in surprise.

I nod, hiding my grief. I *really* hope Erik isn't eavesdropping, as he's prone to do. "There are things we can try, if you want, to help you get your memories back. If you don't want to, that's fine too. No matter what you decide, you can pick a new name, live a new life. If you *choose* Erik as your brother, or not, that's fine. You have choices, you aren't obligated to anyone but you."

He rubs his cheek against the blanket he's nested in, staring me directly in the eyes. "I am obligated to you, Alpha." I open my mouth to protest, but he stops me by stridently adding, "I am."

I settle for huffing out a laugh. "For right now, I want you to get fat and healthy, yeah? You don't owe me anything besides that."

A choked laugh escapes from not-Willoughby, surprising me. He turns his head to kiss the palm of my hand, then settles back in. "Alpha," he murmurs.

One simple word, but the amount of respect and love pouring down the bond between us is crystal clear. He closes his eyes again, drifting off to sleep within seconds. The moment he does, I exhale a heavy sigh of relief. Despite the long road of recovery ahead of him, I have a feeling he'll be alright.

I've no idea what time it is, but I'm pretty sure I've hit twenty four hours of being awake. I need to sleep.

After his breathing evens out, I slip away with ease and softly shut the door behind me. I make it two steps in the hall before narrowly missing Balderik, snoring and curled up in an awkward position against the wall. I sigh, then call upon my power. I bring my hands before my chest and perform the conjuration I need. I'm not well versed in growth like Xylia, I tend to enchant and transform what is already there. Green light spills from my fingertips in a ribbon-like fashion, weaving and transforming into something solid and warm by the time it lays over Balderik.

I smile at my handiwork, a soft blanket of wool and moss that's long enough to accommodate even his lanky figure. I bend down and tuck it around his neck, then kiss his forehead. His lips turn up in his sleep, a quick thing like a baby smiling for the first time, then he turns into the blanket and continues his snoring.

Time to find Xylia. I've hardly seen her today, besides in the midst of chaos. Well, yesterday now, I suppose. Either way, it's been far too long. I need her.

I wander down empty halls until coming upon an iron staircase spiraling upwards, which leads to the rest of the Clubhouse. I fight the urge to wake Hotaru when I pass by our labs, tinkering with them always brings me joy. Hotaru abandoned their given room and has permanently moved into the lab, despite my protests which are nothing more than hollow threats. I have a feeling that despite my exhaustion, I won't be able to sleep. Hopefully Xylia can fix that.

The staircase spills into a corridor which takes me to the Long Room, the last obstacle before reaching our room. All the lights are dimmed. Glitter and confetti litters the floor, thickening as I step into the gathering hall. Sitting at one of the tables is Drystan, nursing a cup of coffee by himself. I glance at the clock tower, it's about to chime three times. He's up earlier than usual, but not by much. I debate on waving to him and moving on, but when he turns and gives me a sad smile, I'm reminded of Hotaru's words to me earlier and the look on Drystan's face when Koa shifted.

I make a detour for his bench.

"Morning." I settle on his bench, albeit backwards with my legs fully stretched out. I rest my head against his shoulder, and a deep purr rumbles through his chest.

"*Ai*, that it is. Xy waited up with me for a while, but she's gone to bed now." Drystan takes a sip of his coffee, then sets it down. "Jaromir said you calmed the little one down. How'd it go with Erik's ... the boy? Felt it when you brought the cat, and him, into the pack. Faint, but there."

I nod, head rubbing against the locs cast over his shoulder. "He's sleeping. Afraid of Balderik. Well, more so afraid of not remembering him and feeling like he should. The fact a stranger is his doppelganger. If they didn't look so alike, it wouldn't be so harsh, I think. He doesn't like his name, either. Up to him now, what he wants to make of himself. Erik will have to ... adjust, I suppose."

"Ah," Drystan says, like that's the answer to everything.

"Everyone have a good time up here?" I stretch my arms overhead, then lean back on the table to get a better look at him.

"Yeah, no thanks to that fuckin' bear dosing the cake with way too much syrup." He mutters. I laugh, which catches the panther by surprise. He chuckles as well after a split second, then sighs and focuses on his coffee cup, which he begins to turn in small circles.

"I'm afraid for Koa. He's not ..." Drystan makes a frustrated noise, abandoning his cup so he can turn on the bench and take hold of my hands. "Don't make him fight, Raj. He's not a predator. I know what it looks like, but please."

"Do you think I would *make* anyone do anything?" I ask in a whisper, no longer angry about this line of thought going through my pack, but hurt. Have I done so wrong by them all?

He flinches as if I'd shouted. "No."

"Koa is a *kid*, and he will be a kid as long as I can help it. When he comes of age, whatever path he chooses to help *our* pack is his and his alone."

Irritation crawls over me and I squeeze his hands still capturing mine. I'm too tired for this. Drystan abruptly shoves away from the table and our bench scrapes along concrete, cracking the silence. He's twice my age, but he kneels all the same. I hate to see it, so I cup his cheeks and kneel with him. I hate standing over *any* of them, they all know this, yet still try to lower themselves before me.

"I know, I know, but ... why a *wolf?* Out of all things?" He whimpers.

I press my forehead to his, a thumb running over his cheek as I do. "We have time, Drystan, and we will keep him safe until he is ready to defend himself. That is the bare minimum required of all Foxes, and we would be negligent if we *didn't* teach Koa how to survive. But that doesn't mean he has to go out on the streets and fight, and I would certainly never ask it of him now. I've always kept my word, haven't I?"

I shake Drystan's face, gently. I need him to understand this. His pupils are dilated, fixated on me. His pulse beats at a strong, rapid pace.

"I won't let him become a weapon in my arsenal, or anyone else's. Not unless he chooses that life for himself, when he's old enough. I don't ... I wish we could keep them young for longer too, Drystan. All of them. But this is our reality, and we can't hide from it. Not always. Not forever. We won't always be there, and they need to know how to stand on their own feet."

He nods, tears overflowing his bloodshot eyes. For a moment we only stare into each other's eyes, and I stroke his face. His hands are tight on my biceps, trembling but firm all the same.

At first glance, Drystan is a menace of a man that prowls in the dark, has more ink than clear skin, and he possesses a strength that rivals the bears. But if you were to look again, you would see past that fearsome exterior and find something much more delicate and passionate. He starts everyday with

Noemie and the youngest children, teaching literacy and facts while Noemie delivers on the creative and innovative side of things.

During the midday break, he checks in with as many people as he can, especially the teens. It may be a simple and gruff *'hello*,' or a head nod to affirm that everything is on the up and up. He's a caregiver, plain and simple, in every sense of the word. During the afternoons, he spends time with the older kits who have been relieved from morning work with their mentors. Drystan fills in the gaps that their mentors, and life, hasn't explained. Perhaps this one didn't learn how to read before arriving, or that one doesn't understand how plants give us precious oxygen.

I say, "You are so precious to me, Drystan. Not only would I be lost without you, but so would the kits, and the rest of the Foxes. I'm finding today that I do not provide the praise I should, and I am sorry for that. I will do better by you, I promise."

Drystan shudders, eyes closing. He nods, taking a moment to recompose himself before looking at me once more. "You do not need to apologize to me, Rajni. It is I who should apologize. I trust you. I do. I know that you are doing what you can."

I give him a small smile, then stand and help the panther to his feet. Before separating, I stand on my tip-toes and whisper into his ear. "Recon. T. Please."

Drystan swallows, then nods upon making eye contact with me. He glances around the empty space, then looks back to me. "Get some sleep, Rajni."

"I'll try." I pat his shoulder, then wander towards a hall which leads to the bedrooms. Before I head down it, I look back and find Drystan where I left him, staring at his coffee cup on the table.

After the Hunt is over, we'll have to do something ... relaxing. Whatever *that* may be. I'm sure Noemie can think of something, she and Xylia are the peace and harmony in this place.

I continue into the dim hall. After passing Jaromir's closed door, I peek in through cracked doors to the kit's rooms, finding beds full of gangly arms and furry legs overhanging mattresses. There are five rooms and each is packed full, organized by age. Jaromir and Drystan's rooms encase the kit's rooms ranging from youngest to oldest, ensuring the best warriors are always close by in case of emergency.

In the first room are four cribs and an endless amount of 'fairy lights' as Noemie calls them, moss, flowers, and other beautiful things that all babies should grow up with. The shift isn't an issue for our toddlers yet, but they're quite a handful for Senka, Galatea, Io, and Lennox as it is. They usually work in pairs, and shifts, supervised by Noemie. Three of them go on missions, too, but we make do.

The next two rooms are populated with kids in Koa's age group, which is evidently the most abundant, numbering almost three dozen. Unfortunately, most of these kids were abandoned by humans who had no clue their child was a shifter, giving them ten to twelve years of a somewhat normal life with parents who *seemed* to love them. Then, the mutation appears and all that love is thrown in the garbage for someone like me to find.

Koa slumbers on a bunk in full wolf form. Most of the kids this age are in a constant state of full or half-shift until they can control themselves, so this room is always filled with fur, much to Madlock's displeasure. I catch a glimpse of Koa's snout tucked under the blankets, then move onto the next room. It's closed, and I don't open it. There's only one occupant in there tonight.

We only have six teens, and it's enough. The time between the first shift and seventeen is fucking hell, pheromones and defiance reigns with an iron fist. The group we have now has been at each other's throat lately. The last group, Hotaru's group, was relatively mild compared to these ... instigators. The shifters who use this room aren't usually here long. Once they're old enough to choose a mentor, they're assigned their own room and official work duties.

Seth is the only one who hasn't chosen a mentor yet, and he's tied with Liam for oldest at seventeen. Those two are quite the pair, and the source of the majority of the tension in the group. I resolve to speak with Seth tomorrow, and as I make the final trek to my bedroom, a satisfied smile plays at my lips.

I will be their Alpha.

I will stay up for endless days and nights.

I will fight the Citadel at every turn.

I will not stop until every shifter is slumbering peacefully like mine are.

I step into a bedroom filled with candles. Xylia is sprawled across our bed like a fucking Goddess, wearing nothing at all. I shut the door and lean against it, heart skipping and air caught in my throat. She's lying on her stomach facing away from me, heart shaped ass in the air, feet kicking back and forth as she reads her book. Xylia is always a vision, but tonight her red curls are shining with a fresh dose of rosemary oil, and her fair, freshly washed skin glows beneath the candlelight.

When her eyes lazily cast over her shoulder, revealing bright green and gold thinly veiled by exhaustion, I shove away from the door. I make quick work of taking my medicine waiting for me in the tins on my dresser. A vial for inflammation, and a vial for hormones. I take a moment to admire the six-petaled beauty growing in its pot beside the two tins. From afar, of course. It's a common flower from the old days, according to the tome, Herbology of Northern Sirione. Xylia brought this particular one to life for me not long ago as she discovered it's a wonder for arthritis, and it has proven to be so. Only when prepared properly, and *incredibly* carefully, though.

I leave the flower in favor of my lover, slowing dropping to my sore knees at the edge of the bed. I grab her legs and drag her to me. She laughs, a bright and beautiful sound that's always reminded me of bells in the wind. She pushes herself up to sit, then her hands drift through the dirty blonde curls framing my face. Her small, white breasts stricken with blue veins and golden freckles tease my face, and I whine.

"May I have you, my dear?" I ask, and the need to please her builds painfully in my bones. A shift ripples through my skin, and I shudder beneath the force of her influence. We've been friends for a lifetime, and lovers for most of that. Xylia was my first, and I hers. There is a certain weight in a well-built foundation, an unshakeable and undeniable thing. Nothing can ground you more than your person.

Your mate.

Your anchor.

Whatever you want to call it.

I simply call her mine.

Xylia raises a thick ginger brow, putting on a good show of being put out. She signs, "Shouldn't you be getting to sleep?"

"I won't be able to until I've had my fill of you." I murmur, taking her hand. I kiss her palm, then drag my lips down to her wrist. I bring her hand to rest on the back of my neck, then lean forward and press another kiss to her soft stomach. Scars have been left behind all across her body from her time living on the streets, and the battles we've fought together.

Xylia inhales sharply, fingers twisting in my hair. She tugs once, and I pull back.

"*Yes.*" The word rings between us and relief courses through me like a heated tidal wave. I rush forward and drown her in soft, gentle passion, withholding my tongue until the last possible moment. I take a handful of breast in one hand, while the other takes solace in her thick curls which hide my calloused fingers with ease. She rolls her hips, grinding against the thickening hardness confined by my jeans. I'm still clad in my leather jacket and all my gear. She whines into my mouth as I pinch her small nipple, rolling it between my fingers.

I bite her bottom lip, almost enough to draw blood, then release her mouth and gently push her back. I worship every crevice and curve of this woman, the fox who has stood by my side far longer than anyone else. There is a short, hellish window of time when we were forced apart, but those dark days are pushed into the deepest recesses of my mind when her whimpers intensify, drawing me back to the moment. She knows this is what I need.

Her.

I leave a biting kiss on her love handle and slide my index finger into her warmth. Her hips buck and she quivers, grinding against my palm the moment I seat my finger inside her. I withdraw, then slowly thrust inside her once again with two fingers. My hips work in slow, aborted movements as I chase friction across the mattress, delighting in how her pleasure heavy voice dances off the walls of our room.

"Impatient, are you?" I tease, barely lifting my lips from her cool skin. I explore her cunt, curving my fingers until they meet the soft pad just inside the peak of her. I stroke across it with a firm and wicked pressure, bringing forth body-wide quakes.

Xylia snaps her fingers twice, and I know without looking she's begging me to stop teasing, that's it been too long. My fangs sharpen as they push through my gums, a painful sort of hot relief. Like washing out a cut. I chuckle, then lower my mouth in torturous increments, thrusting in and out of her in a steadily quickening pace. I lick and kiss her thigh as I travel lower, murmuring, "It's only been a day, love."

"Exactly." Xylia manages to sign, frustration apparent.

I'm pulled out of lust for a moment, wondering where Takara is. She was with us last night, and it was fucking divine. She usually spends most nights with us, but it's not uncommon for her to spend time alone in her own bedroom. I don't want to ruin the moment by asking where she is, or if Xylia knows why she feels *wrong,* or if it's all in my head.

Instead of asking questions, I bring my lips to Xylia's swollen clit and swipe my tongue across it, pouring my entire focus into breaking her apart. This, I can do. *This,* I am good at. My hand quickens, fingers driving into her sweet spot as I suck on her clit and lick between her folds. Pleasure splashes across my face when I slip my tongue inside her but I don't stop, moaning at the taste of her. Her hips roll, back arching as her blunt fingernails scrape my scalp.

I rut against the bed in full force as her moans echo throughout the room, broken and high pitched. I nip on her engorged clit, then go back to sucking on it. When she starts to ride my face in earnest, I add a third finger which stretches her tight slit. I use my free hand to silence her cries, fingers sliding into her mouth. Warmth rushes my face once more as she dutifully sucks on my fingers to keep herself quiet. She goes rigid, heart quivering and muscles tensing with the onslaught of her orgasm. She tightens around me once more, but I don't let up my pace until she's finished.

Once she is, I get off my aching knees and stand on shaky legs. Xylia wastes no time removing layers of leathers, jeans, and dirty cotton. I brace myself over her and dip my head for a kiss, my shaft heavy and leaking against her stomach. The animal in me cries in satisfaction at having pleased my partner, and I can sense Xylia's eagerness to do the same for me.

The *problem* with that, is I fall asleep the moment her lips fall upon mine.

I wake with a start. Smoke and fire eviscerates my nostrils.

I reach for Xylia's arms wrapped around my waist, but a familiar voice stops me cold.

"It's me." Takara whispers, shifting in and out of focus. She's kneeling on my side of the bed, hair damp. I reach a hand out to her, and she takes it. The amount of relief that comes from her hand in my mine is overwhelming. An affirmation that she's here. She's with me. With us.

"You stink." I mumble, thumb rubbing over the back of her hand.

She laughs quietly. "Can I join you?"

"Of course, my *me'od*." I open my arms to her, lifting the blanket as I do. Xylia rubs her face across my spine, making small noises in her sleep.

Takara slides off the clothes she was wearing last time I saw her. What time is it? The Clubhouse is silent and still. I briefly explore my tethers, finding all the pack members either heavy with sleep or lightly stirring, but peaceful nonetheless. Takara nestles into my naked chest, her bare muscles rigid with tension relax slightly when I wrap my arms around her solid figure. She presses a feather light kiss below my clavicle, sighing in relief.

Xylia's hand leaves my waist and entwines with one of Takara's, but she doesn't awaken fully. I kiss the top of Takara's head, and her cropped hair tickles my lips. I close my eyes, already drifting back into sleep.

"I love you both with all my heart, and I'm so proud of you, Raj." Takara whispers, and her promise is lost in the thickening haze of sleep.

Keep Your Enemies Closer

Hotaru, two cups of coffee, and 5:00 AM meet me at the door.

Taru adjusts their beret after I step into the hall and take my mug. Before shutting the door behind me, I peek in at Takara and Xylia's bodies melded in the center of the bed, where I once was. I softly shut the door, then roll my shoulders under the confines of my leather jacket before putting boots to stone.

We fall into step and I side-eye Taru groggily, earning a throaty huff from my apprentice. "Heard you were up until the ass crack."

I scoff. "When aren't I?"

"True." Hotaru takes a sip of coffee, then sighs and gets down to business. "We've got problems."

They pull out a tech pad from the inner pocket of their studded leather jacket, one that is eerily similar to mine. I don't fancy all the studs, chains, and pockets that Hotaru prefers, but they wear it well. Hotaru hands the pad over and I nearly slow to a halt upon seeing Takara's fleeting back come across the surveillance screen. I note the timestamp. 3:03 AM.

Back in the day, long ago when Hotaru first became my apprentice, I instructed Hotaru to install this camera overlooking the alternate entrance into the Clubhouse, and to keep it a secret. There are cameras overlooking the common areas, holding cells, and the front door, along with a few others such as in the labs or training areas. Those are known to all though, unlike this one. As I watch the scene replay over and over again, Takara walking out of the emergency tunnel, I puzzle together what I was doing at that time.

Through the swiftly clearing fog of my mind, I figure that must've been the time I was speaking to Drystan in the Long Room. I wrinkle my nose, remembering how she smelled of fire when she came to bed. I swallow something heavy and hand the pad back over. "How long?"

"Hour and a half." Hotaru's eyes flash blood red, a rare occurrence, then fade to black once more. We continue onwards with purpose, passing through the last stretch of hallway before entering the Long Room. Hotaru's eyes are different from other shifters I've met, their eyes are an endless black pit until emotion is shown. And Hotaru is a master at masking any real emotions, so when they *do* flash, I know it's serious.

They stop abruptly before we enter the Long Room. Hotaru takes my elbow and speaks from the heart, through our own personal bond. *"I'm starting to think there's a reason she had so much intel on those Citadel Labs. It was too easy. The team should not have been able to liberate them so easily. Something's not right, Raj."*

I frown down at the coffee that's spilled onto the floor between us, then drag my eyes back up to theirs. *"I agree, but for now we have the Hunt to worry about. You know what I've always said."*

Hotaru releases my elbow and nods, sighing. *"Keep your friends close, and keep your enemies closer."*

We walk together in thoughtful silence, eventually coming upon a panther and bear sitting across from each other in the Long Room. It appears Drystan hasn't moved at all from where I left him last night, but he *must've* slept at some point.

I sit beside him and find bags under his eyes, proving me wrong. I set my coffee down, then rub a hand up and down his back. Drystan exhales, giving me a sideways smile. Hotaru settles across from us, leaving an entire seat between them and Jaromir. Hotaru doesn't like physical touch generally, and we all know not to take it personally. Even the kids. But, even ice cold Hotaru needs a hug from their Alpha, sometimes.

"Couldn't sleep?" I ask, and Drystan shakes his head. His palms are face down on the table, fingers flexed. No claws, yet. I decide to leave the panther be for now, shifting my attention to Jaromir sipping on his own mug of tea. "How's everyone?"

Jaromir shrugs. "Kids will probably sleep till noon if we let them, they're not worried. Except for Seth, he was asking for you. The rest of us are tired, but we're alright. The teams are assembling for morning drills as we speak."

I shift in my seat. Seth, the oldest of the kids and the only one without a mentor, has given me a wide berth since his arrival. We've only spoken a few times since I found him last Hunt, but not for lack of effort. Some of the kits are skittish around me, which is fine. I blame it on my overwhelming aura and keep a hands off approach with those kits, trusting the caregivers to give them what they need. Eventually, they come around.

But Seth isn't skittish, just ... avoidant. The power of Alpha isn't soothing to everyone, especially those who aren't part of the pack. I know this. But I'd be lying if I said it didn't hurt me a little to have someone so ... afraid?

He's pack, but in a different way. He's anchored to Jaromir, and a few others, and by some metaphysical proxy he's anchored to me. I can feel him, but it's not the same as with the others. It's like seeing his shadow on the wall, something fleeting. My intention is not to make everyone bow to me, or my Alpha spirit. Would I prefer it if Seth saw me that way?

Yes. But in the end, all I care about is his safety and well-being.

"Seth was?" I ask.

Jaromir nods, watching Hotaru play around on their tech pad, doing Gods knows what, then back to me. His voice lowers. "Someone retaliated."

Hotaru's eyes shift to mine, then back down to their tech pad. They pretend to be fucking off, but I know they're listening. Drystan stiffens as I pull away to sip at my coffee, and the frantic energy pouring off him is disorienting. I settle for keeping a hand on his back, using the other to take a drink. After a long sip and a few beats of silence, I ask, "Oh? Someone?"

"Let's go for a walk," Jaromir says.

Drystan stands. "I'm going to check on the classroom. Make sure Taru's glitter hasn't tainted it." His shaky attempt at a joke is thin, but Hotaru rolls with it.

"Listen, once it's unleashed, it will never release you from its shimmery claws."

Drystan rolls his eyes good-naturedly, then says his good-byes and takes off like a shot in the night. I watch him go, and the hairs raise on the back of my neck.

"Ready?" Hotaru asks lightly.

I clear my throat, turning my attention back to the fox and bear. "Yes. Madlock and Raith too."

Jaromir bows his head, and we begin our descent.

We find Raith and Madlock in the firing range. Raith's seated cross-legged on a firing platform, cleaning her black steel pistol. Madlock is doing the same to his rifle, and I marvel at the pair's synchronicity. You can almost count on them to be here every morning around this time, and they're part of my Deadliest.

To the untrained eye, Raith appears to be a delicate and helpless blue-eyed and blonde-haired beauty. That would be your first mistake, as she's trained to kill you a hundred different ways without raising a perfectly painted finger. She's always dressed in immaculate dresses that she makes herself, and today the thin pastel blue fabric is especially low cut. Her curls shine under the fluorescent lights, bouncing across her shoulders as she works. She does nothing else for the Foxes besides field work, which is a mild word for killing and recon.

She left the Roost, not because she didn't like it there, but because she was *bored*. Raith is an incredible asset, and she came to me years ago before Sorin and I were allied. It caused a bit of a sore spot between us, but even more so between him and Raith herself. Raith, Sorin, and Katya are friends in the sense they grew up together, but if they met now, they wouldn't be friends at all.

Unlike Xylia, Balderik, and me. The three of us are codependent, to put it mildly.

And Madlock, well. His world revolves around Raith, they're a mated pair and package deal. I would never tell Balderik this, but he's a better shot than Erik is. Madlock's wide-brimmed hat is tilted down, showing off one of Raith's snow white feathers tucked into the thin leather belt wrapped around it. His pin straight, long black hair hangs around his face, which Raith makes a habit of pushing back, usually while chiding him for being so dramatic.

Raith looks up when I enter the room, then gives me a pastel pink smile. "*Aleph*, you're up early." She dismounts from the firing table and lands on her feet, while Madlock simply nods to the three of us. "What can we help you with?"

"Morning Raith, Madlock. Wondering if you'd care to go on a recon walk with me, and if Madlock could give us some coverage," I say, hands clasped behind my back. Jaromir stands behind me, and Hotaru crowds my side.

Madlock finishes assembling his rifle with a final metallic *clack*. He and Raith exchange a look that lasts less than the blink of an eye, but an entire conversation occurs during that moment. I fight a smile, thinking of Xylia and Takara back in bed.

Then I think of Takara smelling like smoke.

Takara leaving.

And I don't have to fight that smile anymore.

"Sure thing," Raith says. "We can go now."

I bow my head. "Thank you."

After gearing up in the War Room with respirators, a small arsenal split between the five of us, and spray cans, we set off. I lead the way out of the exit tunnel, following the same path Takara took last night.

We walk through a dimly lit, stone tunnel that is so narrow we have to walk single-file. It serves as an entry for the teams, so they don't have to walk through the common areas before or after a mission. It is also an emergency exit, in case the cottage is compromised. Cords, plumbing, and ductwork run along the ceiling. Neatly woven electrical wires which feed off our steam and mutation powered engines, supervised by my head electrician, Namir.

The oxygenation system, which primarily works with the greenhouse, distributes fresh oxygen throughout the Clubhouse via vents. Another system removes excess carbon from the air, delivering it to the greenhouse. The entire thing was birthed by Xylia, and now it's monitored by not only her, but Io and Senka as well. The water filtration system snakes alongside its brethren, a tempestuous beast that has taken some serious innovating. None of us have water mutations, and I've never met someone who does. I suppose the true heart of all life is water. And not even radioactive beings can recreate something as profound as that.

Upon reaching the end, Hotaru affirms once more there is no one outside, as it should be since this immediate area is off limits, labeled as an old and treacherous coal mine. I take a deep breath, then pass through the final barrier between us and the real world. A heavy, camouflaged door recessed into a mound of packed black dirt and stone. I have to push out, and partially up, in order to dislodge the thing from its angled position.

Jaromir is last to exit, and after he shuts the door a series of internal locks take place in satisfying clicks. I nearly sag with relief, which is ridiculous because we're *outside*, where the danger is. Wordlessly, Hotaru takes the lead and everyone falls into their roles as we begin our long trek towards the Chute. Shortly after the debris filled quarry that collapsed ages ago is a series of alleys, which is where Madlock bends down and presses a kiss to Raith's temple, then disappears.

Madlock can scale buildings like it's nothing, and he partially shifts when jumping between rooftops. I'm not really quite sure what his animal spirit is, our history books only have the regional species which once lived in this part of Sirione. Regardless, it's a furred animal that possesses not only incredibly strong back legs, but a long tail and a pouch. He will be our eyes, and have our back.

I comb through the pack bonds and form a closed circuit of sorts between the five of us, then explain the rest of our plan. *"I want to see if there's been any push back from the Citadel, and see how our flora bombs lasted. I've heard rumors of a fire. No force unless necessary, we are gathering intel only."*

"Well you're no fun." Raith whines, but I'm only partially listening because a sudden sense of alarm spikes from Jaromir. I glance at him, but his expression is mostly hidden by his mask. The alleys adjacent to ours fill with the noise of laborers and shift change, and Hotaru takes us down a narrow gap between two shanty homes. Talk of smoke accompanies our steps, and a faint trace of it lingers in the windless atmosphere.

"Has there been any word from Sorin?" I ask.

"Other than last night, no," Madlock says.

We continue on in practiced silence, moving between buildings and side roads in a zigzag pattern before closing in on the unavoidable main streets that spill into the main plaza. Sure enough, the closer we get to the Chute, the more black smoke thickens the heated air. Citadel soldiers move in great troops of two dozen or more all throughout the plaza, and you can tell they've been here all night. Definitely not the lazy patrol of six that usually monitors this area. It's impossible for Hotaru to steer us clear of the majority of them without meeting another band of soldiers armed to the teeth, so we keep our masked faces down.

"I don't think this is a good idea," Jaromir says, but it's lost to the rising crowd. I come to a stop, turning until he and I are face to face. I stare him in the eyes, hard.

"Anything you need to get off your chest, Jaromir?" I ask, and he lowers his gaze.

"No, Alpha."

It becomes too thick with curious onlookers, residents scouring the remains of our creation for scraps, and Citadel officers overlooking the whole macabre thing. The beggars in the streets, the possessed and sick fire eating the nature we left behind. Wandering children scraping trodden upon berries from stone, fighting over the bits they manage to work out of the dirt and charcoal.

We don't need to get any closer, though. The Citadel's fiery message for us is plain to see, even from here.

'Your Move'

Large chunks of nature have been torn from the Concrete Towers, allowing the wealthy to look out their windows once more. Gnarled roots, crisped leaves, and endless vines have been wrought and twisted into letters, stealing from our original message rooted into the ground. The new threat is pinned to the side of a Tin Riser, and the shanty building is being slowly devoured by a brilliant white fire that will burn for nearly two days, at least. Water only intensifies the growing flames, and the surrounding Tin Risers have caught fire. Numerous crowds stand a short distance away from the bases of the skyscrapers, watching their homes and lives go up in smoke.

I rake a hand through my hair, not missing Hotaru's side eye.

"I have a feeling this Hunt will be different from the others." Raith admits, her earlier blood lust subdued.

"We should enact protocol. Now," Jaromir says, fists tightening.

We all look at him.

"The Hunt doesn't start until midnight. Shouldn't we give the kids today, at least?" Madlock counters.

Jaromir bristles, and the tension thrumming throughout his figure is palpable. *"That's how it's always been, but what if today's different? What's to keep them from waiting? We told them last night the Hunt is on, what if—"*

I rest a hand on his shoulder and squeeze. *"You're right. It's better to be safe than sorry."*

Jaromir opens his mouth, then closes it and nods. Hotaru scans the area, goggles on. One of their many grand inventions, able to hone in on various things like infrared, mutation signatures, and electromagnetic shifts. Lenses of various colors click up and down over the main set of their own accord. Thick leather straps are laden with wires, gears, and tiny golden flowers that conduct our power just as well as they do electricity.

The '*o*' falls down in a fiery rush, followed by the '*y*'. Ghost fire, we call it. For a long time we thought it was a shifter from one of the other gangs, but when it started to show up each time we fucked with Citadel troops, we realized someone *there* has a mutation. Hotaru has managed to reverse engineer the chemical tracers so we could make some of our own, but we've never actually used it in the field.

The collateral damage isn't worth it. Not to me. A last resort, that's all.

Some of the soldiers stand before the destruction, gesturing towards the people's plight and laughing. It's then I notice there's a bonfire on the ground too, before them, and I sniff, catching awful whiffs of burnt flesh and hair. Takara came home last night smelling of fire and ozone, the same stench that fills the air now, but not of flesh. A sinking feeling in my gut is what forces out my next telepathic thoughts.

"Did any of you notice if Takara was absent at all, last night, or this morning?"

Raith says, *"Last I saw her was after you went to bed, she said she was looking for you."*

"Jaromir?" I ask, and he stares at me for a moment.

"Last I saw her was when we left you with Willoughby, in the infirmary. She said she was going to find Xylia. Why?"

"Not Willoughby, he doesn't like that name." I mutter aloud, watching the chaos around us. Chaos we brought about. The beginning of the end. I lock eyes with Hotaru, their goggles are resting atop their beret now. We stare at each other for a long moment, then I say, *"I've got a bad feeling."*

Everything is going according to plan.

Children chatter among themselves, lining several of the tables. We had to anchor the benches to the floor, otherwise the kids would rock them back and forth until crashing onto the floor. I stand at the head of the Long Room with a fresh mug of coffee in hand. Takara, Xylia, and Noemie stand in a semi-circle around me.

I haven't made the announcement yet. I will tonight.

Edgar, Quilla, and Galatea, are getting the Bunkers ready to go, along with a few other Foxes that are on a need to know basis. Otherwise, the morning is like any other. Foxes mill about the outskirts of the Long Room, or sit at tables not occupied by kids who have glitter in their hair and whip cream lining their smiles.

Jaromir, that fucking bear, leave it to him to spoil them all rotten with his creative cooking. He had dove into the kitchen after coming back, assisting his former apprentice, Lennox, with breakfast. Flower shaped pancakes surrounded by a river of berries decorate everyone's plates, topped with whipped cream made from oat milk.

I scan those gathered for Seth, but he's not out here yet. My attention falls on Golding and Sallow sitting together with their apprentice Liam. All three men are dressed in sleek black, nursing coffee and tea before training.

Daisy laughs at something Raith said, seated at another table. When the petite and shy Daisy requested Raith as her mentor, I was only mildly surprised. Madlock hides under his hat and trench coat at Raith's side, carving on a wooden figurine that's most likely for her.

Takara smiles at me and Xylia does too, one just as warm as the other.

Noemie goes on and on about today's art project.

The bobcat child sits with two girls her age, Delilah and Avery. Ika is usually with the pair, but they're currently helping their mentor and house doctor, Quilla. Both of those kids are smart and kind, and I'm glad to see them keeping her company. I catch Noemie's eye, then nod to the group.

"How's that going?"

"Oh good, she woke up bright and early, not at all feral but entirely curious. Name's Chloe. A bit nervous, doesn't remember how she got here, or her previous state. But, I explained to her this is a safe house for shifters, for kids like her. She didn't believe me."

"She said that?" I ask.

Noemie chuckles. "No, but why would she? I'm a crazy lady."

Xylia snorts as she signs, "You're not crazy."

Noemie presses a hand to her heart, offended. "Don't you take that away from me."

We laugh together. Takara is quiet this morning but then again, she usually is. It's taken some time for her to become acclimated to our constant teasing and sarcasm. Takara always says what she means, and never has the urge to fill a silence. Whereas Xylia and I are polar opposites, Takara and I are a lot alike in that aspect. I listen, and it makes me good at my job.

Takara works with Mairin on the constructs, is a member of Team Alpha, and one of the first people to dive into danger. She's supposed to be leading the charge with me tonight, but now that's all changed. I need to speak with Sorin, but I can't leave too early without Takara becoming suspicious.

I had planned on visiting the Netherspring with her and Balderik, but now ... I haven't thought of an excuse as to why she can't come yet. When it comes to combat operations, Takara is my second, a decision that may be my downfall. All of ours.

A lanky kid approaches, hands shoved deep in his ripped jeans and mismatched eyes downcast. The lights flicker above us slightly and I pretend not to notice. The fluorescent bulbs do that quite often around the kid, much to Hotaru's chagrin as it flips the breakers. Seth can't help it, though.

Telekinesis is a tricky thing.

"Seth! Ready to throw some clay?" Noemie asks, positively beaming. She's dressed in paint splattered overalls, trousers tucked into her combat boots, and a tie-dye tee. The beads along her neck clatter as she turns towards him.

He shrugs, barely meeting her gaze. "I guess." He glances up to me from under his wild and thick, dirt brown hair, then to Xylia and Takara. "Good morning," he says, attempting his version of cheery.

Which is not very much at all.

"Morning, Seth," Takara says.

Xylia smiles softly, bouncing on her heels. Moving, always moving. "Morning Seth. Did you have fun last night?" She asks, signing.

"Guess so. Cake was good." He lifts a shoulder again, signing his answer.

That makes me smile, and I try to tuck it away before he can spot it. Most of the Foxes are fluent in sign due to the fact Mairin and Xylia both communicate that way, but it's not a requirement. Xylia isn't deaf, but she doesn't speak. I hand my mug off to Xylia and kiss her cheek, lingering so I can inhale her scent. She gives me a brilliant smile, then settles against Takara's side after I pull away. I caress her cheek, then Takara's, staring at them both for a moment.

I clear my throat and turn away, focusing on Seth. I nod in the direction of the main hall. "Seth, could you help me with something?"

He nods, straightening a bit when I give him my full attention. "Yeah. Yes."

I focus on Noemie, because she's the safest to look at. "We'll be right back, don't wait for us to start the day."

She nods, smiling wide. I avoid Xylia and Takara's eyes and leave them behind. Seth falls into step beside me. We walk in silence, then diverge down a side hall that Seth didn't expect. He skids to a stop and turns on his heel. His hands leave his pockets and he glances at me, but I don't say anything. Doors and lights line the stone hall, like they do everywhere else in this labyrinth. This haven.

It's taken years of mutation infused, back breaking, *deathly* slow work to burrow as far underground as we have, and so securely. No one can penetrate our walls, no matter how hard they try, and there's only two ways in. Through the front door of the cottage, or the emergency exit. Even foxholes have a way out, or so I've read from the endless literature I've stolen over the years.

We come to a stop before a wooden door that looks nothing like the rest, painted in greens and purples and reds with no rhyme or reason. I expect Seth to say something, protest a little, but no words escape his stiff figure. I open the door and step inside the art room.

Noemie's room has always been my favorite. A long classroom with 'windows' painted on the walls, depicting a normal, ancient world. Rolling fields, winter wonderlands, circus tents, people dancing, and green, and *life*. Strings of yarn hang from a lazily spinning ceiling fan, whether they're errand scraps or something intentional, I have no idea.

I cross the room slowly, fingers tracing paint splashes and glue stains on wooden tables. Seth follows behind me, his step slower than before. We come to a stop at the back end of the room, where strings of yarn criss-cross from one wall to the other. Paintings are clipped to the threads by clothespins, depicting last week's art prompt.

What makes you happy?

The usual fills most of the pages of pulp paper.

Jaromir's sweets.

Mutations in all their forms.

Colorful eyes.

Paw prints.

Balderik playing his lute.

Noemie is there too, hands on her hips and a brilliant smile cracking her face apart. Most paintings I can't tell whose is whose at first glance, but I find one I can say with certainty is Koa's. It's a close up of Drystan's hands over his, teaching Koa how to wield a paintbrush. And then, in the back, is Seth's. I knew it was the first time I saw it.

"Alpha? I ..." Seth starts.

I give him a soft look. "Rajni is fine, Seth."

He nods, swallowing hard. "Why are we here?"

I shrug, then duck under the paintings until I reach Seth's. I gingerly unclip it from the thread, then make my way back to him. I hold it out to him, but he won't take it. "You tell me."

Seth looks up to me, face pale from under his unruly hair. He's seventeen now, a year older than Hotaru was when they asked me to be their mentor. Most of the kids choose one around sixteen, the others in his group already *have*, but not Seth. It strikes me how much he's grown out of his childhood this year. A defined jaw has made itself known, and there's no baby fat to be seen, there's even a dusting of hair on his cheeks that's a couple shades lighter than his hair.

A sick thought crosses my mind then.

He probably would've been in the breeding program, too.

And like a spark, another takes hold.

Does not-Willoughby have ... children? He did say he made ... contributions.

Oh Gods ....

But then Seth opens his mouth and I listen. I push away all of that, for now, and listen to the boy who has hardly spoken to me in the time he's been here. He says, "There's nothing to paint."

I nod, taking back the paper I offered. I stare down at it, turning the paper over in my hands, considering every angle of this. "I'm going to ask a stupid question."

Seth tilts his head.

"You're not happy?"

And he laughs, like I knew he would. A broken, tired, and wet sound.

Like Hotaru did, once. The day after the failed Hunt. The day all of their friends died, or were taken. The day I found them bleeding out on our lab floor.

I asked '*Why? Why? Hotaru, don't go. Why?*' and they laughed.

Seth says, "The world's shit. *I'm* shit, this place is shit. You think painting about our *feelings* is going to change the fact that we're literally *hunted* for existing? How the fuck can you stomach pretending that everything is okay when it's clearly *not?*"

I wait a few more breaths, ensuring he's done. "That's bull-shit."

He blinks, chest heaving. "*What?*"

"That's not why you're upset, not really. Our shitty way of life is no different than it was when you came here, Seth. You're just older." I set down the paper on a table beside us, then tap it gently. "Is this about what happened with Liam the other day?"

Seth crosses his arms, shrinking into his black hoodie. "*No.*" I raise a brow, and he scoffs. "How do you even know about that?"

I grin, just a little. "It's my job to know when back hall fist-fights happen. Care to tell me your side of the story?"

That surprises him and his arms loosen, but don't uncross. "What ... do you mean? Drystan didn't say anything?"

I lean against a table, crossing my ankle as I stretch my legs out. "Drystan doesn't know what happened. After he pulled you two apart, Liam told him his side of the story, and that's all."

"And ... what did Liam say?" Seth tries, but I shake my head. "You first."

Seth drops his arms and takes to pacing. "My eyes. He gives me shit for ... my eyes. He gives me shit for everything, I just fucking hate him."

"Has he been hurting you?"

"No, never that, he's just … fucking annoying. I was having a bad day, and he got on my last nerve."

"That's what he said, Liam, I mean. Said you needed to punch something better than a wall, so why not him?"

Seth blinks, stopping in his tracks. "What? He said what?"

I nod slowly. "Sounds to me he's looking out for you. His path may be messy, but it's laid with good intentions, I think."

Seth shakes his head, but he's thinking about it. "Does that mean I can't move out?"

"I didn't say that." A cacophony of approaching voices fill the air outside our little world in the art room. "But you do need to choose a mentor to do so. Why haven't you chosen one?"

Seth scrubs at his hair roughly. His eyes dart up to mine, then away. "I dunno."

"Hard to let someone in after you've lost everything, I imagine. It's been a long time since I've been alone, but I remember it. How long were you on your own, twelve years?"

"Yeah," he says, ever so quiet.

So much, so *much* in a word. Alone, on the streets, since five years old. *Five.*

"Well, is there anyone you *know* you wouldn't work well with?"

"Noemie. She's too … bubbly." Seth waves his hands. "Drystan isn't … he's fine, I guess. But I obviously don't have an affinity for teaching. Or people."

"And Mairin? I see you sneaking around her shop. She can handle both you and Tyler."

He looks at me then. "I never see you."

I lift a shoulder. "I check in on all my Foxes, even the ones who don't want to see me. But I have to make sure you're okay, and I can do that from the shadows."

"I want to work with you," Seth says, then his eyes widen as if he can't believe he said it.

I fight a smile. "Oh?"

"Well, Hotaru, really." He mutters, fidgeting with the hem of his hoodie. He reminds me of Xylia, how he never stops *moving*. "I want to blow things up."

I laugh then, full and honest. It surprises Seth, and me, but then he chuckles and a pulse of something warm beats between us, just once. My heart spills over, and I smile. "Why does that not sound like a good idea?"

His face falls, absolutely falls. "Is that a no?"

"You know, Seth, I've been thinking this entire time how much you remind me of them. Hotaru won't be my apprentice for much longer, so how about you hang out with us for a bit, and when Taru goes on their own you can follow them, if they want, that is. If not, you can stay with me."

Seth's lips crack open a shade, then a little further as my words sink in. "Really?"

"Of course, and you've picked a fine time."

"Wh–why's that?"

I stretch my arms overhead, then check my watch. "It's time to cause some trouble."

I find Takara in the constructs lab with Mairin and Tyler, but that doesn't stop me from breaking the news after a bit of small talk.

"Are you sure?" Takara asks, glancing up from the metallic chest she's elbows deep in.

Mairin doesn't pay our conversation any mind, focused on the inner works of the construct's head. Tyler stands quietly beside her, a dutiful mediator between engineer and tools.

His blonde and blue mohawk isn't gelled up today, instead it's freshly washed length drapes across a shoulder. His style is eclectic to say the least, but I like it. He wears a beautiful deep red, shin-length dress, one of Raith's, overlaid with an old denim shop jacket absolutely covered in button pins. All the Foxes trade in pins, but Tyler especially loves to collect them. The laces of his work boots are the same pastel blue as his hair, and they change as frequently as his hair color does.

Leo, the construct that Takara arrived with and essentially raised her during Conlead's neglect, stands beside Takara. Its tall and humanoid, if not lumbering figure nearly scrapes the ceiling in here, but Leo makes do. Takara granted Leo a consciousness, as she is able to do with all constructs, and is a metallurgist. Naturally, mechanics and engineering is where she thrives.

I thought she was happy here.

I clear my throat, leaning against the length of the wall behind Mairin and Tyler. "Yes, we need these ready for tonight, and Mairin needs your help more than I do. Besides, I'll have Taru and Seth with me."

Takara cracks a smile at that and goes back to her work, seemingly placated. "I'm glad Seth finally chose a mentor, and a good one at that."

"Well, I think it's Taru that Seth's after, but either way, I am pleased."

"I'm sure Hotaru's thrilled about that." Mairin takes a break from her work to sign, her fingers sharp through the air. I can only see part of her face as she glances back at me, but it's enough to catch her smirk. Tyler chuckles too, but doesn't say anything. Mairin adjusts the small device situated in her ear as she turns back to her project.

I snort, pushing off the wall. I pace around the work table, standing opposite Takara. "Taru clings to me when they don't need to, confidence is something I cannot give them. Having an apprentice is exactly what they need. No one likes change, but it happens nonetheless. Like these great pieces of technology, always evolving no matter what the world throws at them. Like us."

"And what will you do? Without an apprentice?" Tyler asks, glancing between me, and Mairin as she fetches goggles and soldering equipment from Leo, who had wordlessly begun to gather what she needed. The pink hand print on Leo's chest has faded, but its eyes glow as they hand over the tools needed to bring life to another construct like itself.

I lift a shoulder. "Sleep, probably."

And we all laugh at that.

Isaac's Town

You would think Mairin keeping Takara busy for the day while I plan to fuck her over would ease my worries.

It doesn't.

Even with the burning message, Takara smelling of smoke, the footage of her leaving, and the *wrong*, I still can't help but feel unsure. Like I'm missing something vital. Takara is steadfast, loyal, and good.

Or so I thought.

I try to imagine her standing with Citadel troops while the Clubhouse is ransacked, and I *can't*. I can't picture her watching Koa and Drystan be ripped apart, allowing not-Willoughby to be used like he was, or allowing *any* of them to be hurt.

But I also can't forget the way her face fell when she said, *"I can't believe they would go so low."*

"Alpha?" Seth asks, pulling me from my thoughts.

I shake my head, lifting my gaze from our boots scuffing against the remnants of a stone path. "Yes?"

"You still haven't said where we're going."

Hotaru chuckles under their breath, pulling their beret down to hide the rest of their face not already veiled by a cheekbones to chin mask that appears to be a simple filter, but there's an entire world of technology in that mask. "Just roll with it, Kid."

Seth bristles between Hotaru and me, hair flinging as he turns to Hotaru. "I'm *not* a kid."

Hotaru shrugs. "Could've had me fooled."

"Play nice, kits," I say, earning a glare from them both. I roll my eyes. "We're going for a drink."

Seth blinks, then nearly trips over a discarded mask in the narrow path leading to Village One. "But, I thought—"

I hold up a hand. "You'll find, Seth, that much can be learned by listening, and watching, which is what I want you to do. This is very important, and while I wouldn't normally take a new apprentice on a mission with me so soon, I feel as if I can trust you. Rely on you. Am I wrong?"

Seth flushes, then shakes hair away from his eyes as he adjusts his respirator. "No, I'm listening."

"Good, because I will be testing you," I say nonchalantly, tying my wild curls back at the base of my neck. He sputters and I readjust my respirator, wrinkling my nose at the lack of nature freshening the inside. We're all wearing old civilian masks, nothing like ours.

The Clubhouse's air is 96% fresh, compared to the 27% in the rest of the Dome. The greenhouse and ventilation system works wonders for all of our health, and while the smog out here doesn't kill us fast as it does the humans, long term exposure will harm us eventually.

As we filter into Village One, the air is noticeably thin and the atmosphere dark. While people are out, it's evidently less busy than usual and the less essential businesses are shuttered, light outs. Humans aren't targets during the Hunt, but the Citadel has no love for those who get in their way, or support the shifter population. If you're caught helping one, you're considered fair game.

The three of us weave through the stall market clogging up the main street through Village One. This place is nothing more than a pile of patched together rubble and tin. Homes have been built into the cavernous debris of collapsed buildings taking up street sides. There's small neighborhoods full of tin shanties, a place of squalor, addiction, and visceral poverty that many fear. One in particular is rumored to be an extremely dangerous place to live, but some of the kindest people I've met live there. It's different since the days of my youth, but not enough. There's a few Tin Risers in the village, but they're much smaller than those near the Chute.

And of course there's the Churches of Syzdon, implemented by the Citadel and utilized by very little. Most of those in the Garden believe in the Old Gods, if they believe in any at all. Syzdon is a God of Deliverance, of blood, human sacrifice, and utter bullshit. Another scare tactic to convert people to the Citadel's side. And the Emperor's son is the Child of Deliverance, a devout follower of Syzdon. A miracle for the ignorant masses.

Hotaru flips up the collar of their leather jacket, revealing more fearsome studs of black steel. They lift their chin, turning their nose down at anyone who glances our way. I do the same, and Seth follows suit. He hasn't been outside the Clubhouse since he arrived, but the world hasn't changed much.

Don't show weakness.

Don't make eye contact.

Don't start something you can't finish.

Steam emits from a grate as I step over it, washing the putrid scent of gray water over me. A tell-tale shiver runs down my spine and I casually look around, but don't find anyone out of the ordinary. We turn down a side alley filled with the back ends of soup kitchens and small businesses. Dumpsters line the way, intermingled with people camping out along the minimal shelter of the walls.

I evaluate each scowling, downtrodden, hopeful, or apathetic face as we pass through long enough to deem them shifter or not, and sense none. Seth watches me but says nothing, although that small thread between us bounces with questions. Our alley cuts across a main street, and we continue down it for another block before turning to the left. We immediately come upon the Door, and Seth's light brows pull together at the sight of a gaping hole in the stone, and the top of a spiral staircase.

Chatter, saxophones, and light emanates up the stone steps, escaping in a misty haze of purple and blue. Hotaru catches my attention before nodding to Seth. Although I can't see his face, I can *feel* that he's grinning like a fool as he absorbs the promise of a new adventure.

The Tunnels aren't safe by any means. If it's not a coal mine or oil well, it shouldn't be underground. The Citadel likes to kill two birds with one stone during the Hunt, knocking out all illegal activity, along with the existence of shifters. Otherwise, they don't bother searching the Tunnels more than that, but every few years they surprise Isaac with a raid or two. Tonight will be the last night the Door is here. At 10:00 PM sharp, Isaac will close it all down, then he'll fill in the stairs with rubble.

And then we find it all over again, thanks to the trusted long-tongues Isaac sends out. Salamanders with a penchant for secrets. The Tunnels aren't like the other gangs, because it *isn't* a gang. Isaac doesn't seek extra supplies or territory, nothing beside the safety of the most forgotten. He provides sanctuary for shifters or humans alike, the type of place where you crash before hitting rock bottom, if you're lucky.

Or in my case, a kid down on their luck with too many years spent alone under her belt.

I place a hand on Seth's shoulder and gently pull him out of the way, there's people flowing around us towards the Door. Hotaru snaps at a particularly burly man who tells us to get the fuck out of the way, and the man promptly stalks off. Seth looks up to me with hazy, dilated eyes.

"There's a lot. So much in my head," he says, waving to his head.

"You can go back, if you want," I say, immediately feeling Hotaru's chagrin at the idea of bringing Seth back.

Seth shakes his head, and his eyes clear slightly. "No. I'm ready."

I squeeze his shoulder, then release him. "Good."

Before descending, Hotaru and I shut off our radios. Seth watches us, head tilted. Hotaru says, "They glitch out and make noise beneath the ground, the frequencies get jammed. Better just to shut them off now."

"Isn't that dangerous? What if something goes wrong down there?" Seth asks, looking between us.

"Don't let something go wrong," Hotaru says.

I chuckle, then fix Seth with a more serious look. "It's a risk we have to take, but you'll be fine."

The three of us step descend into the Tunnels, using crude stairs worn down by thousands of footsteps. "He's waiting for us," Hotaru says to me.

"Did you—"

"Yes, I told him we'd be there promptly."

"Jackass."

"Micromanager."

"I do no such thing."

Hotaru laughs then, a small giggle. It's always small with Hotaru, but warm and bright nonetheless. Abruptly, they stop laughing. "*Quit* it."

Seth raises a brow, glancing between us.

"What?" I ask innocently. We reach a well packed dirt floor that diverges into a dozen different corridors, all spread out equidistant from each other as they snake away from the stair's landing.

"You're thinking mushy things. We've talked about this."

"Oh, I'm sorry for caring about you. I won't ever do it again."

"Better not," Hotaru says, leading the way down Tunnel 6.4.

The walls are the same black dirt as the ground and packed denser than rock. The small buildings along the sides are not made of brick or stone, but carved from the compact earth underneath the Dome. I've always felt most at home here, and the urge to pull my boots off and scrape my toes across the dirt is strong, but I resist. The market stalls have fairly large and open storefronts recessed into the walls, and the actual stores are set up inside bubbles of space within the cavernous tunnel. Vibrant curtains either hang down listlessly and scrape the ground, or are tied back to signal the store is open.

Thievery is not tolerated here. Neither is murder, assault, or any of the other Deadly Five, an old, *old* common moral law that all follow while in the Tunnels. I've only seen one person break that law, and the consequences left a macabre stamp on my soul. If anyone is desperate enough to resort to the Deadly Five, they are to see Isaac. Plain and simple.

All curtains are tied back tonight. The vendors won't be able to sell for a few weeks until things settle down, and they need the credits. Not all of the businesses are black market, many of them are simple things like a shoe cobbler's, or a hardware shop. Everything is specialized, general stores are too exhausting to find inventory for. I inhale deeply when we pass by one of mine and Erik's favorites, a certain baker that adores Jaromir. The two flirt via muffins, and I'll be sure to leave her Jaromir's gift before we leave. Half a dozen short cookies.

Hotaru rolls their eyes at my salivating, but says nothing.

"You guys are really like this, aren't you?" Seth asks after a little while.

"What do you mean?" Hotaru snaps before I can say anything.

Seth lifts a shoulder, cheeks flushing behind his mask. "I dunno. I thought you were being jackasses for my benefit, but you two really just rib on each other because it's what you do, isn't it?"

I laugh harder than I have in a long time, startling Hotaru. I say, "Yes, Seth, it's what we do."

Hotaru scowls, slinging an arm around my shoulder. They command Seth to take the lead, which the kid does after sputtering for a moment. We walk the rest of the way in comfortable silence, and I watch Seth take in the world that could be.

The life we could have, if we could hide from the Citadel forever.

Our tunnel comes to a dead end, and there's people ahead of us. I recognize many of them, and one female in particular nods at me, the lines at her eyes crinkled playfully beneath her mask. Seth stands on his tip-toes, trying to see what we're all lined up for. He opens his mouth, then closes it and waits.

After a few minutes, it's our turn.

Hotaru, Seth, and I stand before a trap door.

I grin wide, this is my favorite part. "Hotaru, if you please."

Hotaru nods, and I think they might be smiling a little too. They kneel down and knock on the unassuming wooden door with no handle. They knock three times in rapid succession, then once. Nothing, then twice. Seth watches with intensity as Hotaru steps back, then startles when the trap door flies back and hits the dirt. Hotaru steps forward, then looks back at Seth with a mischievous burgundy gleam to their dark eyes.

Hotaru holds out their gloved hand.

Seth stares at the black leather waiting for him.

Does Seth know this is it?

This is Hotaru giving him a chance. Hotaru doesn't do chances. Hotaru doesn't do friends. Hotaru doesn't do people. Not anymore.

Seth takes Taru's hand, and a violent pulse of excitement rings from Taru's spirit. Hotaru yanks Seth to their side and they both plunge into the darkness below the trap door. Seth's screams resound and I can't help but fucking laugh. How is it during all the shit that's going on right now, I can do that?

It's the little things, I suppose.

Before the people behind me can complain, I jump down the hole and the trap door slams shut behind me, ready for the next person to put in their personal passcode approved by Isaac. Seth isn't screaming anymore, and I can see him and Hotaru speeding down the corkscrew slide ahead of me. The ground beneath me is solid and glass smooth, how Isaac transformed the dirt to crystal is something I'll never know. One of his many secrets.

The darkness is thick through here, but my natural night vision allows me to see well enough. Fresh air whooshes towards us as we approach the last loop, filtering in through my mask with a cold rush. Hotaru lands on their feet, dragging Seth up and out of my way in one smooth motion. I land on my feet too, promptly reaching up to undo the straps on my mask. It hangs down on my neck as the three of us file away from the landing and down a tunnel dimly lit with small torches.

"What *is* this place?" Seth asks, eyes wide.

Hotaru looks at me, but I say nothing, so they take the question. "A friend of ours made this entire place themselves a *long* time ago, it's called the Tunnels. The entrance changes, but everything down here stays the same. Where we're going now is the Netherspring, reserved for VIPs like us."

Seth nods slowly, hands in his pockets. I wait for him to ask why, but he doesn't. Maybe he's taking my words to heart and saving his questions for after. I elbow him softly. "You'll like it. It's a right of passage, you know, for all new apprentices to come here. But it's a secret, you can't tell the young ones."

Seth stares at me. "I can't tell if you're being serious or not."

"She is," Hotaru says, opting to leave their mask on. They smooth out their hair and clothes, becoming fidgety once more.

"Oh." Seth looks between us, then gestures to my mask. "It's okay?"

I nod, tucking my respirator into a jacket pocket. "It's ventilated here, like at home. Hotaru keeps theirs on because they like the dark and mysterious look."

"I do *not*."

"Sure, Taru."

Seth pulls his mask off, revealing an ever so soft smile and red lines along his nose and cheeks. I don't know as if I've ever seen him smile, certainly not like that. Hotaru looks down at him for a moment, then turns their attention to the end of our path. A stained glass vestibule housing the receiving area for the Netherspring, its wide and colorful doors swung open towards us, revealing the line of people we had been behind before.

Seth leans closer to me. "Should I use a ..." He glances at Taru, who is watching the crowd. "A fake name?"

"If you would like, but you are safe with me. Sometimes, it's best for people to know exactly who they're fucking with, and other times it's best to hide until ready to strike. I'll let you decide which is best for you, for today."

He nods. "Okay. I think ... I think I'd like to use S. Just S. Is that okay?"

I cup his cheek, smiling. He straightens, preening under my attention.

Then we move on, leaving the moment behind. We pass through the vestibule, leaving our weapons in the care of Pika, one of Isaac's most trusted sergeants, and our jackets with a butler. Last, but not least, we pass through two tapestries separating the receiving area from the bar.

We enter a crystalline gathering hall of the finest quality, hollowed from the radioactive bones of the earth and transformed into something breathtaking. Floor to ceiling hourglass like pillars are dispersed through the area in equidistant rows, made from the same soft pink crystal as the walls and floor.

Isaac's mutation is crystallography, one I've always admired. Enormous and complex chandeliers hang from the high ceiling in between the pillars, and the surrounding crystals absorb and transform their warm light into a soft pink that slowly dances along every crystalline surface.

Three distinct tapestries mark the doorways, in addition to the one we just passed through, and each depict something sentimental to Isaac such as the old map of Sirione, or the weekly *Meira* ritual that some of my own Foxes participate in. Religion is a touchy subject with most people, but Isaac is a devout follower of the Old Gods. He's the one who taught me about them, and all this time later I'm still undecided. There is one thing I'm sure of though.

If the Gods are still around, they're major fucking dicks.

On the left side of the hall is a raised stage where saxophones, trumpets, a piano and guitars gleam under the largest candelabra, its chrome arms spread over the swing band and illuminate their wild beauty. A man crows with just the right amount of raspiness into his condenser microphone, praising a night on the town. I've heard this song before.

'Go down, down, down, that's where the Misfits and I will be found, in Isaac's town.'

The crowd is happy, a good mix of humans and shifters dressed in their finest. Glimmering dresses of fringe that graze upper thighs, half-buttoned dress shirts tucked into high waist trousers held up by suspenders. Skin, so much skin. If the natural aphrodisiac of a safe place to be yourself doesn't do the trick, the incense burners spewing cones of concentrated *kanah bosem* will certainly soothe your nerves and beckon you to find someone to connect with, whether that be through dance, drink, or good conversation. Most of us know each other and are friends, or at least know *of* each other. Isaac doesn't let anyone he doesn't personally trust inside his haven.

But none of that is the best part.

At the center of the room, is a pool.

A perfectly round, crystal clear body of water, about ten feet in diameter.

The only of its kind, like me.

The Citadel controls the main water supply, from procurement, to distribution and recycling. Not waste, because nothing is wasted. Gray water is used for nearly everything. Households receive a monthly drinking allotment which is of course, barely enough to survive on. Thankfully we can filter our own water in the Clubhouse and piggy back off households that are no longer alive but still receive a water allotment. Another flaw of the Citadel's system.

But *this*—this spring—it's fresh.

The pool is fenced off with delicate iron work that does nothing but keep you from falling in, because everyone knows not to touch the water. An unspoken rule to not taint the one pure thing in this fucked up world. One time, the *very* first time I met Isaac actually, he offered me a drink of fresh water. Despite my severe dehydration, I told him no.

When he asked me why, I said, "Because some things have to remain a mystery, or what will we have left?"

Isaac has had my back ever since.

The three of us drift off just to the side so as to not disturb the flow of people behind us. Hotaru and I wait in silence as Seth takes everything in. His fingers twitch at his sides and his clouded, mismatched eyes dart back and forth.

"I—I ..." Seth starts, then clears his throat.

Hotaru rests a hand on Seth's shoulder, an indescribable expression plays at their eyes which flash the slightest bit. "You're safe here, Seth. We got you."

Seth startles, locking eyes with Hotaru who drops their hand. "Yeah?"

Hotaru nods. "Yeah. Here." Hotaru reaches into their jacket, retrieving a pair of foam ear plugs with a thin wire connecting them. They hold it out to Seth and he takes it, unsure. Hotaru rolls their eyes, then takes the plugs back and gently places them in Seth's ears.

Seth's eyes widen, flashing wildly. One transforms into a blinding, pastel version of its usual deep green, while the other deepens from earthy brown to pure black. I don't allow myself to become unnerved by them, his eyes are one of his greatest insecurities.

"What? What did you do?" He asks, hands opening and closing at his sides.

Hotaru frowns at the grateful, if not confused awe in Seth's voice. "Nothing. You'll be able to hear us, but no one else. Better?"

Seth reaches up to gently touch the earbuds, then nods slowly.

"Don't keep them on after we leave here, you'll need to be alert," Hotaru says, looking away stiffly. "And I'll be wanting them back."

"Don't even." Hotaru warns me through our personal bond.

"I said nothing, Hotaru. Nothing at all." I smile, leading the way to the bar. Seth follows close behind, and Hotaru brings up the rear.

When we reach the bar, three patrons immediately clear their seats for us and I thank them. Each of them nod to me in turn, then leave. Seth raises a brow from his seat beside me, but says nothing. Hotaru taps the rose colored bar twice upon sitting, looking around slowly as they do. I lean forward on my elbows, resting my chin in my hands as I huff out an exhale.

Seth's ears turn red. "So ... can I drink?"

"Nope," Hotaru says.

Seth pouts, glancing sideways at me. I put my hands up. "You wanted Hotaru as your mentor, I'm only a shadow. Their word is law, my friend."

Seth opens his mouth, then thinks better of it and closes it again.

The mixologist works his way down the length of the bar, whipping up drinks for the other patrons faster than I can track. I elbow Seth softly, then nod to the bartender. "Pay attention."

There's a lot to take in and I track Seth's gaze as he scans the mixologist from head to toe. Golden brown and tall, dexterous and built like a dancer. His keen violet eyes flash as he laughs at something a woman dripping in jewels said, and his black hair highlighted in that same hue of purple is hidden beneath the most extraordinary hat.

His black top hat with a fat, purple ribbon complements a fine vest cast in the same shade. Underneath is an elegant, pure white shirt with flaring sleeves that cuff at the wrists. Nothing white lasts in this world, but somehow his clothes are always unmarred. Silver earrings, bracelets, and necklaces finish his eccentric look, along with a pair of ridiculously tight black leather pants.

Seth leans back on his stool, wide-eyed and oblivious to Hotaru's smirk. "That's Isaac." Seth breathes, and as if summoned, the person in question rests their ring burdened fingers on the bar before us.

"Well, hello there. That would be me, myself, and I." Isaac answers in a sing-song voice and a devilish grin. He reaches forward and ever so gently, taps Seth on the nose. "You're new. I don't recall inviting you."

Seth pales. "Oh, I'm—"

Isaac laughs, then reaches under the bar for fresh glasses. "No worries kid, any friend of Raj's is a friend of mine." He lines up four glasses, then glances at me with a more somber expression as he fills three with an amber liquid and the fourth with a bubbling, clear drink. We hardly deal with pleasantries such as hellos and goodbyes, and true to form, Isaac gets straight to the point. "How are you faring, *tchotchke*?"

I shrug. "That depends on the news you and Sorin have for me."

Isaac nods, sliding each drink to their respective owners. Speak of the devil, Sorin floats in beside Hotaru situated on the far side of Seth, along with his partner Katya. After brief hellos, Katya asks, "And who's this kit?"

I rest a hand on Seth's shoulder. "S. Hotaru's apprentice."

Hotaru opens their mouth to let us all know what they think of that, but Katya's excitement has already spilled over in the form of a giggle and syrupy words. "Oh my! You certainly know how to pick them, S."

"You've had all your shots, haven't you?" Sorin asks, which blows Hotaru's lid.

I sigh, listening to the pair bicker. Isaac prepares two more drinks of the stronger variety, sliding them across the bar to Sorin and Katya with a wink. Katya tells me about the party they had last night after the mission, and I halfway listen. Seth watches Hotaru and Sorin's irritable beginning transform into good-natured teasing, as it usually does with those two. Sorin doesn't shy away from Hotaru's brashness. No, he gives it right back.

Isaac primly clears his throat and raises a glass of something red, no doubt a fruity concoction. The chatter ceases and we wordlessly raise our glasses, clinking them all together. We throw our liquor back as one and Seth takes a long drink of his ginger soda, then makes a pleased sound and takes another sip before setting it down on the bar.

"Now that *that's* out out of the way, let's gossip." Isaac leans forward and rests his elbows on the counter, cradling his chin in folded hands. He waves a hand, and a cloud of near translucent pink closely surrounds us. The crowd pays us no mind, used to Isaac's shenanigans, but Seth is intrigued by the sound shield. Hotaru whispers in his ear, while Isaac continues on. "From the sounds of it, you *really* pissed the Citadel off this time, child."

Hotaru scoffs. "What we did has nothing to do with them."

Isaac gives Hotaru a flat look. "The message you left does. You're right, they could care less if you feed the poor, but starting fucking with their Hunt, and *hmm* ... " Isaac trails off.

"Aye, but we're ready," Katya says, resting a hand on my shoulder. "We're banding together, something we should've done long ago."

I reach up and squeeze her hand, giving her a small smile before releasing her. I turn my attention to Sorin, nerves spent before this has truly even begun. "Anything to report?"

Sorin nods, playfulness fading like a light going out. "Our surveillance did ... pick something up, a few hours after you left."

"Well?"

He sighs, raking a hand through his hair. "It was hard to tell for sure, it was dark and—"

"*Sorin*, give it to me straight." I push, using every ounce of self control I have to keep the Alpha at bay. He flinches regardless, and Hotaru reaches across Seth's lap to capture my free hand. Seth makes a noise in the back of his throat, then scrambles for his drink and busies himself with it.

"We left a few people behind to keep an eye on things, like you suggested." Sorin starts.

"And you stayed with them, *unlike* what I suggested."

Sorin gives me a cool look before continuing like I hadn't said anything at all. "Takara arrived shortly after midnight, came out of the dark like it was nothing and went right up to the commander. I don't know what they spoke of, but before she left, the commander asked her a question. I could tell it was because she began to leave and the commander called out to her. Takara looked over her shoulder, said something, then ... well."

Sorin shifts uncomfortably on his stool, exchanging a look with Katya who nods once, biting her bottom lip as she does. I squeeze Hotaru's hand, and they return my fatal grip. Sorin says, "It was like a series of tests. First, she rearranged the letters, and set them on fire. It didn't take long for the Risers to go up, not at all."

I steal a deep breath from the thinning atmosphere, dropping my head to hide my face and the damning emotions that I'm sure are there. I continue to breathe as Hotaru takes control of the situation, all without releasing my hand. "What happened next?"

"I don't think—"

I jerk my head up, staring Sorin directly in the eyes. "What. Happened."

He defer his gaze and shudders. Katya takes over, her tone tinged with the mildest of panic. "The next task was to kill a shifter. They put a shifter on their knees before her, and she snapped their neck without a second thought. It was quick, so quick. I—I—I don't know what you're going to do Raj, but every minute she's with your Foxes is a minute they're in danger. After that, she shifted into her animal spirit and revealed her true form. And then they just ... let her go."

Red taints the edges of my vision.

I try to shake the words out of my head, but to no avail. She killed a *shifter*. For the *Citadel*. I've had suspicions that perhaps her allegiance lay elsewhere, with Conlead still or another gang, but never this. Never did I think she would work *with* the Citadel.

My worst nightmare is confirmed, and the reality of Sorin's words set in. The Clubhouse, she's there, and I'm not. My heart jumps, but then Seth cups my elbow gently, the lightest touch really. I force myself to breathe, just *breathe*.

No one says anything for a minute.

Isaac looks between our solemn group, sighing. "Well, I *do* have a bit of good news."

I don't have the energy to say anything that's not a death threat at the moment.

Hotaru picks up my slack, clearing their throat before speaking. "And?"

Isaac grins, a beautiful thing that outdoes his outfit. He leans in closer to us from across the bar. "You're welcome to use the tunnels this year. I'm leaving them open."

"You're *what?*" I demand over the howl of a saxophone, to which Isaac only smiles. "How?"

Isaac's eyes gleam with mischief. How he's stayed alive for so long, I'll never know, but his risks always, *always* pay off. He says, "I know a guy."

Fang, Claw, and War Cries

Seth, Hotaru, and I stand at the head of the Long Room, waiting for the last of the Foxes to filter in. Takara and Xylia asked if I wanted them to stand with me, and I said no. Neither looked hurt, but Takara maybe was surprised.

She's about to be *very* surprised.

They sit at a table together, accompanied by a few other Foxes. Noemie and Drystan are making their rounds between tables filled with kids coloring and keeping themselves busy with a tub of stackable bricks that an old Fox made long ago, before they passed. Koa sits atop Drystan's shoulders, completely out of his shift now besides a floppy set of ears sticking out of his hair. I watch Koa rest his head atop Drystan's and close his eyes, sighing with a soft smile.

I look away, heart wrenching at the sight. I'm immediately distracted by Not-Willoughby and Jaromir entering the room, accompanied by Balderik who keeps close to his brother's side.

Not-Willoughby's eyes widen as he takes in the entirety of the Foxes, but his hands do not shake and his step does not falter. He's dressed in a loose cream sweater and dark gray sweatpants, Erik's clothes. He locks eyes with me, like he felt me staring, and he smiles.

He looks to Jaromir at his left, then to Balderik and tentatively says something. Balderik nods, then leads his brother over to me. Jaromir leaves the pair and joins Takara and Xylia standing near the front. Upon locking eyes, the bear gives me the subtlest of nods. I acknowledge him, then turn my attention to Balderik and his brother.

Not-Willoughby stands before me, gaze skittering to me first, then Hotaru, Seth, and finally Balderik. Balderik chews on his lip like he wants to say something, but only wistfully stares at his leather boots. After a moment passes, I realize they're both waiting for me to speak first.

"Hello my friend, how are you feeling?" I ask, slowly lifting my hand to Not-Willoughby's face. His whole figure visibly relaxes and his cheek nestles into my palm. He's cold, unbearably so.

"Good, *Aleph*. It is good to see you." He glances at his silent identical twin, then back to me. "It is loud here."

"Yes, it is." I nod, biting back a laugh. "You are very cold, do you need more clothes?"

"No, I am fine." He shakes his head, reaching up to secure my hand on his face as he does. I catch Seth watching us out of the corner of my eye, but he says nothing.

"Erik," I say, and he looks up from the floor. "Did you sleep well?"

A shade of relief colors his face, like he was expecting me to say something else. "Thank you for the blanket, it helped." He looks to Not-Willoughby then, who smiles at Erik a little. Whatever occurred between them this morning must've relieved the tension, somewhat.

"I have chosen a new name," Not-Willoughby says.

Balderik smiles at his brother, and it's sad, but genuine.

His brother says, "My name is Feivel."

"Feivel." I bring my other hand up to his cheek so I'm holding his face with both hands, then kiss his forehead. He shudders, crying through a wide, wet smile. "Welcome to the

Rebel Foxes, Feivel. May I tell them your name, or would you like to?"

His hand reaches for Balderik's, then retreats back to his side. It was so subtle, I doubt Erik even noticed. But I did.

"I ... can?"

"Tell them who you are, and during the next *Meira*, your paw can go on the wall, if you wish." I gesture behind us, and find Seth staring at the wall in question. His print is one of the more obvious ones. When he placed his paw down, sparks and electricity had shot out, burning the area around his print. Pride simmers along the tiny, minuscule thread between us, but I don't acknowledge it for fear of spooking him.

Feivel smiles, then looks at Balderik. "You will ... stay?" He trips on the last word, like it's a foreign thought that he can't fathom.

Erik's lips twitch. "I go where you will have me, Feivel."

I nearly inquire down the bond between Erik and I, curious as to how they're on speaking terms now when Feivel was terrified of him last night, but I don't. Not now.

Feivel nods to him, then turns to face the entirety of the Foxes. The moment he does, the room falls silent. He stumbles backwards a step, taken by the eager faces waiting for him. He does take Erik's hand then, and Erik smiles.

"H–Hello. My name is Feivel." He looks back to me, and I rest my hand on his shoulder. He dips his head, then turns back to the crowd. "I—I would like to be a Fox, even though I'm not really a Fox, I'm a canine, but I—I—*I* would like to s—stay."

Silence follows while the Foxes ensure he's finished.

Then they clap as one, hands raised overhead.

They stomp their feet.

Bare their teeth.

They chant, "Feivel's a Fox. Feivel's a Fox."

I release Feivel and find solace in Hotaru. We stand side by side, and they slowly wrap an arm around my shoulders.

Feivel laughs with Erik through fat tears, and I finally break. The events of the last two days crash down upon me, and Hotaru discreetly pulls me into their chest.

I cry, and it worsens when I think of how I'll have to shatter this long built, delicate peace we have. What do they think of me, crying at a time like this? I have to be strong, I have to—

Another body brushes against my exposed side, shielding me from the crowd which is still cheering for Feivel. Seth's back presses against mine, and his stance is strong as he provides me privacy and dignity. I greedily inhale Hotaru and Seth's calming and ever so grounding scents for five seconds.

Hold it in.

Let it out.

And I do it once more.

Then I lean back, and Hotaru wipes my tears while I rake hair away from my face. *"I'm right here."* Hotaru promises, and I give them the tiniest of smiles. I squeeze Hotaru's forearms, then pull out of their embrace completely.

"Thank you, Seth," I say, patting him on the back. He bows his head, and I step past him.

I take my place at the head of the Long Room, with the Wall of Foxes and my apprentices behind me. My pack is laid out before me, waiting patiently. There's a hint of nervousness in the air, whether it's due to my breakdown or the impending Hunt, or both, I'm not sure. I lock eyes with every single pack member, giving them my attention and absorbing them for a solid few seconds each. In case something goes wrong.

In case I fail. Again.

I dismiss Balderik and Feivel, waiting until they take a seat before I begin. Erik watches me with intensity, no doubt picking up on my anxiety, so I take another deep breath. Then, I change everything.

"Good afternoon, everyone. I have a few announcements to make. As you all know, The Hunt is tonight. We have been planning for this, preparing for *months* to make a true difference this year. I have made a few last minute adjustments that will affect everyone in this room, so please listen closely for your name, and possible adjusted role."

Looks are exchanged between the Foxes. Takara doesn't move an inch, sharp eyes set on me. Xylia searches my face, but I keep my mind closed. I can't risk anything leaking past our bond, and to Takara. While Takara and I aren't mates, we do have a strong bond. Whatever deceit she has planned, you can't fake something like that. You just *can't*. Jaromir taps his finger against the inside of his crossed arm, standing a short distance away from me.

"Team Alpha will be myself, Hotaru, Io, and Galatea. Team Beta will be Xylia, Balderik, Golding, and Sallow. Team Omega will be Raith, Madlock, Quilla, and Edgar. Team Clubhouse will be Mairin, Drystan, Noemie, Senka, and Namir. The objectives for Teams Alpha, Beta, and Omega are the same, but—"

Takara shoots up from her seat. Jaromir's arms unfold. She doesn't even suspect him; she's *so* pissed, and our connection is filled with an emotion I didn't expect. Instead of hot and all consuming rage, only ice cold fear leaks from her. I stare at her, doing my best to keep my face blank, and she slowly sits back down.

"As I was saying, Team Clubhouse's role shall be different than discussed. This year, we are enacting protocol Burrow, and we are doing it *now*." Murmurs erupt then, but I continue and they silence. "Each Guardian in Team Clubhouse shall be responsible for seven kits. Apprentices, you shall accompany your mentors and do as they order. Feivel, you will go with the Guardians and do what you can to help. Kits, do you understand what is being asked of you?"

Avery stands, one of the girls with the newcomer, Chloe. Resolve entwines with her every word, and it makes me so painfully proud. "We are to hide and listen to everything our Guardian says, no matter what."

I nod, and she sits, her back straight. "Correct. Guardians, do you understand?"

Each one nods. Namir raises her tattooed hand. "Why are we burrowing?"

"Excellent question," I say, shifting my gaze to Takara. "And one I cannot answer at this time. I ask only that you trust me, your Alpha."

In unison, they chant their chosen dedication. *Aleph. Alfa. Alpha.*

I raise my chin, and they fall silent. "Guardians, take the kits to their rooms to pack and organize. The rest of you, stay."

A few curious looks are thrown Takara's way as the room empties. Conversations erupt between the children who are old enough to understand, which are most of them. Out of the thirty five, only four are too young to know what's going on and are plenty happy eating their own snot. Seth doesn't move, though.

"Seth, you can go now."

He shifts on his feet, eyes down. "I've been training for this, I'm capable. I want to go with you."

I want to squeeze his shoulder, but instead I give him a small smile. "I know you are, and that's why I need you here." I gesture for him to lean closer, and he does. "You are to go with Jaromir, and you will soon find out why. This is my first assignment to you as your mentor, *listen* to him. Do you understand?"

He nods, then hesitantly takes my hand before I pull back. "Will everything be alright?"

And how fucking hard it is to smile and calm my heart then, to hide the lie.

"Yes, Seth. Everything is going to be fine."

I inhale slow and steady through my nostrils when he leaves my side, then straighten my spine. "There is one more matter, then we shall disperse. It has been brought to my attention that someone in the Foxes is actively conspiring with the Citadel. I have damning evidence, enough to charge the accused with arson, murder, and displacement of hundreds of humans, not to mention the cold-blooded murder of one shifter. Until we can hold a formal trial, they shall be kept in a holding cell until after the Hunt is over."

Before someone can open their mouth to ask who, Takara stands with nothing but panic and fury across her face. "Raj, no. You don't know what you're doing."

Jaromir rests a heavy hand on her shoulder and pushes down. Takara snaps at him, but when he doesn't relent she turns her attention back to me. Xylia stands, looking wildly between us.

"Rajni, you can't be serious!" Takara barks.

"I am."

I nod to Jaromir, and his eyes flash white. Takara's arms are immediately restrained behind her back by his mutation, and although I can't see them, I know his cuffs of relentless stone have hooked her wrists together.

Xylia comes to my side, rapidly cutting through the air to ask, "What's going on?"

"Betrayal." I sign, and that one silent word is louder than all those before it.

"I think we should be on the same team," Balderik says.

I finish loading my clip of mutated bullets. Small steel casings which surround a volatile enchantment which explodes upon impact. Razor sharp thorns, radioactive pollen, and small pale green flowers take hold of flesh, and the plant's dangerous roots find the target's heart within minutes. Something I created, and loathe.

"I want you with Xylia," I say without looking up, starting on my next clip. He and I are straddling a bench in the War Room, solid in the organized chaos taking place around us. Our teammates are gearing up as well, and the thunderous footsteps of those above us are endless as they pack away the best parts of their life and prepare to Burrow.

Balderik sighs, putting his rifle back together. He's an excellent shot and will be providing cover for Team Beta. Same as Io will be for Alpha, and Madlock for Omega. He says, "You could've told me about Takara."

I snap the extra clips into place along my leather belt, then stand. "You could've told me that your brother can look you in the eye now."

He shrugs, cheeks pinkening. "I'm as clueless as you are. He woke up asking for me, then he started talking and didn't stop. It's ...."

"Weird?" I supply, and he huffs out a laugh.

"Well, better to be weird than nothing at all, right?"

Balderik nods, blond curls falling over his eyes as he stares down at his gleaming black steel rifle. Ever so quietly, he says, "I think we should sweep the Woods."

I blink at him, mildly surprised. "There's no pickup points there, and the distance, Erik."

But a few of the other Foxes have stopped now, as our close quarters do nothing for privacy. The large and efficient space is essentially a locker room, headed by several round tables and an enormous pin-board full of our battle plans. At the back of the room is the armory, a storage room locked to the Gods above when not in active use. Currently, it's wide open and spilling its black steel teeth across my Foxes.

"I agree with Erik. Koa was there, and a few of those stuck in the Labs are from the Woods too, right? At the very least we should put eyes on it while we're out," Galatea says, clicking her tongue piercing against the one in her bottom lip. Her neon blue, pixie cut hair is sticking up in every direction, thanks to the gun oil streaking her hands. Like Raith, and some of the others, Galatea's strongest skill is killing.

I think about Chloe. Feivel. I look around the room, wondering how many I will lose tonight. Who can I send? Who can I risk? Is it even *my* decision?

"Team Beta." I call.

Xylia, Golding, Sallow, and Liam join us, each dressed in black tactical gear, the same we're all clad in. Bulletproof vests, leather jackets, and black pants tucked into black combat boots. All of our clothing is warded to the goddamned nines by Noemie and the other weavers, the other shifters whose mutation works best with fibers, enchantments, and charms.

At first glance we could pass for Citadel troops, but there's a lack of gleaming gold detailing on our uniforms. And we don't have patches on our arms, or the standard issue respirators that look like the old plague masks from millennia ago. Instead, a brilliantly detailed fox head is embroidered across all our backs in effervescent green. A painstaking effort by Noemie herself, and no one else.

Golding and Sallow are an inseparable and deadly team. Both males are built like a tank, and their feline spirits are clearly apparent in their human forms. Golding is a jaguar and Sallow a tiger, beautiful yet fatal presences that command all attention. Of course, such dominating forces had to find comfort in each other, much to my daily chagrin when their intense passion transforms into pissing matches that tear the house down, and then back again.

Nevertheless, they're perfect soldiers, and they love to fight for our cause. They are some of the few who abandoned their home territories to live with the Foxes, leaving behind their life in Jungle to pursue the infamous Foxes who say fuck you to the Citadel on a much larger scale. They found me during the last Hunt, and slew an entire platoon of Citadel troops at our side as a way of greeting.

How do you say no to that?

If only we found each other sooner.

"What do you think? Do you want to add the Woods to your list? You're already going through Reptilian, and part of the eastern side of the Chute. There are no pickup points near the Woods, you'll have to go old school search and rescue. And—" I gesture to Team Omega gathered together, specifically Raith at the forefront. "Are any of you willing to meet them at the way points if Beta finds asylum seekers?"

Raith nods. "I'll go. Once the initial path is cleared, we can station Edgar at the center south way point instead of the southeast like originally planned. Quilla can wait at the Chute, and I'll be in Reptilian. But if anyone *does* happen to make it north of Jungle, they'll be on their own."

"I'll cover Raith, and the others, as they set up." Madlock adds, glancing down at the tiny Raith with irritation. He would never argue with her, but his displeasure is plain.

Daisy is there in full gear, her weapons of choice strapped to numerous holsters. Blades. Blades upon blades. I resist the urge to tell the sixteen year old to stay behind. But she's not my apprentice, that's not how this works. We've kept her from this as long as we could, and I meant every word I said to Drystan. They are old enough to fight for their rights, and who are we to keep them from the battle of *their* life?

"Well fuck, I say we sweep the whole cocksuckin' thing. I'm sick of this bullshit." Golding remarks with the usual eloquence cutting through his curses, his voice is always warm, no matter the occasion. His dark skin is cast in a thin sheen of sweat, and a thin bandanna is wrapped around his cropped, black hair.

Liam nods at his side, his figure silhouetted by the compound crossbow at his back. I want to tell him to stay, too. I think about him, and Seth, but it's a fleeting thought pushed to the back of my mind.

"I agree. You say this year is supposed to be different, so let's go all the way," Sallow says, reaching around Xylia sandwiched between the felines to clap Golding's shoulder.

Sallow is cast in a dusting of ginger hair similar to Xylia's, but much lighter, almost more like a strawberry blonde. A full beard, shoulder-length coils, and finer hairs that cover the back of his hands, the hollow of his exposed throat. He and Golding smile at each other, then bare their fangs playfully. Golding ruffles Liam's hair, and the apprentice curses him out.

"Let's do it," Xylia signs while shrugging, unbothered by the fiasco occurring around her. She's mad at me for keeping secrets, and her anger isn't an easily swept away thing like Balderik's. I cannot say I blame her. We don't keep secrets, we never have. She knows I dream of my savior, and she knows my darkest nightmares. The same as I know she lost her first love, and I will never be a match for it, not that I aim to be. Love and connections take different forms, and you cannot compare one to another.

But I didn't want to burden her. I didn't want to trust my gut. I didn't want to believe that I brought the enemy to our bed.

I straighten my spine and nod. "Are there any other concerns?" I gesture to Galatea. "Do you want to go with Beta, then?"

Balderik frowns at that, but I ignore him. Galatea shakes her head. "No, as long as someone is going, that's all I care about. I got your back, Rajni."

"Thank you, Galatea."

I take a step towards Xylia, offering my hand to her. She glares at me. *I'm still mad at you.*

My lips twitch. *As you should be. But I need you, and the pack needs us to stand together. Can you forgive me, for now?*

Xylia rolls her eyes, then takes my hand and pulls me towards her. I wrap an arm around her shoulders and hold her tight to my chest, burying my nose in her hair. I inhale and absorb her scent like my life depends on it, taking a moment to center myself. The bond thrums with confusion, anger, and shades of relief. Comfort.

Love, most of all.

"Alright, let's go over the plan one more time," I say, placing my free palm on the map of the Dome. "As you all know, this year our goal is not only to locate abandoned children, along with any and all others who need our assistance, but to take down Citadel operations along the way. This year, we are wreaking fucking *havoc*."

A few growls and rumbles bordering on animalistic envelope me for a moment, bringing forth the rush of adrenaline and fight that I need right now. I push away the thought of Takara on the floor below us, trapped in a holding cell and most certainly losing her mind. I didn't get a chance to speak with her, but Jaromir and Seth are there, keeping guard.

"This year the pick-up points are here, here, and here." I gesture to the temporary safe houses implemented in Village Two.

Both Villages in our territory possess a concentrated residential population, as do the other cities on ground level in each section of the Dome, but what makes these two cities different from the rest is that they are heavily patrolled. The Citadel has a general idea what portion of the Dome the Foxes are holed up in, but not where *exactly*. This year though, I've laid breadcrumbs for them to find. Where they lead however, is most definitely not the Clubhouse.

"Alpha will dismantle and destroy in Village One, and Beta will gather shifters in Village Two. Omega, you'll flank Beta. Once we're clear, we'll regroup at the Chute where Sorin will be waiting with any refugees he's collected in Jungle. From there we'll split up. He's sending three teams, one to accompany each of ours, including Omega which will be returning to the Clubhouse with the initial wave. You know all his team members, nothing's changed there."

Quilla groans somewhere in the background and I wave her off. "Don't worry, I didn't pair you with Allison."

Without looking up from the map, I *know* she's flushed bright red. Xylia jabs my side and I grin up at the Healer on Team Omega. Usually, Quilla is in the doctor's office, or working shifts caring for the Kits. Since she and Balderik are the only shifters with healing mutations, Quilla lives in two different worlds. A family physician who heals scraped knees and paper cuts, and a field doctor who tends to vicious wounds. Instead of burrowing with her charges, she's stuck with us. Her apprentice, Ika, has begun to show promise in this specialty as well, but their spark is small, growing like wet kindling.

"What, did you want to be with her?"

Quilla tosses a thick brunette braid over her shoulder as she steps up beside Daisy and Raith, accompanied by Edgar, the shortest, and fiercest in our pack. She says, "Whatever, it doesn't matter."

"Ooh, trouble in paradise there, Q?" Raith teases, which earns a swat on the ass from Madlock which is eerily similar to the hit I received from Xylia.

"Don't let her fool you, they made up, and more than once if my ears don't deceive me," Edgar says, immediately earning a kidney punch from his sister. Siblings are a rare thing among shifters, and as such they are near inseparable. He has the same big brown eyes and thick brunette as she does, but he's got a few inches on his sister and affects a more feminine style than she.

Retorts are thrown between the librarian and doctor, and we all laugh at the absurdity of such a trivial thing. The lines between our double lives blur, and for a moment we just *are*. This is it. We're a good team, and there were no casualties last year.

But, that's not always the case.

I clear my throat, getting back to business. "Alright, alright. Edgar, you'll wait for Alpha at the Chute, then we'll make our rounds through Reptilian and the northern region. Conlead isn't going to help us, but he's going to stay out of our way, whether he likes it or not. He's said the same for Jungle, so we won't be fighting them this year, and we'll be able to focus *only* on the Citadel."

Hotaru steps out of the shadows, speaking for the first time. "There is something else." Everyone looks to Hotaru at the same time, heads and boots turning in unison like Taru's the Alpha. They'd be a good one, better than me.

Hotaru shifts uncomfortably, their unease a living thing between us. I asked Taru to stay with the Guardians, offering them an out. Of course, they turned me down, same as they have every year since my failure. Whether it's a death wish or extreme bravery that motivates Hotaru to fight the Hunt, I don't know. Either way, I'm not letting them out of my sight.

Hotaru says, voice strong, "Isaac is keeping the Tunnels open, he's not moving the Door this year. Travel tunnels only. The market, Netherspring, and residential areas are off-limits. So, we can use the Tunnels as a last resort if needed. Isaac insists they're safe from the Citadel this year, but use abundant caution."

"How?" Liam asks. "How are they safe?"

I stare at Liam for a moment, gathering my thoughts.

"Nothing about what we're doing is safe. I trust Isaac with my life, but that doesn't mean someone malicious won't get the same idea and we find them down there. Like Hotaru said, use them as a last resort. I need you to both understand."

I gesture between Liam and Daisy standing on opposite sides of the table with their respective mentors. "You may very well die tonight. I trust your mentors to have made the right decision, and their confidence in your abilities, but the fact remains that you are young, and inexperienced. Your going out tonight has been contested by several Foxes, and I am reconsidering my judgment. In the end, I have decided to leave the final decision to you. If either of you wish to stay and assist the Guardians, I will honor your decision, as will your mentors. There is great honor in protecting those who need it, and no one will think less of you for it. Now is the time to speak."

Daisy raises her chin. "I may very well die tomorrow, too. With all due respect Alpha, I have been fighting my entire life. I want to Hunt."

I nod once, and she bows her head in deference. I turn my gaze to Liam, expecting more of the same. Instead, I find the boy speaking in hushed tones with Sallow, partially blocked by Golding standing in front of them with his arms crossed. I lock eyes with the jaguar, not missing the subtle approval in his gaze. That gives me pause, because Golding and Sallow know that no apprentice of theirs, or anyone's, is required to go on the Hunt. I have never once mandated such a thing. Perhaps he's simply happy with the fact I voiced this fact to the apprentices themselves, instead of their mentors.

Liam steps forward, and both his mentors rest a hand on his shoulder. He does not bow his head, but his voice trembles the smallest bit when he says, "Alpha, I would like to stay."

I nod. "So it shall be done. May I ask why you did not choose to stay before?"

Liam swallows, glancing at Golding who gives him a reassuring smile. "I didn't want to disappoint you."

I try to speak, but I have to clear emotion out of my throat. I gently release Xylia and beckon him forward. The snake shifter stands before me, and I cup his face. He sighs, closing his eyes. I say, "You could never disappoint me, Liam. Every role, every person, matters in this pack. I am sorry you felt that you couldn't tell me."

He shakes his head softly, sniffing. Very quietly, he says, "It's not that. I thought I could do it."

I lean forward and whisper, "Go where you're meant to be. You are temporarily assigned to Jaromir's service. Go on."

Liam's eyes widen, then he quickly nods and turns away. Golding says, "Come here for a minute, kid." He and Sallow fade into the background with Liam, no doubt saying their goodbyes.

"You really think we can reach the north? We haven't been able to get that far in years without getting overwhelmed," Io says. The necromancer's chin is raised, exposing her tattooed throat. She's been here for years, and she lost her apprentice in the Failed Hunt. Like Hotaru, that hasn't stopped her from going out in the field. When she's not exacting revenge, she works with Xylia in the greenhouse.

Everyone in the room looks at me. My watch beeps, signaling it's time to move.

"I *know* we can. With what we found in those Labs, it's more imperative than ever that we find refuge for as many shifters that want the help. And, we'll be causing such a problem out there, that the Citadel won't bother with coming here. Understand me? This is just as much about throwing off the Hunt as it is getting them off our back. I don't know what Takara has let slip to the Citadel, but we *can't* let them get to us. There's no other choice than to *fight* this year. Unleash your mutations, take your animal forms and tear limb from *fucking* limb. Who knows? Maybe we'll take an elevator ride and storm the fucking castle itself, Io. I'm damn ready to."

And the room explodes into a flurry of fang, claw, and war cries.

A Goddamn Hypocrite

Ten to midnight is silent in the Dome.

The streets of Village One are empty, and the alleys are devoid of life. Even the homeless have found scant refuge elsewhere, perhaps in a distant pile of collapsed concrete and tin. We have been planning with our contacts for months, abandoning the idea of picking up shifters in this section. Deliberately leaving behind clues for the Citadel suggesting that our Clubhouse is in the heart of Village One.

We want the battle here, and the rescue over in Two.

But that doesn't mean everyone received the memo, and I hope to fuck that those hiding in their homes stay out of things.

Metal emergency shutters are pulled down over windows, decorated with massive padlocks. There is no movement behind the dark glass of the more ramshackle buildings which lack the useless, false protection of the emergency shutters.

Every neon sign is dead, and in the more well to do areas, only every third gaslamp is dimly lit. No sparking, popping, or humming taints the atmosphere.

We have not encountered a single soul, shifter or human. By now we should've brushed against a bounty hunter or two, or tripped over a half-shifted kit. The *wrong* feeling I've had since dreaming of Takara walking away has reached max pressure, threatening to blow apart everything.

The Rebel Foxes prowl along the carcasses of buildings and dirty alleys, furious and hungry for revenge. Our footsteps are well-placed, and if it weren't for the pack bonds tethering us all together, I would never know my Team is combing through the area. But I can feel every boot step, every exhalation and bead of sweat lost, every angry thump of a heart.

They're ready to hunt.

One by one, the team leaders check in as we settle into position. I take point, leading the way through our planned route to the first checkpoint with Io and her team close behind.

Galatea, our sniper and eyes in the sky, is nothing more than a shadow in the dark.

Hotaru is our head of communications, and they ensure their traps are set along the way. Taru silently works with Mairin in the Clubhouse, and Katya in the Roost, via the tech on their wrist. Katya affirms that Sorin and his teams are on the move in their territory. Mairin confirms the Burrow protocol is complete, and her drones scout the area ahead of us.

The Foxes are locked down.

I allow a singular breath of relief to escape, then turn my gaze skywards. Our sky is nothing more than suspended concrete highways upholding the wealthy, and in the distance beyond is the ceiling of the Dome, which hides the world humanity was once a part of. Supposedly the Dome appears as a mountain to the rest of the world, and the bunker rests at its core. Do the moons still exist, or did my ancestor's transgressions scorch them in a wave of radioactive heat as well?

But there's a pull from *something*, isn't there?

There's an itch beneath the skin, where the fox's claws scratch and gouge in attempts to run wild and free. Its jaws clamp around my heart, teeth gnashing wildly in an effort to tear and rip and *bite*. Where blood should spill, is this intense power that screams Alpha. It would be overwhelming, suffocating, and fatal if not for those who ground me.

My pack.

Megaphones screech throughout the atmosphere, and the intrusive sound overtakes every stagnant molecule. Mounted beneath the speakers on enormous iron pillars throughout the Garden, are television screens, sleek and bulletproof, which power on simultaneously. After the static fizzles out, a live feed of Emperor Drazen ben Matzliach appears, crystal clear and horrifyingly beautiful.

Emperor Drazen has ruled over the Dome for twenty-six years, since he executed the previous ruler, Empress Tamaria bat Mazliach, his grandmother, at the ripe age of fifteen. You would think the stress of running a dystopian society on the brink of failure and revolt would age the man somewhat, but he doesn't appear a day over twenty-five.

He's seated behind an ostentatious desk, one embedded with gemstones throughout the ancient wood. His long, pearlescent hair is woven into an elaborate crown of braids situated atop his head. His skin is whiter than oat flour, stretched thin over high cheekbones and the dramatic arc of his jaw. His eyes are the prettiest shade of blue I've ever seen, perhaps the closest anyone will ever come to seeing the old sky. The Emperor's lips are unpainted, but they are such a natural deep pink that they appear bloodstained. Kohl lines his eyelids, finishing in magnificent whorls where crows feet should be, and his lashes are painted silver which match the powder swept across his lids. He wears a sheer white robe parted in the front and nothing else.

When he begins to speak, I think how much better he would look in red.

"Good citizens of the Dome, may we have your attention. Tonight is the 66th annual Hunt, sponsored by the Matzliach Dynasty. The Hunt is a night of cleansing, one that is vital to the well being of humans. The mutant race known as shifters are a threat to humanity as we know it, and must be eliminated."

Drazen smiles, leaning forward in his upholstered drafting chair. A chill runs down my spine when I notice two things. He's changing the script, and his ever so dutiful son isn't standing behind him per-usual. If he's not standing behind him, then that means he's participating in the Hunt for the first time in nearly twenty years. Drazen goes on, smile sharpening as if he can hear my heart rattling against its cage of anxiety and power.

"Due to the events of this past year, we have decided to ... adjust our Five Star System. Listen very closely, my friends. To achieve a Brass Star and earn visitor's access to the Upper City, one must turn in one shifter to the authorities. For an Iron Star, which grants residence in the Upper City, one must turn in five shifters. A Silver Star grants residence in a Citadel manor, and you need only turn in seven shifters. For only three more shifters, you gain Gold Star status and a household staff to run said manor. And last, but not least, the Crystal Star."

Drazen pauses, folding his hands in his lap. I tear my radio from its holster and smash it against my trembling lips. "Now, Hotaru. Play it *now*. Right fucking—"

"To earn a Crystal Star, one only need—"

With a deafening screech, the megaphones cut out. Drazen blinks and his lips close, then his gaze ever so slightly shifts to someone standing behind the camera. He opens his lips again, but a prerecorded message comes to life over the speakers and overrides the Citadel's frequencies. I'm grateful that I get to *see* the look on his face as I threaten him.

"This year's Hunt is the last to plague our world. If you will not fight with us, then hide in your homes, shut your blinds, and in the morning, you'll wake to a new day. One where the

Citadel is put in their place, because without us, they'd be *nothing*."

The barracks across the street from us comes to life, while the Church beside it is empty and dark. Chain-link gates slide open, releasing armored truck after truck, complete with troops stationed at the dynamic weapons nestled at the top of the beastly machines. The convoy spills onto the main street, and the troops are so close I can taste their sweet adrenaline. Moments later, the purr of airships fills the air. I check my watch, three minutes to midnight. Io nods to me, and I return the gesture.

"The time to roll over and play dead has come to pass, and you must make a choice. You can choose to defend your neighbors, friends, strangers, even though they are different from you. If you cannot do so, I do not blame you, but I ask you to search within yourself, because one day it will be *you* they Hunt down, and there will be no one left to save you if you do not act now. Do not let them tempt you with their lies."

The message cuts out, and for a moment there's nothing but the click of my watch, tires upon the street, and orders shouted by cowards. Drazen stares at me from his safe place inside the Citadel. Time seems to stretch on, and on, until his impassive expression shifts. He picks a piece of paper up off his desk, then turns its towards the camera. Written in bold, red lettering, is a death sentence. Beside it, there's picture of me. It's torn down the middle, and my arm is slung around someone who is no longer in the picture.

Takara.

'Those who capture, and turn in, one Rebel Fox will be granted a Crystal Star, and a place in my court. The person responsible for the live capture of Rajni, leader of the Rebel Foxes, will earn my son's hand, the future Emperor of the Dome.'

A singular chime rings throughout the entire Dome, a high pitched thing that sings and dances along the mile thick walls of granite buried deep within the earth.

Midnight.

A child limps into the road, halfway between my hiding spot and the incoming trucks. A flash of bright blue overtakes the darkness as the child cries out, contorting violently as their shift overtakes them. A cry transforms into a distressed howl, and it's followed by others in the distance.

The night fills with the call of the wild, but those who need help, and those ready to provide it.

The truck at the forefront doesn't slow down, but the soldier in the turret turns. He focuses on the small body twisting at all the wrong angles, readying his aim. A heart shot takes hold of the soldier, courtesy of Galatea, but it does nothing.

It does ... *nothing*.

He grunts, shoulder jerking as the bullet tears right through him, as if sliding through butter instead of flesh and bone. He refocuses on his shot, and there's a flash of red in his eyes. As if slapped, I release he's not wearing a respirator.

"Now, Hotaru!" I shout, running out into the street with black and white fur breaking through my hardening skin. Soldiers, those in Citadel gear and civvy clothes, fall out of the shadows the moment I do. I don't know which of the residents are friends or foe, but I trust my pack to cover me, vision tunneling. Gunshots crack through the air and I pump my arms and legs, faster, *faster*.

"*But—*"

"NOW!"

Two seconds pass.

Two hurried footfalls.

One blink of a red light on my wrist.

I thrust my palms towards the child rapidly shifting between fox and sheep, activating my wrist guards. Vines erupt from the black steel manacles crafted by Xylia and myself, barreling for the kit.

Explosions rock the street occupied by Citadel warehouses, starting at the barracks and rushing towards us with fiery intent. The rear truck flips from the force of impact, then the next, and the next. Screams and the sick crunch of metal thickens the air, followed by the *whoomph* of a gas main beneath the street exploding.

My vines take hold of the writhing child, yanking her towards me. Flames singe my skin, and the kit bites and snarls as I tuck them to my chest. We roll away from the incoming collision, nearly crashing into Io as she fends off two citadel troops with a wicked machete. I unsteadily rise to my feet, keeping the kit close. Io shouts, "Blades, not bullets! Rajni, get her out of here!"

I shake the ringing out of my ears and tighten my grip on the kit who's stopped fighting, but not snarling. Soot, death, and battle cries take the space we leave behind and I don't stop running until we reach the relative shelter of a nearby alley.

"Rajni!" Hotaru's voice repeatedly snapping over the Alpha channel finally sinks into my ears, and their furious heartbeat wipes away the deafening static.

I kneel, gently setting the kit down on their feet. She's wearing an iron collar with tech embedded into the metal, the source of the luminous blue light from before. The once blue indicator is now orange, and something tells me it's about to turn red. Pain flares throughout my right arm and I groan.

"Here." I manage through a cough, but it doesn't matter.

Hotaru drops into the alley from a nearby ladder, as does Galatea from a different building farther down the way. Through the radio she says, "I'm going to help Io, she's checking bodies and it seems like we've gained a few friends. We're clear, for now."

"Be careful."

"Affirmative."

Hotaru approaches me with such fierce anxiety tainting their steps that it affects the shell-shocked kit, who begins to cry. I growl at Taru, and they snap their elongated teeth in return. "That was stupid, Rajni."

"Shh, it's okay," I say to the kit, allowing some of the Alpha to surface and calm her. I turn my attention back to Hotaru, who somehow manages to retrieve a healing pod and glare at me with the force of the universe at the same time. "Can you take this off?" I ask, pointing to the collar.

Hotaru squats, pulling the pin on the fist sized metallic pod housing Balderik's stored healing power. A cloud of silver dust lazily spills out of the canister, then rushes towards the kit and I when sensing our injuries. Healing mutation is painfully cold, but thankfully the sensation is quick. My shoulder pops back into place with a solid *thud*, and the kit shivers as whatever internal injuries she has heals, for there's not really any on the outside.

"Yes, but not here. We should go back, the stakes are too high and everyone knows who you are now. Live to fight another day, right?" Hotaru's pinprick pupils search my face, their voice growing more desperate with every word.

I stand, resting a hand on the trembling kit's shoulder. She presses up against my body, hands hanging at her sides. "Yes, you should."

Hotaru throws their hands up. "I said we. *We.*"

"Taru, I'm not going back. If they take us both—"

"Stop. Stop it right now." Hotaru cuts a hand through the air. Hotaru stares into my eyes, their own are full of tears. I cup their pale face, then press a kiss to their forehead and commit the unthinkable. I inhale, summoning all my strength and power.

"Hotaru, I am ordering you as your Alpha to immediately escort this kit to the Clubhouse. Manage your operations from the safety of the Burrow. This is not a request. You will keep hidden, and you will not put yourself in harm's way, or leave the Clubhouse until it is safe. You are not to argue, try to take me with you, or impede my efforts. I love you, my friend."

Unadulterated rage plays across Hotaru's face, and every single muscle in their body goes rigid. Goosebumps spread across my body in response to the brilliant red fire simmering in Hotaru's usually dark eyes. Spit escapes from their shaking lips, and the cords in their neck stretch taut as they fight the compulsion. Three words make it through Taru's lips and my compulsion, then they take the kit's hand and turn on their heel, leaving me in the dark.

"I. *Hate*. You."

"Team Beta, check in."

"Here. It's just as you said, the barracks are empty and everyone seems to have found the safe houses. We've made it to the second point and acquired a dozen shifters. There's a family of four kits and two adults seeking asylum, but the rest are orphans. Omega's with us. What the fuck happened over there?" Balderik asks.

I stand on the edge of a battlefield, where corpses of flesh and metal cover the street. Airships are closing in, no doubt with reinforcements and artillery. I lock eyes with Galatea and Io, both of whom were given the option to go home, and both told me to fuck off. There are friendly humans standing with them, ready to fight. More of their kind were taken by the wreck, but the only malice they seem to have is towards the Citadel.

The dark, selfish and analytical side of me says, '*You can risk them. Not Taru. Never Taru.*'

What a goddamn hypocrite.

I clear my throat and blink, then tap into the frequency for all three teams. "Ambush, they were using a kit as bait, she had some kind of collar. I sent Taru back with her, they will continue their operations in the Clubhouse."

A beat of silence.

"Are we still doing this?" Erik asks, and there's no fear in his voice. Trepidation, perhaps. As if he's expecting me to back down.

"Is there anyone opposed?"

No one.

"Good. Omega, if you're all safe then stay where you are until Beta has visited the third pick-up. The less trips, the better. Stay out of sight my Foxes, and watch each other's backs."

"There's one more thing," Io says through her radio, staring at the body at her feet. "Half of the soldiers we encountered here are ... hybrids, of sorts. Either they don't have power, or they aren't able to use their spirit, I don't know. But their bodies are physically different. Bullets go straight through them, too much force, and it's like their bodies are made of plasma instead of flesh. Blades seem to be the most effective."

"Noted," Raith says.

"Move out." I order, dismissing the conversation.

"Alpha," cracks over the radio in a cacophony of voices, all except Taru's, and I have to blink away the tears stinging my eyes.

I strap the radio back into my holster and approach my comrades. I'm quickly introduced to the impromptu leader of the rebels, Kevin. He says, "We're here to help, ma'am. What can we do?"

"You're not interested in living up there?" I ask, gesturing in the Citadel's direction.

He shakes his head. "Fuck no, and no offense lady, but we could've taken you in a long time ago." He whistles, pointing a finger in the air and waving it around. All at once, humans slip out of narrow spaces between buildings, crawl out of broken windows and push open creaking doors. My hackles raise and I turn in a slow circle, counting as I go. I briefly wonder how the fuck we missed their heat signatures.

"I count thirty." Galatea murmurs, pressing close against my side.

"Thirty-five," Kevin says, correcting her with a painfully boyish grin. "Can't let everyone come out and play. So, what's the plan?"

"What's the catch?" I ask, and he exchanges a confused look with a woman standing beside him, who appears equally confused.

"There's no catch, we really just want to help. Here, if you don't believe me, how about ..." Kevin reaches into his pocket, causing Galatea and Io to stiffen on either side of me. He pulls out a coin, offering it to me. I recognize Isaac's seal immediately, and my own coin burns against my sternum. "You can believe him, right?"

I nod. "Fine, here's the plan." I leave out Team Beta and Omega's roles entirely, focusing on our plan to take down all the infrastructure from here to the Chute. "There are two power stations between here and the Chute, and over two dozen main water lines. In addition to destroying those, we'll be blockading the Concrete Towers and any Citadel fortifi-cations we come across. We can take Tunnel 5.2 directly to power station A, and Tunnel 6.3 to power station B."

Kevin nods, rubbing his chin. He glances between Galatea, Io, and myself. "I see. So what if we take Tunnel 6.3, and you take 5.2 And instead of going for the lines, why not blow the whole goddamn plant? A few of mine work there, and they could get us in easily enough."

I close my eyes and mentally reach for my pack members beside me. *"Gut feeling?"*

"As long as we don't have to split up, what's the harm?" Io asks.

"They trap us in the Tunnels, and kill us." Galatea answers.

"Hostage?" Io supplies.

"Hostage."

I open my eyes and stare directly into Kevin's, which are an eerie silver that mimics the surface of mercury. "Fine, but you're coming with us."

Kevin shrugs. "Fine with me, not everyday you get to fight alongside the Queen of Foxes."

I roll my eyes. "Shut up, or you won't."

iF i BETRAY you?

It's not long before we come upon the Door I visited yesterday, albeit under different circumstances. I glance at Kevin,
who has been nothing but professional and quiet, patiently
waiting to kill something. He nods to me, and I allow him to
lead his platoon ahead of us. Before diving beneath the earth,
I send my last message to the other teams.

"Team Alpha checking in."

"Beta, here. Found some resistance, but we're okay,"
Balderik says, panting between words.

"Omega, here. We're waiting, no sign of activity near the
safe house," Quilla says.

I take a deep breath. "We're going underground, we're taking Tunnel 5.2 directly to the power plant. We've found some
allies, and they're going for the other plant."

A beat of silence. Galatea and Io press against my sides,
half-shifted like myself and full of nervous rage. Quietly,
Balderik says, "Xylia says to be careful, and I'm saying please.
Please, be careful."

"We will," I say.

"Don't worry Balderik, we won't let her get into trouble."
Galatea teases, and the mood lightens almost imperceptibly.

"We'll make contact the moment we surface. If for some
reason we don't—"

"*Raj—*"

"If for some reason we *don't*, I'm appointing Xylia temporary Alpha, and her word is rule. After her, Balderik. Do not come for us. Be safe, Foxes."

As one, the three of us turn off our radios and descend into the darkness, leaving behind any semblance of the original plan, and our pack's pleas.

The Tunnels are dark and silent. I allow more of my shift to come through, and my vision adjusts shade by shade. Isaac enacts a sort of burrowing protocol of his own, and the abandonment of a main tunnel that acts as a thruway through his world confirms what I already knew. He's already hiding deep within his network of chipped away dirt. Kevin's platoon is gone, but he's leaning against a nearby stretch of wall. When we approach, he straightens. "I sent the rest of mine to scout ahead, make sure we're not the only ones with the bright idea of coming down here."

I exchange a look with Io, and she nods. I say, "Fine. Kevin, take point with Io. Galatea, you're with me."

We take our positions and begin our half-mile trek towards the plant. I can't help but notice how fluid Kevin's movements are. The grace with which he wields that stiletto blade of his is phenomenal, and I find myself entranced by the way he twirls it as he walks. After a few minutes I quietly snap, "Stop, that's annoying."

"*Ai*, so serious." He glances over his shoulder at me, and that shy boyish grin comes to life again. It hits me then, why he's so familiar.

"You—you're the one who rushed Talay."

Kevin laughs, turning his attention ahead once more. "*Ai*, you saw that?"

"I'm pretty sure everyone saw it, pretty idiotic thing to do," Galatea says, and I hum in agreement.

"Ah. Well, wasn't going to just stand there, was I? The way I see it, standing by and doing nothing is the same as committing the devilish act yourself. Besides, I'm more likely to die from tripping over my shoelaces than anything."

My lips twitch. "Is that so?"

"'Tis, an old seer told me so."

"Hm, might want to see about a refund," Io says, glancing sideways at him for just a moment before fixing her gaze ahead. "First intersection coming up. Eyes and ears."

Silence falls until we clear the first opportunity to be ambushed. Tunnel 19.1 intersects ours, and if we were to take a left we'd be traveling towards the market. Right, and we'd be hitting the outskirts of Village One. Kevin's platoon is nowhere in sight, and I'm starting to feel their absence.

"How do you know Isaac?" I ask.

Kevin shrugs. "How does anybody get to know Isaac? Down on my luck, and he helped me turn it all around."

"And your pals?" Galatea asks.

"Ah, not all those guys are so buddy buddy with ol' Isaac, but for the most part it's the same story. Now what about you, Rajni? What would make him trust someone like you?"

Flatly, I say, "He saved my life, and I've spent most of my life repaying him."

"Ah, that'll do it."

We walk for a few more minutes in silence, and after passing another intersection, a thick cold washes over our group. The hairs on the back of my neck stand on end, and Galatea releases a low growl beside me. *"Feel that?"* She asks.

"We're not alone," I say, and Io glances back at the both of us with concern pinching her features. She turns her attention back to Kevin, who casually returns her glare.

Then he sighs, "*Ai*, they're early."

Kevin whirls around, coming face to face with me. A shimmer overtakes the edges of his body, lighting up the darkness. Galatea and Io are right there, poised to strike, but I thrust my arms out and stop them for reasons unbeknownst to me.

I call upon the Alpha and snarl in Kevin's face, which is mere inches from mine.

Kevin only chuckles, undeterred by my fangs. He says, "I *might* have lied to you before. My name's not Kevin."

And then the mercury clears from his eyes, leaving behind nothing but the amber from my dreams. My blood runs cold and I take a step back, crowding into Io and Galatea. The glistening edges of his body explode into a violent white, and upon regaining my vision I'm face to face with none other than Kalypso ben Matzliach.

The emperor's son.

The boy with the amber eyes.

"We're currently surrounded by Citadel troops, and air artillery is stationed at every available exit. Your Clubhouse has been invaded, and there are active forces dedicated to finding your other teams. Beta and Omega, they're headed by Xylia and Raith, right? Oh, can't forget about Sorin and all your new friends, too."

Kalypso ben Matzliach adjusts the cuffs of his shirt, which has transformed like the rest of him. He looks nothing like his father, and although it's been twenty years since we last saw each other, I would recognize him in an instant. He's taller than me and has the lithe body of a dancer, or assassin more like. His skin is a cooler brown than mine, and endless freckles and impossible sunspots are splattered across his cheeks. He stares at me through waves of black overhanging his slim face, and locks curl around his ears. His prominent hooded eyes flash a brilliant gold upon connecting with mine, wiping away the silver entirely.

He's a shifter. A goddamn *shifter*. He has to be. How did I not notice that before? Had he not hit the spark yet last time we saw each other?

Galatea and Io hold my biceps, whether to steady themselves or keep me at bay, I don't know. I tilt my head, listening. There's echoes of people behind us, their words indiscernible but presence as clear as can be. *"Why did you stop me, Alpha?"* Io asks, staring me down.

I swallow my fear and breathe deep, looking between her and Galatea. I've never told anyone but Xylia and Takara that *this* is the person who saved my life. That once upon a time, I truly believed there was a shred of good in Kalypso's heart. Obviously, this is not the case.

"The repercussions are too great. We'll never make it out, even if we use him as a hostage. The moment we turn him over, they'll shoot us in the back. He's kept us alive this long, let's see what he wants."

"She's right," Galatea says, and Io scowls.

"Are you done now?" Kalypso asks, checking his watch. "We're on a schedule."

I straighten, and my Foxes flank my back. "What do you want?"

"Ah, yes. Well, I want many things, but as you well know we can't always get what we want, can we? No, I've brought us together to discuss what I *need*. Really, what you need."

"For someone who talks endlessly, you don't say much. Get to the goddamn point, Kevin."

"Kalypso."

"Oh no, you've done fucked yourself on that one. You're permanently Kevin."

Kalypso sighs, rubbing his temple. "Fuck. Well, we can work on that. The point is, you need to come with me. In exchange, the Foxes will be granted amnesty for their crimes against the Citadel, immunity from this and any future Hunt, and a direct line of resources from the Citadel itself. What's mine is yours, so to speak. Of course, there will be some smaller details to be ironed out later."

"You." I scrub a hand over my face, not entirely sure I haven't fallen into an alternate reality. "I don't understand."

"Alpha." Galatea warns. "You can't be considering this."

I shoot a sharp look. "They have our pack, Galatea."

"So he says! Who's to say there's no one there, or the minute you step inside the Citadel he won't stab you in the back? And his father, what about him?"

"Oh, you can see them if you'd like, and I assure you my father fully intends to keep you alive. It's why he put such a high bounty on your head, after all. But I couldn't risk anyone else catching you," Kalypso says offhandedly, reaching into his trousers pocket. He pulls out a small tech pad similar to Hotaru's—

Hotaru.

I sent Taru back to the Clubhouse, and Omega was going back there. Do they know it's been compromised? Have they already been taken by the Citadel?

Kalypso turns the screen towards us, showing off a live feed depicting the Long Room. The camera appears to be on a soldier's helmet or something, offering a personal perspective of the nightmarish scene before us.

All of the kids are seated at the tables, huddled together and crying. Noemie and Lennox are the only adults present, and the teenage apprentices are doing their best to comfort their kin. I begin to think 'where are all the adults?' when the soldier turns, revealing the people standing with the show of force at the head of the Long Room.

Takara and Drystan.

"As you can see, you have been well and fully invaded. I'm sure the how isn't hard to figure out, Takara has been a wonderful help over the years."

"Years?" I ask, derailed.

"Oh yes, we've been friends for quite some time."

I snarl, and Kalypso holds up a finger. "Ah, none of that. All I have to do is give the order, and your Foxes start falling."

"They're *children.*"

"We were children once, too. Weren't we, Rajni?"

"Stop." Io snaps, baring her teeth at Kalypso. She takes me by the shoulders, turning me towards her. With one word, she manages to effectively make up my mind. Not Alpha. Not please. Not no.

She says, "*Rajni.*"

And I know, because *pack*. How could I ever put myself above pack?

I take in a shuddering breath, then nod. I turn to Galatea and kiss her cheek, wet with tears. She doesn't fight me, only dips her head once. I face Kalypso and take a step towards him. "I want to negotiate."

He laughs. "Oh?"

"Yes. In addition to your previous terms, you will immediately withdraw your militia from the Clubhouse, and you will announce the Hunt finished after my capture."

"I will, I will, I will," he sing-songs. "And what if I betray you?"

"You won't."

"I won't?"

"No, because we're going to invoke a blood bond before leaving this Tunnel."

That damned smirk finally slides off Kalypso's face. In a low tone he says, "That's forbidden."

"Better not tell daddy, then."

Kalypso glances over his shoulder to the darkness behind him, cocking his head as if listening. For the first time I notice an odd detail, his ears. They're slightly pointed at the tip, subtle but distinct. He sighs, then steps forward and offers his hand in the space between us. "How?"

"You only know it's forbidden, but not how it's done?"

"Answer the question, fox."

"First of all, the hand is the worst place. Roll up your sleeve."

Kalypso does as I say, then looks at me with a slight nervousness.

"Tell me that you will keep your promises, Kalypso ben Matzliach, and I will tell you that I consent to leaving with you. Then, I'll mark you. Right here, where it's easily concealed."

I brush my fingers over the back of his arm, just above the elbow, and Kalypso shudders. His thick, arching brows pull together and he inhales through his nose. After exhaling, he nods. I cradle his bare arm in my hands, and the intimacy of the moment strikes too late for me to push away. He stares me in the eyes, and looking away is a feat I could never achieve.

"I, Kalypso ben Matzliach, will honor every promise I've made to you tonight, Rajni of the Foxes, if you honor those made to me. However, I will not withdraw all my men from your Clubhouse. Otherwise, I agree to your terms."

I can't fucking believe I'm doing this. What a goddamn jackass.

"I, Rajni of the Foxes, will honor every promise I've made to you tonight, Kalypso ben Matzliach, if you honor those made to me. I agree to your terms."

My fangs descend as I bend down, coated in a viscous substance that aids in subduing prey, a common factor among shifters. They cause a numbing and aphrodisiac effect to take place instantly, and I wonder if I should warn him. Instead, my lips touch down on the patch of skin behind his elbow. He shudders at the sensation of my mouth on his skin, and I fight back a shiver myself. I harshly run my tongue over the tip of a canine, drawing blood.

I extend an undeserved kindness to him and say, "It won't hurt."

Because for some reason, I feel perhaps that's what he's offering me. A kindness.

"I highly—oh, oh fuck."

The tips of my fangs penetrate warm flesh. Kalypso's blood spills into my mouth, merging with mine. My spirit stirs in delight at the hot taste of copper and gold, and moaning is a near thing. I lick the puncture wounds, pulling away the moment our blood mixes in fear of doing something I might regret. I straighten, wiping my mouth with the back of my hand. Kalypso presses a hand to the front of his pants, groaning.

"It's done," I say breathlessly.

Kalypso nods jerkily. "Yeah, yes, I ... I can feel that." He rises to his full height, throwing his head back and exhaling loudly. His Adam's apple bobs as he swallows, and I tear my gaze away from his exposed throat. "Well, that was easier than I expected."

"Forcing someone to go with you?" I mutter.

"Well, yes."

"You're holding my family hostage." I force myself to give him my full glaring attention, but he only smirks.

"Ah, minor detail." He waves a hand. "Io, Galatea, it was a pleasure fighting with you, and I recommend staying here until we're clear of the area."

"You killed them, your own people," Io says. "What kind of monster does that?"

Kalypso grins. "You're looking at him."

I exchange a look with Galatea, and Io. *Find the others, and go to Sorin's for now. Keep them all safe for me. Please.*

"We'll do our best, Alpha."

I nod, then gesture for Kalypso to lead the way. "By all means, lead me to my death."

"You are such a treat, darling. Oh, too soon?"

I walk beside Kalypso in silence, but he talks enough for the both of us. I only half-listen, entering a sort of dazed state where I evaluate every action and choice that has led to this moment. Every person that handed me to the Citadel, to this man, on a silver platter. Takara. Drystan. And …

"Isaac set me up, didn't he?"

Kalypso hums. "He didn't have a choice, if that makes you feel better."

"There's *always* another choice."

He looks back the way we came, where Galatea and Io's figures are beginning to fade into the distance, then back to me. "You're right. You could've said no, and everyone you loved would have died, and I would've taken you anyway. At least this way they're all safe. Or safer, rather."

I stare at him. "Who are you?"

"Kevin, remember?"

We walk in silence after that, and the closer we get to the surface the more fidgety Kalypso becomes. Gripping the hems of his sleeves, sweeping hair from his face, tapping his fingers against his palms in a staccato pattern. As we near a shaft of light signaling the end of the tunnel, Kalypso looks at me. A cold, solemnity overtakes his once boyish features, aging him.

"What?"

"It's best if you disarm now. After we reach the Citadel, we'll be separated, and you'll be cleansed for three days. Then, you'll be brought before the Emperor, where you will make a pledge of loyalty to the Matzliach family. Only then will he allow you to spend time in the Citadel."

"Cleansing, or torture?"

"It's survivable," Kalypso says, shifting in place. "Rajni, for the good of your people and mine, I need you to trust me, like you trusted me back then."

"Things are different now."

"Are they?"

"Yes, my pack is at stake. You didn't want anything."

"Perhaps I've had an ulterior motive since even then."

"Doubtful."

"Then why did you do it?"

Kalypso smiles, and it's sharp enough to slice apart my heart. "Stick around, and maybe you'll find out. Come now, empty your pockets. You'll lose anything personal, for now."

I sigh, wondering how the fuck I managed to so beautifully ruin everything. I begin with my gun, ejecting the clip before tossing it back the way we came. I unclip my ammunition belt and let it fall around my ankles. Knives. In my right boot, across my chest and along my hip, on a chain around my neck. Finally, the one strapped to my thigh joins the rest in a pile on the ground.

"My, this is quite a show. Not that I minded, but why the fuck did you have to bite me when you have all those?"

"I didn't see you offering up your knife, either."

He grins. "True."

I slip the coin and its chain off my neck, then rub my thumb over its surface. Isn't it sad that through all of this, Isaac's betrayal is what confuses me the most?

"I can hold onto that for you, if you want," Kalypso says quietly, hands clasped behind his back.

I glare at him, tossing the coin with the rest of my discarded things. The last thing of importance is my tech watch, and I gently remove it from my left wrist. I cradle it in my hands, gently setting it down on top of everything else. Better left behind than taken in by the Citadel's engineers.

One last thing to do.

I close my eyes, and one by one, I mute the pack bonds. Not sever, but ... block, in a way. Despite the distance, their feelings and thoughts are a glitching static that has only grown in intensity the closer we've gotten to the surface. After a few moments, there's nothing.

I join Kalypso's side, and he leads me towards the light.

I hesitate, and he grants me one last moment. "What time is it?"

He looks down at his wristwatch. "1:03 AM."

I laugh, and it hurts so fucking bad. "An hour? That's all it took for me to fuck things up?"

"To be fair, I fucked things up."

"*I* trusted *you*."

"While this is true, don't be too hard on yourself. There is … one more thing." He leans in closer to me, lowering his tone. "When the time comes, you need to tell my father you want to marry me."

I rear back. "Are you *absurd*?"

"Yes, but that is besides the point. Rajni, it is so, *so* important that you do this."

"How the hell could *that* be important? You vain bastard."

"Rajni," He says, and it's unfair how my spirit responds to my name on his treacherous lips. "You don't have to believe me now, but you will. Please, just … think about it. I would not ask otherwise."

I shake my head, and he takes that as his cue to leave the conversation behind. We ascend the stairs and before we crest the top, he takes my hand. I try to pull away, but he gives me a look. Nostrils flaring, I painfully tighten my grip on his hand, fully slotting my fingers between his. Without a word or change of expression, we go topside.

Honestly, I'm impressed.

Citadel troops surround the tunnel entrance, a quarter of a mile thick in every direction. The power plant directly ahead of us stands tall, but its proud structure is partially blocked by artillery trucks and a docked balloon ship with black fabric emblazoned with the purple insignia of the Citadel. Spotlights shine down on us from above, where scout ships hover in the small space. There's a quick flash of something green off to the east, but I don't focus on it in fear of drawing other's attention. A drone, perhaps?

A vague sort of fugue settles over my mind, softening the noise and experience. I watch as Kalypso pulls me away from the tunnel and towards an officer with the most stripes on his chest. I watch as he gestures between me and the officer, words muffled. I watch as the officer nods, then barks an order at a soldier with a white band on their arm. I watch as they all scatter like insects underneath my boot. What the hell's going on?

My nervous system is reset with a sharp stab to the neck.

"I'll see you in a while, okay?" Kalypso says, arms tightening around me as my legs buckle. I shake my head, but it does nothing to fight the darkness encroaching on my mind. I claw at him, trying to push and pull, push and pull.

All I manage to do is nick the skin beneath his left eye, and his proud, blood tainted smile is the last thing I see before going under.

A Filthy Beast

I drift in and out of consciousness, assaulted by white, so much goddamn white, any time I surface. I'm surrounded on all sides by bodies and weapons. At one point, there's a distinct inertia of fighting gravity. Marching. A cool, barely there breeze.

My fingers twitch and my gums itch. I test my limbs, finding restraints around my ankles, thighs, wrists, biceps, and neck. A board or something supports my back, and I wonder if I'm being carried. There's a multitude of anchors pulling at my heart, yanking my spirit back the way we came. The sheer emotion that overtakes me is enough to pull me out of the drugs for a small moment, and I groggily blink open my eyes.

A man's face blocks out most of the fuzzy black and purple background.

Unfamiliar. Young. Disgusted.

And I don't know why, but I fixate on the fact he's not wearing a respirator.

He raises his hand, touching his sternum thrice, then his right collarbone and left twice each. The movement orients me further, and every nerve in my body screams to run. The Citadel's militia is nothing more than the clean up crew in its war against the people. The Church of Syzdon is their real weapon, and I'm face to face with one of its priests.

He shakes his bald head. "By the God, this one cannot be cleansed."

A woman's voice barks from behind me. "Yes, she can, and will. Emperor Drazen ben Matzliach and Prince Kalypso ben Matzliach are expecting her, and will not tolerate any delays regarding her acceptance into the Citadel."

"I beg your pardon Captain Tsifya but I highly doubt—"

A woman steps into view, looming over the priest who has not moved an inch. Both of them are beside my stretcher, their stand off comes in and out of focus. In a low tone, the Captain says, "Should I call upon Cardinal Grand Bishop Mincha ben Nissim? Would you like to hear it from him, too?"

"N–no, Captain." A beat passes, then he hurriedly adds, "Captain bat Jeshulun. My apologies. Bring it right this way."

The Captain turns back to me, revealing an eye-patch and a scowl, no mask. She snaps her thick fingers, looking past me to the head of the stretcher. Then, she bends down and brings her face inches away from mine. "And what is so special about you?"

My tongue is heavy and I don't think she's actually expecting an answer, so I close my eyes. Moments later, another sharp stab of pain lances my neck, and I'm dragged back under.

Cleansing is an understatement.

I'm viciously awoken and submerged into a tank of ice cold water. I gasp, limbs tensing against their restraints. I close my mouth just before it sinks beneath the water too, but there's not nearly enough air in my chest. The animal spirit in my heart is dormant, inaccessible, and that sensation alone is enough to terrify me.

They don't bring me up until my body starts to go slack, and a solid slap to the face restarts my brain. My hands are bound behind my back, knobby fingers grasp my chin, turning my head this way and that. Blinking rapidly, I open my eyes and take in my surroundings.

We're centered in an incredibly vast and haunting section of what can only be Syzdon Cathedral, and I've never felt so small. Great pillars of black granite stretch towards a violet stained ceiling of glass with small, intricate panes that number in the thousands. A crowd of clergymen are gathered around the nearby Cardinal and myself, surrounding us in perfect concentric circles that allows everyone a perfect view of my state.

I'm naked, ankles and wrists bound, and the waterline brushes against the collar on my neck. I'm submerged in a white tub that's deep enough for me to stretch to my full height, and even more I bet. A tugging on my ankles suggests a weight and great depth, and the only lifeline is the grip on my chin, and the devilish eyes behind them.

I recognize the Cardinal from his mandated daily prayer readings that broadcast in the Villages early in the morning, and the television screens paint him to be much prettier than he actually is. He's a human past the prime of his life, translucent white skin cast in decades of frowning and screaming. His white hair is cropped short, and his steel blue eyes are the deadest thing I've ever seen. His sweeping white robes are trimmed in four colors, marking his status. The lower status marks never disappear, because according to them, we never truly change. Only expand.

Red is for servants.

Purple is for bishops.

Black is for head bishops.

Gold is for the Cardinal Grand Bishop, and there's only the one.

My life is in the hand of a man who performs human sacrifice on a weekly basis, all in the name of Deliverance. Xylia, Balderik, and I used to plan all the ways we'd murder him, and now I'm staring him in the face.

Loud and booming, he says, "Rajni of the Rebel Foxes, you are awash with sin, transgression, and far from our dear God's Grace and his Great Deliverance. There has never been another has filthy as you, and the honor of cleansing such a foul beast has been bestowed upon none other than I, Cardinal Grand Bishop Mincha ben Nissim, and when I am done with your soul, the Matzliach Dynasty, and God himself, will be blessed to have such a spirit as yours. Praise His name, or suffer His wrath."

I told Kalypso I would go willingly, but I never said I'd make it easy.

"For someone who loves Him so much, you talk an awful lot about yourself too there, priest. And which is it, a beautiful soul, or a filthy beast?"

The moment he releases my chin I'm dragged to the bottom of the tank with intense force, and the icy rush doesn't get any easier this time. Thankfully I stole more air this time, but that plan is quickly ruined when I'm brought above the surface and dunked in quick succession, only moving a few inches each time so water sloshes in with any air I manage to find.

I begin to choke, but he doesn't stop until I vomit all over myself and the water. This time he seizes a chunk of hair behind my right ear, tearing strands out as he lifts me from beneath the surface. "Praise His name, you wicked thing!"

"The only person I praise has a cunt, so unless He—"

It goes on for hours, long after I stop answering at all. I lose consciousness several times, and I'm only allowed enough time to recover before it happens all over again. My ankles feel as if they've been torn apart, and every muscle in my body begs for help. My lungs ache in the most exquisite way, a whole new level of pain I've never experienced before.

The clergymen do not vacate their posts. Their psalms fill the cathedral and my ears, forming a disjointed and bizarre sensation as if they're actually *in* my head. Each time I surface the noise in my head grows, and *grows*, until there's nothing but a tumultuous choir of madmen praising the name of someone who doesn't even exist.

Because how could a God ever exist in a place like this?

After heaving stomach bile for the third time, I choke out, "praise."

The Cardinal stills, then uses his free hand to pet my hair. His other tightens around the base of my neck. He waits, ever so patient. He has not left my side once, performing his duty with the utmost reverence.

"Yes, beast?" He whispers, using the quietest tone yet.

"P—praise Syzdon, G—God of D–Deliverance."

"Is your heart open to him?"

"Y—yes."

"Good."

And I'm thrust under one last time with the boisterous songs of God filling my ears.

I'm pulled out of the water by two clergymen, and they keep me upright since my own legs are temporarily dysfunctional.

The Cardinal impassively watches as a woman in red-trimmed robes dries my naked, inked body with a white towel, which brings forth a whole new wave of pain. She starts at my feet, and the towel is extremely rough which irritates my already shocked skin that stings as it regains feeling, and she is by no means gentle. She works in a quick and professional manner, and when she dries my cock and testicles in the same fashion, her rough treatment draws forth the first growl since going beneath the water.

I'm subsequently whipped across the face, and a thin leather strap catches me in the eye. I cry out, temporarily flinching away from the source of pain and pulling against those holding me up.

"Do you need another, beast?" The Cardinal asks, and I slowly shake my head. "There shall be no more of that forsaken noise, you are not an animal here, not any more. Do you understand?"

I swallow thickly, then bow my head.

"Speak!"

"Yes, I understand."

"Good. You will be released from your shackles, and walk away from them a new woman. Then you shall begin the Cleansing process. Commit any act of disobedience and violence, and we start from the beginning. You are under my supervision, and I do not tolerate rebelliousness. This is your first, and only warning."

Begin? What the fuck was all that for then?

Instead of saying *that*, I say, "I understand."

The Cardinal steps around me, and a few moments later the manacles around my wrists and ankles release with an audible *click*. The clergymen at my sides guide my arms forward, a painfully gentle contrast to their supervisor. Their young faces are blank and emotionless, and their movements near robotic. My feet still do not want to take my full weight, so they continue to effortlessly hold me up.

The woman continues her work, drying beneath my breasts and the hair of my underarms with quick efficiency but less force. Her eyes linger on my breasts longer than they have anywhere else, and I fight a roll of the eyes and a puff of the chest. Balderik's mutation is somewhat more intricate than other healers, working directly with the body and creating and destroying on a cellular level. Thanks to him, I was able to grow into a body that coincided with my mind. I don't mind having a cock, in fact I quite enjoy it, but that doesn't make me any less of a woman. But breasts were different, and I—

Oh, fuck.

Gingerly, I ask, "May I ask what day it is?"

Everyone except for the Cardinal continues on as if I never spoke. He raises a brow, then says, "It is Monday, the fifth day of the eighth month."

"Thank you," I say, and he doesn't bother to respond.

In five days, I'll be due for a treatment, and I still have two more days of this bullshit. And who knows if I can even connect with Balderik, especially not without Kalypso's help. It's a potion that adjusts the hormones in my body, one that I have to take weekly. Without it, I'm so fucked. I start to panic, but I force myself to remain calm. Get through this, find Kalypso. If I can't go back to the Clubhouse, then maybe one of his lackeys he left there can bring it.

After I'm dried, a white robe trimmed in bright blue slides over my shoulders, and my arms are guided through it. The Cardinal ties it off in the front himself, then cups my face and begins to pray. I tune it out, thinking that the luxurious fabric is the last soft thing I will feel for the next three (two?) days.

Kalypso's words come back to me. Has he personally endured this? I had thought perhaps the Cleansing was for shifters only, but maybe it's for all those who commit sins and trespasses.

In short order we march out of the hall, led by the Cardinal Grand Bishop and tailed by the gathered congregation.

We pass by enormous statues of previous Cardinals or other noteworthy bishops, and every once in a while there is an interpretative depiction of Syzdon himself, the God of Deliverance. It seems no one can agree on what he looks like, seeing how the Emperors are the only ones to have ever made contact with him.

Not suspicious at all, right?

We keep walking, and walking, and *walking*. Eventually everything starts to look the same, all black granite and violet glass, and my head aches. The shakes wracking my body have begun to intensify, but I don't dare complain. The air is a biting, vicious thing that makes me want to tear my skin off, and that sweet old panic is starting to return. I must lose time, because next thing I know we're in a dank corridor lined with iron doors.

I glance around, finding there's no one left besides the two clergymen, and the Cardinal. One of them opens the door, revealing an empty room. No bed, no toilet, nothing but stone. I swallow, and he grins.

"You will spend your nights here. Tomorrow will be spent purging and detoxifying your system, from your stomach to your blood. I suggest taking some time to meditate on your newfound love of God. Good night, Rajni bat Matzliach."

That gets my attention. "I'm not part of the house yet, Cardinal."

He grins, and his eyes aren't so dead anymore when he says, "That name is the only thing saving you, so I suggest you begin wearing it quickly."

He turns away, and I'm thrown into a pitch black cell. I catch my fall with my hands and knees, sending jolts of electrifying pain through my limbs. The door slams behind me, then locks me into the darkness. I blink a few times trying to engage my night vision, but it's as fleeting as my mutation.

My arms buckle, and I collapse.

Eventually, after the sobs subside, I fall into a terror-ridden sleep.

The next day is spent as the Cardinal promised. Sleep-deprived, dehydrated and starving, I'm brought back to what I'm calling the amphitheater hall. We are surrounded once more by witnesses, but instead of being submerged in a tub I'm stripped down and made to kneel on a bed of fine stone, spilled directly onto the otherwise pristine floor.

As the gravel bites into my knees, I wonder who has the privilege of cleaning up all this each night. When I try to adjust my position, I'm whipped across the face by the Cardinal Grand Bishop instantly. Lines of heat erupt across my cheek, but I do not cry out like I did yesterday.

"Hands behind your back," he says, boosting his voice into that showman's tone again.

I do as he says and raise my chin for good measure. He stands before me with such a smug look on his face I want to spit on it, but I'm ready to get this over with. I can't waste time.

"Open your mouth, and accept Syzdon's Deliverance."

I hesitate for only a second, then obey. He smirks, then reaches into his pocket. He pulls out a coin-sized, lustrous yellow disk, showing off both sides of it to me. He takes his sweet time approaching me, all the while my mouth is open and waiting.

He says, "You will not move from your place, even when your sins spill out of your guts. And then, we shall cleanse your blood, and you will not move from your place. If you move, we start over. Through pain, discipline, and sheer will, the strongest will survive. I have to wonder, is that you?"

I respond by saying nothing, moving little.

"Only time will tell, beast." He places the disk on my tongue, which immediately dissolves into the nastiest and most sour thing I've ever tasted. "Close your mouth."

I do as he says, having to fight and keep the growing saliva back.

He stands, facing away from me and towards his people.

I scowl at his back, eyes watering and nose running. My stomach twists as the foul substance begins to run down the back of my throat, and I cough in response to the sort of numb tingling it brings. It feels as if my throat is closing, but that can't be the case, can it?

Out of the corner of my eye, I catch a flash of amber. My head jerks, attention drawn to a clergyman in the first circle surrounding us. He doesn't appear familiar, but his gaze is intense and furious, and while there's no gold now, I swear it was Kalypso's eyes flashing. Am I seeing things, or is he really here to watch my downfall?

And that's when my stomach gives out.

The thing is, I haven't eaten in over a day now, and yesterday's drowning already caused me to retch a few times. But somehow I vomit an intense amount of ... *something*, my stomach itself perhaps? The heaves are enough to turn my lungs inside out, and once they start it's an unending thing. I gasp for air between them, and it feels like I'm sucking through a straw. Tears join the puddle of saliva, blood from my shredded knees, and vague vomit before me.

The choir's voices lift higher, and higher. My ears ring with the sheer force of it, and I scream in frustration and rage after a particularly brutal purge. Every muscle in my body stretches taut, and my nails half-shift just enough to puncture my palms, hidden by my closed fist. The relief from being able to shift even that much, and the warmth of the blood I brought forth, dulls everything else. Eventually, the retching subsides and I manage to straighten my spine, all without moving my massacred knees.

I lock eyes with the Cardinal, and the corner of his lips lift. Beside him is a boxy machine on wheels, laden with clear tubes. "And now, your blood."

When I'm brought to the cell that night, I'm gently set down instead of thrown, but it doesn't matter because I can't feel a fucking thing. Is this what it's like to be hollowed out?

For the last day, I'm allowed to keep my clothes on and walk of my own accord, however slow that may be. I have to assume the collar around my neck is similar to the one the child in the street was wearing. Not only is it keeping my mutation at bay, but it restrains my self-healing abilities as well. Every part of me is sore, beaten, and emptied out.

Instead of a tub or a patch of stones, I find a stretch of simmering coals. At the opposite end, is an altar. Thankfully, or not, there is no person strapped down to it. The Cardinal leads me to the closer end, and after coming to a stop he offers me a necklace of black rosary beads complete with a pendant depicting Syzdon's tri-spiral sigil. It is incredibly heavy, and each bead has hundreds of facets.

Loud enough for all to hear, he says, "To complete today's Cleansing, one must walk across the coals whilst counting the number of rosary beads on their necklace. Once at the end, if your number is correct, you will make your final oath to the great Syzdon, completing the Cleansing process. If you are wrong, however, you must go back to the beginning and walk the fires until counting correctly. You have three chances, and if you fail, we start again with the baptism."

I nod. "Understood, Cardinal Grand Bishop."

"Begin, Rajni."

On cue, the witnesses gathered begin to chant, "Rajni, Rajni," and my already sensitive stomach flips. I take a deep breath, wrapping the length of the rosary around the knuckles of my right hand, then step onto the coals.

Fuck.

I grit my teeth and capture the bead beside the sigil with my thumb, using that as a starting point. I count fourteen beads before stepping on a particularly searing chunk of coal, and a fresh wave of burning flesh fills the air. Black smoke thickens the world every time I disturb the coals, and I begin to cough persistently around a third of the way. The end seems to get farther and farther away, and I don't remember the necklace being this long. Was it thirty-five? No, thirty-four.

I trip, landing on my hands and knees. I scream, horrified by how quickly my hands crisp beneath the hellfire. The wounds on my knees tear and blister. Footsteps approach and I hoarsely shout, "No! I'm not done."

I push myself to my feet, arms quaking. I find the same two clergymen who have been responsible for me this entire time, one waiting on either side of the coals. The Cardinal stands beside the altar and he takes a moment, allowing my feet to burn and *burn* before he says, "Continue."

One step, one bead after another, I walk across the unbearable. Upon reaching the end I collapse, crumpling onto my side. The clergymen are there in an instant, tending to my feet. It strikes me as funny how quick the church is to heal the pain they've caused, only to do it again and again. I hold back my laughter, if only because I'm too bodily tired to move.

The Cardinal waits quietly until my feet are bandaged, but the crowd has no such compunction. Gossip, anticipation, and anger radiates in the clergymen around us, but he does not ask them to quiet down. When I'm pulled up to standing, held up in a similar fashion as the first day, they all silence at once. The Cardinal takes the necklace from my hand, having to pry my shaking and contorted fingers apart to break it free.

He dangles it before me, eyes gleaming. "How many?"

"A–a hundred and—and f–fifty."

He reels back, all smugness gone. "Do it again."

"I—I'm right, I know I am."

"DO IT AGAIN!" He roars, and the clergymen holding me up exchange a look before turning me in the direction I had just come. Tears prick my eyes and I open my mouth to protest, but for what?

"And what is this?" A lofty voice calls from behind him, stopping even the air from moving.

The clergymen at my sides go dead still, and there's a fleeting irritation, not fear, but *irritation* on the Cardinal's face. He turns, revealing none other than the Emperor himself, accompanied by his son. He bows from the waist, and after straightening to his full height he says, "Your Grace, we are honored to have you present at such a small event as this."

The Emperor breezes past him, waving a hand vaguely. His son keeps a few steps behind him, hands clasped behind his back. All traces of the man in the Tunnel have been wiped clean, and he pays me no mind. The Emperor tucks his arms into the wide sleeves of his robe and stands before me, evaluating my state. He says, "Evidently, or you would not be behaving as such. Did you count the beads correctly, darling?"

I bow my head, seeing how I can't bow of my own accord. "Your Grace, I believe it to be so, but I shall walk across the coals and count again if it pleases you."

"You may lift your face."

I do as he says, looking up in time to see the sharp look he throws the Cardinal. "Is she wrong?"

The Man of God clenches his jaw, which is a moment's hesitation too long for the Emperor. Without breaking his gaze he says, "I believe it has been too long since you indulged in the Cleansing yourself, Cardinal. Do not let your pride overshadow your faith. Come now, let her make her mark and take pride in the most impressive Cleansing to date. Thanks to you, isn't that what you said?"

The Cardinal dips his chin, hiding his pale and drawn face. "As you wish, Your Grace." Without raising his head he gestures towards the clergymen holding me up. "Bring her forth."

"If I may assist?" Emperor Drazen asks, gesturing towards me.

His question stills the room completely, and after a moment the man at my right answers when it seems no one else will. "Y–Your Grace, if it is your wish," He says, offering my side like I'm a piece of furniture to be moved.

"Oh, it most certainly is," Emperor Drazen says, effortlessly taking the clergymen's place. Every hair on my body stands on end, and I'm overwhelmed by a wave of nauseating heat. Drazen gives me a curt nod, then I'm led through the tightening crowd, committing what feels like a walk of shame. Kalypso walks behind us, his father's silent and emotionless shadow.

We make it to the altar where the Cardinal and his choir are waiting, singing their praises to the God above. My name is entwined with their words, and it's all so damn disorienting. A crimson stain marking the breadth of the stone knocks out my knees. Drazen's hold is firm, as is the remaining clergymen's.

Quietly, Drazen says, "My, my. What a bizarre set of circumstances we find ourselves in, lovely Rajni."

I turn my head slowly, mind jumbled and tired. "Bizarre indeed, Your Grace, but no less exciting."

He chuckles, a soft and breathy thing, almost rusty and hollow, but enough to catch me off guard. It's as if there's no one else in the room, and he can say whatever he likes, make them all wait for however long he likes. In a low tone, he asks, "We are going to have fun, aren't we?"

"I do hope so, I've been waiting a long time."

"Oh, you have no idea what waiting is, dear. I have been expecting you for quite some time, and the plans I have for you are endless."

That ties my tongue, and he smirks.

"Rajni, hold out your hand," The Cardinal says, loud and even.

My attention is forced ahead, away from the mischief in the Emperor's eyes. In the Cardinal's hand is a wicked curved dagger with a freshly polished blade and bone handle. I extend my right hand over the stone altar, fighting my imagination working on how many human sacrifices have been committed here.

I'm reminded of Koa, and how he made his mark only days ago in such a different way than this, surrounded by his pack and love, such love. No pain, no despair.

The Cardinal takes my hand in his, then uses the other to saw the blade back and forth across my palm. It bites deep, and I can't help but whimper. I manage to stay still, but only just. My gut churns and mind swims as I watch a steady stream of blood pour from my hand onto the altar. It doesn't drip, but spatter and spit.

A crystal glass is set beneath the stream after the stone has absorbed enough of my life.

The Cardinal asks, "Rajni, do you pledge your soul to Syzdon, our beloved God of Deliverance?"

"Yes."

He takes my hand, turning it face down. My palm touches down in the middle of the puddle. The blood is cool and thick, further disorienting me. Despite this, I'm unable to tear my gaze away from the Cardinal bringing the cup to his lips. I begin to sag, tunneled vision shifting between the filling cup, and the Man of God before me. He must find something amusing, because his lip curls.

In a booming tone he says, "Our beloved God of Deliverance, please accept Rajni's fealty and gift of life, and accept her into your heart."

And he drinks, a full and long swallow. He pulls the crystal away, revealing blood stained teeth and lips. The Cardinal offers the cup to the Emperor, who shakes his head. Drazen says, "Kalypso, take the treasure you have earned, and waited for."

Kalypso ben Matzliach does not make his father wait. He crowds the clergymen's side, taking the glass of blood with a small bow of his head and a quiet, "Thank you, Cardinal Grand Bishop ben Nissim."

The Man of God bows his head to Kalypso, then addresses me. "Rajni, do you pledge your loyalty to the Matzliach family, our beloved God chosen rulers?"

"... Yes."

Kalypso gently lifts my hand from the stone and returns it to my side. I'm too tired to fight, and he's blurring in and out of focus. Kalypso stands directly between me and the altar, fully facing me. He lifts the goblet of my blood high above as the Cardinal says, "Our beloved Child of Deliverance, envoy of the Matzliach family, please accept Rajni's fealty and gift of life, and accept her into your hearts."

Kalypso drinks, closing his eyes as the blood flows down his throat which works once as he swallows. The last thing

I see before collapsing is a drop of my blood escaping from the corner of his lips. It trails down his jaw, along the strained tendons in his neck, and the exposed part of his chest before disappearing lower, and lower, and lower ....

A Good Man

I'm cold, and I pull the blankets up around my neck in efforts to steal them back from Xylia. Then, I remember. I cry myself back to sleep, not bothering to extricate myself from the blankets or take in my dark surroundings. I'm in a soft bed, that much I know, and I'm safe now.

Safer than before.

The next time I awake, I'm warm and hungry. I wearily blink open my eyes and gather the energy to take in my surroundings. They are less, and more, than I expected. While I'm most certainly a hostage and it's clear they need me, that doesn't mean they need to spoil me, only keep me alive. I expected it would be one of two ways. Disgustingly wealthy to convince me how good life in the Citadel is, or a dungeon cell to convince me living in general is good.

But what I find is a studio apartment of sorts, humble and well decorated but by no means opulent or cast entirely in gold. The blankets I'm tangled in are layers of fine stuffed comforters, patchwork quilts, and silky soft sheets. All of the furniture are antiques from before the blast, polished and well taken care of, and the bed is an enormous four post frame with a headboard full of books.

In a rocking chair beside the bed is a wisp of a young man. He's watching me, quiet and calm, hands folded in his lap. His ginger hair is cut short but still manages to curl up a little bit in the front, and his hazel green eyes are the brightest thing I've seen in this place yet. The right side of his face is marred by burn scars, and part of his throat. The burns remind me of Koa, and my stomach turns. His clothes are plain, his cream colored, v-cut tunic reminds me of a medical scrub top, and his pants are similar. On the back of his right hand is a black symbol inked directly into the skin, one I don't recognize. A star surrounded by six overlapping circles.

I swallow, and it's painfully dry.

Without moving, he says, "There's a glass of water on the bedside table if you would like, Dame Rajni. It would be my honor to assist you, if you would allow. My name is Corvin ben Lahav. I am Prince ben Matzliach's personal attendant, and now, yours. I am here to answer any questions you may have, and to make you as comfortable as possible."

"I—" I cough, then try again. "I would allow."

He nods, then slowly rises. As he unfolds, I'm struck by just how damn tall he is. Even taller than— no, abandon *that* thought. There will be plenty of time for her later.

The chamberlain assists me with sitting up, and while there are no external injuries, or internal, so I'm told, it feels as if I've been ran over. After taking a drink of the freshest water I've ever consumed, I ask, "What day is it?"

The chamberlain sets my glass down on the bedside table, then clasps his hands before him. "It is currently the third hour past noon on the tenth day of the eighth month, my lady."

"*Fuck.*" I scrub at my eyes with my free hand, the other grips onto the mattress with all I've got. Through all my haze, there's one thing I know for sure. "I need the Prince. Immediately"

"Of course, my lady. Prince ben Matzliach is currently occupied in a trade meeting, but he did say you were free to call upon him when you were ready. Would you perhaps care for a bath, first?"

I look down at my body, dressed in a simple white nightgown that hangs around my ankles, which are dangling over the side of the bed. While my body is visibly clean, there's an unmistakable stench of days spent in a festering hell. I look back up to him. "Was this you?"

He nods, cheeks flushing only the barest amount. "Yes, my lady. You were ... rather indisposed upon arrival, and Prince Ka–*ben,* excuse me, Prince ben Matzliach, insisted that the remnants of your stay in the Church be cleansed from you."

I note that little slip up and continue on. "And where have we arrived *to?* Is this the Prince's quarters?"

Corvin bows his head. "Yes, my lady. Or rather, a wing of it. Your apartments are adjoined by that door there," Corvin vaguely gestures in a direction, "and may be locked from either side, to ensure you have total privacy. We are on the uppermost level of the Citadel, where the Dynasty lives. This will be your permanent residence."

"And is everyone else like you?"

Corvin blinks, mouth opening and closing a moment before he says, "My lady?"

"Nice."

"Oh." He looks away, then back to me with a wry, almost hidden smile. He whispers, "No, my lady. I am honored to be in Prince ben Matzliach's service. He is fair, and a good man."

I fight an eye-roll, if only because I'm warming up to Corvin. He's most likely a spy in addition to a servant, but I can't fault him for that. I reach up to absently tug on a curl of hair, then brush against the collar still around my neck. I extend my hand to him, fighting my disgust.

"I will keep that in mind. I hope you know I'm going to take advantage of your assistance, Corvin, and that you meant what you said, about it being an honor and all."

Corvin smiles, for real this time, and takes my hand. His own is cold, covered in calluses. "I did, my lady. I truly did."

Corvin leads me through the space, and while I don't exactly need his help there are a few times when his steadying grip is welcome. The room is clean, and the vintage decorations extend from not only the furniture but to the excessive paintings and gaudy curtains as well. I briefly ponder what the hell such large windows could offer a view of, and vow to keep all six curtains closed. The front door is abutted with a foyer which opens to the main area. A sitting room on one side, and a dining area on the other. A hall splits from the dining room, leading to a bathroom, guest bedroom, and empty storage space.

The bathroom is bigger than my entire room at home, and that thought makes my heart ache. My dear Xylia, and Balderik, Hotaru. Koa, Seth, and all the other Foxes. *Goddamned* Takara and Drystan. What the hell do they have staked in this? Leadership of the Clubhouse? Takara was essentially already in power, and Drystan ... he makes a little more sense. He was protecting the kids.

From me.

Standing here, watching Corvin fill a porcelain claw foot bathtub with steaming water, oils and soaps, I've never seen things clearer. Every conversation, every silent plea to listen before he felt he had to do something rash. All Takara had to do was whisper in his ear, that was it. But *why?* Are she and the Prince truly friends? Years long friends, at that?

"My lady," Corvin says gently, and I snap my attention to him standing beside me, no longer at the tub. "Are you ready? The ..." He clears his throat. "The collar is waterproof. It is a means for the Emperor to dampen your magic, and ensure your safety by knowing where you are at all times."

"Yes," I say without looking at him, clearing my throat full of emotion.

I don't even go into the magic versus mutation argument I love to have with Isaac, my soul is too tired for it. Without preamble I drop my robe, then step into the water. I sigh, sinking into the hot water that smells of rosemary. How I have no idea, but I don't rightfully care at this moment. I slip entirely beneath the water, and upon surfacing I slick my hair back away from my eyes.

I lean back, pushing against the opposite end of the tub with my toes, barely reaching as the thing is enormous. Corvin stands a few feet back, hands clasped before him. "Would you care for privacy, my lady? Or assistance?"

"Privacy, if it's all the same to you."

He bows his head. "Of course, my lady. Shall I call upon the Prince now?"

I breathe deeply, then nod. "Yes. Please. There is something else, but I'm not sure if you can help me."

"Anything, my lady."

I give him a tight smile. "What were the results of the Hunt?"

"Oh." His face falls, but he continues with a professional calm. "After your departure the Hunt ended, given your agreement with the Prince. But there were still sixteen tags claimed, and three deaths, my lady. I am not sure who was tagged, but I do know the Prince ensured none of them were yours."

"And is my agreement with the Prince common knowledge?"

Corvin flushes. "N–no, my lady. Merely commentary between master and servant, if you would. The only news to have been aired thus far is the Citadel, and Church's acceptance of your fealty. Nothing else."

I wince. "Is there footage? Of me?"

He bows his head. "Yes, my lady. Specifically, when you made your mark and vow."

"I see. Can I ask you one more thing?"

"Yes, my lady."

"No one wears respirators, why?"

"The Citadel is sealed off from the Upper City, and we have our own private oxygenation system that is shared with the Church. As long as you are in the Citadel itself, you do not need a mask, my lady."

"Of course. Thank you, Corvin."

Corvin nods, then leaves the bathroom and shuts the door behind him.

There are several things of note in which he said. There were *still* sixteen. He could have said only, which would imply not enough. But still implies too many, and a disagreement with the Citadel's policies. And if the Prince is keeping our deal a secret, then what does his father know? It's clear that the Prince has a good rapport with his chamberlain, and perhaps Corvin works for him in a far greater capacity than I initially thought.

And the three deaths. Were they mine?

I wash my hair, using the bar soap Corvin left in a dish on a small table beside the tub. It smells of rosemary, of Xylia, and my heart crumbles while my hair softens. I physically ache for her. I need to know she's okay, that Kalypso held up his end of the deal. My mind works in vicious circles, analyzing and taking apart every moment of my life, but nothing is clear. I shift my thoughts away from the Xylia and the Foxes, if only to keep me from going insane.

Where do they get their essential oils from? There's no fresh produce anywhere but the Clubhouse, so either these oils are eternally old, or we're not the only ones. And if they're weaponizing shifters, why not put them to work, too?

I wash the rest of my body in a fugue state, searching the swollen red of my knees for evidence of my punishment, but find nearly nothing. There are no needle marks along my arms or on the top of my feet and hands. My feet, though. The bottom of my feet are the raw, fresh flesh beneath a ruined wound. They don't hurt, but it seems like they should. The same as my hand.

Another clear reminder that my mutation is 'dampened' as the cut has mostly healed, but not as much as it should be. The edges are red and puckered, angry from the Cardinal's viscous sawing treatment. Who the fuck would buy into such a dangerous and malicious religion that requires blood, and bodily sacrifice?

Like a freight train I'm struck with the memory of a single drop of my blood inching down golden brown skin, and my dick swells in response. What the *fuck*?

No, the response we're looking for here is fight, not fuck. I do *not* want him to fuck me. I don't. It's the Alpha, screaming *mine* and *yes* and drink it drink it drink it it's me it's mine it's yours i'm y—

I wrap my fingers around my cock and tug upwards once. A body-wide shudder wracks my body and heat unfurls in my stomach. Fuck it. My other hand palms my breast, and I moan softly.

Of course, that's the moment a knock sounds on the door. "My lady?"

I groan and sit up, curling in on myself to hide my now painfully hard erection. When the door doesn't burst open, I call, "Yes?"

"I merely wish to inform you it has been thirty minutes, and the Prince is expected shortly."

Thirty minutes? What the fuck?

"Oh, oh. I'll be out in a moment."

I step out of the bathtub, sloshing water all over the black and white tiles. I look around and find a towel, but no clothes. "Clothes?" I ask while drying off, watching the shadow of Corvin's feet on the other side of the door. I wrap the towel around my chest, then pick up the wide-toothed comb on the vanity and work it through my freshly oiled curls.

"I have several options laid out for you, my lady. I was not aware of your preferences."

"Preferences." I mumble, like all this illusion of choice will wash away the fact that I was bribed, blackmailed, and threatened to get where I am. I think on it for another moment, wrapping the towel around my chest. I open the door, revealing Corvin standing on the other side with his hands clasped before him. He blinks in surprise, but says nothing. "Show me these choices."

With each step I take, the stronger I feel. Corvin reveals the outfits he promised, each precariously laid out on the freshly made bed, no longer a nest of pillows and blankets. I brush my fingers over the hem of a dress on the far right, a sheer thing that reminds me of Raith. Everything is white, so goddamn white.

Corvin says, "Do you have a penchant for dresses, Dame Rajni?"

I toss him a sideways smile. "Sometimes, but not always. I'm usually working, and dresses tend to get in the way of that. I'm a practical woman, Corvin."

"If I may, my lady, perhaps this outfit would be to your liking?" Corvin gingerly lifts an outfit from the bed by its hanger, revealing a billowing and gorgeous pantsuit, the bodice of which has thick straps and a drape cut, cinching a multitude of white layers across the chest.

To my surprise, he demonstrates several pockets, those hidden and obvious. "This one in particular, my lady," He points to a pocket on the inside of the bodice, accessible only through the top, "is ... protected." He raises his brows, tapping the pocket for emphasis.

My brows furrow. "As in ...?"

He nods. "Yes, my lady. The tailor will be here in the morning to take more accurate measurements for tomorrow's outfits, this was the best we could do while you were indisposed."

I look around the room, then back to him. I gesture to my ears. "Are there any?"

"Yes, my lady."

"Interesting. Corvin, I think I might like you."

He dips his head. "My lady, I am pleased to hear you find my service satisfactory."

Corvin assists me with getting into the contraption known as a pantsuit, unbothered by my nudity, or rather the lack of matching parts. I expected to get a small reaction out of him, something to gauge the attitude towards such things in this place, but there's nothing. He dutifully zips the back of my bodice, then aligns my length of admittedly happy curls down my back.

He stands before me, hands clasped once more. "My lady, is there anything else I can help you with?"

The echo of a door opening freezes my blood, but it only draws forth a tiny smile from Corvin. He dips his head. "If you may excuse me, my lady. You are ready now, correct?"

I nod, voice stolen. He opens his mouth, then closes it again and allows that little smile to come back before he turns away. I watch Corvin cross the apartment in record time, curious to see how his master treats him and how my theories pan out. He stops in the archway separating the foyer from the living space, then bows at the waist.

Corvin says, "My lord, thank you for coming on such short notice. Dame Rajni will see you now." He steps off to the side, gesturing for the Prince to enter. Does he ever look the same way twice, and do I look much different than the last time he saw me? My brain catches up with that thought, and I internally grimace at the circumstances he saw me last.

Kalypso enters the living space, flanked by two silent guards who take up their posts on either side of the entry. They are dressed in black tactical gear trimmed in subtle purple, complete with tech goggles, dual pistols, an arsenal of strapped knives, and radios. Their hair is shaved and if not for their stitched on name tags, I would have no idea which one is which. I can feel every second of their hard evaluation, but there's no time to spare them a second look.

Kalypso is dressed in high-waisted white trousers secured with a belt of conjoined, tiny golden chains that match the gold powder decorating his eyes. His shirt isn't a shirt at all, but a white vest that's open in the front. Somehow it doesn't expose more than the delicate golden chains hanging over his toned stomach and sternum dusted in dark hair.

Upon seeing me he bows at the waist, a move reserved only for those who deserve the utmost respect. I do the same, and after straightening I close the distance between us. As if he didn't uproot my life and completely fuck me over, he says, "Hello, Rajni."

My plan has been to gain favor, but I can't help saying, "Hello, Kevin."

He laughs, and when his guards bristle, he waves them off. "Ah, yes. Tell me, how do you feel? Are you comfortable?"

"I am fine. Comfortable, yes. Corvin has been most accommodating."

His eyes twinkle with mischief as he looks over his shoulder. "Has he now? Corvin, not trying to steal my lady, are you?"

The servant bows his head from his place beside one of the guards. "I'm afraid so, my lord."

"Oh, good," Kalypso says, then turns back to me. "I was told you needed me."

"Yes." I glance at the guards, then back to him. "In private."

"Oh? Well, I'm afraid this is as private as it gets. Would you mind if we sat?" He gestures to the plush seating arrangement.

I fight back the words *why are you asking me?* and nod once, which is all the consent he needs. He takes a prim and proper seat on the edge of a loveseat, hands gripping his knees. As I sit opposite him in a similar seat, I note the bloodshot tinges in the corner of his eyes, and the sweat dampening his collar.

I look at the guards again, and Kalypso smiles. "These two are part of my personal guard, *Chayal* Esmeray bat Rakia and *Chayal* Xivan xir Gabi, and there is no one I trust more explicitly than them. Tell me, what do you need?"

I wring my hands, then immediately stop. "You were there, during the Cleansing."

He nods slowly. "Yes, I was. I participated in it, if you remember."

I fight the urge to stare at his throat. "The second day. You were there the second day."

"Oh." He leans ahead, but there's still a good few feet between us. In a remarkably different, dead serious tone, he says, "No, I wasn't."

"You–"

"*No*. However, for the sake of argument, what are you getting at?"

I stare at him for a moment, and he stares right back. I search for answers, but all I find is more confusion. I sigh. "I was naked."

"Yes ...?"

"If anyone were to be paying attention, they would notice that my ... I don't match, so to say. It does not seem to be an issue for anyone thus far, not that I particularly care, but I bring this up *because* there is medication that I take to assist with the way I live. I need it. As in, today."

"I see." Kalypso taps the arm of his chair. "And let me guess, you would like to return to your Clubhouse to retrieve it?"

"Is that possible?"

"No."

"Then what *is* possible?"

"My connection in the Clubhouse can secure it and bring it here, tonight at the latest. Is that acceptable?"

No, it is not acceptable.

"Yes, thank you. It's with ...."

"Yes?"

"It's only that I don't know who is there, and who is not."

"Ah, I see. Well, as of this morning there are still six known Foxes missing. It is suspected they have found refuge elsewhere. Takara is the interim leader of the Foxes, and Drystan is her second. Wonderful man, big heart on that one. Nothing has changed, Takara explained how everything works and the roles people play, so I left her to it. Fresh supplies have already been delivered, and another delivery will come next month."

Who is missing? Who did I lose? Who did I fail? True, unbridled anger rises as he talks about my life, my people, *my* home. "You were *there*?"

"Yes, of course. Do you really think I would trust the safety of your livelihood to anyone else? I know you are angry, and confused, but I swear I do not wish to harm you, or your people."

"Then why have you and Takara been planning on taking me out of the picture? What do you want me with, Kalypso? What do you *want*?"

"Freedom." He whispers, so quiet I nearly miss it. "I ... I didn't know. She didn't tell me that you two—well that is to say you *three*— were together. I—" He shakes his head and rises from his seat. "Will Takara know where it is? Your medication."

After a bewildered moment, I stand too. Reluctantly, I say, "Yes. She will know. But you didn't answer my question."

He smiles thinly, eyes dancing around the room before landing back on me. "You will find out soon enough. Dinner is in one hour, and the Emperor is expecting you to make an appearance."

"Why?"

"Not now. If you'll excuse me." Kalypso bows at the waist once more, then departs, or flees more like, for the door joining our rooms. His guards, the *Chayal*, follow without giving me a second glance. Kalypso reaches for the doorknob, then abruptly turns and tucks his left hand into his pocket, sweeping back the side of his vest to reveal dark, lean muscle stretched over his ribs.

He says, "Your situation is not as uncommon as you think, and if anyone bothers you, I would like to know *immediately*."

Then he leaves me behind, softly shutting the door behind him.

Silver Lining

My apartment is a haven from the mockery of the Citadel.

Kalypso meets Corvin and I outside my door, joined by the same two *Chayal*. He's dressed the same as before, but his hair is wet and freshly combed back, curling at the nape of his neck. He gives me a quick wink, offering his arm to me. "May I escort you to dinner, Dame Rajni?"

"You may." I bow my head, then slip my arm through his. I'm immediately accosted by the scent of wet wood and something unfamiliar but sweet, and my spirit rages against the confines of my collar. The Alpha wants to pin Kalypso down and breathe him in, explore every facet of the man I've been building up in my head for twenty years. He's different, and altogether the same. While our encounter was brief, it spoke volumes to his character, or so I had thought. I want to take him in, every detail and twitch of the fingers.

And I want to take him apart.

Kalypso escorts me through the halls of the royal quarters, unbeknownst to blood and lust building in my heart. I do my best to ignore the animal inside, focusing my attention on the world around us. The Citadel seems to be nothing more than an inverse extension of the Church. White marble architecture with high ceilings and statuesque pillars. Epic arches mark one hallway from one another, detailed with the tri-spirals of Syzdon and the Matzliach insignia. Enchanting chandeliers the size of a small car are perched overhead every fifty feet, and ornate gas lanterns mounted to the walls fill the spaces in-between.

Kalypso asks, "Are you familiar with the Citadel's layout?"

"Yes."

"Oh?"

"I thought I could breach it, once."

He chuckles. "So honest. Tell me, does seeing it in person match up to your expectations? Given we're only in a small section, and the uppermost level at that."

I sigh, glancing at the bodyguards behind us. Corvin stayed behind in the apartments, unfortunately. I decide to tread carefully. "It is impressive. I'm sure that one of those chandeliers could feed the entire Garden for a year. But they are pretty, aren't they?"

"That they are."

"Tell me, will there be anyone else in attendance besides your father?"

Kalypso's lips push thin and his heart kicks up a notch, echoing in my ears. I don't understand why it's so *loud*, and it's all I can do to focus on Kalypso's words instead of his pulse. He says, "Yes, the Emperor Consort will be accompanying us, but private dinners are not the usual. For instance, tomorrow there shall be a great feast, where all are invited to look upon the Matzliach Dynasty."

I say nothing on the matter, because it is a statement that does not deserve an answer. Silence follows our footsteps. We find no one in the halls, not a soldier or a servant. Kalypso quiets, tensing further with each hall we traverse through. Eventually we come to the end of our current hallway, and before turning right, the soft laughter of a man reaches our ears. Kalypso's arm tightens, inadvertently pulling me even closer against him.

He looks at me, lips parting as if to say something.

Then he shakes his head and leads me on, into the belly of the beast.

After turning the corner we only have to walk a short way before passing through an elaborate archway detailed with the Matzliach Dynasty crest. There have been no doors in this place besides our bedrooms, and the dining hall is no different. The scene inside is plain to see, disturbing me with how ... *regular* it is.

Kalypso escorts me through the relatively modest dining room that is the size of the Long Room, but doubled. The decor and furniture is a detour from modernity that shows itself in the centuries old wood pieces trimmed with gold hardware, such as the twelve person dining table, closed velvet curtains with golden pulls, and one gigantic chandelier, the only light in the room.

Cream wallpaper covers the marble in here, a faded floral pattern that puts me on edge for some reason. Canvas and paint masterpieces of all sizes decorate the walls, and there are two large hutches full of dishware on the longest sides of the room. There are no windows, and three exits. The one we came through, one on the opposite end of the room, and another on the middle right side of the room.

For all of this, only one thing piques my attention.

At the opposite end of the room, beside a door which I'm quite sure is to the kitchens, a large demilune table is situated against the wall, beneath a large painting of a forest. An aerial view, revealing hundreds of trees in the midst of their fabled autumnal change. On the table is a ceramic pot, quite plain really, which plays house to a violet, six-petaled flower. Unassuming, and my potential ticket out of here.

Of course, the Emperor is not to be outdone. He stands from his place at the head of the table, and so does the man at his left. They both bow their heads, then Drazen gestures to the seats at his right. "Dame Rajni, what a pleasure. Please, make yourself comfortable. I trust that my son has been treating you well?"

Kalypso pulls back the second chair for me, leaving the one beside his father for himself. I demurely accept, taking a seat as he scoots the chair in. "Your Grace, he has." I fold my hands in my lap, tucking my thumb between them so I can scratch it against my palm. The Emperor and his companion sit as we do, and the vague familiarity I found before in his face is crystal clear now.

Black-Hearted Daniel.

About eleven years ago Black-Hearted Daniel was the first, and youngest, person to claim the reward for turning in fifty shifter tags. A place in the Emperor's court, and it would seem he's most certainly earned that. The scars of his old life remain, a hairless line runs through his right brow and his right ear is missing, but otherwise he is immaculate. Crisp black hair slicked back into waves, flawless pale skin and glaring blue eyes. How did I not know that Black-Hearted Daniel is the Emperor's consort?

For that matter, that he had a consort at all.

Drazen takes Black-Hearted Daniel's hand in his, and smiles are exchanged between the cold-blooded killers. He says, "Dame Rajni, may I introduce you to the Emperor Consort Jedediah ben Matzliach, my husband."

Of course he would have changed his name. Pain spreads throughout my palm as I dig my thumbnail in, keeping my rage at bay. I bow my head once again, shifting my deferred attention to the consort. "Your Grace, it is an honor."

Jedediah smirks, his free hand taps a short pattern on the table. "Oh, I'm quite sure it isn't, *shifter*, but I do love to see you pretend. Is that all it takes to domesticate you beasts, one simple Cleansing? Kalypso completes his weekly Cleansing without so much as a complaint, but you just couldn't handle it, could you?"

Simple? Weekly?

I glance at Kalypso, only to find him giving Drazen an indecipherable, blank look. "Now dear, let's put the past in the past, shall we?" Drazen says, patting Jedediah's hand. "Tonight is about new friends."

"Of course, my lord." Jedediah bows his head, but that arrogant glint in his eyes doesn't fade.

"Good. Now Rajni, where should we start this wonderful discussion awaiting us? Ah, and of course. Here comes the food, I find words are softer over a good meal, are they not?" Drazen raises his glass to me, full of a golden liquid that all our crystal goblets share. "Let us drink, and toast to new beginnings."

Kalypso straddles the vine of his cup between his trembling middle fingers, glancing at me when he notices my stare. I quickly shift my attention back to my own cup, and I take it with all the wariness Hotaru would with a bomb. I raise it in unison with the Matzliach family.

Drazen says, "Kalypso, if you would."

"As you wish, father. To the new world," He locks gazes with each person in turn, leaving me for last, "and those brave enough to build it."

We drink as one, and I hope to hell my drink isn't poisoned. Then again, I could have been killed ten times over already, or dragged to a laboratory or back to the Church. The liquid is sweet, bubbly, and rich with the bite of alcohol. I don't drink much as it is, and I keep my sip minimal. Kalypso fills Drazen in on his trade meeting, something about Trading House and Alchemy House, but I'm only half-listening.

No less than a dozen servants work in unison, emerging from the door beside the flower. These servants do not wear the comfortable, bright clothes that Corvin wears, but all black, skin tight clothing that stretches from ankle to wrist. Gold masks cover the bottom half of their face, providing grotesque and permanent smiles. They are all barefoot, no louder than a whisper and harmonious to say the least. They settle platter upon platter at one end of our table to the other, and I'm so distracted by the servants that I don't notice what's served for dinner.

Meat and vegetables.

Produce is rare, a gift first revealed to me by Xylia and her mutation. All the Foxes have fresh vegetables and fruits year-round thanks to the greenhouses and Xylia's team, but not meat. There are no animals, and we're no fucking cannibals. For the longest time we consumed the same protein as the rest of the Dome, a powdered form that's stirred into water and quickly drank before you can change your mind.

Until the day Xylia brought forth a plant Edgar identified as soy, using his extensive library that has been added to over the years by Foxes old and new. We managed to process soy in a hundred different ways, and while it doesn't taste the best, it's a hell of a lot better than powderized *something*.

I have already suspected that the Citadel has greenhouses of its own, considering they are using shifters for other means, but the *meat*. What is it?

Or rather, *who* was it ....

After the platters are delivered, the servants disappear like they were never there at all. Never acknowledged. Never seen. There is more food here than even twelve people could eat, what is done with the leftovers? The thought of it becoming waste is sickening, but my traitorous stomach isn't on the same page as my mind. It grumbles and twists on itself, but I wait as Kalypso fixes my plate in the same fashion Drazen does for Jedediah.

Once the four of us have plates, Kalypso, Drazen and Jedediah clasp hands. Kalypso offers his free hand to me, as does Jedediah from across the table. My heart stutters, and I do my best not to let my fear and anger show. Kalypso's hand is cold and light, while Jedediah's is overheated and firm as it envelopes mine.

They bow their heads and close their eyes, so I do the same.

Kalypso says, "Dear Syzdon, our beloved God of Deliverance, please bless this meal and those around it, including our esteemed guest Dame Rajni bat Matzliach, the Alpha of the Rebel Foxes."

I retract my hands, snapping my attention to him, then Drazen in quick succession. Drazen lazily smiles, unbothered as ever. "Oh yes, we know. Why else do you think you're here?"

"I ...."

"At a loss for words, Dame?" Jedediah asks.

"Father," Kalypso says, meeting his father's eye. A move that would have anyone else punished immediately, and it seems that single word is enough to get things back on track. A word that Kalypso won't utter when in a separate room from the Emperor.

"Yes, always so serious, my son. Rajni, I have waited for you for far longer than you can imagine, or rather, a version of you. *The Alpha.* For the longest time, I had no clue what that even meant. What *is* an Alpha? A person? A thing? A concept? Such is the way of God, for if He were to give us all the answers, how could we rise above?"

"Your Grace, I don't—"

Something dark flashes in Drazen's eyes, and he holds up a finger. "Don't interrupt, dear. It's unbecoming of a Lady of your standing."

I swallow, bowing my head. "Yes, Your Grace."

"Good. Now, where was I? Ah, yes. The day I was given the greatest gift, and greatest riddle." Drazen smiles at Kalypso, who returns it. It's not the same as that grin in the Tunnels, though. "The day Syzdon came to me—"

I dig my nail into my palm harder. What a fucking lunatic.

"And delivered not only His son, but a great puzzle. One that was not solved until my dear boy brought back the news of an Alpha in the Underworld. I am a patient man, but I must say the moment he told me I was prepared to drag you out of whatever foxhole you were in right then. But I left it in Kalypso's hands, given it is his destiny. He did not disappoint, but then again, he never does."

Drazen reaches up and caresses Kalypso's face, and the Prince does not move a single muscle. The move should be sweet and kind, full of love, but it turns my blood ice cold. He says, "Just as promised."

I brave the following beat of silence and ask, "Your Grace, am I hearing you properly? God—Syzdon *Himself*—came to you and ... delivered a .. demi-God? Then what, told you to come find me?"

"To be exact, He said, 'You shall unearth infinite power if you nurture, love, and raise the boy, keep him safe, and find the Alpha.' I have kept my first part of the deal, and now I have found you."

"I don't understand," I whisper, because it feels as if the rug has been pulled out from beneath me.

On the one hand, I want to call him an idiot for believing that he spoke to an actual God, but on the other hand, Kalypso is sitting *right* there. No one knows how Drazen obtained a teenage son at such a young age himself, but the most popular rumor is Kalypso is a child born of wedlock, and his teenage mother was 'dealt with.' They are nothing alike, not from their mannerisms to appearance, and it makes so much goddamn sense, but yet it doesn't. Kalypso The Demi-God?

Gods don't exist. If they did, why would they deliver 'infinite power' to someone like Drazen? Why wouldn't they save us?

Why would they give anyone, let alone a child, to a monster?

Again, I whisper, "I don't understand what I'm to do. Aren't you powerful enough?"

"Rajni," The Emperor whispers, placating and soft. I lift my gaze, focusing only on his chin and mouth. "You've seen the worst of this world. You grew up in the shanties, did you not? Your parents were burned alive before your very eyes, because of *you*. Your mate was stolen from you and raped by three–"

I stand, then am immediately shoved back down by two *Chayal* I don't recognize. Drazen waves them off, and I *crave* to make him feel something other than careless and aloof. He says, "There is no need to get upset, it is done and over with, is it not?"

"She was assaulted by no *less* than three Citadel troops, *your* soldiers, and left permanently disabled due to the attack. Not to mention—" I inhale deeply through my nostrils, reeling in my anger. "Something like that is *never* done and over with. Do *not* bring it up again. Your *Grace*."

"As I said, you have seen the worst of this world. What I have isn't power. It's a privilege, one that does not extend to those who need it most. If I could change things on my own, I would, but wiping a system clean is not without its hardships. As you've said, the militia are untrustworthy at best, and what I have in mind will never be accepted by the Counsel. But, with you leading my latest ... project, it won't matter what they think. They won't have a *choice*."

"Cleansing ... the system?"

"Yes. The Dome was never intended to accommodate this many people, Rajni. We need to cull the herd, so to speak. I have been collecting some shifters of my own, and while they're powerful, nearly ninety percent are feral and therefore, uncontrollable. That's where you come in."

"I'm not killing innocent people, or forcing shifters to do the same."

"Of course, of course, however I'm afraid you don't have much of a choice. You see, Jedediah is the supervisor of your Clubhouse until further notice, and if you so much as say no, there will be consequences. Your Foxes are currently exempt from the programs, and they can stay in that cozy bunker you've made for them without a care in the world, just like you wanted. Do this for me, be the Alpha to my shifters, and you all live in peace."

My fury is an unfathomable, barely controllable thing. The thought of Black-Hearted Daniel being in the Clubhouse is enough to make me retch. "And Kalypso? Where does he come in?"

Drazen chuckles, patting Kalypso's hand. "Ah, yes. Kalypso is my heir, and everything I do is for him, as everything he does is for me. The two of you will be working closely together, as these programs are his children, so to speak. Ever since he quit the Hunt on me, that is."

Kalypso says nothing, but the glitching edges surrounding his figure speak volumes to his rising emotion. Of *course* he's in charge of the shifter programs. Is that to have an up close and personal opportunity to hurt shifters, or save them? I can only imagine what they go through, with programs like Super Soldiers and Breeding. How could you run something like that?

Carefully, I say, "I will not be able to influence the other shifters, Your Grace."

Even Jedediah stiffens when Drazen leans ahead in his seat. Ever so quietly, Drazen asks, "Oh?"

"Not with this collar on. I have to be able to access my mutation."

A singular crease forms between his brows, barely there, but the delight it brings me is endless. "You must think me an imbecile to suggest that I remove it."

"No, Your Grace, I am merely stating a point of fact."

"Does this mean you agree, otherwise?"

Jedediah leans forward in interest as well, while Kalypso is straight-backed and stoic. When our eyes meet, he gives me a quick wink. *Fuck*. This is the moment, isn't it?

I sigh, sitting taller. "I have a proposition of my own, one that may neutralize the issue regarding my loyalty."

"Do you now? This should be good," Jedediah says, taking a sip of his drink.

Drazen gestures towards me. "Go on."

I decide to stretch the moment, opting to take a long sip of my own drink. After setting the goblet back down, I fully lean back in my chair and gesture towards Kalypso. "If our fates and lives are entwined so thoroughly, then it only makes sense for us to take the next logical step. Marriage. It cements my position in the Matzliach household, and subjects me to Martial Law should I choose to harm any of my kin. Of course, the Prince has the privilege of choice, seeing how he captured me and earned the reward."

Jedediah flushes red. "This is absurd, she could never—"

Drazen's flash of anger cuts through the air. "Jedediah, your *tongue*. One more word and I shall have it."

Jedediah dips his head immediately.

Drazen turns to me, all pretense of civility gone. His airy presence hardens, and I finally feel as if I'm faced with a true foe. It would seem that Kalypso is his weakness, evident by the way he utters, "You wish to ... marry Kalypso?"

I provide honesty, as any good deception requires a shred of truth. I whisper, "I wish to stay alive, and keep those I love alive."

Drazen hums. "Interesting. It would certainly send a message to the damned Houses ..." He studies Kalypso, who seems to be unaffected by the whole affair. He searches his son for something, and only when Kalypso nods the smallest bit does Drazen seem satisfied.

To me, he says, "So be it. In the morning, you will meet the Council. They are a constant thorn in my side, and they are ... skeptical of Kalypso's destiny, at best. But this will do nicely. You will announce the engagement, and your fealty. Two weeks, I think, yes. That should be sufficient for planning. We can iron out the details of your collar in the morning, for now, let's eat. I feel we've made good headway, have we not?"

"Yes, father," Kalypso says, swiftly finishing off the conversation.

"Thank you, Your Grace."

Kalypso does not look at me once during the entirety of dinner.

I don't touch the meat, and no one forces me to. Silver linings, and all that.

I'm escorted directly back to my room after dinner, sans Kalypso. It would appear I have my own pair of *Chayal* now, they were waiting for me outside of the dining hall. One leads the way whilst the other walks close behind me. The lead guard opens the door for me, bowing at the waist. I enter the room, disappointed to find Corvin isn't there. Instead, a meek servant girl waits in the sitting room with her hands clasped.

She bows her head. "Dame Rajni, how many I assist you?"

I glance at the closed door leading to Kalypso's room, then back to her. My instincts prickle and I decide she's nothing like Corvin, so I hold my question. "Nothing, I'm turning in for the night. I would like to be left alone."

"As you wish, Dame Rajni. If there is anything you need, don't hesitate to pull the servant's chime just there." She points to a thick, braided rope hanging beside the bed with long golden tassels. She bows once more, then leaves the apartment without a fuss. The *Chayal*, however, are another matter. One stands with me near the foyer, while the other stands beside Kalypso's door. The only points of exit.

"I suppose you two equate alone?"

The one who bowed at the waist before and now stands only a few feet away says, "Yes, Dame Rajni. We are to stay with you at all times, as are all *Chayal* assigned to the service of the Matzliach family."

"So I'm not a special case then?"

"Not in this instance, no, Dame Rajni."

"Alright, well. Don't feel as if you have to be statues the whole time, as long as you don't kill me in my sleep we'll get on fine," I squint at the patch stitched onto their chest, "*Chayal* xir Dasi."

"Yes, Dame Rajni."

If I'm not mistaken, there was a quirk of lips there.

I leave *Chayal* xir Dasi's side, tentatively exploring the room. I take the long way to the bedroom, which is now curtained off. I tug on the heavy brocade, studying the long, curving runner above as the curtain moves back and forth. I step inside the bedroom, then shut the curtain completely. Another nightgown like the one I wore earlier is laid out on the bed, along with lounge pants and a loose shirt, all white. The illusion of choice.

I shed my pantsuit, groaning as soreness makes itself known in my joints and muscles. For a moment I consider taking another hot bath, then chastise myself for falling into the Citadel's indulgent ways so quickly. At home it's every other day, unless a freshen up is needed, of course. I leave the barely worn outfit on the floor, then slip on my trousers.

When the fabric crests my thighs, I freeze.

I have several tattoos, courtesy of Drystan and Namir, and most of them are functional. On my right thigh is a garter, and tucked beneath the inked fabric is a piece of paper. At first glance it could pass for a piece of ribbon from the nearby bow, but it is far more than that. For the first time since my capture, there are small words written there. Indecipherable, until brought to life.

Xylia has a matching tattoo on her left thigh, providing us a way to communicate when separated. After the last time I swore it would never happen again, but Xylia, ever the realist, came up with the idea.

Do I have enough power to activate it?

I sit down on the edge of the bed and breathe, pants slid down around my calves and breasts pebbled against the chill. I had already assumed my tattoos would be restrained by the collar, so if this doesn't work nothing changes. But that doesn't stop the damned thing called hope from saying, 'what if?'

I brush my fingers over the tattoo and rub in a clockwise circle once, then counterclockwise. I tap the black outline of the paper and green sparks emerge from my tattoo in response. The small note painlessly sprouts out of my skin, and red-hot tears stream down my cheeks. I carefully turn the strip of paper over, holding my breath as my eyes scan a column of perfectly printed words.

ABANDON SHIP.

ROOSTING.

2 DOWN. SA+DA

E+X=Y

GENESIS.

2 WEEKS.

WHAT IS HE LIKE?

I exhale a portion of my worries. Erik and Xylia are safe with Soren, but I lost Sallow and Daisy. Oh, *Daisy.*

Fuck.

My hands shake, and the tears don't stop assaulting my soul. They splash onto my bare thighs, and the paper quivers in my tightening grip. I killed Daisy. I killed Sallow. I should've listened to Drystan and made her stay behind. I should've listened to Hotaru and gone back when they said. And Genesis? That's a fucking suicide mission, there is *no* way they can pull that off. I told Kalypso the truth, we once contemplated storming the Citadel, we called it Plan Genesis, but even then we knew it was too much. But with everything I know now?

Unless all the gangs band together, then maybe … no, it's too risky.

"Dame Rajni, Prince ben Matzliach calls upon you. Do you accept?" One of the guards asks from the other side of the curtain, startling me. I hurriedly press the tiny paper against its home in my skin and repeat the initial process, but in reverse.

"I … I am not decent, give me a moment."

"As you wish, my lady."

Footsteps trail away and I quickly dress. Did Kalypso say he was coming? No, I would remember if he did. After straightening out the pants and shirt, I pull back the curtain. I don't move any closer. *Chayal* xir Dasi stands in the living space, hands clasped behind their back. "I'm ready now."

The other *Chayal* unlocks the conjoining door, and opens it.

Kalypso slowly enters the room, dressed in lounge pants and a bathrobe undone in the front, quite similar to how his vest rested earlier. I tilt my head, studying the subtle limp he carries. When I open my lips, he softly smiles and beats me to it. "I wanted to say goodnight, and thank you."

"Oh. What for?"

He stands before me, giving me a flat look. "Your marriage proposal."

I cross my arms and huff, desperately wishing I could speak plainly. "It is the least I can do, I suppose."

Kalypso buries his hands in his trouser pockets, tugging the hem of his pants down ever so slightly to reveal more of that *interesting* dark and thick trail of hair that leads beneath the waistband. "You are quite the creature, Rajni. Well, that is all. We have a long day tomorrow, the sooner we can soothe those shifters, the better."

I step closer, and I can't help the grin that comes to life when Kalypso's heart quickens. "Is that so?"

He shifts closer, too. His eyes drift to my bare feet and linger for a moment, then slowly drag upwards, cataloging every inch of me. "Why yes. Our wedding is in no less than two weeks, my dear. Such a grand event, and everyone in the Upper City will be there. Everyone will be looking to us, to the Citadel, and it's an opportune time for things to go awry. Which we can't allow, of course"

Kalypso pauses, staring me directly in the eyes. His hand rises in the inches between us, and I stiffen. He raises a brow, and when I don't back down, he licks his lips. The pad of his index finger sweeps back and forth over my bottom lip, then settles in the middle and gently taps. I watch him study my lips under his touch, and despite the fact that Kalypso himself has only shown me vague kindness, the fact that he is dangerous, absolutely and completely, remains.

"Kalypso." I whisper against his finger, and his pupils blow wide. I remember a trail of blood going down, *down*.

His hand falls back into his pocket and he takes a step back. "Forgive me, Rajni. I—I—" He shakes his head. "I believe it is time for me to turn in."

Kalypso takes another step back, and my fingers wrap around his wrist. Movement occurs in four points of the room, but halts completely when Kalypso firmly says, "Stand down." He looks down to my hand, then back up to my face. "Yes?"

"Is it true?"

"Most likely, but what in particular?"

"What Black-Hearted Daniel said, about you. Do you really go through that every week?"

"Don't call him that." Kalypso whispers, pulling out of my grip. He gives me a grim smile. "It's not as bad for me as it is for others."

"What the hell does that mean? You go through the same trials, don't you?"

"Well, yes, but—"

"Just because someone has it worse than you doesn't mean you are invalidated, Kalypso. *Every* week? For how long?"

Kalypso jerks as if struck by electricity, and that mercurial pool shines behind his amber irises for just a moment. His jaw ticks once before he storms off. "I'll see you tomorrow afternoon. Remember, Rajni. Two weeks" He turns around, something I'm finding he does quite often, and grumbles the entire time. After stepping back into the bedroom, he shuts the curtain and hides us from the guard's view.

Then, to my surprise, he begins to viciously sign, and they're mostly the same signs that we use in the Clubhouse. Did Takara teach him? Xylia was taught by her parents before they died, and over time we made our signs for things, too. Plus, there's one single book in Edgar's library. There are some signs of his I don't understand, but I get the gist of it.

"Do *not,*" He cuts sharply through the air, "do this with anyone else unless I say they are good. *Listen*. I need you to kill Snake (?) and I am planning a — (?). I want to use our wedding as a cover. We can get your people and mine in, and if you take control of the animals (shifters?) stuck here, then we have a fighting chance. I have friends but what I don't have is you. I need to know I can trust you, and that you trust me."

I answer him in sign, stepping closer. "The number one rule to surviving is to *not* trust anyone. That's how I ended up here."

"Mechanic (Takara, and *damn* him for knowing her sign) did not — you because she wanted the —. She did what I asked her to do, because she believes in me. She believes in a world without Snake (Drazen ?), without the Church. The outside is liveable Rajni, I have proof of it, but Drazen will never let us live out there, not while he has power here. We need to tear it all down. I can show you if you don't believe me."

A tiny smile escapes me at what I can only assume is his sign for me; fox.

I sign, "I believe you. I don't trust you. But I believe you."

He smiles. "Fair enough."

Hesitantly, I ask, "Are you ... a shifter, too?"

He shakes his head, then signs, "No," for good measure.

I open my mouth but Kalypso holds up a hand, then reaches into his pocket. He reveals two familiar tins, wiping away the questions on my tongue. I exhale a shuddering breath and take them, opening the one I need most to ensure everything is inside. I can suffer through the pain, but not the loss of this. The relief I feel upon seeing six glass vials safely nestled into a bed of moss, full of a steel-blue liquid and stoppered with cork, is indescribable. Balderik's greatest creation, accompanied by a note face-side up.

I'M SORRY, AND I DON'T BLAME YOU FOR HATING ME. BUT I WANT YOU TO KNOW MY FEELINGS FOR YOU AND XYLIA ARE GENUINE, AND A MISTAKE I DO NOT REGRET. IF THERE IS ANYTHING YOU BELIEVE ABOUT ME, LET IT BE THAT I TRUST KALYPSO WITH MY LIFE, AND I THINK HE'S DOING THE RIGHT THING. THERE'S A WORLD WAITING FOR IF NOT US, THE KIDS, TO RUN FREE. I'M KEEPING THEM SAFE, I PROMISE.

I snap the lid shut, glaring at Kalypso who has been pretending to be very interested in the curtain. I whisper, "I hate you."

"I know. Now muss my hair so it looks like we've been fooling around."

Later, long after I kick Kalypso out and take both my medications, I lie stretched out beneath layers of blankets. I pull them over my head and activate my right garter tattoo, heart racing as the green sparks emit from my skin. I partially shift one fingernail into a claw, then scratch my message on the now blank strip of paper.

GO GENESIS. 2 WEEKS. ALL HANDS ON DECK.

K=ALLY. BIZARRE.

BE SAFE. I LOVE YOU.

I dream of Takara.

She sits on the floor inside the prison cell I last saw her, and she's in her unique fox form. Her black and white fur is flat against her body, and her calm eyes are set on me. I stand on the other side of the reinforced glass, shifted as well.

But I am not calm.

"How could you do this?"

"Why didn't you tell me?"

"I would have believed you."

"We could have done this together."

"Did you not trust me?"

"You really didn't love me, did you?"

No matter how many questions I hurl at her through the bond connecting us, she does not move, and does not answer. And doesn't that piss me off more? We have a *bond*. How can you form a bond with someone you never truly wanted? It's not a mating bond, but it was close. She said her feelings were genuine, and the bond should be proof of it. But I feel as if I am nothing more than a means to an end to her, and to Kalypso, even.

So why can I feel her rapidly beating heart?

WARFARE OF A DIFFERENT SORT

Panic, a crowd of people, and the distinct stench of fire and ash waits for me when I awake. Corvin slides the curtain back as chambermaids work in the dining room, delivering this morning's breakfast. My *Chayal* are posted on either side of the foyer, and there is a mannequin in the den being fussed over by the tiniest person I've ever seen, perched on a step-stool.

I scramble backwards in bed and Corvin holds up his hands placatingly. Smooth and even, he says, "My lady, I apologize for the rude awakening, but you have a long day ahead of you and must rise early. Breakfast is served, and the Head Tailor is preparing for you. Afterwards is the Council meeting at ten o'clock, then your visit to the lower levels with Prince ben Matzliach."

"Corvin, one thing at a time!" I scrub at my face, heart racing at the prospect of awaking in a new place, again, and surrounded by strangers. "Okay. Breakfast. Clothes. Tell me more as we go."

When I enter the dining room the servants shift into the bedroom with their heads down, promptly stripping the bed and putting on new sheets. These ones are different from Corvin, or even the servant I met last night. These remind me of the ones who served dinner, nothing more than emotionless shadows. They wear the same skin tight black outfits, and the partial gold masks. Breakfast consists of warm bread, berries, eggs, and small crisped links of meat. The sight of meat alarms me, and Corvin takes notice of how I poke at the eggs, something I've only read about.

Quietly, he asks, "My lady, is something wrong?"

"What is this?" I point to the links.

Corvin shifts on his feet, standing a short distance away. "Sausage, my lady."

I give him a flat look, and irritation seeps into my tone. "And where does the meat come from, Corvin?"

He bows his head. "Slaughter House, my lady. There are animal farms there, where all the meat, eggs, and dairy originates from. The Garden, as you refer to it, or the Underworld, as the Upper City refers to it, is not aware of its existence, most likely due to the fact ground level citizens receive dehydrated meals, the ingredients of which are the recycled, or extra, materials from Slaughter and Green House. The output of the combined Houses are not enough to provide everyone with the same quality, but this is an effective alternative."

Anger is too futile a word to describe my emotions, and the force of them is so great that Alpha rears its head, proven by the green glow cast across Corvin's figure. I grip the arms of my chair and close my eyes, breathing heavily. It's not Corvin's fault. It's not his fault. After recomposing myself, I ignore Corvin completely and eat the bread, along with the berries. With great disgust, I drink the entire glass of fresh water.

The moment I declare that I'm finished, Corvin ushers me into the den where the tailor is still working, humming to themselves. Only once I'm in their bubble does the tailor give me their attention. They are half my height and dressed in an all black, skin tight outfit with excess fabric draped fashionably across their chest and shoulders. They have steel rings in their septum, along the shell of both ears, and through the middle of their bottom lip. Their neon green hair is cut into a short asymmetrical style that frames their petite face, contrasting their pitch black irises. Their sleeves are rolled up to their elbows, revealing black tattoos that encase both arms beautifully. The same symbol that Corvin has on the back of his hand is hidden in one of their ink sleeves.

They extend their hand to me. "Sybil xir Yadir, at your service, my lady."

I shake Sybil's hand, appreciating their firm grip. "Rajni, but you already know that."

"As that may be, we are allowed the right to introduce ourselves, are we not?"

"I suppose so. Is this the part where I stand here like a doll? I've only ever been fitted for a dress once before."

"Clever you are, yes it is. Although," Sybil gently takes both my hands, guiding me to the center of their workspace, beside the mannequin, "I was under the impression you do not prefer dresses?"

I shrug, slightly flushed. "I merely do not wear them often, for practicality. I leave the decision in your capable hands. It is my understanding I'm going to war today, and I need every advantage I can get."

"War, my lady? Here I was thinking you were attending a Council meeting." Sybil remarks. The *Chayal* are interested as well, but neither move from their posts or comment, simply watch. I do not recognize either of them, they must have changed shifts while I was sleeping.

"In my experience, meetings are nothing more than a different type of battleground, this is merely warfare of a different sort. I have changes to make around here Sybil, and a duty to the Emperor to uphold. If there are those who do not like it, well ...." I trail off dramatically, and Sybil chuckles.

"I'll see what I can do."

I find myself curious and eager to meet the heads of the Houses that make up the Citadel, and my constant questions regarding the people and their roles seem to have perked Corvin up. He further proves to be invaluable, and I resolve to thank Kalypso for allowing him to be in service rather than his. The information he gives me is common knowledge and casual, but he highly touches upon key points that others may not find useful. Gossip is a wonderful thing, and the flaws in the Counsel are my weapons.

I wonder about Sybil, as well. They frequently talk of the Prince and his personal interests in multiple Houses, including Alchemy, Education, Library, Green, and Trading. Sybil has a table on wheels which plays host to a sewing machine run by foot pedal, and I find it fascinating. Sybil stands on their step-stool as they finish altering my last article of clothing, apparently they had started on my wardrobe while I was asleep, but there were some measurements Corvin could not take while I was in bed.

Corvin makes quick work of the gold buttons along the front of my black dress shirt, and for some reason it reminds me of Balderik casting a shield of protection on the teams before we leave the Clubhouse. The gilded paw prints and tri-spiral symbols of Syzdon beautifully embroidered into the shirt's fabric in gold do nothing to abate my heartache. Corvin does the buttons up to my sternum, leaving quite a bit of skin on display. I opted not to wear a brassiere, and the sleeves are rolled up to my elbows, similar to Sybil. My trousers are high-waisted, accentuating my wide hips and thick thighs, and are pure black with deep pockets that I cherish.

And like the pantsuit I wore last night, it has secret 'protected' pockets on the side. I still haven't quite figured out what that means, whether it's because they're warded or hidden. Considering the guards are watching and the walls are listening, I'm only notified of them by a quick, subtle tap of Sybil's bright green nails.

Corvin clips suspenders to the back of my trousers, then brings the straps over my shoulders and does the same to the front. This close, I can fully appreciate the extent of his injuries. I assumed before it was from acid, and there's no way to deny it now. I suspect it wasn't washed off immediately, because the pits in his stressed, constricted skin are deep.

Sybil speaks as they work, breaking me from my stare. "Nitza xir Maron has been proposing an alliance between their nephew, Nathaniel ben Tshuva, and the Prince for quite some time now. Considering their relations, it made perfect sense. But the Prince always insisted he was saving himself for someone different. Someone who was going to change the world. And he did not say this unkindly, merely a point of fact. It's almost as if he knew you were coming."

"Is that so? Are you telling me I have competition, Sybil?"

Sybil chuckles, a light thing that tickles a small smile out of me. "There is no competing against you, my lady. Merely an elder rambling on, as we tend to do. You know how it is."

That causes my smile to fade, because most people don't grow old in the Garden. Jaromir is one of the oldest people I know, and he's only in his fifties. Whether Corvin or Sybil notice my shift in demeanor, they do not comment. Sybil leaves their sewing machine, passing what I now recognize to be a cloak directly to Corvin. I'm temporarily confused, because aren't cloaks a one size fits all sort of thing?

But then he turns it around and holds it up, showing me the back. A star surrounded by six overlapping circles, the same insignia Corvin has tattooed on the back of his hand, is embroidered across the breadth of it in honeyed gold. There is a key difference in this design, though.

Inside each circle is a neon green print, each vastly different. A paw. A slither trail. Talons. Imprint of butterfly wings. Dual wavy lines. A human footprint.

"What is that symbol?" I ask quietly, gesturing between the cloak and Corvin's hand.

He exchanges a quick look with Sybil before answering. "This is Prince ben Matzliach's insignia, my lady, the one bestowed by Syzdon, but we thought it could do with some adjusting, given your alliance."

It's our future, or what it could be.

If Kalypso's right. If I trust him. If we get everything right, and it's enough.

But even if it's not, I think I could face the end knowing that I did everything I could. That I didn't cringe away from the weight of responsibility, from a chance to do something more. Because Takara is right about that part. This is bigger than the Foxes. And if I gave up now, I would always wonder; what if?

I breathe deep, then nod.

Corvin gently covers my shoulders with the weight of the cloak and my duty, then clasps a simple penannular brooch closed, finished with one single crystal, a rainbow opal. Gemstones are unearthed sometimes in the Garden, if you're able to manage cutting through the stone-hard ground. In the Citadel, it's all preserved wealth from life before, same as their food sources, apparently.

He takes a step back, standing beside Sybil, and there's a hint of wetness to his eyes. I swallow thickly, then kneel and take Sybil's hands in my own. I press them to my bowed forehead and whisper, "Thank you."

This time Kalypso does not meet me outside the apartment, but rather at the private elevator lobby down the hall from our rooms. His back is turned to me, hands clasped behind him. I'm able to catch the way his thumb briefly presses against each fingertip, beginning with his pinky, before the person he's speaking with nods my way. Kalypso turns around, and his arms fall to his sides. His lips part, and that mercurial haze makes an appearance not only in his eyes, but around his figure, making it appear as if he's vibrating.

I'm sure it's quite the dramatic effect, cloak billowing behind me as I stomp towards him in my old combat boots, chandelier light dancing across the golden details of my outfit. Upon meeting him I bow at the waist, and the long braid of dirty blonde fashioned by Corvin swings over my shoulder. Kalypso responds in kind, then reaches for my hand. I oblige him, and he kisses my knuckles. When he straightens, releasing me, the haze has disappeared and his smile is tight.

"Dame Rajni, you are especially striking this morning. I trust that Sybil treated you well?"

I nod, giving him an appraising look. He's dressed in an outfit eerily similar to mine, but instead of gold, the paw prints and tri-spirals detailing his shirt are silver. It's completely unbuttoned, and his suspenders are a tad loose, sliding partway down his shoulders. He dons a cloak identical to mine. I say, "*Ai*, they did, and you aren't so bad looking yourself this morning, Prince ben Matzliach. I wanted to thank you for lending me your staff, they are most hospitable, but Corvin especially."

The man in question shifts behind me, and I can only imagine the blush creeping across his face. Kalypso simply bows his head. "Of course. Only the best for you, Dame Rajni. Shall we?" He gestures towards the elevators, and the person he was once speaking with is gone. All that remains is his guard detail, standing close behind their master.

I nod in acquiescence, and together our envoy boards the next elevator car. Kalypso and I stand in front, flanked by Corvin, and each *Chayal* takes a corner of the massive elevator furnished with plush couches and pretty sconces. I note there are seven levels according to the control panel, two more than I was initially aware of. B1, and B2. The button currently lit up is C4, and I don't miss the irony. The fourth level is the main hub for all things political.

Kalypso follows my gaze and his jaw twitches. There's a fine layer of stubble there, as if he forgot to shave this morning. I glance back at Corvin, then to Kalypso. Hesitantly, I began to make a joke, "Kevin—"

"Prince ben Matzlaich, *Dame* Rajni." The *Chayal* in the back right corner barks, startling me as their voice reverberates off the white walls with ease.

Kalypso turns on his heel, slides past Corvin, and comes nose to nose with the offending person. It happens so quickly and with such violent force that I'm shocked into silence. In a low tone more forceful than the royal guard's previous outburst, Kalpyso says, "She will address me as she damn well pleases, and you will shut the *fuck* up, lest I recommend you for Cleansing or far worse, a visit to the Emperor's Consort. Do I make myself clear, *Chayal* xir Lironic?"

"Yes, Your Grace. My apologies."

Kalypso leaves *Chayal* xir Lironic behind and joins my side once again. He glares at the control panel as we near our destination, and an unfamiliar urge passes over me to fill the silence. Casually, I say, "I'm most looking forward to meeting your friends, Kalypso."

He blinks at me, completely thrown and anger temporarily forgotten. "Friends?"

"Yes, it's my understanding that you are quite close with Nathaniel, at the very least." I give Kalypso my best smile, and it seems to do the trick.

He chuckles quietly, shaking his head. "That old bat. Yes, well, I suppose he's a friend of sorts. Nothing to worry about there, I assure you. You'll meet him shortly."

"When we announce our engagement."

"Indeed."

"Are you nervous, Kalypso?"

He draws in a long, shuddering breath, then gives me a grim smile. "Only fools are fearless."

The elevator's quiet humming is interrupted by a loud rumble and the doors slide open, revealing a long, narrow hallway of white marble with gold veins and rows upon rows of tiny but effective chandeliers. People fill the hallway as far as I can see, and I can tell right away not all of them are magistrates, council members, or some other political nonsense. Cameras flash the moment we're visible, and journalists begin rambling all at once before we even set foot outside the door.

As the guards in front begin clearing the way, Kalypso offers his arm to me. I loop mine through, focusing on the sound of his racing heart instead of the mob awaiting us. For some reason, I never considered the press. It's not an issue where I come from, we're only fed propaganda from above. No one cares about what's happening to us, and it's never filmed or investigated. The Garden is merely 'the extras,' all those who don't fit. It's like they were cast aside and forgotten about, left to their own devices, and what I've learned so far has only solidified that line of thinking.

Everyone dresses in bright colors here, and the only white is the marble of the floor and walls. Piercings and flamboyant hair is common as well, and there's so much exposed skin. We're escorted out of the main hallway and into a circular auditorium, where the officials wait for us in many more layers of clothing, but in no less vivid colors. On a distant wall are racks of respirators, locked in a glass case that reads, '*EMER-GENCY*' along the top.

"Doesn't the Church have some rule about modesty?" I whisper to Kalypso, and the corner of his lips twitch.

"Not quite. It's all about indulgence. Survival of the fittest, and living ruthlessly. On the face of it, it can be an attractive thing. Living however the fuck you want."

"Half my crew like to dye their hair and pierce their faces too, Kevin, but they're not selfish jackasses. I'm just saying, I thought they wouldn't want so much ... *skin* out and about. The old churches used to preach abstinence and modesty."

Kalypso smiles for real this time. "Appearance has nothing to do with whether you're an asshole or not. They encourage all the skin, actually."

The auditorium is full of curved metal desks which serve as stations, one for each House, and on the ascending tiers behind each station are the noble members of that House, which number in the dozens. The modest room is packed, no thanks to the few journalists situated in the distant corners of the room.

We approach the station situated directly before the podium, and all eyes are on us. I sweep my cloak beneath me and take a seat, opening my mouth to retort, but the Emperor's appearance silences me. Kalypso rests a hand between my shoulders, opting to remain standing. His touch comforts me more than I care to admit, and I breathe through the encounter.

Drazen's seneschal, Orioz ben Sarig, is with him, and the fact that he was not at our impromptu dinner last night does not evade me. Orioz is an elder, heavy set man with thick ginger curls and beady black eyes. He proudly wears a gaudy pendant depicting Syzdon's sigil, and dresses more conservatively than his peers. I do not like him at all, and I haven't even heard him speak yet.

Black-Hearted Daniel (*Jedediah*, I remind myself) is with them as well, and his outfit matches his partner's, a sheer black gossamer suit, shirt entirely undone. My ears ring and it hits me how vulnerable he is, Drazen. His stomach is *right* there, his aortic pulse pounds just beneath pale skin stretched over a soft layer of fat.

Kalypso's hand travels to my shoulder, squeezing once. I breathe, blinking rapidly as my senses return to me. The conversation filters into my ears just as Drazen says, "Are you ready, Dame Rajni?"

"I—Yes. Ready, Your Grace?"

Jedediah releases a long suffering sigh. Drazen merely smiles at me like one might a child. He says, "To address the assembly with the Prince. As we discussed."

The doors are shut, did that happen during my blood lust fantasy?

"Oh. Yes."

I rise from my seat and my achy knees, elbows, and ankles already miss the short relief I'd found. Kalypso's hand slides down to the small of my back before linking with mine, and Jedediah's eyes track the movement. I bow at the waist and say, "Thank you for the honor, Your Grace."

I resist the urge to shoulder-check Jedediah when passing, and I keep my chin held high as we take our place at the steel lectern centered in the room. There is no vintage wood here, only harsh metal, bright lights and everlasting white. Attached to the lectern is a microphone, and I exhale my bone weary grief. It's only a microphone. It's not like Hotaru invented the goddamned things.

Kalypso opts to go first, and I'm grateful for it because once again, I've been thrown to the wolves unprepared. What the hell am I supposed to say? In two week's time I'm going to kill your leader and break apart life as you know it? Yes, that's the one.

Whilst still holding my hand, Kalypso confidently addresses his people with a layer of charm I'm finding to be no more than a mask, not that he isn't charismatic in his own right. "Members of the House, I am thankful to have you all here, as today we celebrate new alliances and breakthroughs that will change life in the Dome as we know it. As many of you know, I am a Child of Deliverance, and the prophecy delivered upon my arrival has finally come to fruition. It is my pleasure to introduce my fiance. We are to be married in two week's time, and you are all invited, along with the rest of the Citadel. Under my father's guidance, we shall usher in a new age that will benefit all of us. What say you?"

My eardrums writhe beneath the chaos of hundreds of people clapping and shouting, both in outrage and joy. Trembling but determined, I raise our joined hands and Kalypso quickly picks up on the cue. After a moment, we lower them and separate. I take my turn at the mic, and Kalypso stands behind me. The lights blind me and sweat beads upon my brow, and *how* did Kalypso make this look so easy?

I rely on the large, neon signs attached to the front of every station. They depict the names of each Head and as I search the room, I lock eyes with each one. On the first two circular levels are the oldest Houses which are considered 'domestic', and they carry the most nobles. There is the Head of Power House, Orin xir Tinit.

Head of Public House, Temon ben Lon.

Head of School House, Rasha xir Delone.

Head of Kitchen House, Liron ben Hadoram.

Head of Chamberlain House, Elipaz xir Shamir.

Head of Health House, Leah bat Tal-Or.

My heart drops upon seeing Cardinal Grand Bishop Mincha ben Missim, the Head of Syzdon House. I do my best not to let my bodily fear show, but that smug fucking grin of his makes an appearance regardless. I look away, immediately finding a man who can only be a teenager. Head of Alchemy, Eliram ben Avichen.

Sybil told me a little bit about him, including the fact he works with Kalypso on the shifter and pharmaceutical programs. He reminds me of Seth so much that it's a wet slap to the face, and I have to grip the sides of the lectern. Kalypso shifts in my periphery, but I breathe through the panic and ignore him.

I cannot be prey.

I'm surprised to see Captain Tsifya bat Jeshulun's station beside the Cardinal's, and even more so when I receive a curt nod from the battle worn woman. She is the Head of Militia House, and her station neighbors Fleet Admiral Reshef bat Benli, who is the Head of Airship House. Reshef is far older than her counterpart, a stout wrinkled woman with jaundice taunting her swollen eyes.

Next is the Head of Trading House, Nitza xir Maron, the person who's been trying to marry their nephew off to Kalypso. An elder with glowing onyx skin and white hair shaved close to their scalp, and hauntingly dead green eyes. Many layers of pearls decorate their bare and nipple-less chest, and a wrap-around skirt is the only article of clothing they wear. They might have been handsome or even beautiful once, but now there's only a lingering air of malice that has hardened anything once pleasing.

The Head of Slaughter House, Orli ben Yoratan, frightens me. He's young, perhaps only a few years older than me, but there's a ... cloud, almost, of overwhelming dark energy surrounding him. He has thick blond curls and steel-blue eyes, and his white complexion is dotted by a multitude of freckles. He appears outwardly friendly, conversing with the Head of Green House, Avidan ben Zisi. Avidan appears older than his comrade, a thick man sporting a brunette braid and beard, and somehow he feels safer to look at.

Last but not least is a pretty young woman with bleach blonde waves and long fingers tipped in blood red nails. The Head of Library, Cilia bat Farah. According to Sybil, she has a crush on Kalypso. If she resents me, she doesn't let it show, rather she gives me a little wave and smiles upon seeing me.

Who is enemy, and who is foe? Who opposes Drazen's ridiculous plan of genocide, and who favors it? Are Kalypso's allies here, or do they reside only in the lower classes?

While every station is full, I can't help but notice there are two key players missing. The heads of the shifter programs, but it makes sense considering it's an underground operation. I'll be meeting them, one way or another.

I fill my lungs with courage, and my mind with the faces of all those who deserve better than this. Better than these people who have so blatantly failed them, sitting on their houses of endless resources. Words sharp as blades and threats heavier than bombs, I introduce myself.

"I am Rajni, leader of the Rebel Foxes. I am a fox shifter, an Alpha to my people, and I have accepted the honor of joining the Matzliach family. I believe in what they are building, and I will be working closely with them from here on out. It is high time there is a voice for shifters here, and I understand there is some disagreement regarding their place. I'll get right to the point on that matter. There will come a day when there is a feral force far greater than yourself, and you will have to make a choice. Will you be standing behind that force, or in front of it?"

Emperor Drazen is the first to stand from his station and clap, and the entire room follows suit. His glacial stare follows us the entire way back to the station, and I say nothing as Kalypso pulls out my seat for me once more. He sits beside me, a meager shelter between Jedediah and Seneschal Orioz. The Emperor bows at the waist to me, a gesture not lost on the populace. He takes his place at the lectern, and it's all I can due to focus on his words full of promise and propaganda.

Kalypso whispers, "You were born for this."

"I don't know about that, Kevin." I whisper back, body trembling with the aftershocks of adrenaline.

He smiles, tongue darting out to wet his bottom lip. "Do you think we could have lunch together? Before this afternoon?"

"Are you asking me on a date?"

"A non-required one." He shrugs, staring down at his hands in his lap. His right thumb taps his fingertips in that same pattern he seems to do when nervous. "As friends, that's all."

Tentatively, I reach over and take his hand. His pupils dilate, and his heart is so *loud* as it quickens. My own heart rate kicks up in response, because *a drop of blood trailed from the corner of his lip and—*

I clear my throat. "Friends. Food. Yes."

Kalypso laughs, and I hold onto the sound with all I have.

HE'S SAFE. HE'S GOOD. HE'S MINE.

Kalypso and I don't go on our non-required date.

Immediately after the long and drawn out meeting concludes, one of Kalypso's personal *Chayal* approaches and whispers in his ear. Kalypso draws in a big breath, then nods. The Emperor and his Consort have faded into the political background, but the Seneschal is close by, watching us intently.

Kalypso turns to me and whispers, "We're needed downstairs. Immediately."

"Oh. Okay," I say, feeling oddly terrified for a moment. I glance at one of the iron caged clocks, surprised that it's well past lunchtime. "Lead the way."

The mob of interested civilians and journalists has only grown, and our guard contingency increases to a dozen instead of the mere four *Chayal* we came with. The new additions are general military, marked by the colors trimming their tactical gear. Kalypso keeps close to my side, the two of us sandwiched between the small platoon clearing the way. By the time we make it back inside the Matzliach's personal elevator, Kalypso's heart rate has skyrocketed exponentially. Outwardly, he appears no different than his usual self, save for his jaw. I can't tell if he's grinding his teeth or chewing on his cheek, but either way it seems to be the only thing saving him.

I brush my fingers against his ever so gently, and his attention snaps to me. I ignore him, focusing on the buttons of the control panel, watching as they change color. His pinky and index finger trail up the back of my hand, and I inhale deeply. Honey and pine. A single drop of blood trailing down.

I capture his hand in mine, a completely unnecessary gesture, and watch the buttons as we near our destination.

B2.

The guards tighten their formation around us, and the four in the front, standing between us and the door, unholster their guns. I glance up at Kalypso. "What kind of emergency are we walking into, here? I'm not quite sure what to expect."

He gives me a long look, then stares dead ahead. His fingers twitch in mine. "We're visiting S-Block, which is where all shifters in possession of the Citadel are kept. Any shifters turned into the Citadel alive, end up here. The two main programs are the Super Soldier—"

"Or Breeding." I snap, and he glances at me for a small moment before nodding.

"Yes. But there are some individuals who are not suitable for either program, and they fall under an improvised alchemy program which studies the magic of shifters, their anatomy and physiology."

"Experimentation. And that's with Eliram ben Avichen?"

Kalypso stiffens, but doesn't try to pull out of my grip. For reasons I don't care to explore, I don't release him, either. Our light finger hold has become full on clasped hands, and our combined grip is anything but subtle. "Yes. It is integral to the Citadel's well-being that we have a complete understanding of what we do not know. Eliram is an incredibly talented, and emphatic, alchemist. You'll like him."

I scoff. "I believe our ancestors spent quite some time trying to name such a thing as magic, I don't think you or him will have much luck. Especially considering our powers do not lie in magic, but mutation."

This quirks his attention. "Mutation? Is that what you think?"

"It's what I know, what I live. Only those who ..." I trail off, staring at him anew. Isaac believes in the Old Gods, and as such has frequently tried to convince me that the creation of shifters is of the Old God's doing, and we've been granted magic as a means to survive. Is that what Kalypso believes?

Then again, he said that he's not a shifter, and yet he possesses power of his own. How else would he have it? What else would you call it *but* magic?

"What?" He asks, tilting his head.

I shake my head, and once again the elevator car releases a warning rumble to signify we've reached our destination. I pull out of his grip and the loss is palpable on both ends, if the wounded look on his face is anything to go by.

"Nothing. Let's get a move on."

The guards oblige my command and Kalypso efficiently drops the subject, and conversation, all together. B2 reminds me of the Clubhouse, and the similarity punches me right in the chest. All concrete and fluorescent lights, its subterranean depths are a heavy presence made known by the loss of windows, something the Citadel seems to pride itself on. There is no decor, nothing to denote one hallway from another. Only after walking in near silence, besides the march of boots, for about five minutes does anything of interest begin to appear.

Distressed howls, barks, and ferocious yowling echoes off the stone walls, their origin hidden by the upcoming curve in the hallway. The animal in me pops its claws, curious and angry all at once. I haven't even met these shifters yet, and I already feel a strange possessiveness over them. I ask a question that I most definitely should have asked before now, "How many are there?"

Kalypso hesitates as we turn the corner. Thick metal double doors and a shrewd old man come into view, and I slow instantly. Only then does he answer me. "A hundred and twelve currently live in S-Block, and there are sixteen more currently in quarantine. There are several ... cliques, if you will, and every single one of them have become unsettled since your arrival. Unhinged, one might say. This had led to some interfighting, which shouldn't be able to happen."

"And why is that?"

"They wear collars, which not only repress their shift, but can cause the individual to submit through a series of electrical shocks which increase if the behavior does not cease. It's as if they feel nothing."

"Speaking of which, I still won't be much help with this on." I tap the side of my collar, irritation rising further. "You think someone might have told me I have to soothe over a *hundred* shifters before now? You all made it seem like there's a small pack here, but I've never even been in the presence of a hundred shifters at once, no thanks to all of *you*. I can't do this, Kevin. Not like this. I'm not their Alpha, they don't know me."

It takes Kalypso's hands falling upon my shoulders to make me realize I'm hyperventilating. I breathe deep, hating how much he grounds me. It's only because he's the only person not actively trying to kill me. Not the kinship I find in his spirit, or anything else. Very quietly, he says, "They may not know you, but they can feel you. Listen."

I do as he says, finding there's no more cries of distress. I fight the urge to itch at my messenger tattoo, as it's currently burning like a fucker. Instead, I straighten beneath Kalypso's hold. "If you insist. And my collar?"

He gives me a grim smile. "I don't have the power to remove it, but after tonight it shouldn't be an issue. Just make yourself known, give them something to tether to. You don't have to do anything else other than that."

"Are you sure ..." I trail off, because it's a question I already have an answer to. There's no animal spirit within him, nothing calling out to mine. If you don't count the way his heart sings to me, that is. I blame it on destiny, on our fates being apparently twisted together, because any other answer is unacceptable. You can't be mates with someone without forging a bond, and sealing it in a way I've only ever done with Xylia.

"Never mind. I'm ready."

Kalypso nods, hands leaving my shoulders. We approach the man waiting for us, and I don't miss Kalypso's mask falling back into place. Upon meeting us the man thrums his chest with a gnarled fist, bowing his shaven head. "Lieutenant Doron ben Galoi, at your service, Prince ben Matzliach and Dame Rajni. Thank you for coming so quickly."

Kalypso does not bow his head an inch, or bother with bringing his fist to his heart, so I follow his lead. He says, "Of course, Lieutenant ben Galoi. Are there casualties?"

Doron shakes his head. "According to the vitals systems, no. But there are several that are severely injured, and the aggression has not lessened."

"If I may," I say haltingly, and when I'm not told to shut up I continue, "when did this spike of aggression begin?"

"Since your arrival, Dame Rajni," Doron says. "There are several in the block who consider themselves to be pack leaders, and they especially have been acting ... off. We don't know how it works, the dynamics of an Alpha and Betas, but it would seem they are reacting to your presence. But is this an accurate statement, considering they've never met you?"

I glance at blank-faced Kalypso, then back to Doron. "It does not surprise me. I've been known to have an influence on packless shifters that aren't bonded to me, and when in times of stress, that influence can be greater. I don't know what the bonds are like between these 'Groups,' but they're clearly built on fragile ground. Do they attack on sight?"

"Yes, my lady."

"Swell. Let's do this, then."

Doron opens the double doors, flanked by our soldiers with guns at the ready. He leads us into an expansive room with spectacularly high concrete ceilings. On either side of the landing are what I belatedly recognize as living spaces, and in the distant right corner of the communal space is an enormous kitchen fit with a refrigerator, stove, and cupboards upon cupboards.

Overturned bowls of fresh fruit and blood decorate a length of counter island separating the kitchen from the rest of the room, and that's not the only place blood touches. There are several crumpled bodies on the ground, but their faint heartbeats alert me to the fact they're alive, but injured.

The place is far more expensive, and free, than I initially thought. I expected shifters to be kept in cages, prison cells, or even worse, isolation. Instead, it appears they have nearly all the creature comforts one could want, even television and books, art easels and musical instruments, all of which are destroyed.

In the back left corner are rows of tables that stretch to fit twenty-four people, and it takes four benches to do the trick. Most of the seating is overturned, and a number of shifters stand on top of the tables, bloodied claws and fangs bared. In fact, every shifter in the room, whether it be in the living room to my right or a den of sorts to the left, stares us down with sharpened edges exposed. They're more than half-shifted, and full of danger.

I whisper, "I thought they couldn't do that."

At the sound of my voice, countless eyes flash in a cacophony of vivid colors.

"On guard," Doron says. The guards in front raise their pistols and begin to fan out.

Kalypso releases a quiet but firm, "No. Stand down."

"But Prince—"

"Do as he says, you incompetent fucks." I bark, startling those around me. Approval sharpens the animal gazes set on me and for a moment it's overwhelming, because I *can* feel them. Little pinpricks investigating my mental defenses, seeking out my spirit. I glance at Kalypso and he nods minutely, an exchange that takes less than two seconds. With his approval, I push past the guards and stride forwards until hitting the center of the room. I'm not shot in the back, so I take that as a plus.

Every shifter stills, and the violently blinking lights on their collars threaten to distract me. Just above each collar are numbers, the very same I found on Feivel's neck. Every flash of red and green reminds me of my purpose. My *true* purpose. I draw on as much of the Alpha as I can, and it's absolutely excruciating. Like a truck has parked on my chest, crushing my heart and lungs as they struggle to fill with blood and air. A ringing overtakes my ears, and a sharp pain lances through my temples. Despite this, I don't stop. Not until the bloodstained concrete at my feet is washed in a vivid green light, and my heart opens completely.

And only once the moment is right, do I speak.

"I am Rajni, Alpha of the Rebel Foxes. Some of you may have heard of me, some of you may have not, and in either case you most likely don't trust me, and I don't expect you to. Not today. I can't pretend to know what your life has been like until this point, neither before your capture or after, but I do know what my life has been like. And I can tell you that I'm tired. I'm so fucking tired of fighting to live. I want a place in this society, and I will do everything it takes to make it so. To do this, I need your help. Not the Citadel, but *me*."

Like a crack of the whip, the first accusation flies, its origin unknown. "But you're with them!"

I touch the collar around my neck. "As you can see, I am held here the same as you. I would not be here if it wasn't for your benefit, and trust me, that is all I care about. I know you can feel it, the Alpha." For good measure, I shove my influence outwards one more time. An exquisite twinge of pain seizes my neck, and a warm stream of blood escapes my right nostril. A few of the shifters tilt their heads, exposing their necks towards me despite the distance. There are far more who do not, but I honestly didn't expect any type of submission this early, and certainly not with my damned collar on.

There is a small cry from behind me and the source of it surprises me, but not enough to disrupt my focus. Louder than before, I ask, "Who is the leader here?"

A familiar woman pushes through the crowd, the same height and apparent age as me. She has black skin and un-naturally white hair, and there are patches of vitiligo on her neck. I can't place her, but I immediately think; *'Lynx.'* She's barefoot and dressed in the same standard issue outfit the rest of the shifters are, a sleeveless white tunic and cuffed trousers. She's one of those who did not immediately submit, and her dislike of me is plain to see, let alone feel.

"Serena," she says, and it's a punch to the gut.

I open my mouth to say, *'Takara's mother. You are Takara's* mother. *You left her in a dumpster, and she had to claw her way out of the garbage just so she could* breathe, *and then she wandered home to her drunk of a father in the dark. You are the problem with shifters, abandoning your own so harshly.'*

I swallow my resentment and anger, not to mention a mouthful of hot blood. I take a step towards Serena, then another, and another, until we're nearly touching. She stands battle ready, one foot shifted ahead and weight on the balls of her feet, not unlike myself. Lowly, I say, "I know who you are, and you would do well to stand aside. I don't take kindly to those who abandon their kin."

Serena bares her elongated fangs at me, and I do the same. Somehow, I'm able to partially shift and *roar* in her face with my entire fractured chest. Her arms raise, shoulders bunching, but I knew what the verbal jab would do. My fist connects with the side of her head, right above her ear, and she goes flying. Quite literally, her body arcs through the air and collapses into a pile, surrounded by shifters who had hurriedly jumped out of the way.

But she's not the only one falling through the air. I'm finally brought down by the radioactive power that I can only get small pieces of, like sucking a thick liquid through a straw and it finally gives way, choking you. I don't crash to the ground, though. Instead I'm drawn into the arms of a tall shifter with long red hair, and for a moment I imagine it's Xylia, because the curls are so beautiful and I *miss* her and—

A sharp growl cuts through my haze. It ruminates from the body against mine, and it's directed at Kalypso. While I can't focus on him well through my blurry vision, I can feel that it's him close by, pissed off and worried. I can feel him more than the rest, and I want nothing more than to be close to him. To smell him. To feel him. To know that he's real.

Because how can any of this be real?

I manage to say, "He's safe. He's good. He's mine. Let me–" I cough, splattering blood across the shifter's clean whites. "Him. I need ... him. I'll be ... back. Promise."

"*Aleph.*" The shifter growls, then reluctantly passes me over to Kalypso's waiting arms. He holds me close, but I push against him. He opens his mouth to tell me what he thinks of *that,* but I beat him to it.

Quietly, I ask, "Put me down. Let them see me walk out of here."

He grumbles, but does as I say. He holds me up and whispers, "Your face, Rajni, there's burns all over you."

My vision and consciousness continues to ebb and flow, as do my muscles. I grit out, "I went too far. You s—shouldn't be t—touching me. Radioactive."

"Oh fuck you." He tightens his hold on me, like *I* might run.

"N—not here." I laugh, but it immediately sets my throat on fire.

Little hooks barb into my heart with each shuffle-step that Kalypso and I take, weak connections between the strange shifters and myself that tug me back towards them. I shouldn't be leaving them. They need me, and I need to bond with them. It hurts, like leaving a child behind.

And we all know how I feel about that.

The moment we step back into the hallway and the double doors are shut behind us, Kalypso sweeps me off my feet, bringing me to his chest with an arm behind my back and knees. My forehead crashes against his heart, and I immediately pass out.

I awake with a start, effectively punching Kalypso in the face. Thankfully my energy is non-existent, but it's enough to twist his head to the side. We're in my room, shrouded by the curtain. I have no idea what time it is, but the shadows beneath Kalypso's eyes have darkened immensely.

"Are you alright?" He rubs at his jaw and focuses on me once again, unbothered by the patch of red blooming on his cheek. His shifted, silver eyes dart so fast back and forth across my face that I have to shut my own to keep from getting dizzy. I check in with myself, then nod.

"I think so. Sick and sore. I pushed it too far, this fucking—" I reach up to tug at the collar, only to find it's gone. That wakes me up a little bit, and my eyes fly back open. Kalypso is right where I left him, kneeling at my bedside. He's dressed the same as he was earlier, and his black waves are a twisted, knotted mess. He gives me a small, unsure smile.

"You got worse. When we got to the elevator, you started to seize in my arms, so I ..." Kalypso clears his throat. "I brought you right to him, and after hearing the guard's reports, along with my own, the Emperor decided you had earned the privilege of the collar being removed earlier, and privately. The shifters are calm, even more so since your collar was removed. Can you ... feel them, now?"

"You're okay?" I ask, studying him for evidence of radiation burns.

He shakes his head in disbelief. "Going to need more than that to take me down, Rajni. I heal on my own, similar to how a shifter does."

After a moment of processing, I nod. "Good. I can't feel all of them, not by a long shot, but there are some that so desperately wanted somebody to follow that wasn't ... Serena." I spit out her name, then stare at Kalypso with fresh eyes. "Do you know who she is?"

He swallows, then leans back on his heels and raises his hands to sign, which he does so slowly. "Before I met you, I met Takara. She had Leo (he uses the word gear, Takara's sign for Leo) with her, and both were ready to fight me to the death. I don't really know how it happened, but I let her go. I couldn't stop thinking about her, though, so when I got a little older, I found her again. We started trading papers (information?) for papers, and I did my best to keep her safe, but she was always packless. Sure she had fucking Lizard (Conlead?) but ... well, I don't have to tell you. Being around people is not the same as being bonded to them. But anyways, yes. I know who her mother is, not that anyone else does, because it doesn't matter."

There's a green monster rearing its ugly head in the confines of my heart, and I don't dare do more than acknowledge it. So what if I'm not the only one who was saved by Kalypso? So what if he thought of Takara for years?

So what if my most prized memory has been thoroughly shit on?

I sit up in bed, slowly, and bury the jealousy deep within me. It's not an emotion I'm familiar with. I've never been jealous, not of Xylia's lovers or anyone else, and it doesn't serve me. Takara isn't mine anymore. I inhale sharply, as if the thought had penetrated my heart for the first time. For some reason, that hasn't really settled in 'till now. I mean, it's obvious it's over, isn't it? Whether or not she thought she was doing the right thing, she still manipulated me, lied to me.

I raise my hands and focus on the questions I've yet to ask Kalypso, and seeing how we're shrouded from this crazy world by nothing more than a curtain, it seems the best time to ask. "Who are you, Kalypso?"

It takes a moment to recognize that last word, and upon realizing that my sign for him is a wolf, he blushes immensely. He signs, "What Drazen said is true. I am not from here, but I do not remember where. I remember very little of my life before, but I remember the prophecy being given to Drazen by ... *someone*, fuck. It's hard to explain like this. But I did hear it. I have power. I would call it magic, but you don't believe in that, so I don't know what to call it."

"I believe in you."

He ducks his head, trying and failing to hide that painfully boyish smile that I caught a glimpse of in the Tunnel, before all this started. "Thank you."

"How old were you?"

"Eight."

"What do you remember? Where did you come from?"

"I remember my parents. I–" Kalypso inhales sharply, hands stilling for a moment, then continues. "I remember that I had parents, anyway. When I think of them, there are five faces, but they're always just out of reach, always covered in ... shadow. Sometimes it's water, or snow, or a rainbow. I don't know how to explain it other than dreaming when I'm awake, for all the bizarreness of it."

"Five?" I affirm, and he nods. "Do you think you'll see them again?"

He laughs, and it's so broken that my spirit cries in response, wanting to stitch him back together. "Considering I don't even know where I'm from, no. If they're in here, I haven't found them, and if they're outside of the Dome ... how could I ever search all of the world? I have no idea what's out there, other than the fact it's out there, waiting. It will take all my life, but I think I just might try, when this is all done."

Stupidly, I say, "I'll help you."

He gives me a look, hands dropping. Not exactly accusing, but wary. We stare at each other for a long time, until he haltingly signs, "If we win, you'll want to take your pack as far away from me as possible, and I do not blame you."

I shrug, feeling oddly flushed. "*When* we win, the pack will want to run. Explore. What better way to do that than helping you search the world?"

"And what about Xylia?" Kalypso asks, using the sign for a corkscrew. Tears sting my eyes upon realizing this and I sniff, but don't look away.

"As long as you don't kill me, or betray me, I think we'll all get along just fine."

"Why are you saying this?"

"I ..." I huff in frustration. "Must you make me explain everything? You saved my life once, and while you might not have thought twice about it, it changed my entire fucking life."

He stares at me, bewildered. He cuts sharply through the air as he signs, "Is that what you think?"

"It's what I *know.*"

Kalypso stands, looming over me. His freckles stand out against his now mercurial eyes, and the way the chandelier casts its light over him is unfairly beautiful. Aloud, he says, "Rajni, you have consumed me from the very first moment that I met you. I knew then you were the Alpha I was supposed to find, and I refused to go on Hunts after that. I didn't want him to find you, not until you were ready. I had this crazy idea that we were drawn to each other, because why else did I feel this magnetic pull to you? One that physically *hurt* me to ignore, one that *still* does. I do not think of you, because I do not have to. You are always on my mind, ingrained into every thought, dream, and awareness that I have. I ..."

Kalypso looks away, hands bunching into fists at his sides. He says, "It's late. Get some sleep."

He practically flees the room, sneaking through the gap between curtain and wall best he can without opening the divider any further. I groan in frustration, and only when the adjoining door shuts hard, not *quite* slams, do I shove the blankets down, locating my messenger tattoo. The parchment is full, and calling it out of my skin is effortless now that the collar is removed.

TA -> WANTS A MEETING. Y/N?

KA-> CAN YOU TRUST?

HU-> LOSING IT W/O YOU.

There is a gap, as if she wrote the next few messages some time later.

WHAT HAPPENED?

WE FEEL ... SOMETHING BIG ...?

R?

R?

R?

My nails shift, elongating and darkening as they transform. Hastily, I try to fit as much as I can in as little space, and with as much vagueness, as possible. When it comes to the question about Kalypso, I try to be as objective as possible.

Y, BUT BE CAREFUL.

Y, HE IS GOOD.

TELL THEM I SAID STOP WORRYING.

The last encounter I had with Hotaru, *'I. Hate.You,'* derails everything, and the tears finally escape. The writhing, unsure ends of the new connections I've picked up recoil at my emotion, and it's easier to reel in my sadness this time than it was last night. I continue, unsure about the damning last bit, but I desperately need to talk to someone about it, and if not Xylia, then who? I cannot lie to myself anymore than I can lie to her.

001+ NEW

I ... FEEL FOR KA.

I recall the words I said to the shifter downstairs, knowing damn well that like is an understatement. What I feel for Kalypso isn't love, either. But the possessiveness I hold is uncalled for, and the thought of anyone touching him is enough to draw a partial shift out of me. And the things he said to me, it's like he pulled them out of my own damn heart. There's something between us, and I'm not calling it love, but I'm not calling it hate anymore, either.

With great difficulty, I get out of bed and take my inflammation medication. Both my tins are right where I left them, in the relative safety of my bedside drawer. The inflammation vials are precisely filled with a viscous, deep purple liquid that tastes like garbage, but is effective nonetheless. Xylia is the only person I know of that can safely process this plant, and it's antidote. If I can get Drazen to ingest the plant in his dining room, then he's as good as dead. I suspect he either knows it's toxic and is making a statement with its presence, or he simply thinks it's pretty. And besides, I have my medicine, too. Not that matters, because how would I get him to ingest either without revealing myself? It's simultaneously too simple a solution, and too difficult.

I return to bed, mind full of murder.

Most Talented

I awake before Corvin arrives in the morning, and I spend some time staring at the message Xylia sent me in the night.

YOU'VE FELT HIM SINCE THE DAY YOU MET HIM, RAJ.

PART OF YOUR HEART HAS ALWAYS BELONGED TO HIM, ONE WAY OR ANOTHER.

FIND OUT WHY, AND DON'T LET HIM GO THIS TIME.

IF YOU DON'T, I WILL MAKE YOU REGRET IT.

I write her back, trembling the entire time.

I DON'T KNOW IF HE FEELS THE SAME, BUT I'M WILLING TO TRY.

I quickly go through the motions of rising for the day in efforts to keep from thinking myself into an attack. I dress in an outfit similar to the one I visited the shifters in yesterday, a long sleeve shirt tucked into high-waisted trousers. By the time I pull my boots on, Corvin pokes his head through the curtain. Upon seeing me he immediately stills, unsure whether to withdraw. "My lady, my apologies. I did not realize you were already awake. Would you like me to ...?"

I stand, giving him a warm smile. "What can I say? I'm excited for today's adventure." I gesture towards the cloak I had previously laid out on the bed. "Do you mind?"

Corvin smiles, obliging me. He sweeps the cloak over my shoulders, and when he begins to pin it together I ask, "How many people live in the Upper City, Corvin?"

Corvin's fingers pause for a brief moment, then continue securing the crystalline closure. "At the last census, nearly two-hundred thousand people were estimated to occupy the Dome. The Upper City lays claim to approximately two-thirds of that number, my lady."

I stare up at him, searching his scarred face for a long moment. I desperately wish to know his story, who he really is. He is far more than Kalypso's personal servant, or perhaps that is *why* he's so knowledgeable and ... kind. How does someone like that survive here? There's only one answer, really.

Finally, I whisper, "We never had a chance on our own, did we?"

Corvin bows his head. "My lady."

"Can I ask you something else, Corvin?"

"Anything, my lady."

"You're Kalypso's only servant, aren't you?"

Corvin blushes, ducking his head in efforts to hide his expression. "Yes, my lady. He insists that he does not mind, for Kalypso—the *Prince*, excuse me—did not have servants before me. He wishes for your utmost comfort."

"I see. Well, you have certainly provided that. Thank you."

Corvin lifts his head, revealing a tiny smile. "Are you ready for breakfast, my lady?"

"Ah. I suppose so. Will the Prince be joining us?" I pull the curtain back, revealing today's *Chayal* at their posts and masked servants working in the dining room. "Good morning, everyone."

Corvin effortlessly keeps up with me, unbothered by my energetic pace. "Prince ben Matzliach is currently in a trade meeting, and has requested that you work with the shifters again this morning. You also have an invitation to a luncheon afterwards with the Emperor and Council in the Pink Room, as does the Prince."

Another trade meeting. I slide into a stool at the counter island, nodding to the servants in thanks before loading my plate with steaming eggs and toast, one of the many options laid out on platters before me. I address Corvin waiting patiently at my side, hands clasped before him. "And who will be escorting me?"

"Your *Chayal*, those assigned to you today are *Chayal* xir Dasi and *Chayal* xir Gabi. The Prince made it clear to the Emperor that you were responsible enough to perform your duties without supervision, and accepted the punishment should you not."

I scoff. "When the hell does that man sleep?"

Corvin chuckles. "Not often enough, my lady."

"Say, isn't *Chayal* xir Gabi on Kalypso's service?"

"The Prince requested some of his personal guards to be in your service, in efforts to best accommodate you, my lady."

"And what he says just goes, hm?"

"Quite often so, my lady. He is the Child of Deliverance, if I might add."

I give Corvin a thin smile. "This is true."

We make it to S-Block without incident, and extra security waits for us, along with Eliram ben Avichen, at the elevator landing. His dirt brown hair sticks up in every direction, and when he extends his right hand towards me I notice the ink smears that extend from fingers to wrist. He leans heavily on a sturdy walking cane with his left hand, where I find Kalypso's sigil tattooed in the same fashion as Corvin's.

Interesting, for two reasons. The tattoo, which isn't discreet to say the least. And I've yet to meet anyone in the Citadel that has a disability. Until now.

He inclines his head, grip tight. "Eliram ben Avichen, at your service. I was hoping we would be able to meet yesterday, but it sounds like you had quite the time down here."

I shake his hand with the same amount of force. "Rajni. I hear you're the man who's playing God."

Eliram blushes furiously, and his hand retreats into one of his overcoat's deep pockets. "Only trying to understand Him, that's all. Anything I can do to help the Matzliach Family is time well spent. I think after you see my work, you might agree."

"Noted," I say, all traces of my good mood gone. "I thought today's agenda was bonding with the shifters. Is that not the case?"

"Oh, it is. But I thought I could walk you there, ask you some questions? I'm working upstairs this morning."

Let him talk if he wants to talk.

"Lead the way, Ben Avichen."

"Please, Eliram is fine." He bows his head, then leads the way towards the shifter quarters. He keeps a slow pace, his gait unsteady due to his lame right leg.

"Alright, Eliram. Let it rip."

"Um. Okay. How did you connect with the shifters yesterday? According to the monitoring system, over a third of them bonded with you when you exerted your influence. That is far more than we hypothesized, to be honest I thought it would take more time."

"They need someone to follow. Not all shifters *require* an Alpha, but in times of great stress, it's the only way to keep the animal tethered to humanity. It's a pretty cage they're in, but a cage no less. That's enough to put anyone on edge, not to mention what's involved in your ... programs."

The moment I finish talking, he starts. "I'm not disagreeing with you there, but when you say *the* animal, are you saying your forms are ... two different entities?"

I study Eliram for a moment, recalling what Kalypso said about him. I can't wrap my head around the fact that this person who experiments on shifters, could be an ally. I don't sense anything malicious about him, and I'm starting to think the tattoo is a calling card of sorts. But why make it so visible?

We turn a corner, and while there's no distressed cries echoing through the halls, the unease waiting for me is strong. I focus on my words, treading slowly. "Not quite. Think of a shifter's soul as two different spirits. The animal is there in the back of my head, but quiet. Territorial, emotional. Primal and base. When I'm a fox, I'm still present, but everything is ... easier. Simpler. You're able to be what you cannot as a human. You can't have one without the other. Some people see no difference, and this is all my opinion, of course."

"Interesting ...." He taps his cheek, lost in thought. I leave him be for about ten seconds, then bombard him with questions of my own.

"Tell me about the hybrids. The ones I fought against."

Eliram startles, and him falling is a near thing. "Oh. Yes ... they're a branch of the Super Soldier program." He glances at me, and I'm reminded of a kicked dog. "They're humans who have been treated with shifter blood, those ones in particular shared DNA with a jellyfish shifter."

"How?" I ask roughly.

He swallows. "You cannot obtain the mutation through a traditional bite, it has to be injected directly into the heart. They don't have the self-healing abilities, or increased stamina or strength, but they are able to partially shift. They imprint on whoever administers the treatment, and while they have some free-will after, it's ... they're not the same, the people."

"Great," I say, thankful that we're coming upon the doors to the shifter quarters.

Eliram takes hold of my arm, his grip demanding. My *Chayal* advance, but I shake my head. "No, he's fine."

He fixes me in his watery gaze. "My Ma."

My brain doesn't compute for a moment, and I stare at him until it kicks in. *Oh.*

"I'm the most talented alchemist of my generation, all our scores are reported, you see. The Emperor made me the Head of Alchemy, along with all the ... protection that comes with it, because of how much he approves of my work. And this," He gestures to his leg, "people like me don't make it. Not unless we're useful."

I rest my hand over his. "You're wrong."

His eyes widen. "What?"

"You're the second most talented, because my apprentice is first."

"Oh." Eliram laughs a little, shoulders slumping.

"Besides, there's more to a person than what they can do, isn't there?"

Eliram gives me a tight smile, pulling his hand away. "Maybe one day that will be true. Thank you for making time for me, I'm sure we'll be seeing each other again soon."

He leaves and I watch him go, then turn to *Chayal* xir Gabi. She straightens her already stiff posture underneath my attention. I ask, "Is it possible that I can go in with just you?"

"My lady?" They ask, glancing at *Chayal* xir Dasi.

"I want just the two of us to go in."

"You are my superior, Dame Rajni, but I do not know if it is safe to do so."

"So I'm allowed?"

"Yes, my lady."

"Good. Let's go play with the animals."

The guards unlock the doors and as I follow *Chayal* xir Dasi inside, my fingers twitch for the absent radio at my side.

The inability to reach and feel my Foxes *physically* pains me, even more so now that the collar has been removed. What surprises me is the incredibly strong tug pulling me into the shifter's quarters, one that is familiar but dulled, hard to reach and identify.

The scene we come upon is much more docile than yesterday. The bowls are right side up, full of unblemished fruit. There's no blood stains or bared teeth, and the living spaces are full of lounging, mostly relaxed shifters. There's a few groups on the fringes, wary of our entrance. I scan the room, noting that Serena isn't in the common areas. When my eyes land upon the dining area filled with tables, my heart stops.

A large man with a shaved head that was once thick ginger curls sits alone, staring down at his hands resting on the table. He's dressed in the same white pants and shirt all the other shifters have, along with a collar and no doubt a number. His back is turned, but there's no mistaking him. "*Sallow?*" I ask through our bond, which is as heavy as it was before. He doesn't turn, and I speed walk over to him.

Chayal xir Dasi keeps close behind me, a silent shadow. The other shifters watch, freezing in place in response to my high tension. I reach his side and quietly say, "Sallow?"

He turns towards me, revealing strong facial features that I haven't seen in months due to his thick beard that he takes pride in, which is gone now. His eyes are no longer bright green, but dull and dazed. '*789*' is inscribed above the collar, ink fresh and angry.

"Yes?" He asks, once strong and playful voice only a hoarse whisper.

I kneel, taking his hands in mine. He allows me to, but the gesture clearly confuses him. I can *feel* his relief, even if he can't feel me. "Do you know who I am?"

He searches my face, then shakes his head. I inhale a shaky breath before continuing. "Do you know where you are?"

"I ... home? A better home. A better place. They said I'm in a better place, and I need help. They're going to help me," he says, tears welling in his bloodshot eyes.

"Oh, dear Sallow." I bow my head, pressing his hands to my forehead. I take a moment to recompose myself, because I'm ready to rip and shred. How did he end up here? Xylia said he was dead, but maybe she only thought he was, and they couldn't recover him. I'll be damned if I let Drazen take Sallow from me, too. Not when he's right in front of me. I breathe deep, then do the only thing I can think of. I think of Golding.

Sallow makes a chuffing sound, fingers twitching against my head. "What did you do? I saw ... I remembered someone."

I lift my wet eyes, focusing on him. His own are wet and wide, darting across my face. "Yeah? Was it a big guy in a bandanna?" He nods furiously, and I choke on a laugh. "I'm going to try something. It might hurt. Are you ready?"

"Yes. Yes."

I close my eyes, and reach for Sallow. I take hold of his heavy yet slippery thread, using all my willpower to bring him back to me. I think of the day I met him and Golding, and the times I made them put the Clubhouse together after they knocked out parts of it during their love fights. I think about Liam, and the pack. Oh God, how I miss them. It's enough to drown me, but I hold onto Sallow, physically and mentally.

He gasps, a tiny thing that speaks volumes. "Alpha?"

"Yes," I cry. "I'm here, I'm right here."

Sallow sweeps me up in his arms, holding onto me for dear life. He cries onto my shoulder, fat heaving sobs that break apart my own grief. He asks, "Where's Gold? Where is he? I don't—it *hurts*, Alpha. He's too far. Too far. He was hurt, and I—I think I unleashed my mutation, and I don't remember what happened after. Is he okay? Please tell me he's okay."

"He's okay, and so are you. Everything's going to be fine, I've got you." I murmur, surprised that he's alive at all. Sallow doesn't make it a habit to use his gravity bending mutation, considering its radioactive blowback is more intense than most. No wonder why they thought he was dead.

We hold each other for the longest time, and no one interrupts us. *Chayal* xir Dasi stands with their back to us, and the other shifters remain in the periphery, watching and waiting. Eventually I whisper, "You're going to have to trust me. Can you do that?"

Sallow nods, still holding me tight. "Homework?"

"Homework," I say, affirming the code word for Plan in Progress. I pull back, cupping his face. His stubble scratches my palms. "And I need you to be strong for me."

"What can I do?"

"Make friends."

We spend the rest of the morning doing just that, sitting side by side at his table in the dining area. After a while the shifters who bonded to me yesterday make an appearance, including the tall one who growled at Kalypso. Her name is Lilo, and she's one of the leaders, an opponent of Serena. She explains to me that the 'strongest' shifters either look out for the weaker ones, or kill them. She falls under the former category, while Serena tends to prey on those she deems inferior.

Which is why my stunt yesterday won so many hearts, especially considering it landed Serena in the infirmary overnight. Today she's licking her wounds in her private bedroom, something I learn each captive here has. There is no schedule for them, besides for four hours in the afternoon from 1:00 PM to 5:00 PM where they spend time in their designated program. Sallow hasn't been assigned one yet, which will remain the case if I have anything to say about it. Lilo is part of the alchemy program, and while she doesn't enjoy being at the doctor's all afternoon, it's the preferred alternative among the shifters, apparently.

Choosing the lesser of evils doesn't change the fact it's still an evil, though.

I manage to learn some about the Breeding program, but it takes some enticing to get Lilo to talk about it. She says, "They can't keep the babies alive. It's considered unsuccessful, as of right now, but they keep trying."

"And do they ...." I trail off, asking the obvious question. Lilo shifts uncomfortably, and I hold her hand. "It's okay, you can tell me."

She tucks a curl of ginger behind her ear. "They're ..." Her voice drops even lower than before as she says, "I had a friend who was a part of it, and after he came back, he wasn't the same, couldn't handle knowing he had done that to someone, let alone the fact he was forced to."

"Have I met him yet?"

Lilo squeezes my hand so tight, my knuckles pop. She cries, but the tears are silent and angry. "He killed himself two days later. I heard his ... I heard that they lived for two days, before the baby and mother both died."

"It's the bonds," I whisper, which surprises Lilo. "You can't grow something out of nothing. They'll never make it work this way."

Before leaving, Sallow takes me aside. He takes my hands, and his own are shaking. Fear, and anger, reaches me from his side of the bond. "Come back, Alpha. Please."

"I will tomorrow, I promise. And you can feel me now, right?"

He nods, squeezing my hands. "Right."

"And you'll look after them? I know it's a lot to ask, but it makes me feel better, knowing they have you."

Determined, Sallow says, "Alpha."

I'm escorted to the Pink Room in silence, which is just as well. I'm in no fucking mood to have lunch with Sallow's captors, and I'm tired of this game already. Kalypso is waiting for me as promised, accompanied by his *Chayal* and several of the Council members. He stands especially close to a giant of a man who takes up the entire world before me. I look up, and up, and *up*.

A broad, blue-black chest encased in nothing more than a black leather halter top, and tight leather pants that leaves little (or much, depending on how you look at it) to the imagination. Long locs of black with dozens of chrome and gemstone beads lay across rippling, thick pectorals. Broad shoulders double the breadth of the man's tapered waist, and his large nipples are pierced with steel hoops that are connected by a silver chain. Interwoven tattoos cover the impressive column of his throat, stopping just beneath a strong jaw covered in a thick black beard. Kalypso's sigil is there, branding the side of his neck. Last, but certainly not least, prominent tawny eyes that are *absolutely* alight with mischief.

After bowing to Kalypso I extend my hand towards the man, expecting a handshake, but he takes my wrist and flips my hand over, leaving a gentle kiss on my palm. Upon straightening, his fingers glide down my arm. He says, "Dame Rajni, it is a pleasure to meet you. I am Nathaniel ben Tshuva, a noble in Trading House, and a good friend of your fiance's."

Unable to help myself, I smile and cock my hip, if only a little. "Nathaniel, the pleasure is all mine. I've heard much about you, but nothing compares, I'm afraid. And let's be honest, good friend is a mild term, is it not?"

He laughs, a loud barking thing. I glance over at Kalypso, only to find him flushing immensely. Nathaniel throws an arm around Kalypso and kisses his cheek. "Better not let this one get away, Kay, she's a firecracker."

Kalypso smiles at Nathaniel, and some of the tension leaves his shoulders as he does. "I have no intentions of that. Dame Rajni, I hope you are well this morning."

Nathaniel gives me an appraising look, followed by a salacious wink. I return it, then focus on Kalypso. "Quite."

The following beat of silence is cold, and Kalypso clears his throat. "I see. Well, I believe it's time for us to go in."

Nathaniel bows his head, taking his leave ahead of us. "I'll see you later, Kay. And it was nice to meet you Rajni, save me a dance at the wedding, eh?"

"You can have as many as you like." I call after him, then Kalypso's offered arm. "I like him. I wouldn't be offended if you wished to continue whatever relationship you have, if there is one. I'm only relying on gossip and all those rippling pectorals.

Kalypso chuckles, and we squeeze through the throng congregated just inside the Pink Room. "We are friends, that's all."

"So you've never slept together?"

He gives me a dry look. "I didn't say that. We're friends who have enjoyed each other's company a few times, but there's nothing romantic involved."

"Ah."

"And what about you?"

I raise a brow. "What about me?"

Kalypso tugs at his ear with his free hand, eyes darting to where the Emperor sits with Jedediah. We wait on the opposite side of the room with pink crystal walls painfully familiar to the Netherspring. There's even a live band and a stage, and exotic dancers wearing nothing but body paint that glitters beneath the chandelier lights. Kalypso whispers, "How does it work? Are you ... allowed to have friends like that?"

I laugh, even though it hurts to think of Xylia. "Yes, I am, but I don't seek them out. To me, sex is ... it's better when it's with someone you hold dear, I suppose."

We hover on the outskirts of the room, waiting for everyone to take their seats at a table laden with platters and goblets, buffet style. Kalypso doesn't seem keen on entertaining, and I'm happy to aid him in procrastination. He asks, "And ... she can too?"

"Oh, yes. But that's not the case for every polyamorous relationship, just us."

Kalypso rolls his eyes, mouth twitching. "I'm familiar with the concept, but I thought with shifters it would be ... different."

I grin. "Because we're possessive and territorial?"

He ducks his head. "Most are, you can't fault me for that."

"This is true, but that doesn't really have anything to do with how we love. I feel territorial over all my Foxes, even if we're not romantically involved. Sure it's more with Ta—" I shut my mouth so fast my teeth click together.

Kalypso grimaces. "Does it make you feel better to know she kept your relationship hidden from me? We weren't together, not like that, but ... we were friends. She was the first one I ever had."

"It doesn't really matter now, does it?"

Kalypso opens his mouth, but Drazen beckons us over without breaking his conversation with Orioz ben Sarig. We dutifully take our seats to his right, while Jedediah and Orioz sit across from us. Avidan ben Zisi sits beside me, and he gives me a nervous smile which I return.

"Friends, I'm so glad you could join us today. Kalypso, if you would." Drazen gestures to Kalypso, who bows his head.

We don't join hands this time, but everyone listens as Kalypso leads the table in prayer, praising Syzdon and other bullshit. I take the time to study the thirty-two people gathered around the enormous, rich walnut table.

Every House Head is here, along with one guest, including the Heads of the shifter programs, Doron and Eliram. He avoids my eye, and I don't linger on him for too long. Some of the dancers revolve around the table, sashaying as they go, and Rasha xir Delone, Head of Education, takes the wrist of one and pulls them into their lap. The dancer doesn't fight it, merely shifts gears and dances provocatively in Rasha's lap. It occurs a few more times, several of the Heads and their guests drag the dancers into their orbit like they're a doll. I tell myself to stop watching, but I find it hard to look away from Temon ben Lon shoving his tongue down the throat of a dancer who has gone practically limp, allowing the Head of Public House to what he wishes. A short ways down the table I spot Nathaniel sitting with Nitza, and he winks at me. Thankfully he's not accosting anyone who can't say no.

Kalypso finishes the prayer and we all begin to eat. I quickly learn this luncheon is not an uncommon thing, and it seems to be a more private version of yesterday's meeting. Almost like a social club, given the way everyone seems to be enjoying themselves. Nothing like politics behind closed doors.

There's a person I don't recognize, she wasn't present at the Council meeting but seems to be held in high regard. She's young, around Eliram's age, with short black curls and red fingertips. She's dressed in trousers and a blouse, and a white coat. After catching me staring at the woman for the third time, Kalypso takes a long drink of wine and says, "Shaike bat Tal-or, I don't believe you've had a chance to meet my fiance yet."

Shaike inclines her head. "I have not. It is a pleasure to meet you, Dame Rajni. Or is it Alpha Rajni? I'm unsure of the specifics."

I chuckle, but it's full of heat. I immediately don't like her. Thumbnail digging into my palm, I carefully say, "If it's all the same to you, Dame Rajni works just fine. Tell me, what is it you do here?"

Shaike smiles. "I'm Head of the Breeding Program."

Perfect.

"Ah, I see. I hope there's no hard feelings about your labs in the Garden, they needed some renovations, to say the least."

Shaike laughs. "Oh those? Overflow, if you will. Really, you did me a favor, that place was a money pit."

Kalypso's knee gently bumps mine, but I ignore him. "You know, I'm quite curious. What do you do with the babies, after they're born?"

"Well, we used to incinerate them." At my outrage, Shaike waves me off with a laugh. "Truly, you must think us monsters here, don't you? I think you of all people would be happy. Isn't that what you want, for more shifters to live among us?"

"There's plenty enough that need you already. Why not help *them*? Why force people into becoming a broken factory for—"

Kalypso's hand rests on the back of my neck and firmly squeezes once. He doesn't say anything, but the look on his face is clear. *You're going to get us killed.*

I glance at Drazen to gauge his reaction, but he's merely enjoying the show, feet propped up in Jedediah's lap as he munches on some sort of pastry. He gestures towards me. "Go on, by all means. This is much better than the usual droll."

I shake my head. "My apologies, Your Grace, and Shaike bat Tal-or. It was wrong of me to make assumptions. I look forward to seeing your work."

Doron laughs, no longer meek like he was yesterday when it was just Kalypso and I. He says, "Prince ben Matzliach, it would seem you've tamed the wild."

Kalypso's fingers tighten, pulling on my curls. He shrugs, lazily taking another long drink with his free hand. He says, "Or has she tamed me?"

Laughter spills, breaking the tension. I pick at my food and listen to the conversation, bristling beneath all the stares. Orli ben Yoratan, Head of Slaughter House, lifts his lips from a dancer's neck to address Kalypso. He says, "We missed you at the Revelry last night, Your Highness, I thought you weren't to be married for another week and a half."

Kalypso chuckles. "Unlike you, I have values and responsibilities."

Orli clutches his chest, and his other hand squeezes the dancer's side. "Values are underrated my dear friend."

I ask, "Revelry?"

Orli grins, clearly pleased I've seemingly fallen into his trap. "Oh yes, the Sensual Revelry, or rather the celebration of this year's Harvest, and the Hunt of course. It's all rather public, and anyone in the Citadel is free to join. Our very own Prince is quite fond of it, but then again, he's fond of anything that requires no clothes and all his favorite vices."

Orli is clearly trying to bait Kalypso, but the Prince merely shrugs in agreement.

I ask, "So tell me, what is a sin then, if exhibition and lewdness is not?"

Orli bows his head, gesturing to Drazen. "Whatever the Emperor decides, for he's Syzdon's prophet. Currently, there are three that warrant punishment. Murder. Acedia. Weakness."

The urge to look at Eliram down the table is strong, but I resist. "Weakness? How do you define such a thing?"

Avidan stiffens, and it would be imperceptible if I wasn't sitting next to him. Orli says, "Any way that you can. It is Syzdon's belief that only the fittest shall survive, and as such those with physical, or mental, hindrances are a target. Unless they are useful, of course."

Kalypso vehemently signing, *"Do* not *repeat this with any-one,"* takes on a whole new meaning.

"Indeed," Drazen says, raising his goblet. "To the strong."

I raise my glass and take a long drink, but I don't repeat his sentiment.

I successfully manage to be a silent observer for the rest of the luncheon and avoid making contact with the Cardinal, but that doesn't stop him from staring daggers at me. He's going to be the first one I kill, I fucking swear. Well, I suppose it depends on which one of these fuckers I can get my hands on first, but I hope it's him.

Kalypso leaves my side to speak with Drazen privately, and I fight a grimace when Jedediah immediately takes advantage. He offers his arm to me. "Allow me to escort you back to your room, Dame Rajni."

Pinpricks of fear run up my spine at the prospect of touching Jedediah. I have not missed the fact that he is responsible for a great deal of the shifters living here, though years have passed since he claimed his fifty tags and they're probably dead by now.

But he wants something, evident by his newfound respect and addressing me properly. I glance towards the group Ka-lypso is part of, then sigh when he doesn't look my way. I say, "Thank you, Your Grace," and slip my arm through Jedediah's.

He gives me a sharp grin and leads me out of the Pink Room, and nobody stops us. His guards and my own fall into formation around us, that constant line of protection between us and everything else in the Citadel.

Jedediah remains silent until we're a safe distance from the Pink Room, then he teasingly whispers, "You don't like me."

I look up at him, gauging his amused expression. "And you don't like me. Or anything with a heartbeat, besides for the Emperor, it would seem. Then again, we both know what you're really after."

Jedediah laughs. "I much prefer you with your claws out. Have me all figured out, do you? And what is it I'm after?"

I shrug my free shoulder, the other is cinched close to his side, due to the fact his arm is vise-tight where it's looped around mine. "The same thing we're all after. Freedom. And the only way to do that is to be the most powerful person in the room, or in your case, close to it. Close, but not quite there."

"It would seem we're in the same boat, my lady," Jedediah says quietly. His guard contingency doesn't seem to mind his borderline treacherous words. I wonder how many different factions there are in this noble life. Do they follow him, or Drazen? Or do they simply not care what we talk about, because it will all be reported later anyway?

We turn the last corner, entering Kalypso's hall. "We're in the same ocean, nothing more than that. I'd rather cling to my liferaft than be in your boat."

Jedediah chuckles. "You might change your mind, my lady."

I give him a dangerous smile of my own. "I doubt it, Your Grace."

"And have you forgotten who keeps an eye on your beloved outcasts?"

I pull away, not able to make it the rest of the way latched to him. He shakes black hair away from those stinging blue eyes, clearly pleased with my reaction. I lower my tone and say, "You do anything to them, and you'll have to answer to the Prince, in addition to me."

Jedediah shrugs. "But at that point, what's done is done, is it not? If one of your shifters goes feral, no doubt suffering from your lack of presence by now, I'll have no choice but to defend myself. You've proven how vital an Alpha is to shifters, how *crazy* they can be without one. Especially those little ones. They're cute, but claws are claws, and they're by no means harmless. Kalypso may be the Emperor's gift from God, but don't underestimate how valuable I am to the Emperor as well."

My hands tighten into fists. "What do you want from me?"

Jedediah reaches forward, brushing curls away from my cheek. I don't flinch, but my nostrils flare as red hot anger boils every ounce of blood my pissed off heart pumps out. He leans closer to me, bringing his lips to my ear. "I know what you're doing."

I breathe, slow and steady. My hand drifts to my left thigh, where my dagger stored in ink lies. It'll rip my pants coming out and the guards might kill me for retaliating, but it's time for him to fuck off. I quietly ask, "Serving your master?"

Jedediah chuckles, hot breath washes against my cheek. His hand settles on my waist, gripping tight. "I think—"

"Hands off. *Now.*"

Jedediah stills, his fingers dig into my side painfully hard before retreating. He slowly straightens, and a blade remains pressed to his throat the entire time. *Chayal* xir Dasi stares Jedediah down, and I fear for their life until seeing who's standing beside them. Kalypso, eyes wildly flashing between gold and silver, body shaking in fury.

Jedediah's guards are poised to attack, guns trained on *Chayal* xir Dasi and Kalypso. Jedediah holds up his left hand and snaps once, which causes his guards to lower their weapons. I guess that answers my earlier question regarding fealty. He ignores *Chayal* xir Dasi completely, focusing on Kalypso instead. He quietly asks, "What is this? Are you threatening me, little Prince?"

Chayal xir Dasi drops their blade and takes a step back, deferring to Kalypso as he steps forward, coming face to face with Jedediah. Kalypso quietly says, "When I'm threatening you, you'll know it. The next time you touch what's not yours, you won't live to regret it. Get the fuck out of my sight."

Jedediah scowls, and when he opens his lips Kalypso pulls a small, flat radio out of his back pocket. I've not seen it until now, and it's different from the ones the *Chayal* use. Kalypso holds it up to his mouth and clicks the button, which is all it takes for Jedediah to turn tail and flee at a barely dignified walk, flanked by his soldiers.

None of us move until Jedediah is out of sight, and then I'm accosted by Kalypso. He goes to cup my face in his hands, then thinks better of it and drops his hands. He doesn't back up though, and there's only inches between us. Both *Chayal*, Kassif xir Dasi and Xivan xir Gabi, stand close behind him.

He asks, "Are you alright? I turned around and you were gone, and so was he. I thought—" Kalypso shakes his head. "I thought he hurt you."

"I'm fine, I like to think *Chayal* Kassif xir Dasi wouldn't have let him go much further."

Kassif bows their head. "My lady, I apologize. I am not allowed to intervene unless your life is in immediate danger, or by the Prince's directive."

I scoff. "I'm quite sure my consent was in immediate danger."

Kassif does not raise their shaved head, and Xivan bows theirs.

Kalypso sighs, tugging at his ear. "You heard what they said, at lunch? Assault is ..." His jaw works, and he has a hard time meeting my eye. "It's not a sin. Taking what you want is encouraged, and that extends to all things. I thought that he wouldn't be so stupid, but apparently not. It doesn't matter what title you hold or ... who your kin is, there's no protection from predators other than you protecting yourself."

"Well that's fucking great," I say, all pretense of formality gone. "So it's sanctioned hell is what you're saying. And what those soldiers did to—what they did to *her*. They were never punished for that? That's *encouraged*?"

Kalypso whispers, "I'm sorry. I don't know what to say. I don't—" He takes in a long, shaky breath. "I don't think I should've brought you here. I thought I could protect you."

I close the distance that Kalypso is afraid to. I step forward, taking his face in my hands. My breasts brush against his chest, and he breathes me in. His eyes brighten, darting back and forth across my face. "And who protects you, Kevin?"

Kalypso laughs, broken and quiet but there all the same. "I hope you never stop calling me that." Tentatively, one of his hands comes to rest upon mine, and the other cups my elbow.

I smile. "I won't."

We stand there for a moment, holding each other in the middle of hell and an empty hallway. Kalypso's lips part, then he closes them. A crease settles between his brows. He asks, "Do you ... do you want to see something?"

"Is that code for something? Because I'm well beyond the days of cheesy pick-up lines."

He laughs, and the crease gives way to heartwarming dimples. "No, it's not code for anything. Come with me. Unless you wanted to rest, or go back downstairs. I heard that one of the shifters they had quarantined was yours. I didn't know, otherwise I would've told you. By the time I found out, you were already down there."

His dimples fade, and I decide to use the rest of the day to be selfish.

"I believe you. I told him I'd come back in the morning, based on the assumption that my mornings will be spent down there. I'd like to see them train, though, and the other programs that take place in the afternoon. Could we do that tomorrow?"

"Oh, of course. Yes, that's what I intended, but the Emperor had other plans for me this morning."

"The trade meeting?"

He sighs. "Yes. Nitza's House is in charge of distribution, and the price of her services has exponentially increased since the announcement of our marriage."

I chuckle. "I can't imagine anyone charging the Emperor. Why doesn't he just force her to do it for nothing?"

He gives me a dry look. "He may be the Emperor, but he relies on his Houses. Think of them as states, and they have their own systems and military. While they won't last against the Citadel's forces, they could cause enough of a problem that it disrupts the other Houses, and in turn, us."

"And why haven't you married Nathaniel then, if it's such a big deal?"

Kalypso rears back, offended. "Because I haven't been waiting my whole life for Nathan."

"You weren't waiting for *my* hand." I state more than ask, confused.

When Kalypso flushes, it's a beautiful thing that the Alpha responds to instantly. I hold my breath, swallowing down an extreme surge of lust. He quietly asks, "Do you want to come with me or not?"

"Yes," I say, because I think that's always been my answer to him.

Little Prince

We take the elevator to C1, the ground level of the Citadel, so to speak, which mildly surprises me. There's no mob, but there are wealthy common people milling about in the main hallway. The *Chayal* rest their hands on their guns and remain vigilant, allowing Kalypso to lead the way. I itch to take his hand, but I don't.

No one speaks to me, but Kalypso receives several warm greetings and bows along the way from those who are clearly of higher status with their fine, eccentric clothes and bared skin. I like watching him talk to them, he's curt but not unkind. He introduces me time and time again, but no one gives me a second look which seems to grate upon him after some time.

After a good twenty minutes, I'm good and lost in the heart of the Citadel. The halls are like urban city streets complete with businesses in pretty stone domes, each building a piece of the larger puzzle that is the Citadel. We pass by giant spires that play host to vertical neighborhoods, a more modern version of the Tin Risers and Concrete Towers. The spires are a part of the larger, structural architecture that is the Citadel as a whole. The Dynasty's upper levels are literally built on the homes of their people, in more ways than one.

We travel down a few narrow halls that are much different than the main ones, like comparing an alley to a highway. There is no hard packed dirt, only white stone and endless light. Eventually we come upon an especially thin hall filled with open doors, and people. But they are not like the rest.

They do not wear over the top fashion. Ripped jeans and dirty t-shirts, boots, and sneakers. Some sport piercings, tattoos, or dyed hair, but that's as wild as it gets. There are no young people here, only the middle-aged interspersed with a few lucky elders. Tables and awnings line the walls, one to a door, which play host to crafted and baked goods. There's brass and wood phonographs at the first table, along with stacks of vinyl discs. I'm immediately drawn there, thinking of Namir.

Kalypso hovers over my shoulder, hands clasped behind his back. Without looking at him I say, "One year a Fox of mine made one of these, or something like it. It was kept in the Long Room, that's what we call the common room, and we had to make a schedule because everyone wanted to use it. Music played at all hours of the day and night, and the poor thing only lasted a week."

He laughs. "I can see that. I—" He clears his throat. "When I was little, I liked to dance. It's just small bits in my head, but ... there was a big window with different colored glass, and I used to dance in the sunlight, trying to catch the colors."

Dancing in the sunlight. What a thought. "Do you still dance?"

"Uh, no. It's been awhile. Do you? We're expected to, at the ... at our wedding."

"Really? Who would have thought?"

"Okay, smartass."

"Oh, look at you. Name calling and everything. I'm so proud of you. But yes, I can dance. My apprentice actually taught me, they're quite good. I ..." I shyly look up at him. "I hope you meet them. I think you two would get on pretty well."

"Why, are they fabulous like me?"

I laugh, and it's the lightest I've felt in days. If his laughter is anything to go by, he feels the same way.

We don't buy anything, but we take our time fawning over beaded jewelry and intricate wax seals, painted ceramic dishware sets and handwoven swatches of fabric. There are tapestries painfully similar to those in the Netherspring, and leather works. Several of the leather vendors are dedicated to 'bedroom tools,' and Kalypso gets all flustered when we begin browsing there. When I pick up a nine of tails, he tugs at his collar.

"What? Aren't you supposed to be the quiff here, Mr. Revelry?"

He shoots me a look. "I don't—I only watch when I attend, okay? I think it's … interesting."

"Oh, really?" I can't help the purr that creeps into my tone, and I leave the whip behind in favor of crowding Kalypso's space. To his credit, he doesn't move a muscle. "Are you a virgin?"

"*No*, but I haven't—" He gestures to the tables, then abruptly starts walking. I keep close to his side, waiting for him to finish. "I'm not *experienced*, one might say. But I've had sex. With Nathaniel, like I said before."

"Interesting," I say, using his own words against him.

He glares at me. "No, it isn't. It's not interesting at all."

And the fondness I feel for him right then is overwhelming. For a moment, we're just two relatively young people going for a walk in the market, teasing the edges of flirtation. "You're cute when you get flustered, you know that?"

Kalypso fights a smile, avoiding my gaze. "All right, all right. We're almost there, come on."

When Kalypso darts inside the second to last door on the left, he takes me by surprise. I have to backtrack a step, narrowly avoiding a crash with the *Chayal*, and the smug look on Kalypso's face tells me that was payback for working him up. We enter a storeroom of sorts, full of metal crates and wood shavings. This piques my attention, and I expect Kalypso to pass through the cracked door leading to what appears to be a storefront. Instead, he opens a closed door which reveals a spiral staircase.

"What's this?" I ask.

He smiles, then shifts his attention to our guards. "*Chayal*, keep watch, will you?"

"As you wish, Your Highness," *Chayal* xir Gabi says, bowing at the waist.

Kalypso takes me by the hand and I hold on tight to him as he leads me down the stairs. His hands are cold, but they don't shake. Gaslit sconces are inlaid into the white granite walls, dim beacons that play on Kalypso's many freckles and sunspots. They must've been from his life before, when he danced in the sun.

We make it to the bottom of the stairs, and the room we come upon is not what I was expecting. At all. It's a workspace achingly similar to mine and Taru's, at the very least in size. There's metal work tables and rolling stools, but the tools and materials are all different. Thin, curling wood shavings and fine dust coasts nearly every surface, and there's a neatly stacked pile of wood rounds cut into several different lengths.

Chisels, hammers, rasps, files, and knives, so many knives, are neatly organized on a shelf that takes up the main wall, evident by the largest and relatively empty work station situated beneath all the tools. There's a block of wood with a long-handled spoon drawn onto it, the bowl carved out but not sanded. Rolls of sandpaper rest on another wall, slid onto a dowel so they can spin freely.

Kalypso slowly walks into the room, avoiding my eyes again. He lightly runs a finger over a thick patch of wood dust on his work table. "This is the only thing I've ever had that's mine. The only secret I've ever had. Besides you."

"Kalypso," I say, trailing off as I meander through his workspace. There's a tub full of carved but unsanded utensils, one with broken pieces and another with finished and sealed masterpieces. Right on top is a baby spoon, and I find myself drawn to it. I carefully pick it up, studying the fine detail poured into such a small chunk of wood.

And that's the other thing, isn't it? This is a piece of *wood*.

I laugh quietly to myself. This is his joy. This is what he smells like.

"I don't know what to say, other than this is gorgeous work. Where does the wood come from?"

Kalypso slowly approaches me, tapping a work table's surface as he passes by. "That one there is white birch. It's one of the fastest growing trees we have in the ark, along with red maple and a few others. But I like working with those two the most. Avidan is a good friend of mine, saves me scraps."

I tear my gaze away from the spoon in my hand. He's close, and his eyes are bright. "What's the ark?"

"It's the seed bank the Matzliach family brought with them. That's how Green House is possible. The animals, they're all descendants of the first ones that were brought here."

I shake my head, turning my gaze back down to the spoon. "They could have done so much better. Things don't have to be the way they are."

Kalypso lays his hands over mine, closing them over the spoon. I look back up to him, and there's a determination to him that wasn't there before. His figure shimmers, and his eyes are dual pools of mercury back-lit by gold.

He whispers, "I think we can do this. And I might be wrong. Then again I might be right, and it still won't be enough. But I'm starting to think that it doesn't matter. Because I have never felt more alive than I do when I'm with you. You make me feel ... well, that's just it. You make me feel, Rajni. And I think I make you feel, too. You look at me like no one else has, and I don't want you to ever stop. I know it's too much to expect, but is it too much to ask? Can I have a place at your side?"

"Are you ... asking me to marry you, Kalypso?"

He smiles, bottom lip trembling. "No. I'm asking to be your mate. I know I'm not a shifter, not like you, but ... I would be honored to be yours, in any capacity you'll have me."

And that hits me harder than anything he's said before. I feel as if my entire life has been culminating to this moment, ever since the day he set me free. Like a key settling into its lock, gears clicking as the pair work in tandem to open something extraordinary. My heart throbs, aching for Xylia, aching for the man before me. Aching for the woman who betrayed me, because *damn* her. I can't stop loving Takara no matter how hard I try.

The Alpha watches intently, waiting for me to make the choice that was decided for me (us) over twenty years ago. To take this man as mine (ours) and protect him from all those who would do him harm. To run with him in the lands of a new world. To reunite him with his family, and make him part of our own.

I close the already meager distance between us, trapping our joined hands between our swiftly beating hearts. "You understand that I am mated already? If you ... if we did this, that doesn't mean you two would have to be anything, but her and I ... we're for life, Kalypso. You have to understand that. I don't hold my love back, I never have."

Kalypso nods, and it's like the sun is setting just beyond that pool of mercury, because his eyes flash so bright that I have to close my own. He whispers, "I'm sorry, you can open your eyes again." When I do, his eyes have completely changed to a white gold, and his chest heaves with the effort it takes to restrain his power.

He says, "I know, and yet I still ask."

I lift my chin, looking up at him through my lashes. "There is something else you must understand."

He shudders, then carefully takes the spoon from my hands and slips it into his pocket. His hands twitch at his sides, so I make the decision for him and reach forward. He does too, one hand settles on my lower back while the other rests between my shoulder blades. I wrap my arms around his neck, bringing my lips a feathers-width away from his.

"What?" He breathily asks, and it's so damn intoxicating that my fangs extend in response. At the sight of *that*, his pupils blow wide which does nothing to help the animal taking over.

I keep it together long enough to say, "I've been yours since the day we met, the same as you've been *mine*. Nothing would make me happier than to have you as my mate, Kalypso."

Kalypso jumps the gun. His mouth crashes onto mine and my canines nick his upper lip. He moans into my mouth, hands sliding and grabbing with purpose. We stumble backwards and I tangle my fingers in his hair, trusting him to keep me upright. The waves of black are softer than my dreams lend me to believe, and my heart wrenches with some odd feeling I can't name.

His blood coats my lips, and I whine at the sweet taste of it. I lick his mouth, then slide my tongue inside and meet his own. My back hits a work table and Kalypso effortlessly slides his hands beneath my thighs and hoists me up without breaking our kiss.

My cock is painfully hard and apparent through my trousers. A fleeting sense of worry hits me for the first time, because what is he expecting? He didn't seem to care before, but we never really—

His lower stomach brushes against me and I gasp into his mouth. Kalypso chuckles against my lips, hands skating my thighs at a respectable distance. It's a near thing then, swallowing his laughter whole. "My, what big eyes you have," he says, gaze cast downwards to most definitely *not* my eyes.

"Are you jealous, Kevin? It doesn't suit you." I tease, and he laughs again.

"You forget that I can be whoever I want. If I wanted a big cock, I'd have one. I actually don't mind it, sometimes.

I told you before, you're not the only one who identifies ... differently." He gently reaches up and takes my hand, kissing my palm. "Can I show you?"

Everything about that statement begs for more details, but I only say, "Yes."

He places my hand on his bare stomach, his shirt unbuttoned in the usual style. His dark hair is soft there, too. He quivers beneath my touch, and Alpha paces impatiently, ready to mark and claim and take—

I breathe, watching as he skirts my hand farther down, sliding it beneath the waistband of his trousers. More soft skin, and the hair is coarser, thicker. Then my fingers slide across a wet heat that is most certainly not a dick. I stop breathing, wholly focused on how he skates my fingers back and forth, using my hand to please himself.

"Oh, fuck, Kalypso. Please, let me—"

He pushes my fingers into his cunt, forehead colliding with mine as heavy breaths punch out of him. "Oh." He breathes.

"That's it, you feel so fucking good, love. Touch me, you can touch me."

"Rajni." He murmurs, releasing my hand in favor of undoing my trousers. I curve my index and pointer fingers inwards, firmly massaging his pleasure spot. He temporarily stills, moaning as he tightens around my fingers. With great difficulty he fends off the orgasm and frees my cock, which slaps against my clothed stomach the moment it's released.

"Rajni," he says again, fingers tracing through the dark curls at the base of my length before lightly wrapping around me. "You're beautiful." He watches, enraptured by the way my uncut shaft moves in his hand, fingers effortlessly sliding in the sticky warmth leaking from me. "There's so much."

"I want you." I whisper, withdrawing my fingers. I pinch his clit before pulling away completely, and he moans against my shoulder before bringing his lips to mine. I kiss him gently, lingering for a moment because I need to breathe, try to fathom how we got here. "We need to come together, with open hearts. I'll bite you, and that will seal it. The mark will scar, but it can be anywhere. Where do you want it?"

He inhales sharply and pulls back a little, reaching up to touch my lips. He searches my eyes, and I kiss the pad of his finger. "Do I have to bite you?"

"No, but you can if you'd like."

"Okay." He nods, nose brushing against mine. "I'm ready. Do it on my shoulder."

I slide off the work table and bend him over it. I slide his trousers down, palming his firm ass dusted in dark hair, just like the rest of him. With my other hand, I take hold of his shoulder and pull his back flush to my breasts, snaking my arm around his chest. My shaft slides between his cheeks, and he sighs. I kiss his shoulder, then whisper in his ear. "Are you sure? We can wait, if you want."

He reaches back, sliding his fingers through my hair. "We've waited long enough, haven't we?"

With that, I take hold of my length and line up with his wet cunt, sliding in slow and steady this time. I need him to know what he means to me, I need to keep the animal at bay just a little bit longer. He gasps, tightening around me immediately. I groan, forcing myself to still until he adjusts. I take a hold of his ass and gently spread, which causes Kalypso to shiver. I kiss his neck, which he beautifully exposes to me the moment I search for it.

"You're so fucking tight, love."

Kalypso tightens his fingers in my hair and his other hand takes a firm hold of mine settled on his chest. He curls his hips impatiently, and I watch my cock slip in and out of him. He whines, "Rajni, please."

"Please, what?"

He tugs on my hair particularly hard, and I roughly thrust into him. My balls slap against him as I drive all the way inside. He cries out, "Oh, yes."

I slide my hand from his chest to his face, taking a gentle hold of his jaw. I turn his face towards me and kiss him fiercely, rutting into him the entire time. "Is this what you want? You want to feel me for days?"

Kalypso bites my lip and tugs, then shoves his tongue inside my mouth. He's so passionate, so much more confident and unafraid here, with me. The thought drives me wild, and especially so when he says, "Yes. Yes, fuck me, claim me. Make me yours, I need it. I need *you*."

And that's it. My last thread of sanity snaps, and I begin to partially shift. Claws extend into flesh, digging into his face and ass cheek. My groans transform into growls, and there's nothing left but the beast as I drive into Kalypso relentlessly. I have the sense to take my hand off his face, and then I realize how much I need to *see* him.

I unceremoniously pull out and spin him around, his vest falls to the floor. He rips off my shirt and wraps his arms around my neck, like he wanted the same thing. I lift him up and those long legs wrap around my hips, locking me in place. I bring him down on my cock, much less kinder this time. His orgasm follows moments later, and his entire body shudders as he squirts around my length. Wet heat trails down my thigh and I groan, but it's overshadowed by his nonsensical cries.

"Your cock, it's—oh fuck! Rajni, Rajni."

There's resistance this time, my knot swells in time to each of his whimpers and moans. He slowly rides out the after-shocks of his orgasm, rolling his hips and grinding against me with expert intent. I do my best to keep still and kiss his cheek, licking away the blood. "You're doing so well, darling. You're almost there, can you do it? Can you take all of me? Don't tell me you forgot that I have a knot."

"I can do it. I can do it. I need all of you." Kalypso whimpers, beginning to ride me in earnest.

I pull back enough to render his efforts useless and quietly ask, "Are you sure?"

Kalypso full on glares at me. I laugh a little, which only makes it worse. He opens his mouth to berate me, but in a single thrust I work my knot inside him, stretching him open completely. I moan, doing my best to keep my nails from scratching up his ass too much. I kiss him through sharpened teeth. "Oh, Kalypso. You are everything."

He smiles, and it's so beautiful. "Make me yours, then."

"As you wish, love. Hold on."

I fuck him with complete abandon, and it's a blood bath. He tears out my hair and scratches up my back better than a shifter could. My nails scrape his ass, and the scent of blood and sex fills the world. He palms one of my breasts, rolling the hard nipple between his fingers. My grunts and his moans are enough to shake the Dome down, and I distantly wonder if the *Chayal* can hear us.

Let them try to interrupt us, for it'll be the last thing they do.

My orgasm builds until I can't hold it back any longer. With great difficulty and through many teeth, I ask, "Are you ready?"

In answer, he kisses me and says, "Yes."

He leans ahead and wraps his arms around my neck once more. His pulse point brushes against my lips and the urge to bite him there is near overpowering. My knot swells once more and to his credit, Kalypso stifles his cry by latching onto the back of my neck. Not enough to mark, but enough to hurt.

His heart is as loud as it's ever been, and it hits me then that his heart has always been open to me. Waiting.

I sink my teeth into his shoulder, hips stuttering with the force of my release. His blood spills into my mouth at the same time I fill him, and I greedily drink him down. He bites me harder, and my knees shake beneath the weight of a new bond settling into place, linking his soul to mine.

Because shifter or not, I can feel him now.

Without lifting his teeth from my flesh, or I from his, he explores the bond and says, *"Hello, my love. Hello, I am yours, and you are mine."*

And I say, *"You are mine, and I am yours. Always."*

"Always."

I lick his wound and Kalypso kisses the spot he bit me. He rests his head on my shoulder, breathing into my neck. It only takes a few minutes for my knot to relax enough that we can separate, and during that time we say nothing. We hold the other, and breathe. Absorbing and memorizing the moment, because when we surface, nothing will be the same.

My shift recedes finally and I withdraw from Kalypso. He groans, arms tightening around my neck. I gently set him down, keeping an arm around him as he's shaky. "Are you alright? I ... I should have warned you."

He gives me a bizarre look. "I don't think I've ever been loved like that in my life. I've never been fucking better. Don't worry about all this," He gestures to his face, "it'll be healed in a minute. It ... caught me off guard, but I didn't mind it. Are you ... I mean, is it like that every time?"

I laugh quietly, and he does too. "I'm not usually so ... wild, but you know all the right things to say, it seems."

After cleaning up and waiting for Kalypso's scratches to heal, which they do but I don't feel any less of a monster for it, we ascend to the world we left behind. I'm acutely aware of his feelings. Not his thoughts, as I can't even read Xylia's thoughts unless she projects them onto me, but Kalypso's emotions are incredibly strong. Vivid flashes of color dance across our bond, eventually settling into pure gold.

We make it back to the storage room and find the *Chayal* posted on either side of the door, right where we left them. Kalypso says, "Well, time to go home, don't you think?"

Kassif gives us a wry smile. "Of course, Your Highness."

Our walk home is uneventful, and we don't rush, but Kalypso doesn't take as much time to speak with people, either. We walk hand in hand, and the entire time I worry over a hurdle I hadn't quite thought of until now. But of course, Kalypso already has. Before opening the door to my apartment, he gives me a sheepish look and squeezes my hand.

He says, "If you don't mind, I think I would like to sleep with you tonight."

I exhale relief, the thought of sleeping apart from him after all we've done is unsettling to say the least. "I would like that."

"We missed dinner, but maybe we can—"

Corvin, a dim atmosphere lit only by candles, and a table set with dinner for two awaits us. He brightens immensely upon seeing us and bows at the waist. "Your Highness, Dame Rajni. Per your wish to dine in tonight, and spend time together undisturbed before the wedding, you will find that you have the rest of the evening to yourselves, and that you were excused from family dinner tonight. Is there anything I can assist you with?"

Kalypso's shoulders relax, and he finally releases my hand in favor of stepping forward to cup Corvin's cheek with both hands. He kisses him on the forehead and says, "Ah, Corvin. What would I do without you?"

Corvin smiles, ducking his head. "I don't know, Your Highness."

Kalypso pats his cheek, then makes quick work of pulling out a chair for me, which I take. "Correct. I will be staying here tonight, if you could bring me night clothes and something for tomorrow?"

I don't think Corvin's smile could widen any further, but it does. He says, "Of course. Dame Rajni, is there anything you need?"

"Nothing at all, Corvin. Nothing at all."

We eat quickly and in near silence, but it's not uncomfortable. Anything that we have to say to each other isn't for the guard's ears, and I have a feeling Kalypso is as tired as I am. We take turns in the bathroom and I freshen up with a wet washcloth, reluctantly washing away the evidence of our mating.

When it's time for bed, Kalypso shuts the partition, blocking off all four *Chayal* from our sight. He wrings his hands, standing near the curtain while I make my way to the other side of the bed. I take the initiative, undressing without a word. Kalypso watches me, and he hums when my shirt hits the floor.

He slowly paces towards the bed, slipping his vest off along the way. I slip my underwear and trousers over my hips, sliding them down. He does the same, but he's not wearing anything beneath his pants. His night clothes and mine are laid out on the bed, and I toss them to the floor before crawling into bed, sprawling out on my back.

Kalypso shivers, and goosebumps spread across his arms, dark nipples hardening. Silver emotion spills into the pool of gold. He whispers, "I can't believe this."

"Come here." I open my arms to him. He obliges me immediately, and the animal within preens. He lays directly on top of me and I laugh, kissing his temple. "What's wrong?"

He sighs, knees settling on either side of my hips and hands sliding into my hair. He listens to my heart for a long time before answering. "At this moment, nothing." He shifts, laying on his back beside me. He raises his hands, and I watch intently as he signs, "I've never had anything to lose. Not really."

I respond in kind. "You matter, you know."

He glares at me, cutting through the air. "Let me have this."

"No, I won't. You matter, you always have. If not to yourself, then you have to me. And one day, I will make you see yourself the way I do."

"And how is that?"

I don't hesitate, and my hands work quickly as my emotion rises. "Kind. Different. Other. Trustworthy. Strong, and courageous, most of all. I could not have lived in your place, Kalypso. Once, I thought I could. I thought it would be easier to live here, but it's not. Give yourself credit. I see you, even when you think others don't."

Kalypso kisses me, soft and tender. It's not a collision like before, but a gentle greeting. He threads his fingers through my hair and licks my bottom lip, then pulls away a meager inch. He whispers, "Thank you."

"Can I ... show you something?" I whisper back.

"Of course."

I bring my right thigh up across his waist, showing off my garter tattoo. He immediately begins to explore, cold fingers skimming over hot skin. Upon seeing the strip of parchment, he looks up to me with curiosity brightening his eyes. "What's this?" He whispers.

I bring my power to the surface, and emerald light plays across Kalypso's golden freckles. A tiny, awestruck smile overtakes him and he has to drag his attention away from my face, to the strip of paper coming to life. "Go on, take it," I say, and he hesitates before doing so.

"There's words." He mouths, and I nod.

Kalypso stares at me for a hard moment, then turns his attention to paper, keeping it positioned so we can both read it.

CD ON BOARD.

MET T AND ... SOMETHING UNEXPECTED. M BOND FORMED, BUT NO BITE. SHE LET ME SEE EVERYTHING, EVEN BEFORE US.

I KNOW YOU'RE ANGRY, AND I AM TOO, BUT ... I CAN'T LET HER GO. IT HURTS TOO MUCH.

GENESIS IS 75% READY.

DETAILS I NEED TO KNOW IF THE WAIT WAS WORTH IT.

I laugh upon reading that last line, and it's a choking, wet thing. Kalypso pulls me against him and holds me close, petting my hair. "I miss her. I miss her so much."

He kisses my eyebrow. "I'm so sorry you're not with them."

"Me too. But I'm glad I'm with you, and I mean that."

Kalypso's arms tighten around me, and I listen to his heart. It's solid and steady, and he's all gold again. He whispers, "I am too. What ... I didn't understand half of that. Did they ... do what we did?"

I sigh, then say, "Yes, it sounds like it."

"Aren't you ... angry?"

"No. Maybe I should be, but I'm not. I ... I think I forgive her. I'm angry that I was kept out of things, but I understand it, at least a little. I know that Takara only had the pack's interests at heart. Her and Xy, they've always been close, it doesn't surprise me that they mated."

"And you two weren't? Close?"

"We were, but it was different for us, same as it's different for them. And there was always ... something. A distance, but I thought it was her past. I never thought it could be our future."

Kalypso gently takes my chin, lifting my face from his chest. He stares deep into my eyes, searching. Quietly, he says, "Would you like me to tell you about it?"

"What?"

"Our future."

"Yes."

We lay on our backs, signing late into the night and mid-morning. I tell him about Balderik and Hotaru, because it hurts too much to think of Xylia and Takara any more tonight. I wasn't lying. I'm not angry. But the Alpha demands that all our mates be together, and it won't rest until they are.

I tell him about Seth, and Liam.

I tell him about Daisy, and how I killed her.

I tell him about my parents, or the little I remember of them. They were loving. Kind. Exactly what the Citadel crushes on a daily basis.

I tell him about Isaac taking care of me, and how it'll take longer for me to forgive him, because his lies and deceit hurt the most. He laid a trap, just for me.

When the conversation turns quiet here, Kalypso tells me about the time he and Nathan were 'exploring' the Citadel, looking for a discreet place, and instead they found a door. A simple man door constructed of thick steel, hidden in an unassuming and forgotten alley in C1, not far from where we were today. It's bolted shut and locked, and while there are no guards posted outside, there is a security system.

He tells me that he found Corvin after a vicious sexual assault that nearly killed him, and this attack is what permanently disfigured him. He was left to die, and Kalypso brought him home like a lost puppy, demanding that he keep him. Of course, Drazen allowed it. When he signs, "Black-Heart," I kick the Cardinal out of first place on my kill list and replace him with Jedediah.

He tells me that Eliram is a close friend of his, and that he personally ensures that his mother is protected. Eliram is in charge of the oxygenation systems, which filter the radioactive air pulled in from the outside. Thing is, the air pulled in for the last few months has been clean, and anything fresh is pumped directly into the Citadel.

"And he can't tell people the truth, because of his mother."

Startled, Kalypso signs, "Yes. This is the case with Avidan (Plant Man, which takes me a moment to understand) and Captain. They have people to lose."

"I ..." I hesitate, hands held above us. Our heads are pressed together, legs tangled. "I have an idea."

I tell him about my inflammation medicine, and its deadly side effects. The lines in his face deepen the more I talk. I finish by signing, "I can't figure out how to get him to ingest it."

"What you have is enough?"

"Yes," I slowly sign. He thinks about that, and something tells me he has the answer to my puzzle. "What?"

Kalypso grimaces. "At the wedding, we have to take a vow of fealty to him as a married couple, and since it's officiated by the Church, that means it will be the same type of vow as during your Cleansing."

"He'll drink our blood, you mean? Both of us?"

"Yes."

"Interesting," I say quietly.

He immediately begins berating me, and I can't help but notice how handsome he is when he's focused on chewing me out with his hands. "You said so yourself, we don't have good medicine. (Antidote?) If you take enough to make him sick, you'll make yourself sick. That defeats the purpose of everything."

"No, the purpose is to free the Dome, I don't need to be—"

Kalypso looms over me, moving quicker than I can react which is saying something. He takes my wrists in one hand, pinning them above my head. He braces himself, glowering down at me. Aloud, he says, "You will not finish that sentence."

I want to smile at him, but I feel like that'd be condescending. I know he means well. I do.

But is one life worth hundreds of thousands?

WITH A PASSION

The days go like this.

Kalypso and I stay up late and wake early, unable to keep our hands still, or our mouths closed. We haven't had sex again since the evening we spent in Kalypso's workshop, neither of us willing to do more than play under the sheets when the walls and *Chayal* are listening. Kalypso doesn't risk frequent trips there, but I enjoy the slow exploration, finding the places that make Kalypso shiver. He particularly likes when I kiss between his shoulder blades, and I love when he falls asleep with his head on my chest, palm to my breast.

Last night he had asked, "How did you know?"

"Hm?" I asked, twisting my fingers in his inky curls.

"The rosary beads. You didn't lose track, that was the fastest anyone has crossed the coals and counted properly."

"Oh." I sighed, allowing memories of Isaac to come to the surface. "Isaac taught me about the Old Gods, and the new. He had beads of his own, and on days he was busy, I'd count them. I'd make a game of it, counting by twos or threes. Make odd patterns of numbers in my head, but I'd always end up with the same number, in the end. Anyways, I knew any rosary of Syzdon's was one of three numbers. Eighty, a hundred, or a hundred and fifty. Isaac had all three types."

"He believes in you," Kalypso whispered. "He would never have gave you up if he didn't believe in you."

I said nothing, and that was the way we fell asleep. His head on my chest, my fingers in his hair, and memories of my childhood playing like an old reel behind my eyes.

Corvin is ecstatic about our sleeping arrangements to say the least. I feel bad for initially keeping him from Kalypso, especially given their history. While Kalypso assures me that there are no romantic feelings between them, it's clear Corvin thinks the world of Kalypso. Then again, Kalypso often makes a point of saying that he wouldn't be where he is without Corvin, not only because of his friendship, but his knowledge and ability to blend in. He takes good care of us both, and I have a feeling wherever Kalypso decides to go, Corvin will be there too. Not because he's required to, because he won't be, but because he wants to.

I've befriended Kalypso's *Chayal* and my own, particularly Kassif and Xivan. Even *Chayal* Ben xir Lironic is warming up to me. Why the change of heart I'm not quite sure, but Kalypso doesn't trust them. I, on the other hand, think they feel protective of Kalypso and simply disliked me.

I only refer to Kalypso as Kevin when we're alone, now. Or what alone means for us.

I spend my mornings with Sallow and the shifters, and besides being with Kalypso, it's the most at ease I feel all day. There's only one group that outright does not like me, Serena's, but that's fine by me. Each day more and more shifters meet me personally, edging in from the sidelines of the common rooms. I listen to their stories, which Hunt they were brought in and by who. I learn about the people they've lost, and left behind. I recognize a few, and they form bonds with me the easiest.

While the Foxes are a big pack, nothing could prepare me for the weight of so many new, heavy connections. While I'm grateful for their trust, the burden of their traumas, worries, and hurts, grows heavier with each promise I make. It's a redacted version of our own induction ceremony. There's no

Wall of Foxes, no nature brought to life by Xylia's hand, no howling and chanting, no mark.

But there are hearts reaching to mine, and mine reaching back, promising safety, and hope. Over and over I take hands in mine, and through the newfound bond we've made, I say, *"I am your Alpha, and you are mine. I will keep you safe. I will protect you. I will free you. I promise, if you fight for me, I will fight for you. Fight for the Prince, because he fights for me, and all of you. Trust me. Please, trust me."*

A ferret says, *"I trust you, Aleph."*

A lion says, *"I fight with you, Alfa."*

A snake says, *"I will keep you safe, Alpha."*

A tiger who desperately wants to go home says, *"I will continue to follow you, Rajni, Queen of the Foxes, wherever you may lead."*

We break for that damned luncheon everyday, but the Emperor is happy to let me remain as a decorative fixture during the whole affair. Kalypso wears his mask beautifully, and it hurts my heart to watch, especially now that I can feel his hidden nervousness and fear. Oh, there's so much fear in Kalypso when it comes to Drazen. Whenever Kalypso thinks of Drazen, has to be in the same room with him, or talk to him, there's nothing between us but a cold abyss.

But he's not the only one who has a walking terror. The Cardinal never lets me out of his sight during the lunches, and I'm waiting for the day he stands up and throws a knife at my forehead. Every time he moves my instincts hone in on it, and one night Kalypso said my fear was like an explosion, choking his throat.

The drama between the House Heads is interesting to say the least, but I stay out of it, opting to mostly listen. Except with Avidan. The seating arrangement does not change, and I'm perpetually between him and Kalypso. The first time I struck up small talk with him he was quite shy, but he perked up the moment I showed interest in his work. He twists his beard when he thinks, and when he talks his hands sweep through the air.

Nathaniel is another face I don't mind seeing. I learn much about him, but most importantly that he's more than a friend. He's an ally, an accomplice, a spy. He's charming, the perfect child of the Citadel from an esteemed House, and a player in the black market clubs known as Easy Alley. An ear for information of all kinds, and a heart that belongs in a shifter. He has people of his own who want out of the Dome, and they'll be the ones clearing the elevators for the Gardeners, as I've taken to calling the joined forces from down below.

After lunch, Kalypso and I spend time in one of three places, all of them on B1. This level is like the one beneath it, a concrete fortress with several large, multipurpose rooms, but no shifters live here. It's completely utilitarian, equipped with more obvious defenses and visible security cameras. Special forces are stationed outside every room, not to mention inside them, and they patrol the hallways every few minutes.

Before passing into Eliram's lab, you have to go through a sanitizing airlock which sets my teeth on edge every time. Nevertheless, I prefer visiting Eliram ben Avichen as opposed to anyone else. After passing through the airlock to the lab we enter a comfortable main room fit with navy upholstered furniture, tables, bookshelves, and a phonograph that cycles through the same four vinyl disks.

The room serves as a waiting area of sorts, as Eliram works with one patient at a time, as he calls them. Regardless, the shifters for the Alchemy program are brought up all at once, made to wait while Eliram does his work. He only works with three assistants, all of them wear white coats trimmed in his House color, pink. One of the assistants keeps the waiting shifters company and brings out snacks every hour, on the hour. The shifters are free to move about the space as they please, but then again, you can't run far with high security watching your every move.

He reminds me of Noemie the more time I spend with him. The concrete walls of the lab are painted in abstract blues, greens, and smears of white, like someone had used their hands to slap the paint up there and spread it around. He's constantly without a pen, even though there are cups full of them throughout the space. His assistants are kind, and I'm suspecting friends that he handpicked from his life before, if their camaraderie and familiar rapport is anything to go by. All three assistants have Kalypso's sigil tattooed somewhere on their body. Behind an ear, or on their wrist.

Doron ben Galoi's Super Soldier training is the complete opposite. The moment you enter the training arena, the oppressive atmosphere punches you in the gut. The shifters, and hybrids for they are included in this program as well, do not have a cozy place to rest and snack. A running track follows the perimeter of the ring, wrapping around sparring rings and a gymnasium complete with punching bags and everything you could want for exercise equipment.

There are three side rooms, one for lockers and the bathrooms, a firing range, and a weapons testing area. The testing area is no more than a place for the shifters to exercise their abilities, which is near impossible to do without removing their collars. There are a few considered 'trustworthy,' or brainwashed as I call it, whose collar's effects are minimized, allowing them to access more of their mutation while training.

Doron constantly yells at them, and I'm about to my wit's end with it. His sergeants are no better, but at least they offer praise for a job well done. Four humans to fifty-three shifters, and seventy-six hybrids. The humans are armed with what Doron calls 'shifter killers,' a type of bullet infused with a chemical that shuts off a shifter's mutation, or more importantly, their self-healing. They are similar to my own bullets in the sense that they will kill a shifter, but the exact how of it is much different. The hybrid's collars are different from the shifter's in the sense they don't provide punishment, only relay vitals and tracking information.

The only person in charge of the collars and vitals systems is Eliram, and that is one room in his lab I am not allowed to see. Kalypso has assured me they've made a plan for the shifter's collars on the night of our wedding, but I'm still wary of everything working out so smoothly. I'm only bonded to about half the Super Soldiers, and the hybrids are completely unreachable, a variable I do not like.

Seventy-six variables, to be exact.

Sallow was recommended to the Super Soldier program and I pulled rank on the matter, however little rank I may hold. Drazen already knew Sallow is one of mine, and I managed to convince him that Sallow helps move the process along, since he and I are so closely bonded. It's not an outright lie, but I suspect the Emperor knows my ulterior motive, one he could never understand.

Love.

Shaike bat Tal-or hates me with a passion, and it's entirely mutual. I've only visited the Breeding program once, and I hate myself for how strongly I react to that place. I need to be strong, an unshakable pillar for the other shifters to look up to. I thought I knew what to expect, and perhaps if I didn't see Feivel everywhere, it wouldn't hit me so hard.

Structurally, it's identical to Eliram's lab. The main room is full of exam tables and makeshift medical rooms divided by thin curtains, and there's so much equipment and technology that the paths between the rooms are a meager two way path. The walls are painted a stark, disorienting yellow which match the trim on the white coats that Shaike's team wears. Team is a meager word, she has six times the amount of staff than either Eliram or Doron's programs.

And you can't find an ounce of bedside manner between them.

The side rooms are where conception occurs, according to Shaike. They are heavily guarded and during the time I visited, occupied. I couldn't bring myself to watch the process, and she enjoyed watching the blood lust build within me when I refused. I gave no opinions as to why her program is failing, and she does not seem bothered by the fact she can't keep any babies alive.

According to her, "It's all progress."

And she didn't lie, before. They don't cremate those who have passed.

They send them over to Green House and bury them deep beneath the compost beds.

On the day before the wedding, our routine breaks.

We're in the main room of our apartment, accompanied by Corvin who's busying himself with tidying up, and four *Chayal*. The usual entourage. Kalypso pins my cloak over my shoulders, and I study the crease forming between his brows as he works the pin closed. His fingers are not nimble like I originally thought, but clumsy, and his shakes don't help. He slept restlessly and said little last night, only easing when laying in his favorite place. Directly on top of me.

When he catches me staring, he asks, "What?"

I chuckle. "Nothing at all, Kevin."

He softens, shoulders deflating. "Is it that obvious?"

I reach up, cupping his cheek. He leans into my palm, eyes closing. I breathe, then close my eyes and try something. Our bond isn't nearly as close as Xylia's and mine is, but it's strong, steadfast. In the space between our hearts and minds, I say, *"Don't be frightened. I'm proud of what we're doing, and I think we have a shot."*

Kalypso startles against my hand, but I keep my eyes closed. His breathing quickens, after a moment, he responds. *"What if we fail?"*

"Then we died trying, and the only regret I'll have is that I didn't find you sooner."

"I don't want to lose you. You're the only thing I've ever wanted. We could...."

But Kalypso doesn't finish, and I can feel his self-mounted frustration. Because he can't lie to me, or himself. He can't keep living like this, and my being here doesn't change that. Not really, not when it means we would be letting others suffer.

I open my eyes and take my mate in. His eyes are closed, his features pinched but determined, not worried. I sweep my thumb back and forth across his cheek, then whisper, "I love you, Kalypso."

His eyes fly open, revealing glistening silver. His heart stops, if only for a moment. Quietly, he says, "You mean that. I can feel it."

"I do. I think I always have, even if I didn't know how to name it."

"Oh, Rajni." Kalypso's arms snake around my shoulders and waist, pulling my body flush against his. Inky hair falls over his luminous eyes and stark freckles when he dips his head, and I'm momentarily transfixed by him; is this what the moons looks like? His lips brush over mine, and he doesn't pull away when he says, "I love you."

We kiss, deep and slow. His fingers thread through my curls, mine grip the nape of his neck. There's need there, and desperation, but it's different than the first time. We leave our mark on the other with intent, tongues exploring mouths and teeth drawing the barest amount of blood from errant lips. When my hardening length rubs against Kalypso's hip, he groans into my mouth and I greedily swallow the sound.

A loud rap on the front door breaks the moment. We pull back, and Kalypso presses his forehead to mine. He sighs, then says, "Corvin, would you please?"

"Of course," Corvin says, sniffing as his footsteps echo through the room.

I give Kalypso a smile, then kiss his cheek. "Ready to face the day now?"

He smiles back, albeit slowly. "I believe I am."

We part ways, facing the foyer just as Captain Tsifya bat Jeshulun walks through it, accompanied by a small troop of Citadel soldiers. More wait in the hallway, evident by the front door being left open. Tsifya bows at the waist to us, and her team does the same. She says, "Your Highness, the Northeastern Outpost has been breached by an overwhelming force of protesters, Sergeant Ivin ben Loch is requesting immediate backup. The Emperor has ordered that you accompany us down there and mediate the situation."

Kalypso looks to me, shoulders straight and posture unbreakable. The pride I feel then is staggering. I have no say in this. If I said no, he'd be made to anyway. And yet, I'm the one he looks to.

I nod. "I will go with you."

Tsifya says, "I'm afraid that won't be possible, Dame Rajni. The Emperor gave specific orders for you to tend to the shifters as usual."

I stiffen, bristling at the red flag. "They're protesting our wedding. They think I'm being forced into this, when it was my idea. I don't think keeping me in the corner will help here."

Kalypso asks, "How many are there?"

Tsifya stares at me, then shifts her attention back to Kalypso. "By my estimation, thousands. We have an hour, and if we can't defuse the situation, then Admiral Reshef has the go ahead to engage."

Kalypso takes my hands in his, bowing so he can bring my knuckles to his forehead. He says, "Forgive me for abandoning you, but duty calls. I won't be long."

"Be careful."

He releases me, and I'm equal parts relieved and worried to see that mischievous smile of his coming to life. "I'm always careful."

Chayal Ben xir Lironic and Kassif xir Dasi escort me to S-Block, sans Kalypso. The elevator lobby is empty, and the halls devoid of life, which isn't unusual in itself. I've learned that the servants use their own corridor system to travel throughout the Citadel, which is why they're rarely seen throughout the day going about their work. By all rights, today seems no different than the days before it.

But by the time we board the elevator, I've decided there's something off. Maybe it's because Kalypso's presence is fading the farther away he gets, or the shifter's restlessness grows stronger with each level we sail by. I glance at Ben and Kassif standing at attention on either side of me, and they both nod in turn.

"Is the Prince often called upon to mediate situations?" I ask.

"Yes, he's the People's Prince, so to speak, my lady," Ben says.

"I see."

"Is there something bothering you, my lady?" Kassif asks.

I hum. "I don't like coincidences. We haven't been separated for nearly two weeks now, something I know the Emperor is pleased with, and now the morning before our wedding he chose to send Kalypso without me? Wouldn't it make sense for the Gardeners to see us as a united front? They think I'm a mindless captive here, and Kalypso speaking for me isn't going to help with that."

"It is not our place to question the Emperor's motives, my lady," Ben says, resting a hand on his pistol.

Kassif does the same, but for an altogether different reason, I think.

We exit the elevator, encountering the usual security forces permanently stationed down here. There's no fanfare, and none of the shifter program Heads are down here. Sometimes I encounter Eliram or Doron on the way, but then again, it's not uncommon for them to be absent this time of day. Kassif and Ben take their positions among the other soldiers standing guard outside the doors leading into S-Block, and I slip inside.

Everyone is waiting for me, inconspicuously gathered in the den and on high alert. The moment I enter the room, sixty-three shifters make their move. I remain in place, allowing them to touch, smell, and feel me. *Really* feel me, and not just through the bonds we share. I exhale, and a small burden tumbles off my shoulders as I reconnect with each person. The anxiety brewing in the pack is strong, but outwardly they don't let it show.

Sallow and Lilo are on the inside of the impromptu huddle, Sallow's hands settle in my hair and Lilo crowds against my back, chin resting on my head. It takes a few moments for the group to relax, and even then we don't disperse. I kiss Vic's forehead, a bear shifter, then muss the hair of a canine shifter named Kitten. Pez, one of many adolescent shifters, stays close to Sallow's side.

Sallow has taken his role seriously, doing his best to connect with the shifters and tell them stories of our life, our pack.

The pack that they can be a part of, should they choose. But he is especially protective of the younger shifters, a fact that isn't lost on the kits. Through our bond, Sallow says, *"They've canceled this afternoon's programs. I have a feeling they're going to separate us or something."*

"Why?"

"Yesterday during training, Doron let it slip to one of his sergeants that they'll be working late tonight, as in today's tonight. Vic said they looked right at him when they said it, and they all had this ... look."

"Fuck. Okay. I'll stay here. They can't do anything if I stay here."

Sallow's tiger comes through as he chuffs, deep and low. *"They'll suspect you."*

"It sounds like they already do. I'll think of something. Keep them calm until I get back." I turn, taking Lilo's hand in mine. I smile at her and squeeze once, then release her hand. I expand my next words to all the bonds, and it temporarily unsteadies me to have so many receptive hearts ready, and their emotions.

I say, *"I'll be right back. Listen to Sallow. I know you're scared, but we only have to hold on until tomorrow, then you can bite, and rip, and tear. Look after each other."*

Then I turn my back on them, and it's never felt more wrong.

I rejoin Kassif and Ben, leading the way back to the elevator car without a word. I slap the button for the upper level, fuming. When the light doesn't come on, I smack it again. It still doesn't come on, and before I can hit the button once more, Kassif simply presses it. I glare at them, and Kassif chuckles.

"It's a button, not a body."

"It will be." I mutter, stepping into the car the moment the doors open. Both *Chayal* assume their positions, and we begin our ascent.

"Is everything alright, my lady?" Kassif asks.

"Fine."

When Ben doesn't make a crack, I glance at them. They stare dead ahead, sweat building on their brow. They are utterly, completely still.

In the span of a moment, three things happen.

I reach for my dagger embedded in ink.

Ben turns, drawing their pistol.

Kassif catches on, but it's too late. One bullet after another tears through their throat, blowing their neck apart.

Alarms scream and the car is bathed in flashing, blood-red lights. Respirators fall from the ceiling and air whistles through the bullet holes in the gore ridden wall behind where Kassif once stood. I dance backwards, putting meager distance between the *Chayal* and I, unsheathing my blade as I do.

Its brilliant emerald glow temporarily blinds *Chayal* xir Lironic which is all the time I need. They fire, eyes screwed shut, and the first bullet whizzes past my ear as I lunge. I wrap my legs around their waist and drive the blade into their neck with both hands, tearing down and in until bone stops me.

Chayal xir Lironic screams, but has the sense to try shooting me again instead of dropping their gun. It goes off, ejecting a bullet directly into my gut. Pain blooms in a hot rush and I shout, voice animalistic and full of rage. I forgo the dagger, leaving it stuck in place, and dig the shifted claws of both my hands into the gaping wound.

I rip, and I tear, screaming through the pain and fury.

Chayal xir Lironic falls to their knees and I go with them. Both halves of their upper body collapse atop me, pinning me to the floor. I shove them off with the last of my strength, groaning with the effort. I inhale, but all I receive is a mouthful of hot blood. I reach down, feeling for the wound. More blood waits for me there, spilling from the bullet hole. I call upon my mutation to draw the embedded bullet out, but there's nothing there.

"Fuck." I choke out. They hit me with a shifter killer.

The elevator doors ding, but I can't lift my head, let alone exit the car.

I stare up at the rapidly fading ceiling, pissed off that this is the way I go. We hadn't even gotten to the hard part, and I let fucking *Chayal* xir Lironic kill me.

Shaike bat Tal-or's face comes into view, hovering inches over mine.

"Well, that was too easy. Such a shame, really. I—"

The world disappears in a cloud of blood.

Husk

I wake in our bed.

I can't feel Kalypso.

I've become so attuned to him, and even when we're apart during my time with the shifters, I can feel him. But not now. Now everything's … cold. Something's there on the other end of the bond, but it's too cold to touch or investigate. I have to find him. I have to know he's okay.

The room is quiet and dim, untouched by Corvin's morning rituals. I remain still, listening, but there's nothing. I slowly shove away the blankets tucked around me, grimacing at the tenderness in my stomach. I lift my sleep shirt, one someone must have changed me into, investigating the bullet hole. Except, there's no hole. Oh sure, I'm all bruised to fuck like an elephant kicked me, but there's no hole, no blood. Someone got the bullet out in time, and my bodily healing took over the rest.

Everything's fucked. My first instinct is to say that Drazen put out the hit and separated Kalypso and me, but Shaike was there. Maybe she did his dirty work? Or was she working on her own? Drazen has done everything in his power to keep me happy and bonding with the shifters, so why would he try to kill me *now*? The wedding? That doesn't make sense. Not quite.

My dagger is back in its place, hidden in the ink on my thigh. I check my messenger tattoo and find eight words.

GENESIS STILL ON. BE READY. I LOVE YOU.

Genesis *still* on. Xylia must know something I don't.

I quietly, and with great difficulty, slip out of bed. I dress for the day in a pair of trousers and a plain shirt, both made by Sybil, then lace up my boots. I release the charm on the lock in my bedside table and take out my medicine tins. I stare at the vials of anti-inflammatory, there's still only the one missing, as my body knows well. I sigh, shoulders sagging as I shut the lid.

I quickly take my hormones, there's two vials left now and it hurts my head to look at them. I can think of them in two ways. I won't be needing them, or it'll be nice to have them until I'm able to reconnect with Balderik. I put the tins back, but find it hard to shut the table and lock it once more. My instincts prickle, and my fingers twitch as I contemplate.

I take all seven vials and coalesce them into one, strengthening the bonds between molecules to ensure they don't break. There's a brief flash of emerald light, but thankfully the curtain is closed. I shove the vial into the pocket hiding in the hemline of my trousers, feeling marginally better.

It's always good to have a backup plan close at hand.

I take a final centering breath, then pull back the curtain separating our bedroom from the apartment.

It's empty, save for Sybil in the den and four *Chayal* I don't recognize.

"Where's Kalypso?" I ask. After three seconds pass, I march over to Sybil seated on the couch, waiting patiently with their materials and mannequin. My entire body screams at me, and my march is more of a stomp, but I'm not taken any less seriously. The *Chayal* tense, but their hands remain firmly clasped behind their backs instead of reaching for their guns.

"He's attending Conditioning," Sybil says, staring directly up at me. "Conditioning is a process reserved for those who commit a sin but are pardoned by the Emperor, as long as they are conditioned properly. It is not the first time Kalypso has been conditioned, but it is ... it's an extensive treatment. Only the strong survive it, death is not an uncommon side effect." They grimace, fiddling with their rings.

I whisper, "He killed Shaike, didn't he?"

Sybil nods. "Quite thoroughly, if I might add. If it had been anyone else, perhaps it could have been overlooked, but he went ... feral, as you would say, upon finding you all in the elevator. The timing was ... precise, if you don't mind me saying. But even the Prince must have consequences."

I scratch at my palm with my thumb, mind whirring. Drazen knew that Kalypso would kill Shaike if he found her, why else have *Chayal* xir Lironic do it in the elevator and Shaike waiting for us? Why not the apartments, where Kalypso wouldn't find me until after it was done? No, he wanted Kalypso to be caught in the act, to do whatever *this* is.

"And the treatment? Do you know what that entails?" I ask quietly, sitting down beside Sybil. They offer their hand to me, and I take it.

"No, but I do know that he's quite ... listless, after. Exhausted, but unable to sleep. Almost in a daze, if you would. Under normal circumstances, he would be bedridden for several days. He'll be able to manage the ceremony, I think, but ... it'll be hard for him."

I inhale sharply, pieces falling to place. "Where is Corvin?"

Sybil gives me a sad smile. "We don't know. He didn't report for duty this morning."

Fuck. Drazen knows. Kalypso's most trusted *Chayal* aren't here, in fact I don't recognize the guards at all. Did Drazen take care of Xivan and Esmeray too? Will I find Nathan at the ceremony, or has he been exposed, too? Eliram, Avidan?

There's one thing for certain. Draven is disabling Kalypso, taking his pieces off the board.

And I'll be damned if thinks he can subdue me down so easily.

Sybil says, "Why don't you get freshened up, and we'll get started?" They pat my thigh, alerting me to the hidden vial. I search Sybil's face, then do as they say. I quickly wash in the tub and oil my hair, then dry off roughly. I retrieve the once hidden poison from my trousers, then transform it once more.

Sybil dresses me in a daze, humming quietly to themselves. All the while, I think of all the ways this could go wrong. What if the Gardeners aren't able to breach the elevators? What if Nathaniel and Captain Tsifya's forces, all those loyal to Kalypso, aren't there to back them up once they reach the Upper City, and keep the navy from blowing them to bits with their artillery or airships? What if the signals don't go off at the right time, and one of the many moving parts gives away another? What if Eliram's gone, who will release the collars? What happened to the shifters last night? Can I reach them?

Sybil reminds me to breathe, and I do. I close my eyes, searching for my newfound pack. Apparently they were searching for me too, because the moment I open my heart they're all there, even closer than before. The ease with which I can find them startles me. They're not in S-Block, but somewhere much closer. I calm my racing heart, but the bonds still simmer with anticipation and fear.

Fuck.

Sybil says, "There. A masterpiece, if I do say so myself."

I blink, coming back to reality. I take in my physical state for the first time, heart racing. My hair is captured in a series of braids which tickle my spine, but several errant locks around my face are held back by pins. A multi-tiered white dress trails behind me, and crystalline straps complete with tassels rest over my shoulders. Silver embroidery details the dress, a perfect match to Kalypso's eyes when they are alight with magic.

The Emperor Consort turns the corner of our hall, accompanied by his usual dozen guards. Every hair on my body stands on end as he approaches, but I bow at the waist like I should. He does the same, disturbing layers upon layers of gossamer and lace. His ball gown is magnificent to say the least, and my first thought is to tell Raith about it. I shut it down, forcing pleasantries through my lips.

"Your Grace, you look exquisite tonight. If I may ask, where is the Emperor, and the Prince?"

"As do you, Dame Rajni. Emperor Drazen is on his way to the Great Hall with Kalypso, we'll be arriving just after them. Are you ready?"

"Oh, yes. Tell me, how is the Prince doing?"

Jedediah chuckles, offering me his arm. I take it, ignoring the revulsion boiling in my stomach. He leads me to the elevator lobby, and his guards surround us. My own stays close behind me, which isn't a comfort anymore. Kassif's neck bursting apart takes over my vision for a moment, and my ears ring with the phantom sound of a close-quarters gunshot. I flinch, but if Jedediah notices, he doesn't remark upon it.

Jedediah says, "Oh, fine. He's nervous, but the treatments help with that, too."

I grind my teeth, fighting the animal inside me, and say nothing.

Jedediah seems content to let me stew, smirking. When the elevator's doors open, I hesitate. He glances at me, then to the waiting car. He leans over and whispers, "I heard it took hours for the servants to scrape Kassif off the walls."

I try to pull away, but his arm cinches around mine tighter. I glare at him, and the hearts of my pack beat ever so loud. "*Chayal* Kassif xir Dasi deserves to be treated with respect, even in death."

"Oh, of course, of course. Tell me, did they even have a chance to scream?"

"I know what you're doing."

"And that is?"

"Trying to piss me off."

"Is it working?"

I shove him away from me and the *Chayal* move as one, all drawing their weapons on me. Guess that answers the question of loyalty regarding my own guards. Jedediah holds up his hand without breaking my gaze, then lowers it slowly. I gather the layers of my dress and turn, keeping Jedediah in my sights, and walk into the elevator backwards.

"We'll see, won't we?"

Jedediah laughs, following me into the car. He keeps close to my side but doesn't try to take my arm again, and all the guards manage to fit inside without stepping on my dress. With each level we pass, the stronger my connection to the pack grows. We exit at C1 without incident, and I'm glad to have survived the ride. There is no mob waiting for us, for our destination is nothing more than a narrow, white marble hallway. There are more guards, though. Over a dozen wait for us, and our extended contingency keeps close as we're escorted through. The babble of a crowd intermingled with swing music rushes through the hall, and I grow tenser with each step we take.

This is it. Do, or die.

Jedediah stops at the mouth of the hallway and turns towards me. I stop too, and when he reaches for my hands, I reluctantly offer them to him. He kisses the knuckles of each of them, and the gesture is shielded from the screaming populace by our small army. The urge to slap him is strong, but I resist. He straightens and gives me a wink, then we fully enter the Great Hall.

The endless ocean of people are held back from our path by nothing more than low steel fencing, and Doron's hybrids are stationed along it every six feet, armed to the teeth and fully geared out. I try to reach for the hybrid's hearts, but there's nothing to reach for. They're hollowed out husks, narrowly focused on one thing. Doron's orders. They're not what I'm feeling.

Bulbs pop and smoke rises into the air as paparazzi capture our arrival. Hands stretch towards us, interrupted by distance, fencing, and our enveloping military presence. The Great Hall is a ballroom on steroids, complete with multiple levels of balconies which overlook the main floor, full of waving people. The domed cathedral ceilings are distant enough that a Tin Riser could stand tall in here. Hundreds of chandeliers alight the space from massive to small arrangements, accompanied by naked acrobats.

I'm nearly struck dumb by the vulnerable beauty of the people twirling down great lengths of white and gold fabric, hauling towards the floor at breakneck speeds before catching themselves at the last second. They occupy hoops, performing dynamic and provocative moves that would break my spine in an instant. Even more still swing back and forth from one pillar to another using trapezes, and no protective nets to keep them from falling to their death.

I imagine a small village could fill the breadth of this room, and it's easy to do given all the *people* gathered in it. The last time I saw this many people, we were claiming the Chute. Our fenced off path cuts down the center of the room, leading to a raised stage at the head of the space where the Emperor waits on his throne.

But he's not alone.

Three more impressive chrome thrones accompany him. One is clearly intended for Jedediah to the right of the Emperor, while Kalypso sits at the Emperor's left with an empty seat beside him. Cardinal Grand Bishop Mincha ben Nissim stands beside an altar of sorts, decorated in his finest black and gold robes. The Emperor's personal *Chayal* are posted at equidistant points on the stage, and a small crowd stands behind the thrones.

Oh, no. No.

The moment I lock eyes with Sallow, he bursts into my head. *"He knows everything. You have to tell the Foxes to abort the mission, tell them* now.*"*

"Don't be afraid, Sallow. I told you I would protect you, and I will."

"Rajni, surprise was our only advantage, we can't win. The forces you can see isn't even half of what this hall is filled with, not to mention we all have a gun to our backs right now."

"As your Alpha, I'm telling *you to calm the fuck down. As your friend, I'm telling you to trust me."*

A beat of silence passes, then he says, *"Alpha. I trust you."*

I extend my influence to the others with him, promising what I can. *"You will be safe. Trust me."*

Then I close my heart before it's all too much.

We approach the front lines of the crowd, where the Heads of Houses and their following take up space. I'm relieved to see Nathaniel and Eliram there, and both nod to me. Most everyone else gives me dirty looks, and I ignore them. They're isolated from the Emperor, but close enough to watch him take all the credit for their joint decisions.

I swallow my fear and take the first step, then trip on the second. I fall forward and catch myself on the steps, hands scraping against the stone. The crowd's cheering dulls, taking a moment for those in the back to realize the perfectly planned day has had a misstep, literally. Once pinned back hair comes undone, and the pins fall between my hands. I quickly take the glass one and shove it into my mouth, the movement hidden by wild mane.

Jedediah offers his hand and I take it, allowing him to help me up. Power warms my eyes as the glass turns wafer thin and cracks against the pressure of my tongue, but it's similar enough to the glow that occurs when my emotions get the best of me.

Quietly, he asks, "Are you alright, my lady?"

I swallow glass, blood, poison, and pain. I nod to Jedediah, tightening my grip on his hand. He helps me up the steps, and the crowd's cheering renews. Meanwhile, the shards of glass strengthen again as they go down, slicing apart my esophagus.

I can practically *feel* the poison entering my blood, and my body tenses against the assault. Under normal circumstances, perhaps my natural healing would be able to filter it all out, but not this much, not so quick. If anything, it'll help me make it through long enough to watch the light leave Drazen's eyes.

When we make it to the stage, Jedediah releases my hand and bows to me, then approaches his husband. I shift my attention to Kalypso mutely sitting in his seat, back ramrod straight and dead eyes set straight ahead. He's dressed in a three-piece suit, all black with a white undershirt and silver embroidery. The shell of his ears are laden with overbearing diamonds that match the gaudy necklace tight around his throat. His hair is slicked back, curling at the nape of his neck and restrained by wax. My heart reaches for his, but there's nothing. A hollowed out husk, like the hybrids. What the fuck did Drazen *do* to him?

Jedediah kneels and takes Drazen's offered hand, then turns it over and kisses his palm. Drazen smiles at him, then gestures for Jedediah to take a seat. I'm unsure what to do, so I stand before Drazen and bow at the waist.

"Your Grace, it is an honor to be standing before you today, and I thank you for the privilege of joining your court."

Drazen stands, hair neatly coiled up into a series of braids that form a stiff, pearlescent crown. His fingers are cast in rings, and his white robes trimmed in gold trail the ground as he walks closer. He takes my face in his hands, then kisses my forehead. Before pulling away from my skin, he whispers, "Oh, Rajni. All you had to do was play along."

He retreats, only just, giving me a broad smile which I return twice as sharp. We are nose to nose, sharing the same filtered air.

"You can't fault me for trying, can you?"

"That's what I admire about you, Rajni. You never stop trying, even when it kills those around you." Drazen laughs, gesturing towards the shifters. I can now see the soldiers standing a short distance behind them, once hidden by my lower viewpoint.

"You wouldn't kill over a hundred innocent people in front of a crowd, not while half the Dome wants you dead."

"Innocent? No. But over a hundred *feral* shifters? I think that would set an example, don't you? It would paint me as a hero, no doubt, not a villain. All it takes is the click of a button, and they all become nothing more than what they always were, what *you* are. A beast."

"What do you want from me?"

"I want you to fuck off." Drazen leans forward to whisper in my ear. "And if you don't call off the attacks and marry my son, there will be hell to pay. The Clubhouse is rigged to high heaven, and the moment I give Jedediah the order, he'll blow it to pieces. And when Xylia comes for you, I'll let you have her, but only after Jedediah has chewed her up and spit her out. Maybe I'll let him have Takara at the same time, I'm sure it's quite the experience. I need an heir, Rajni. I need you to stop *fucking* around, and do what you promised. What Syzdon promised. *Quit* fighting this."

By the time he's finished, I'm shaking in rage and excruciating pain, stomach clenching and muscles contracting. I take the few playing cards he's offered to me and grit out, "Okay. Okay, I'll do it. Don't hurt them. Please."

"Call. It. Off."

I shift my gaze to Sallow and shake my head. I pointedly look back to Drazen before closing my eyes, and I inhale sharply. I allow a few moments to pass before opening my eyes once again, and when I do Drazen is still there, wearing that damned smirk of his. I whisper, "It's done."

Drazen chuckles, reaching forward to sweep a curl away from my eyes. "You're so pretty when you submit, Queen of the Foxes."

I bow my head in deference, then allow him to usher me to the Cardinal waiting for us at a stone slab painfully similar to the one in the Church. Drazen gestures towards Kalypso who stands abruptly, wavers, then approaches with a slow gait. Drazen quite literally maneuvers Kalypso before me and takes his hands, sliding them into mine. This close, I can see through the makeup failing to conceal the severe bruising around Kalypso's bloodshot eyes. What appears to be blackened and crisped skin mars his temples and all around his throat, beneath the necklace. I stare into twin pits of dull gold, searching for a spark of life.

But there's nothing.

The Cardinal addresses the crowd, Nathaniel and Eliram's cue to get the fuck out while they can. I force myself not to look, not *yet*, and pay attention to the Cardinal. A hearing device is settled into his right ear, the same as Drazen, and when he speaks his voice is projected throughout the entire room via the structural pillars playing host to sound systems.

He says, "What a blessed day, one that we bear witness to the union of Syzdon's Child of Deliverance, Kalypso ben Matzliach, and the Alpha he was promised, Dame Rajni of the Shifters. Blessed be our God, He who created the Universe, He who created Humankind. Blessed be Him for delivering us mirth and joy, rejoicing and companionship. Today we ask him to bless this union, and the fruits of his Children's labor. Praise be Syzdon!"

The Great Hall shakes beneath the force of all those chanting, "Praise be Syzdon! Praise be Syzdon!"

The Cardinal holds up his hands, the sleeves of his robe slide down to his elbows and reveal years of scars along his forearms. The crowd silences, and I take the opportunity to discreetly scan the people. Nathaniel and Eliram are gone, a relief that is overshadowed by the person now occupying the space they once stood.

Corvin. He's ashen and disheveled, white robes wrinkled. Upon making eye contact with him, he immediately looks away. What the fuck?

There's no time to dwell on it, because the Cardinal steals my attention with his booming demand. "Dame Rajni, repeat after me. Prince Kalypso, you will do the same after." He gestures to Kalypso while keeping his dead eyes set on me. "I am your Beloved, and you are mine. I take you as you are, if you take me as I am. I am no one else but myself, and this is what I offer you."

I breathe, looking at Kalypso. His fingers tighten around mine, and I give him a little smile in hopes of drawing him out of the haze he's trapped in. His lips quirk, and he dips his head. I say, "Kalypso, I am your Beloved, and you are mine. I take you as you are, if you take me as I am. I am no one else but myself, and this is what I offer you."

Kalypso hoarsely whispers, "Rajni, I am your Beloved, and you are mine. I take you as you are, if you take me as I am. I am no one else but myself, and this is what I offer you."

My heart quickens, and I squeeze his hands.

The Cardinal says, "Bring your right hands over the stone, palm up."

With great reluctance, I release Kalypso's hands and turn towards the altar. He does the same, and his hand shakes terribly. Nausea sweeps through me in an intense rush and my knees nearly buckle, but I manage to stay standing. Just a little longer.

Drazen stands beside the Cardinal with a gleaming ceremonial knife in hand, its bone handle polished and blade no doubt sharp. The Cardinal begins to chant, but there's no room in my head for anything else but Drazen's hand cupping Kalypso's. He asks, "My son, Kalypso. Do you commit yourself to Rajni?"

Without hesitation, he says, "I do."

He slices swift and deep. Blood immediately wells to the surface and begins to pool in Kalypso's palm. He grunts in pain, but says nothing as the Cardinal guides Kalypso's hand over the waiting goblet. Drazen closes his hand into a fist and squeezes, pupils dilating as Kalypso's blood steadily pours into the glass. My nostrils flare and I fight back burning rage.

Because now it's my turn, and this will all be over soon.

Drazen takes my hand and murmurs, "My lovely Rajni. I'm so proud of you. Tell me, do you commit yourself to Kalypso, and the Matzliach throne?"

"I do."

He draws out the pain, cutting across my palm ever so slowly. Drazen takes in a breath upon seeing my blood tinged with oil-slick green, and the corner of his lips turn up. He guides my hand over the goblet and squeezes, filling the half-full goblet the rest of the way. The Cardinal wraps my hand with a length of cloth bandage in the same fashion he had done with Kalypso, and only once we're tended to does Drazen raise our blood to the crowd.

I feel it, finally. Kalypso's heartbeat.

Or maybe it's mine, ringing in my ears and threatening to ruin everything.

Drazen says, "With this sacrifice, our beloved God blesses this union."

He brings the goblet to his lips, and drinks. Long, full swallows of hot, poisoned blood. I exhale satisfaction, watching him finish the entire thing in one go. He lifts the empty glass once more and grins, showing off teeth washed in the blood of his enemy, and downfall. He announces, "I declare Kalypso and Rajni to be husband and wife. You may kiss!"

The crowd's applause is world shattering. I unsteadily turn to Kalypso and he catches me by my forearms, but he's not the most steadfast right now, either. We hold onto each other for dear life and regain our footing, and only then do I lift my eyes to his. Kalypso smiles, then leans down and softly kisses me.

But it's not right. It's chaste, and ... unfamiliar. Like kissing a friend, not someone you've laid with. I lean back, but the movement disorients me.

"Kalypso?" I ask, or try to, but it's choked and wet. Blood splatters across his suit in a spectacular pattern, flecked with gelatinous clots and tiny shards of glass. My legs finally give out and Kalypso holds onto me, but his knees buckle too.

The sweet sound of retching and screaming fills the atmosphere. I'm not denied the pleasure of watching Drazen going down. He collapses in a pile of blood and clot-ridden vomit at the Cardinal's side. His skull bounces off the stone, cracking audibly. I watch the life slowly go out of his eyes, and his blood edges towards me. Jedediah shouts orders to the *Chayal* who are finally pulling out their guns, and he runs towards us with glacial fury written across his face. I try to push Kalypso behind me, but my limbs won't obey.

But then time slows and I relish every second, watching as a bullet penetrates his forehead. A cloud of neon green emerges from the hole, reminding me of the barrel of a smoking gun. Ivy and thorns latch onto bone and flesh as they explode outwards from the place Jedediah's head once was. I sigh with relief as he falls, nature and blood spilling from his neck.

The gunfire doesn't end there, but it's all fading. I use the last of my energy to take in Kalypso one last time, but when I finally manage to look at him, he's not there.

It's Corvin holding onto me.

Black hair gives way to ginger in a quick rush, once smooth complexion puckers and contorts as it settles into place. His right ear shrivels until it's no more, but the exhaustion and dullness to his eyes, now their usual hazel, doesn't disappear. He says, with great difficulty, "Hold on, my lady. Hold on."

"Wh—where's Ka—" I cough, grip loosening on Corvin.

And then he's there, sliding to his knees and crashing into us. Kalypso pants, sweat and blood dripping from his brow as he digs through his pockets. "Don't fucking die on me," He says, hurriedly unstoppering a vial. "Drink, Raj. Drink."

I open my lips, unable to do much more than that. His heart thunders in my ears, in addition to two more rapidly approaching. Oh. Oh.

Cold liquid spills onto my tongue and flows down my throat, numbing the pain. Two foxes, one black and one red, come into view behind Kalypso. Moments later, a golden canine is there, too.

I smile. *"You came."*

Then I fall into nothingness.

Searching. Trying. Loving.

Nothing isn't cold, not like I thought it would be.

It's warm, and soothing.

A heavy presence suffocates my ear drums, and my heart beats ever so slowly. I blink several times, and the world starts to come into focus. I'm standing on hard ground, and the surrounding darkness is broken by a single spotlight focused directly on me. I hold up a hand, shielding my eyes from the intense light.

"Welcome, Alpha," An encompassing voice says, neither female or male, young or old. I lower my hand slowly and with great trepidation. The spotlight remains, silhouetted by an enormous serpentine figure, one I have no name for.

They have extraordinary plumage decorating their main body, feathers longer than I am cast in vibrant sunset shades. Scales cover their long neck and tail in the same sunset complexion, along with their black-taloned feet. Black fur encircles their throat and ankles like jewelry, and orange crystals protrude from their spine and the length of their tail like horns. Massive bone white antlers extend from their narrow forehead, covered in moss, crystals, and a net of ivy woven between them. Their eyes, dotted with a horizontal pupil, are the brightest shade of pink I've ever seen.

They bow their head to me, and I do the same.

But that's as far as my respect goes.

"Are you Syzdon?"

A bone deep hum emanates from the being, followed by a series of bizarre clicks. Is that laughter, or anger? They say, "No, but I am the one those around you *believed* to be Syzdon. He exists, but not here. Not in this place. We all exist, in one time or another. I do not have a name, not since my son took up my mantle, but I still ... interfere, when I can."

"So you ... you're the one who brought Kalypso to the Dome? Is he your son? That's true?" I ask in a rush, taking a step closer.

"I am, but he is not my son. His father made an oath to the Gods, to *me*, one that promised Kalypso to us long before he was born. We have been fighting Syzdon for eons, but without a proper weapon. Kalypso is that weapon. *You* are that weapon. The first step was to free you, and everyone else imprisoned here. To do that, we needed Kalypso."

I ball my hands into fists. The connection between Kalypso and me vibrates, like a golden string plucked once. I ask, "Why him? Why not break open the Dome yourself?"

The being lowers their head, bringing their eyes level with mine. "Even Gods can be bested by humans, little one. Drazen ben Matzliach's love of blood is not by coincidence. His family were all devout followers of Syzdon long before the nuclear blasts, and when they crafted the Dome they imbued it with their blood, providing a safe haven for their God, while keeping the rest of us out. Human sacrifice and blood magic is the most powerful way for a God to gain power, but it corrupts and twists us into we're nothing more than a maelstrom of destruction and hate, which is all that Syzdon is. Knowing this, I delivered Kalypso under the guise of Syzdon, and ordered Drazen to unite you two. I left enough gray area in my demand, allowing Drazen to believe he was in the benefit. Then again, he *did* have power, if only for a moment."

"And Syzdon? Where is he if not in this so-called safe haven?"

"This is not the only one, and he has not lived here since its early days. You are not the only one hidden from the world, Rajni. It is time to set the others free. Can you do that?"

"I don't want to fight anymore." I breathe, overcome with emotion. "Is there no rest for us?"

The being makes that purring and clicking noise again, something I'm betting is laughter, now. "A domestic life doesn't suit you, Rajni of the Foxes. You have always been meant for more. Besides, didn't you make Kalypso a promise?"

Energy rises, urging me to move. "I did. To find his parents. Do you know where they are?"

"Seek, and you shall find. All you have to do is open the door. Go now, little one. Keep my grandson safe."

A glacial wind rushes me, and the spotlight flashes and pops like a camera bulb going off. Before I'm taken away, I reach out towards the being. My fingers brush against their forehead, and in that moment I experience hundreds of lives, hundreds of worlds, and hundreds of loves. In that moment I am everything, and nothing.

I come back to myself as a fox.

Life blooms slowly.

Warm bodies against mine, those in fur and otherwise. Dual steady huffs of air against my neck. Pack surrounds me, a heavy scent and presence like no other. I don't smell the Clubhouse, or the apartment, but both packs are here. Wherever here may be.

I groggily open my eyes, first taking in the ceiling of S-Block. Oh no. Why are we here? We shouldn't be here. We did it, we killed him—

"Shh, it's okay. You're safe," Kalypso says, fingers sliding through the fur between my ears. "We're all here. It's the only room big enough to fit everybody."

My head rests on his stomach and my back legs are between his, my stomach is stretched across his groin. Hotaru and Xylia lay on either side of me in their fox forms, one across each of Kalypso's thighs. Takara, also shifted, lays curled up between my side and Xylia. Balderik is close by. I can't see him, but I can feel him. Perhaps on the other side of Xylia?

Kalypso whispers, "We're all here. It's the only room big enough to fit everybody."

I sigh, then close my eyes and draw upon my power in attempts to shift back. Or rather, try to, but it's all sluggish and weak. I chitter in annoyance and Kalypso chuckles, scratching between my ears once more. "Save your energy. Balderik says your body heals better as a fox, and you're still 'pretty fucked up' according to him. You stupid idiot. What were you thinking?"

I huff, turning my face away. I speak to him the only way I can as a fox. *"A thank you would be nice. Did we do it? Did we win?"*

Kalypso responds in kind, breathing quickening as he recounts his version of events. *"Yes. We won. I couldn't ... I didn't tell you the entire plan, Rajni. And then everything went south when fucking Shaike tried—"* He inhales sharply. *"There was no time to tell you anything more. And I had a pretty good feeling you were going to go ahead with your plan anyway, so I told Takara to bring the antidote.*

"Tsifya and I met with those on the ground, and your people were there. An attack was staged, and I was able to extend

my power towards Takara, Xylia, Hotaru, and Balderik. I ... glamored them? It's hard to explain, but it worked, in the chaos we all made it back. But then we found you as you were and I—I lost it, Rajni. Takara and Xylia were there seconds later, tearing her off of you. But all I had to do was look at Shaike and think 'Dead.' And then she was. I don't know how I did it, but it just happened.

"Then I saw it for what it was. A trap. So Corvin and I ... it was his idea, I hated it, but ... he endured the Cleansing and lived as me for a short, terrifying while. I am forever indebted to him, even more so than I already was. He's right there, at our feet. I can feel him, now. Something about you changed that for me, because I feel them all, but him especially. So we traded places, and I was in the crowd with the others, waiting.

"I couldn't ... I couldn't feel you, Raj. None of us that were ... not ourselves, I suppose, we couldn't feel anything. It was like the ghost of you. I hated it, and I hated standing by, watching you get weaker and weaker. I'm so sorry for that. But it's all done now. I hate to say it, but it worked. He's dead. They're all dead. Jedediah. The Cardinal, the entire church is disbanded until further notice for that matter. Orioz is gone, and Orli and fucking *Doron. I had them all executed. I think ... I think I might be a monster now? But everyone is celebrating, and it hurts my head because there was so much blood and—"*

"Am I married to Corvin, now?"

Kalypso laughs aloud, the sound freeing and everything I fought for. I don't have the strength to shift back, but the hope he gives me then is enough to keep going. To keep fighting. Searching. Trying. Loving.

Living.

With my pack safely tucked around me and the world ready to be explored, the lifelong fractures in my heart begin to heal, and the hearts of all those I love beat as one.

We plan to open the door in three days.

During the time I slept, Isaac was elected the ambassador for the Garden. He and Kalypso have been working closely in their efforts to assist those who have decided to stay in the Dome. Since most of the Council was eliminated during the coup, dissolving the Matzliach Dynasty, while not an easy thing, was certainly easier than it would've been. Captain Tsifya bat Jeshulun has been temporarily elected leader of the Upper City, per Kalypso's recommendation.

His abdication that immediately followed the coup surprised the entire Dome, but no more than his and Eliram's announcement that the outside world is inhabitable. Since then, all those on the ground have been given access to the Upper City, and its warehouses of fresh food and top-tier oxygenation systems. There are many who are skeptical of leaving the Dome before the hundred year mark, but as Kalypso has stressed, no one is being forced to leave.

He simply is.

He fits in with the Foxes better than I imagined. Balderik isn't very happy with him still, but Xylia adores him. Seth is ... Seth, but not without the ever optimistic Liam permanently attached to his side. Golding and Sallow have been reunited, an affair that I'm sad I missed. Hotaru and Kalypso have actually talked a few times, but ....

Hotaru and I still haven't talked.

While Takara and I might not ever have the relationship we had before, I've forgiven her. It's not romantic between us, not now and perhaps not ever again, but I'm glad that she's here, and that her and Xylia bonded. I can see the five of us living happily together, including Corvin because he is Kalypso's just as much as I am, if not more. There's nothing romantic between them, but there's certainly a bond, there's no denying that. And I care for Corvin, too.

At the end of the first day, I blame Hotaru's avoidance on the chaos. On the second day, I blame it on me. The night before we're supposed to leave, I'm downright pissed.

I seek Hotaru out first, having to trek a ways to find them in their new hidey-hole.

Kalypso's workshop.

I'm not accompanied by *Chayal*, which have been disbanded and merged into Captain Tsifya's new force that serves the general public. While Xylia wanted to come, I told her this was something I had to do on my own, and she stayed behind with Takara. Kalypso is with Nathaniel, who was shot in the chest by one of the hybrids, his lung punctured. While Quilla was able to stabilize him, he's still holed up in the infirmary.

And keeping him there is a full time job, one Kalypso is happy to share with Edgar and Quilla, as it seems the siblings have taken a liking to Nathaniel.

I travel through a new world with a light heart. There are shifters and humans in the streets, and everyone has enough to eat. I think back to when this whole thing started, and I'm thankful no one will have to stoop to cannibalism as a means to survive ever again. While our problems haven't entirely gone away, as dissent and discrimination will always thrive in the dark cracks of the world, there's more hope than ever before.

And it's up to Kalypso and me, and all the rest of us, to spread it like wildfire.

I pass through the storage room and down the stairs, finally cornering the fox in a trap. Hotaru faces away from me, back hunched over a work table. I keep a small distance between us, leaning against a nearby wall. Kalypso has cleared the space of the things he wishes to bring, which is only a tool roll full of chisels and his best knives. The wood shavings are still here, the log rounds are stacked neatly beside the place where Kalypso and I mated for the first time.

The silence that stretches on is painful and oppressive, but I won't be the first to break it. Finally, Hotaru's shoulders bunch up and they exhale heavily. They say, "I thought that I lost you. I thought that I lost you, and the last thing I ever said to you was that I hate you. Not how much you mean to me, or how much I love you. How much you keep me afloat and steady, and that I'm proud to be your beta?"

Hotaru sniffs and my muscles coil, but I force myself to remain still. I whisper, "You're not a good liar, Taru. I know you didn't mean it."

Hotaru explodes like a spring gone off. They push away from the table and march over to me, bringing their face inches before mine. "I meant it at the time. How *dare* you separate us? How dare you *force* me to leave your side? I'm still so fucking mad at you for that."

Their hand slams against the wall beside my head. I reach up, slowly, and caress the bags of exhaustion beneath Hotaru's dark eyes. Hotaru shudders, shaking their head. "No. You can't just do the Alpha thing and think everything is better."

I swallow hot emotion, fighting back a smile. "It's not better. But I really missed you, Taru. And I hope that one day you can forgive me. I don't know what your plans are, but I ... I'd really like it if you came with us."

Hotaru rolls their eyes, and that's what finally breaks the dam. They say, "You must be crazy to think I'm going any-where without you. Big Bad Alpha my ass, get over here."

We hold each other and cry for a long time, but it's the healing kind. The type of cry that tears you down, and builds you back up.

Kalypso and Corvin stand at my left, while Xylia and Takara stand at my right. Eliram and Hotaru stand at my back, flanked by Balderik and Feivel on one side, and Golding and Sallow at their other. Drystan stands behind them with Koa up on his shoulders, accompanied by Noemie and Jaromir. Avidan is with us, along with Cilia ban Faran, the former Head of Library. Kalypso's former *Chayal* Esmeray bat Rakia and Xivan xir Gabi are here too, along with Kassif's ashes kept in a small urn which they want to bury outside. Sybil opted to stay behind, but the cloak they gifted me is tight around my shoulders.

Nathaniel stands before the door to the outside, breathing heavily. I exchange a look with Kalypso, then nod towards Nathaniel. He obliges my silent request, temporarily leaving me and Corvin behind. I take Corvin's hand, and he immediately crowds into my side. Together, we watch as Nathaniel and Kalypso embrace each other, then open the door.

The door cracks and stagnant, cold air washes in. Together, the pair peek through the sliver like a couple of kids spying on something they shouldn't be. Then they look back, and the dual grin is enough to make my heart sing.

"There's a tunnel," Kalypso says, and I can't help but chuckle.

Of course there is.

Nathaniel and Kalypso lead our caravan of shifters and humans into the tunnel, one that supposedly cuts through the mountain and to the surface, which is dark until all the shifter's eyes glow to life. When I glance at Corvin, he smiles upon seeing mine lit up. He says, "We're going on an adventure."

I laugh. "We sure are."

After many hours, we find the last obstacle. A thick steel door. Plain and practical, not what one would expect.

This time, Kalypso turns to us and says, "I think you three should open it." He gestures to Xylia, Takara and me.

Xylia signs, "I won't say no."

Takara glances at me. "I don't know."

I roll my eyes, taking her and Xylia by the hand. There's a flicker of warmth in the pack bond between Takara and I, while Xylia makes her satisfaction known by humming. When we join Kalypso and Nathaniel, Xylia stands on her tip-toes to leave a kiss on Kalypso's cheek. He flushes, bringing his fingers to the place she kissed him. He tentatively kisses the corner of her mouth, still unsure how to act around Xylia even though she loves him to pieces already. Then Kalypso kisses me gently, smiling against my lips. My bond with Xylia vibrates with happiness, and I've never felt Kalypso more calm than he is right now. I never thought I could have it all, but I do. Right here.

Before stepping away with Nathaniel, Kalypso rests a hand on Takara's shoulder. He says, "You earned this, and I am so proud to be your friend."

For the first time since I've known her, Takara cries. It's silent and soft, but she nods and presses her forehead to Kalypso's. Then he backs off, and it's just the three of us. I give Takara a smile, which she returns. I look at Xylia, who is brimming with excitement. She speaks in the space between our hearts, connecting the three of us. *Are we ready?*

Takara nods, and so do I.

We each take hold of a spoke on the old door's massive cog-like handle, and turn. And turn. And turn. Just when it seems like the door will never give way, the mechanism releases with a *click*, and the door groans outwards. The air that spills through the gap this time is ... I can't describe it. Cold but wet. Fresh, undoubtedly so. I nearly feel high from the small gusts of it escaping through the crack.

Together, the three of us push open the door the rest of the way, and step into a new world covered in something I've only ever read about.

Snow.

We wander out in a cautious daze, mesmerized by the landscape. We're ... high up, on the top of the mountain, I think. All around us are great towers that can only be trees, taller than the Tin Risers and flush with green needles that smell like Kalypso. It's nighttime, but the moons—

I drop to my knees in the snow, and as the shifters spill out of the tunnel and behold the half-full moons, they do the same. They are so close, it's almost as if I could touch them. One enormous gold moon ringed with brilliant stardust, and a smaller silver one that shines even brighter than its larger counterpart. The effect they have on the snow is dazzling, and I imagine during the day it would be blinding.

Human and shifter alike, we all howl at the moons.

Epilogue

Three months later and our people, the *Chaya,* have explored the world no farther than the base of the mountain. The snow has melted, cascading down the alpine hills until crashing into a brilliant lake, the same one that gives life to our village.

It began as small and temporary, ready to be picked up at a moment's notice. But as more people made the arduous trek down the mountain and joined us, in addition to the surprises unearthed as thick snow gave way to thin patches, the more permanent our place in the world became.

I share a longhouse with Xylia, Kalypso, Takara, Corvin, Hotaru, and Seth. Our longhouse is different from the rest, because it's a motor vehicle that collapses inwards to form a long bus fit with all the amenities for traveling. It's Hotaru, Seth, and Takara's love child, along with the occasional help from others in the pack, like Nathaniel and Mairin.

Quilla is with his child, and we're all excited for the first child of the *Chaya*, part shifter, and part human. It's been interesting, the pairings that have occurred since we settled by the lake. While the first two months were a boom of doing and moving and building, the last month has been ... too domestic. The seven of us are feeling the itch, the urge to put paws to the earth and move.

Kalypso and I especially. The destiny laid before us by the celestial being we simply call, 'Them,' is a physical thing, a pull that is just as real as the pull from the moons. The triple suns that warm Sirione amplify that feeling. The lush grass and violet wildflowers beneath our feet beg to be walked upon, explored until they give way to something else. The world whispers, 'What is beyond the grove protecting our little place beside the waterfall?

What is beyond the mountain?

What *is?*'

We find them by accident, but the moment is no less sweet for it.

Kalypso and I walk through the woods together, scouring the earth for fresh growth. Seth and Liam found a berry bush not far off, but none of us have tried them yet as Hotaru tested the handful they brought back a hundred different ways, effectively smashing what we had to pieces.

Kalypso swings his rainbow woven basket, a birthday gift from Noemie, back and forth, whistling as we walk. His other hand is entwined with mine, and his heart beats steadily. I smile at him. "You seem awfully happy today."

He grins. "It's a beautiful day, and I'm with you."

I pull him over to me, stealing a kiss. Our lips smash together in an echo of our first embrace, and I laugh against his mouth. When we part, I say, "It is? Isn't it?"

We continue walking, breathing fresh air and listening to the birds sing. I don't know how I ever lived without it. There's always noise. Always life moving, from the birds to the rabbits and the insects. There's even a small herd of deer that live close by, growing more bold now that the snow is gone.

Xylia and I usually spend a few hours every night laying on the roof, counting the stars. Sometimes Takara or Kalypso join us, but oftentimes it's a moment that just the two of us share. Every once in a while Balderik will come over, and those moments are the most surreal. The three of us laying together, watching the sky turn.

Kalypso says, "You're thinking awful hard over there."

I chuckle, squeezing his hand. "Taru thinks there will be a meteor shower tonight. I was thinking it would be nice if we all watched it together, lay out on blankets on the Common Ground by the lake."

"Oh, I like that idea. You always get bitey when the stars come out to play."

"I'm always bitey."

"Yes, but especially—"

A loud crack almost like thunder jerks our attention to the right. In a clearing not far away stands a fox the size of a wolf, shaggy black fur streaked with iridescent blue. Three men stand with it, each one vastly different from the other but all vaguely familiar. The tallest has cool black skin and tight inky coils tied back at the nape of his neck. He's dressed in light traveling clothes made of linen, and scars. A particularly nasty one cuts across one of his eyes. Tucked beneath one of his arms is a bundle of fabric.

The fox stands between him and another man, one with long blond curls and great wings, the elegant feathers black tinged with green and blue. He's dressed in plain traveling clothes similar to his companion, and he has a prosthetic right hand that shines in the sunlight breaking through the canopy. There's something ... *more*, about him. Something I can't describe, something that wants to make me cower, and come closer.

The last man is nothing like the other two. His tight copper curls dance across his face as they catch the wind, and he's dressed more like my people. Jeans and a hoodie, the hood pulled up. His hands are buried deep in his pockets, but upon seeing me, he gives me a little wave.

The fox shifts, but it's not ... it's not like how shifters transform. There's a rainbow aura that overtakes the edges of the person's form, shimmering bright as they change. It's like how Kalypso changes.

Kalypso's heart stops as the transformation takes place, and his knees buckle. I hold him close to me, petting his hair as we watch.

In the place of the fox stands a person with black hair curled around their ears. They are shorter than their companions but strong in their own right, with olive skin that is a shade lighter than Kalypso's. They're naked, but the tallest of the group offers them a change of clothes. Shakily, the person dresses in clothes similar to their companion, then faces us once again. The man in a hoodie stands a little ways off to the side, and something tells me he's not part of this. At least, not in the way I think the others are.

After dressing, the fox shakily says, "Hello. I don't know if you know who I am, who we are, but—"

Kalypso takes off running, crashing into the arms of his parents.

I join the odd man out, bowing at the waist to him when we're face to face. Through tears and a bursting heart, I say, "Thank you. I don't know who you are, but thank you. Did you bring them here?"

The man smiles, extending a pale freckled hand towards me. He says, "I did. We've been looking for you for a long time, and I think the person you should thank is yourself. I never would have been able to find you inside that place." He gestures towards the mountain, grimacing. "Besides, I ... I don't get involved with matters involving *Him* anymore, or I try not to, but They give the orders, not me. Anyways, I think it was worth it, in the end. We can't hide forever."

He gestures to Kalypso and the others, and I'm torn between watching the reunion and interrogating. But the man watches on fondly, clearly pleased with the outcome. He's so ... bizarrely normal. He appears my age, but there's something cosmic and old about him, like a meteor hurtling through space. He looks tired, but happy.

Hesitantly, I say, "I don't know what you've been through, but I'd say it was worth it."

After a few moments, he quietly asks, "Do you think it was all worth it? Everything you endured? The years you spent alone? The torture you experienced at the expense of ... of Him?"

I listen to love and life break apart Kalypso's heart and put it back together. I say, "Yes."

Glossary

The Foxes; identified by animal form and mutation, if applicable.

Balderik – Golden Retriever. Healing.

Chloe – Bobcat.

Daisy – Owl. Gravity.

Drystan – Panther. Mild Enchantment.

Galatea – Fox. Increased senses.

Golding – Jaguar. Super Strength.

Hotaru – Fox. Enchantment and Electrical.

Io – Fox. Nature.

Ika – Hedgehog.

Jaromir – Polar Bear. Super Strength.

Koa – Hedgehog.

Lennox – Fox. Nature.

Liam – Snake. Telepathy.

Madlock – Lion. Increased senses.

Mairin – Racoon. Enchantment.

Namir – Fox. Electricity.

Noemie – Sheep. Affects bodily sensations.

Quilla – Fox. Healer.

Raith – Owl. Super Hearing.

Rajni – Alpha, Fox. Enchantment.

Sallow – Tiger. Super Speed.

Senka – Lizard. Nature.

Seth – Fox. Telekinesis.
Takara – Fox. Metallurgy.
Tyler – Goat.
Vienne – Bull.
Xylia – Fox. Nature.

The Roost; identified by animal form and role, if applicable.
Allison – Blue jay.
Katya – Blackbird, Sorin's second.
Sorin – Owl, head of the Roost.

Others.
Conlead – Leader of Reptilian.
Isaac – Leader of the Underground Tunnels.
Talay – Leader of Jungle.

Matzliach Family; identified by familial ties and lore.
Drazen ben – Son of Silvana, made Emperor at 15 years old when he executed his grandmother for her sins and transgressions during her rule.

Jedediah ben – Emperor Consort, also known as Black-Hearted Daniel, a hunter who claimed over fifty tags.

Kalypso ben – Adopted son of Draven, responsible for House affairs. Also known as the Child of Deliverance, which references his origin story and prophecy.

Revena xir – Child of Tamaria, regent during the four-year reign of Silvana, and she served as Drazen's regent for sixteen years until she was publicly executed.

Silvana bat — Daughter of Revena, made Empress at 12 years old when Tamaria passed, her final decree. Died at 16 in childbirth.

Tamaria bat – The Dome's creator, Drazen's great-grandmother and a devout follower of Syzdon.

House Members; identified by their title, if applicable.

Avidan ben Sizi – Head of Green.

Cilia bat Faran – Head of Library.

Doron ben Galoi – Head of Shifter Militia and Hybrid Training.

Eliram ben Avichen – Head of Alchemy and Shifter Research.

Elipaz xir Shamir – Head Chamberlain, also Drazen's personal attendant.

Leah bat Tal-or – Head of Health.

Liron ben Hadoram – Head of Kitchen.

Mincha ben Nissim — Head of Syzdon, Cardinal Bishop.

Nathaniel ben Tshuva – Nobleman in Trading.

Nitza xir Maron – Head of Trading.

Orli ben Yoratan – Head of Slaughter.

Orin xir Tinit – Head of Power.

Rasha xir Delone – Head of School.

Shaike bat Tal-or – Head of Shifter Breeding.

Temon ben Lon – Head of Public.

Tsifya bat Jeshulun — Head of Militia, Captain of the Guard.

The Chayal.

Declan ben Zamir

Esmeray bat Rakia

Kassif xir Dasi

Trent xir Lironic

Xivan xir Gabi

Citadel Staff; identified by role.

Corvin ben Lahav – Kalypso's personal attendant.

Orioz ben Sarig – Seneschal.

Sybil xir Yadir – Head Tailor.

About the Author

Noah Hawthorne (he/they) is a fantasy punk author who craves inclusive stories with wild adventure, flawed characters, queer love, and found family.

Noah originally began publishing under the Aelina Isaacs pen name, and after some self-discovery adopted the new pen name Noah Hawthorne, which is dedicated to writing books with trans leads. Visit neshamapublishing.com for information on his other books, playlists, and more.

* 9 7 9 8 9 8 7 0 1 0 6 3 1 *